OVERGROW

OVERGROWN

BETSY PRICE

First published in the UK in 2020.

Copyright © 2020 Betsy Price
All rights reserved.

Cover design by Karen Barnes pinkglasses.co.uk
Typeset by Phillip Gessert

ISBN: 978-1-8380033-1-9
Ebook ISBN: 978-1-8380033-0-2

For those who thought they were alone.

1

H OW HAD I let myself get into this habit? My only work-free, child-free day and I was slumped in a post pasta carb crash. A second glass of wine sat patiently in front of me, awaiting my decision. Wardrobe decluttering and six pack abdominal workouts would have to wait for yet another week, a week when there was more time, or a week when I'd sleep through the night and bound out of bed at 6 a.m. ready to take on the day. I was being a dutiful niece of course, let's not forget that. It was important that she had this time to offload, to try and make sense of everything. But if she referred to my uncle's genitalia again, I was going to have to speak up. I empathised with her plight, I really did, but I wasn't sure how much more I could take.

'He can swing his pendulous testicles in someone else's face for a change,' Aunty Georgie drained her glass and returned it to the table with a thump. 'All I care about is keeping the house.' A perfectly Shellacked fingernail pointed toward the waiter and then into her empty glass.

'Let me do that,' I said. 'He looks busy.' I reached for the bottle—a foolish move.

'It's not your job.' She smacked my hand away and I followed her gaze to the approaching waiter.

'I'm so sorry, madam,' he flustered, struggling to coordinate bottle and glass. 'Do you want...I mean, would you like—'

'Another bottle. Well, if that one's empty, then of course I want another bottle. And what is your name?'

'Jacob, madam.'

'Tell me, Jacob. How old are you?' She scanned her eyes up and down his, to be fair, rather lovely physique.

I had witnessed this behaviour before and knew better than to intervene. In her mind, she was Mrs Robinson. Any moment now, she'd stick out the tip of her tongue and give him a slow, knowing wink.

In his mind, she was a knackered old lush in a Wonderbra.

'Nineteen, madam.'

Out came the tongue.

'Nineteen. Did you hear that, Eliza? *Nineteen*. Well then, young Jacob, you'd better run off to the wine cellar and fetch me another bottle of Pouilly-Fumé.'

Now the wink; better late than never. Jacob scurried away unharmed—for now.

'Watch and learn, darling. Don't ever think that you're too old for a little flirtation. I know you're married, but come to think of it, so am I.'

'I'm not married.'

'You're as good as. How is darling Will? Working as hard as ever?'

'He's booked up with weddings every Saturday until October.' I tried to deliver the news with enthusiasm. Will detested weddings: week after week of lining up guests on church steps, trying to make everyone laugh so he could capture arty shots of staged joy when all he really wanted to do was gun them down and go to the pub. Bridesmaids marinated in prosecco threw themselves at him after the speeches. You couldn't blame them, Will exuded cool and didn't wear a ring. If I'd been in their glitter-encrusted stilettos, I would have done the same. It was infuriating, said Will. He was there to work.

I'm not sure when young flirtatious women started to infuriate middle-aged men—another of Will's placating tools. I wasn't jealous, or unreasonable. Far from it. But I needed placating from time to time. Who didn't?

'He's working every weekend? I doubt you two find time for much, well, you know…intimacy, do you?'

A rhetorical question, I hoped. I took a sip of wine and pretended not to hear her.

'Let's hope Will's not like your uncle—one headache and he's humping the first thing in a pencil dress.'

'The Pouilly-Fumé, madam. Would you like to try?'

'Oh, Jacob, Jacob, Jacob.' She clasped his hand in hers and looked up to him like a disciple unto Jesus. 'I'm sure this one's equally as delicious as the last. Just pour it and we'll all loosen up a little, shall we?' She emphasised the idea by shaking her shoulders, luring Jacob's gaze into the province of her cleavage, which, at sixty-eight, was not at all bad.

Jacob's face flushed and he made an excuse about a temperamental corkscrew before rushing off to the safety of the adolescent bar staff. Georgie was triumphant—her work here was done.

'You see, darling, never too old. I'm proud of my girls and you should be too. Start looking after them now with proper, tailored exercise; absolutely no jogging. Get yourself a personal trainer and tell him that your breasts are your utmost priority. You need a good bra and an expensive sunblock. You don't want to hear the words décolletage and Grand Canyon used in the same sentence, do you now? Anyway, where were we?'

'We were talking about Uncle David and the house.'

'That broken old record? I'm sick of thinking about it. No, I think we were talking about you and Will. Now, it's important that you maintain a healthy relationship both in and out of the bedroom.'

'The Pouilly-Fumé, madam.' Hervé, master sommelier, didn't take any crap from anyone.

'Hervé, what a lovely surprise. Have you been jetting off to Chile again or was it California this time?' Georgie shot me a look, an *I know stuff about wine regions* sort of a look.

'Tokyo, madam.'

'Tokyo? In Japan?'

Hervé inhaled deeply through his enormous French nostrils and offered a simple smile. 'The Japanese have been producing wine for over one hundred and fifty years now.' *You stupid bitch.* 'The Koshu grape delivers an elegant white. You really must allow me to tempt you out of the Loire Valley one of these days.'

'I'm not sure I like the sound of that.'

'Loire Valley it is then, madam.' *I shall leave you there to rot.* 'How is Mr Hamilton?'

'Mr Hamilton is very well, thank you for asking.'

'Excellent, I was going to invite him to our next tasting. He has such a willing palate, but I haven't seen him lately.'

'London, Hervé,' Georgie snapped. 'He's in London working. This is a very busy time for him.'

'Of course. I will ensure he gets an email. *Bon appétit.*'

Hervé spun on his heel and waltzed back toward the bar, stopping briefly at a table of octogenarian ladies to compliment them on their outfits.

'Hervé knows.'

'Hervé knows what?'

'Hervé knows about my bloody husband, Eliza. Did you see how smug he looked? *"Ooh and how is Mr Hamilton?"*' Georgie tried her hand at a camp French accent, but ended up somewhere in Scotland. 'He always gets bitchy when I chitchat with the waiters. He's like a vigilante, protecting his precious boys from any *fun.*'

She had started to raise her voice to the point where it was grabbing the attention of other diners and options needed to be weighed:

I could pour us some mineral water and suggest that she was exhibiting the classic white-wine-induced symptoms of paranoia and righteousness at a higher-than-average volume. If she carried on, she could end up dancing or crying and it was only 2.30 p.m.

Or I could plough into the wine myself, which limited Georgie's consumption but increased mine, leading to less embarrassment all round. Although I needed to factor in the school run in just over an hour: I wasn't a huge fan of the *oops-I-overdid-it-at-lunchtime* playground pick-up scenario; one needed a fast foot, large sunglasses and a staggering amount of extra-strong mints. Due to the paranoia and righteousness mentioned previously, it was far from ideal.

I sat silently, listening to her venomous chatter. She hadn't always been like this. She had always been gracious and kind. My own demons chanted to me: water or wine; good versus evil? Which would it be? I took tiny sips of each, hoping the correct choice would spring out and declare its victory.

2

SUSANNAH HASTINGS: DISORDERLY mane of golden hair, face of a goddess. Once I'd got past the impertinence and scent of horse manure, I'd found myself a gem of a friend. Today she stomped across the sports field toward a playground of waiting parents, parading a blazer in one hand and a grass-stained sock in the other. She thrust the blazer into the air on an index finger to make the announcement, our bland gossip grinding to a halt as we waited to hear which pitiful child would be named and shamed today. I couldn't help but feel morbidly excited—none of us could; just a crowd of meddlesome villagers at a witch trial.

'Charlotte Hamilton.'

Shit, it was mine.

'Ah, Eliza, there you are. Would you look at the state of this?' She tossed the blazer at me in disgust. 'You really need to talk to Charlotte about the importance of looking after her belongings. She's almost six for goodness' sake. Now, about those *National Geographics* you wanted. They've been sliding around in the back of my car since Thursday and I'm about ready to burn them.'

'Like a witch?' I said, without meaning to.

'What? No. Where did you park?' Susannah smiled. It was a *You're odd, aren't you?* sort of smile. I'd been getting a lot of those lately.

'No car today.' I gave what I considered to be a convincing

pat on the hips. 'Summer's just around the corner. Got to get my fat arse into gear.'

'Did you get drunk at lunchtime?'

'What? No.' I laughed, a little too much. 'I just thought, you know...nice day, fresh air, less carbon dioxide for us all to breathe in.'

'Oh, Liza, I love you dearly, but do shut the fuck up.' Susannah squeezed my shoulder and I was left feeling sinful yet warm; a cute little disgrace of a person. 'Let's find Charlotte and I'll drive you home.'

'I'm absolutely fine.'

Susannah moved closer. 'Were you drinking at home, on your own?'

'No, I had lunch with Georgie today and you know how much she likes her wine. I had two glasses and then drank gallons of water.' It was unnecessary to mention the second bottle. It had little relevance to the conversation.

'Well I'm taking you home anyway so I can get rid of these blasted magazines. You get the girls. I'll grab Teddy from the nursery and dump this filthy sock in the bin.'

'Whose is it?' I asked.

'Not labelled. Honestly, what kind of parent doesn't label their children's socks?'

Susannah's standards were, generally speaking, unattainable. Most of the mothers here struggled to even look her in the eye. Me included, initially. That had all changed during the first term at school. Susannah had organised a night out, thought it would be good for us all to get to know each other a little better. She invited twenty, but only three turned up. They drank wine spritzer, talked about how blessed they were and went home at 9 p.m. Susannah and I did not drink spritzers or go home at 9 p.m. We did what we set out to do: we got to know each other a little better.

Susannah had moved to London at twenty-one, where she

proceeded to wipe the floor in corporate advertising. At the age of forty-two, with an array of inadequate men blundering in her wake, she had approached Simon, a junior executive in the firm. She'd had her eye on Simon for quite some time. He was thirty-one and athletic with a strong jawline and a mop of flaxen hair. He was passionate and driven, thoughtful and sensitive.

She asked him out to a chic Soho bar for an evening of champagne and oysters. She had a teensy little favour to ask and had prepared what she considered to be the perfect pitch:

'Simon, I'd like to discuss the possibility of you fathering my children without the constraints of parental responsibility. I've consulted my doctor and other fertility professionals and I'd like to present you with a brief synopsis of the procedure involved.'

Simon howled with laughter before informing Susannah that he was unequivocally homosexual.

'I know,' Susannah had said. 'And you're perfect.'

Simon listened to the pros and the cons, the ifs and the buts. By the time they'd finished the second bottle, the thought of the clinic seemed cold and expensive. Simon suggested that, if Susannah was happy to pick up the bar bill, he was happy to go back to her apartment and deliver his goods into a turkey baster. And considering her basal temperature was holding at 98.1 degrees, it seemed crazy not to.

Simon had been so enchanted by the idea of fatherhood without the pressure, that after Tilly was born, he offered Susannah a second helping.

When Teddy was born, she moved to the coast and renovated a barn on some land just outside of town where she was raising the children, along with a horse and three chickens. Simon's role as a mere sperm donor evolved: he had a key to the house and visited whenever he could, sometimes staying for the weekend. He took the children swimming or back to his flat in London, where they'd see a show or an exhibition at one of the big museums. There were no maintenance payments, no custody issues, no competition, no jealousy. As Susannah said, 'It just bloody well works.'

'Mummy, you smell all minty. Can I have a mint, Mummy, please, please, please.' Charlotte tugged at my bag as we climbed into Susannah's muddy 4×4. 'Tilly, would you like a mint? Teddy, you can't have a mint cos you're too young. Mummy, is Teddy too young to have a mint?'

The lunchtime joy of languishing around in the bosom of the Val de Loire was fast wearing off: a headache, irritability and an unquenchable thirst were now putting their feet up and making themselves at home. Susannah's frenzied productivity with the children and the magazines and the flawless parking skills seemed to amplify my incompetence.

'Right, you put the kettle on. I'll shift these magazines straight into your car. Where *is* your car?'

'I left it at the restaurant,' I said. 'Better safe than sorry these days.'

Susannah leaned in for another patronising I'm-fabulously-together-and-you're-clearly-not whisper. 'Are you *sure* you're okay? I could take Charlotte home for a bit of supper and you could have a rest if you like.'

Yes, please. Take my daughter off my hands and let me sleep for a week, without waking up hot and drenched, heart racing, consumed with angst. It's just a phase, stop thinking about it.

'Absolutely not.' I whirled around the kitchen in a pathetic attempt to demonstrate the sort of efficiency I presumed was expected of me by Susannah. 'Thank you anyway. That's very kind, but she needs an early night.'

Forty-five minutes and a couple of painkillers later, I was down to one child refusing to read, on the basis that she didn't like words; she only liked Barbie.

'But Barbie is very good at reading,' I said, trying to thrust a book under her nose. 'I'll read the first page.'

'What's for dinner?'

'What about something easy like cheese on toast?'

'Yummy, cheese on toast. Can I eat it on my lap while I watch *Barbie*?'

Sod it, why not.

Barbie had found herself in a princess finishing school where all the girls were catty and vindictive. Barbie must prove she is the heir to the kingdom before she and her family are forced to live a life of poverty.

I considered millennial Barbie to be a pretty decent role model. In many of her films she overcame adversity by bestowing kindness on others, using strong core values to help the misfortunate. These qualities were all the more admirable considering her appearance, where she could just as easily doss around a hotel pool in a bikini, sipping cocktails while everyone ogled her hot body.

My issue here was not with Barbie, but the sheer volume of malicious behaviour from so many girls in one school.

I hit pause.

'Mummy, why did you do that?'

'Because I want you to remember that this is only a movie, and in real life most people aren't mean like this. As long as you respect people and are nice to them, they will treat you the same way.' I only realised I was lying when I'd said it out loud. Too late now.

'But, Mummy...' Charlotte's eyes began to fill. I didn't like her film and I was disappointed with every single one of the princesses in the royal palace.

'Oh, darling, come here.' I reached out to hug her but she pulled away.

At that very moment, Charlotte's real-life knight in shining armour bounded in and swept her up into his arms, where she fell limp and helpless, weeping with relief at being rescued from the wicked queen.

'What's up, angel-face? Why the tears?'

'Mummy paused *Barbie* because she thinks that all the princesses are horrid.'

'Really?' Will frowned at me. 'Maybe Mummy needs to chill out.'

Once Prince Charming had heroically restored peace within the kingdom, I sloped off to the kitchen to prepare a resentful concoction of tired leftovers for his dinner. Ten minutes later he was hovering over my shoulder, blatantly judging my ability to peel an avocado. 'Hey, Liza, drink too much wine at lunchtime, did we?'

'No, I did not drink too much wine at lunchtime Will.'

'Okay.' Will treated himself to an eyebrow raise and a sly smile. 'Just wondered where the car was, that's all.'

'It's at the restaurant because I had *two* glasses of wine and I am responsible. I'll pick it up tomorrow.'

'And how is Georgie?'

'She's fine. How's your white horse?'

'What the hell are you talking about, Liza? Are you okay?' I decided that Will was the male version of Susannah and I wondered idly if they were having an affair.

'Sorry. I...'

Tears. Giant hot blobs of them, saving me from my self-induced shipwreck.

'Oh, Liza, come here.'

And so another, not-so-fair maiden crumbled in his arms. He made a pot of tea and I told him the latest news from Georgie. He told me about one of his more unusual clients, a man in his late fifties, who wanted to be photographed in neon-pink hot pants emptying the dishwasher—a present for his wife's birthday.

I tucked Charlotte up in bed and apologised for saying that the princesses were mean. She said that it was okay because, in the end, all princesses were nice; it was only the mother who was mean and that was because she was getting old.

Will made some outdated grunts about me working too

hard, that I should drink some water and have an early night. He offered to cycle down in the morning to get the car. He also asked me if I thought drinking at lunchtime was really suitable, as if I was trying to pull off haute couture on the school run or clown shoes at a funeral.

I made a firm decision to rise at dawn, dust off my bike and collect the car myself.

3

It was 6.30 a.m. on a beautiful spring morning. I was a balanced forty-five-year-old mother and partner, perfectly capable of juggling my own business, Will's accounts, longstanding friends and colourful relatives. As of today, I would begin a simple morning fitness regime, starting with this morning's cycle ride. When I returned home, I would drag the Nutri-Bullet out of the dark corner cupboard and make us all a nourishing smoothie before anyone in my happy little household had even fluttered open their eyelids.

Bessie creaked and strained with seasonal neglect. Cobwebs and dried-up insects coated her chain, the lack of lubrication causing her to hobble with martyrdom toward her destination. Spring, however, had arrived, Bessie's hibernation was over and once we'd warmed ourselves up, had a hose down and some WD40, we'd be able to enjoy the warm months ahead of us: two well-oiled machines barely ruffled by ageing mechanics.

The ride was shorter than I'd remembered, comprising, for the most part, a gentle downhill gradient until the very last corner, where the road drops down, giving the first sweeping views of the harbour. I put my legs out to the side and freewheeled all the way to the bottom, hoping to channel a degree of exhilaration. I drank in the fine sea mist and, for the first time in weeks, I felt grateful—grateful for my health; for Will and Charlotte; for my home.

Then, just as the clouds began to part and the sun burst its first shards of light onto the receding tide, it happened—a divine revelation: I'd left the fucking car keys on the kitchen table.

No, no, no. I did not leave the car keys on the kitchen table. My heart picked up. There was absolutely no point panicking about the car keys now. In the highly unlikely event that I did forget to bring the car keys, I would simply throw my head back with laughter, hop back on the bike and pedal my way up the gruelling incline, relishing the challenge, entertaining myself with the thought of retelling the tale to the girls some-time soon, when we got together for that tapas night I kept meaning to arrange.

I rested the backpack on the bonnet and began to remove items in a serene manner: phone, bottle of water, purse, empty crisp packet, Charlotte's charm bracelet, last year's diary, some acorns and three lollipop sticks.

I allowed myself a short scream, just the one. Fine, I'd made it to the car but the keys were at home. Hahaha. No big deal.

The first steep hill was not as tough as it looked, but the subtle slow incline home: that was the one that laughed in my face. *Skipping around the kitchen making a wholesome breakfast for the family are we? No, I didn't think so.*

'Hey, you've been ages, did you get the car?' Will and Char-lotte were lounging around the breakfast bar in their dressing gowns, eating cereal straight from the packet. 'What's up? You look like you're about to pass out.'

'I don't think I've been that long.' I managed to talk casually and suppress the coughing fit that loitered in my burning windpipe. 'Have you seen the car keys? They were right here on the table.'

'Oh, Liza, you didn't, did you? Hilarious!'

I steadied my breath and pictured myself beside a still lake listening to birdsong. The lake was surrounded by gently sway-ing willows and smooth white rocks. I imagined picking up a rock and marvelling at its pure beauty before lobbing it in the general direction of Will's head.

They both stared back at me like I was the single most absurd human they'd ever seen. Will shuffled around some newspapers and a packet of granola. 'Nope, no car keys here. Sorry.'

I cupped Charlotte's face in my hands. 'Did you move Mummy's car keys, darling? Tell Mummy where you put them.'

'No, Mummy, I don't know where they are.'

'It's okay. Mummy isn't cross. It's just important that I know where they are, so we can all get to school and work on time.' My teeth gnashed together beneath my smile. 'Try to think, Charlotte, please.'

'I don't know, Mummy. I told you.' She slid onto Will's lap; her relaxed expression now wary.

'Liza, she didn't move them, okay. Have you checked the backpack?'

'What? Of course I've checked the bloody backpack, Will, it was on my back. Do you think I'm some kind of bumbling *idiot*?' Another, shrew-like woman had taken control of my voice box, making my tone bitter and shouting the word 'idiot'.

The silence that followed was only broken by Charlotte having the nerve to crunch down on some cornflakes she'd been holding in her mouth.

'They must've fallen down here.' I dropped to the floor and scrambled around on all fours, rubbing my eyes frantically to ward off the threat of tears.

Will peered under the table and jangled the keys above my head. 'You obviously didn't check the front pocket, did you?'

No.

'Yes. I definitely checked the front pocket.'

Will stood up and headed toward the stairs. 'For the record, I don't think you're an idiot, but I could easily change my mind. I'll chuck some clothes on and go down there now. It'll take me five minutes.' *Because I'm so smug and effortlessly fit.*

'By the way, Johnno just called on the landline and asked if you could pick up three more pink azaleas for the Andersons.'

'Why can't he do it?'

'Because he's already there and you probably don't pay him enough.'

I crawled back up to the table and hugged Charlotte, the free-wheeling euphoria of earlier now a hazy memory. 'Sorry, darling.' She squeezed me tight around the waist and I was instantly forgiven. I couldn't bring myself to apologise to Will, but that was okay because he'd taken the higher ground, rendering himself indifferent to apology anyway.

'Mummy?'

'Yes?'

'How can you cry and smile all at the same time?'

'It's something that mummies can do because we are very clever,' I said, kissing her on the head.

The high point of today was remembering the Andersons' azaleas: the right size, colour and amount. They were at home and in their usual high spirits when I eventually arrived. 'Here she is. Had a nice lie-in, eh, Eliza? Poor Johnno has been hard at it since before eight. Ha ha.' Mr Anderson: pencil-thin, late seventies, spent his days pondering over his immense garden and laughing hysterically at his own jokes. 'Now, let me sort some coffee, so we can discuss my exciting idea for the west lawn. You might want to fetch your sketch pad.'

The Andersons, at times draining and eccentric to the point of confusion, were my favourite clients by far, always keeping us busy with unusual designs while plying us with top-notch fresh coffee. They never quibbled an invoice and always sang our praises at the bridge club.

Mr Anderson appeared on the front terrace wheeling a nearly defunct hostess trolley loaded with coffee and plates, and what looked like a large femur resting across the top. He threw a giant tartan rug at Johnno. 'Do the honours would you, old chap? I need to get this beauty down to some manageably sized portions.' He took the bone off to a tree stump where he produced a cleaver and split it into three neat sections.

I looked at Johnno and briefly imagined him and Mr Anderson sitting on the tartan rug, gnawing bones and discussing the population problem. I could hear a commotion up at the house before the loud creak of the heavy barn door: Winifred, Daphne and Queen Mary, the resident cocker spaniels, ran in frantic circles around Mrs Anderson as she walked down carrying a plate, which I hoped was holding her infamous lemon drizzle cake. 'Girls, calm down and go and see Daddy. Shoo!'

The excitable barking was followed by a ruckus over one portion of bone which was evidently superior to the others. It was soon replaced by peaceful snorting and slurping. Queen Mary scurried off, head down, to her covert burial site.

'Get those plates ready, Mr A.' They called each other Mr and Mrs A, but I knew their first names were Audrey and Harold because I had nosed at a wedding invitation pinned to the fridge. I'd only heard her call him Harold once, when she was scolding him for flirting with the postwoman.

'So, Eliza,' Mr A eased himself down next to me on the rug. 'I've been contemplating what to do with the west lawn for some time now, as you know. The grandchildren have all gone off to university and it seems pure lunacy to keep it like this. So, you'll be glad to know that I've made my decision.' He paused to rub his hands together, adding to the suspense. 'I would like you, Eliza, you...' Another excruciating pause. '...to create for me...a Persian carpet garden.' He clapped his hands together with glee, almost to suggest that I could knock one up, just like that. Of course, we'll start this afternoon and have it in the bag by lunchtime tomorrow.

I had been concerned that something like this was coming.

He'd been to visit the gardens at Highgrove last summer and had been fidgety ever since.

'So, what do you think? Up to the challenge?'

No, not really, Mr Anderson. There were plenty of other gardens at Highgrove that you could have chosen, like the Cottage Garden or the Wildflower Meadow. How the hell do you expect me to recreate a Chelsea Flower Show Silver Medallist on your lawn when I can't even find my car keys?

'Wow, are you kidding? Of course I'm up to it. What an amazing idea.'

4

WILL KICKED THE pile of *National Geographic*s, which had been in the hallway for the best part of two weeks. 'Are these magazines going to live here for ever, Eliza?'

'I can't move them now, Will, I've got five bags of grass cuttings in the car. I'll do it tomorrow if I get time.'

'Only asking. Could you call the suppliers for me today and chase up that flash gun?'

'I'm heading straight to the Andersons' to go through this design. That could take all day—you know what they're like. Charlotte, shoes on now, please, we've got to leave in one minute.' I walked over to the magazines and straightened them, hoping that their temporary home might add an air of cultural awareness to the hallway. 'Can't you phone them?'

'Not really,' Will said, his shoulders slumping in such a way that made me want to slap him. 'I'm out on a job all day.'

'So am I.'

And here we are, back on the merry-go-round of who is busiest or more exhausted, which one of us had the least amount of sleep or whose work was most physically tiring: *me, always me.*

'You've got the day off tomorrow, can't you do it then?'

'Day off? Will, let me tell you what I do on my day off.'

'Okay, okay.' Will held his hands up in a pitiful attempt to guard himself from the flurry of banality that was about to spew from my mouth.

'I'm getting up at 6.30 to start the laundry. *Then* I will

scrub the bathroom. *Then* I will make your lunch. *Then* I will take Charlotte to school. *Then* I will vacuum the entire house. *Then...*'

I knew I should stop. Self-respect aside, it was just such a pointless exercise. Will wasn't listening and why would he? He'd pulled down the shades, pushed play on some abstract Pink Floyd track and gone to a happier place. All he could hear now was a mild droning of 'tip, socks, dinner, toilet, laundry' in the background.

But I could not and would not stop. Not until I had squeezed out every last drop of righteousness, right there onto the hallway floor. And why not? I was the one who'd be mopping it up later. I had officially become one of *those* women, as Georgie would say. Last time I looked, I'd been planning my status as Super-Mum, merrily pureeing carrots and dreaming up an infallible business plan. I didn't recall the shrew creeping in, weaving her way silently through my veins and setting up home in my prefrontal cortex.

'My admin, your admin, award-winning Persian carpet gardens... *Charlotte, have you got your shoes on yet?*'

Will looked at something on his phone and sighed. All he wanted to do was kiss his daughter goodbye and get out the door as soon as possible. 'Do you know what, Eliza? I'm just going to do it myself.'

'Good. Thank you.' Why was I thanking him?

'I take it you're not out with Georgie tomorrow then? Not with that to-do list.'

'I might pop out for a quick lunch, just to see how she's getting on.'

'Right. Well, don't let her bleed you dry.'

'She's hardly bleeding me dry, Will. She just needs a non-judgemental ear, that's all.'

'Yes, but you're her niece. Shouldn't she be talking to her friends about this?'

'You know what? It's actually quite nice to spend time with

her *and* to be treated to lunch out every now and again.'
One–Nil to me. As I was standing on the bottom stair and
he was not towering over me, I kissed Will on the forehead.
'We're late. Come on, Charlotte.'

'Mummy, I can't find my shoes.'

It was rewarding to take the higher ground and I could see
why Will made such a habit of it. I felt superior in a way quite
foreign to me. I had the ability to float back upstairs, recover
the lost shoes and still get to school on time without a harsh
word to be heard. The bin liners full of grass cuttings would be
going to the dump before I did anything else, not staying in the
car for another week, forming mushroom rings and small com-
munities of centipedes. I would simply call the Andersons and
tell them that I would be arriving twenty minutes later than
scheduled, with no need to crash in, gasping for breath, blaming fictitious roadworks or perfectly innocent barcode scan-
ners at Garden Depot.

Except that I didn't really take the higher ground. I stood
on the stairs and ranted like a banshee for five minutes while
everyone pretty much ignored what had become standard
behaviour.

Will was probably right about Georgie; she could be
exhausting, but she refused to speak to anyone else about it,
so what was I to do? She forged on with that perpetual smile
gushing about the weather, the lighter evenings, the tennis
club—and the grandchildren.

5

'Not all three of them?'

'Yes, all three of them. What the hell am I going to do, Eliza? You *have* to help me.' Georgie took a gulp of water and looked around anxiously for the waiter.

'You'll be fine. You're a fabulous grandma. How old's Leo now?'

'He's twenty-two weeks.' Georgie allowed herself a smile, but she was far from thrilled. This was a big setback in the quest to keep her head in the sand.

Tom and Tara did this about every three months so they could have 'us time', which typically involved business-class flights and five-star hotels in Switzerland or some Eastern European country I'd never heard of. But Uncle David had always been here before, and now there was a baby thrown into the mix.

Tara, to the untrained eye, was a dream daughter-in-law: polite, chatty, gracious. Why, the last time they had visited, she'd even had the forethought to bring her own thousand-thread count Egyptian cotton bed sheets.

'She's not breastfeeding then?' I asked.

'Breastfeeding? Darling, she practically gave birth on the trading-room floor and sent little Leo home on the Central Line while she closed a deal. Tara doesn't breastfeed.'

'You'll have a great time with them,' I said. 'Don't worry about the baby. Just cuddle him and feed him, he'll be fine.' I thought back to Charlotte at that age—night after night of pacing the floor with wind or teething pains. 'What's it for? Two nights?'

'Three.'

'Three? How lovely. You'll really get to bond. Where are they off to this time?'

'Poland.' Georgie sighed. 'I'm not worried about the girls, it's just the baby. I'm going to be up half the night. I'm too old for this, really I am. And where's your uncle when all this is going on?'

Should I, as a blood relative, be offering an explanation for his conduct? What if there's some unspoken genetic responsibility that I'm completely unaware of?

'Why don't you ask him to come home that weekend?'

The audacity of me.

'Oh yes, Eliza, what a fabulous idea, why didn't I think of that?' She made a telephone out of her hand: '*Oh hello darling, it's me, your wife. Sorry to bother you, but our grandchildren are visiting and I thought you might like to drag yourself away from the boudoir of that plastic-titted slut to sing nursery rhymes and change nappies with me, for old times' sake.*' She glared at me. 'He'll be down here like a shot I'm sure.'

'Sorry, Georgie, I didn't mean—'

Georgie reached for my hand. 'No, I'm sorry. Don't listen to me, I'm just sounding off about the same old nonsense. It'll be fine.'

'It's important to open up about everything, it'll do you good.'

I needed to tread carefully to avoid any unnecessary orders from the bar. Georgie had a tennis lesson at 3 p.m., so we were on mineral water. We could have a productive, sensible conversation, instead of a wine-fuelled rant.

'No point. Nothing can be done at present, so I'm making the best of a bad situation. Worse things happen at sea.'

'Divorce him.'

Georgie tutted and averted her eyes, making a big display out of rearranging her napkin.

'I don't really think—'

'Phone him right now and tell him you're filing for divorce on the grounds of adultery. Do it. Then call some agents and get them to value the house—this afternoon.' The shrew had made an executive decision to step in and take over the reins. Someone had to.

'Eliza, darling, you must understand something.'

'No, Georgie, *you* must understand that I am not ten years old anymore. I'm not happy to see you in that house, night after night, on your own, while he's swanning around up there stuffing his face with foie gras or whatever it—'

'And silicone.'

'Yes. No. Not silicone. I don't want to think about that, okay? Stop talking about sex all the time.'

Georgie folded her arms. 'I was only making a joke, Eliza. What's got into you?' She was becoming agitated, but the shrew forged ahead.

'This is madness and you're letting him get away with it. You should be out and about, having a great time.'

'I *am* having a great time, thank you very much.'

'No you're not. You're pretending to have a great time. In reality you're hoping it'll all just fizzle out before anyone from the tennis club gets a whiff of it. I wish Dad were here to read him the riot act.'

Georgie dropped her eyes to her lap. 'Excuse me,' she said and headed off to the ladies. I noted that the shrew had made a swift exit too. No hanging around to pat me on the back and congratulate me on a job well done. No 'Good work, Eliza, got to be cruel to be kind.' None of that; just the familiar sense of regret and uncertainty over opinions I should probably have kept to myself.

'Alright, darling, I've paid already.' Georgie was back at the table but there was still no eye contact. 'Shall we go? I've got my lesson in an hour and I need to change.'

She declined a lift home. 'It's only ten minutes from here if I get a march on. It'll be a good warm-up for tennis.'

'I went too far, I'm sorry,' I said, as I kissed her goodbye.

'Nonsense. I'll call you in the week.'

6

MR WITHERS: ONE of Elm Tree care home's loveliest and liveliest of residents.

'Not more bloody primulas.'

'Yes, Mr Withers, more bloody primulas, I'm afraid. I have made alternative suggestions, but...'

'It's her, you know, not him.' Mr Withers gestured toward the house. 'There's something wrong with her. She's got an IUD.'

'What makes you say that?' I asked.

'I know the signs. My niece has got one.' He nodded wisely, screwing up his forehead. 'Cleans anything and everything all day long, she does, just like Linda.'

'Do you mean *OCD*?'

'That's what I said—IUD. Day in, day out, can't move this and don't touch that. She's the mad one around here. I said to Margot: She's at it again with those yellow gloves on. Don't be leaving anything lying around, it'll be in the bin, you mark my words.'

Mr Withers still spoke to Mrs Withers. They had both come here for respite care eight years earlier when Margot broke her hip, but she'd struggled to recover and had passed away six months later. Her slippers were kept by her side of the bed and her clothes still took up half of their small wardrobe.

'Talking of gloves, have you got yours handy?' I asked.

'Of course.' Mr Withers fumbled around in his trouser pocket and pulled out his tweed gardening gloves. 'Always prepared on a Thursday, highlight of my week. What are we doing today?'

The bags of manure that needed to be moved from the back of my car to the greenhouse were a little weighty and Linda would be furious if she saw Mr Withers helping me.

'I've got this, my dear,' he said, dragging one of the bags across the lawn. 'This is man's work. I don't want you hurting yourself. Are these from your friend with the horse?'

'Yes.'

His face lit up. 'She's the one with those *National Geographic* magazines you were going to bring me. Have you got them?'

'Yes...well no, actually. She forgot them again. Sorry, I do keep reminding her.'

'That's a shame. My nephew brought me a copy last Christmas and it was all about the giant redwoods of California. I wanted to read it to Margot cos I know she can still hear me, but I can't because bloody Linda threw it in the bloody bin.'

'I'll nag her about them. She's terribly forgetful.'

'That's the trouble with you youngsters: you're always rushing around with so much to do. You don't stop to smell the blossom on the tree until you've slipped on the autumn leaves and broken something you really need.' His face dissolved into a faraway thought. 'Next thing you know, it's a long, dark winter.' Without saying another word, Mr Withers disappeared back up to the house and I didn't see him again for the rest of the day.

Evidently my goal of the week was to upset pensioners: two down and it was only Thursday morning. I'd still got this afternoon and a full day tomorrow to score a hat trick. Maybe I could vandalise a mobility scooter or reprimand a kind old lady in the supermarket for dithering over the rhubarb.

I'd just finished packing twenty-two hanging baskets with primulas and was about to sit down in the greenhouse for a flask of tea and an emotional outburst when Linda appeared.

'Everything okay out here?' she asked, slightly short of breath.

'Yes, great thanks, Linda. So much pollen around at the moment,' I said, wiping away a tear and gulping back the stale lump of hysteria that had been threatening to leap out and scream at someone all morning.

'Don't talk to me about pollen: it's all over the house and I've got enough to do with all these care plans.'

And she was off: the bathrooms, the laundry, the idiot cook. Her rubber-gloved hands gesticulated wildly around flushed cheeks, her face contorted with resentment and exhaustion. It was like looking into an illuminated mirror.

'Lucy's refusing point-blank to study for her exams and what's Brian doing? Playing golf, that's what Brian's doing.' She threw her hands up in despair. I remembered a good joke about golfers but I held back, deciding to offer something far more inappropriate.

'Linda, how old are you?'

'I beg your pardon?' She looked stunned, but I'd said it now.

'Sorry. If you don't mind me asking, how old are you?'

'I heard you the first time, Eliza. I'm fifty-two. Why do you ask?'

'Because you always seem so stressed. Did you ever think that life might've turned out, you know, a bit differently?' I observed the line of professional conduct and strode on past, risking an eight-grand contract along my merry little way.

'Huh?' Linda seemed bemused and remained motionless for a moment, staring at the bags of manure. The stuffy air in the greenhouse pinged with silence.

'That was quite rude of me actually, Linda, I didn't mean to—'

'Well, it's to the point, I'll give you that.' She slowly took off her gloves and I was unsure whether she was going to hug me or slap me. 'Look, this place is a big commitment. There's a lot of work involved and it's tiring.'

'Yes, I can imagine. It's just that women these days...we do a lot. Life's so manic and we're all a bit crazy, don't you think?'

Linda was frowning at me and nodding her head, but also smiling, probably with disbelief at my inability to shut the fuck up. 'Eliza?'

'Yes?'

'There are a lot of dandelions sprouting up in the beds around the decking.'

'Okay. I'll get to that this afternoon.'

'And the conifers near the fence need some more wood chip.'

'I did put some down there last week.'

'Well, it's not enough. I can still see dirt around the base.'

'Of course, I'll bring more next week.'

She lowered her eyes to the manure. 'Is *this* for the vegetable garden?'

'Yes. I'll lay most of it this afternoon, but Mr Withers would like to keep some for his tomatoes.'

'Charming. Well when your young boy comes, maybe he can put a fence around the vegetable garden—health and safety. Anyway, I can't stand around chatting all day; some of us have got care homes to run. I'll see you next week, Eliza.'

On the upside, I didn't lose the contract.

7

I PULLED UP outside the school in my battered diesel hatchback at the same time as Organic Emily glided in on her electric bicycle. She told me about her plans for the Easter holidays, which included hiking on Exmoor and volunteering at an animal shelter. I told her about my plan to work for most of it and put Charlotte in holiday club or in front of the TV, but she didn't see the irony and I was left feeling like a bad mother instead of a dry-witted businesswoman. Emily informed me about The Earth Salon, where I could get a non-toxic manicure for half price until the end of March. I admired her cuticles and promised to book an appointment the minute I got home.

But I didn't. After showering and sorting out laundry, I meandered through the threats and bribes of homework, unloaded the dishwasher and replied to text messages. I played a game of *The Little Mermaid* with Charlotte, where I was cast as the Sea Witch. I protested as I wanted to be the mermaid's mother, but the mermaid did not have a mother and we weren't allowed to pretend, so the Sea Witch it was.

Five minutes in I lost the will to live and used my evil powers to freeze Charlotte and the co-starring toys so I could go into the kitchen, pour myself a nice glass of wine and get on with dinner. Halfway through chopping the coriander, a turn of emotion found me back in the greenhouse at the crying episode I'd embarked on earlier—the one I would've had if Linda hadn't so rudely interrupted me.

I wondered if Organic Emily ever had a clandestine sob in her kitchen while chopping up organic herbs and knocking back a glass of organic red?

Organic Emily would have exactly the same after-school routine as me, but with three children and a husband who worked away in Paris. This did not faze Organic Emily. Her children would sit quietly around an old oak table scattered with kooky little vases of lavender, doing their homework as efficiently as possible, so they could all be rewarded with a nice crunchy organic apple. Once they'd played a game where she was cast as the fairy godmother, they would all skip off to bed without any fuss or last-minute toy dramas.

Organic Emily wouldn't slam cupboard doors, despair about her failure as a mother, girlfriend, niece and landscape gardener. She wouldn't panic over assignments or fabricate images of her husband being spanked by gorgeous French prostitutes.

Organic Emily would be in a complicated yoga pose by now, or working on her Open University degree in Environmental Science and sipping turmeric tea with her squeaky clean, non-toxic fingernails.

Will crashed in through the back door, grubby and sweaty after his weekly early evening cycle with a load of other middle-aged men who were conscious about keeping fit and who used this as an excuse to disappear for hours on a Sunday morning so they could indulge in what they liked to think of as 'healthy competition', before stopping off in a retro cafe for a macchiato and smashed avocado on toast while completely avoiding anything remotely family or chore related. We paused to gauge one another's mood: I saw irritation; I'm pretty certain he saw madness. He sighed. 'What's the matter with you?'

'I'm a total arsehole.'

'You're not an arsehole. You're fab.' What a stupid thing to say.

'I am not fab, Will. I am an arsehole.'

'Let's compromise—you're a fabulous arsehole.' Will smiled to himself, delighted by his own humour. 'Glass of wine?'

'I'm already on it.' I raised my glass. 'There's some chilli in the pan.'

'I'll get Charlotte into bed, then you can confess all.' Will thrived in this environment: the white knight returned to his castle just in time to rescue the damsels before their entire world collapsed.

I could hear Charlotte and Will upstairs, giggling over a book. I poured water onto the burnt rice at the bottom of the saucepan and gave it a feeble scrape, wishing it was someone else's job. I left it to soak and sat down, the wine lolled around in my empty stomach, sending fleece-coated signals up to my brain, smoothing out the edges of the day.

'I'm letting her have thirty minutes of a *Barbie* movie,' Will said. 'And she wants a kiss from Mummy.'

I tip-toed into Charlotte's bedroom: a haven of soft lilac with fluff and love hearts and kept promises; a place where unicorns danced on rainbows and beautiful fairies with skinny legs and perky tits breathed sparkles of optimism into the air around them. 'Love you, darling. Nighty-night.' I kissed her cheek and squeezed her tightly.

'Mummy?'

'Yes?'

'Can the Sea Witch break her spell and unfreeze all of my toys now so they can go to sleep? They're very tired and frightened.'

'Of course. I'll do that right away.'

With an elaborate swish of my hand, the spell was broken. Charlotte smiled and snuggled beneath her covers.

'Thank you, Mummy.'

'Don't thank me; thank the Sea Witch.'

'So, what's up?' said Will, more focused on stuffing chilli into his face than my imminent breakdown.

'Well, let's start with how much I *love* upsetting people.'

'Yeah, you're good at that, aren't you? Is this about Georgie? All you did was hit the nail on the head. She'll get over it.'

'It's not just Georgie, it's everyone. Clients, you, all the mums at school are disgusted by my fingernails and Charlotte thinks I'm the Sea Witch from *The Little Mermaid*.'

'Whoa.' Will paused for a gratuitous chuckle. 'Firstly, Charlotte is only five, so give her a break. And when did you start giving a shit about what mums from school think? As for me, I'm here for you. I just don't like being snapped at.'

'When do I snap at you?' I snapped.

Will shrugged. 'On a daily basis at the moment.'

'Well, why didn't you say something?'

'Because sometimes it's easier not to. It's like you have this wall of fire around you and I don't like getting burnt, that's all.'

'*That's all*? Great, now I feel even worse.'

'Just talk to me normally so I know the score, rather than all this mental shit you rant on about.'

I pushed my dinner aside. Will carried on eating and we sat in silence for a moment, his coarse words perched like a lump of raw meat on the table between us.

Sometimes I wished Will was a woman. I'd recently had lunch with an old school friend who'd divorced her husband to marry a woman. Whenever she had a bad day, her wife instantly picked up on her mood and dropped everything so they could sit on the sofa with a glass of wine and talk it through: 'I feel so calm now—she just gets me.' It sounded like heaven.

I let out an exaggerated sigh and returned to the present situation. 'I'm constantly worrying about everything.'

'Like what?'

'I don't know—work stuff, Georgie, paedophiles, stupid people texting when they're driving.'

'Liza, remember that you've taken on a lot more work recently. Maybe it's a bit too much?'

'I should be allowed to grow the business now Charlotte's at school. It's not the 1950s. Anyway, it's nothing to do with work. I just don't feel like I used to.' I forced out a few more tears because Will was not taking me quite as seriously as I would have liked.

'Go on.'

'I'm not sleeping well. I'm always waking up agitated and hot.'

'Why don't you just open the window?'

'Will, can you stop trying to come up with a solution and just listen? I'm snappy because I'm tired and then I feel guilty for being snappy. Then sometimes I feel so *angry*, it's really scary. I don't know what's happening to me.'

Will stared at me, perplexed. I didn't know what to do next so I hurled myself slightly too dramatically into his arms and stayed there until there were no tears left. He found a tissue, lifted up my snot-covered chin and gently wiped away all the chaos from my face.

'Liza?'

'Hmm?'

'Is your period due?'

I did not know how to react. The crying had left me void of emotion. I got up, threw my barely touched dinner into the bin and glided upstairs without saying goodnight. I needed sleep. Sleep and the clarity it would bring to look at things afresh in a new dawn.

I lay awake for hours, starving. Going downstairs to eat now would simply be saying to Will that I had overreacted; a silly little hormonal outburst. I was humbled by the thought of Marion Wallace Dunlop, the first suffragette to go on hunger strike in 1909. I imagined Marion and Emmeline in their celestial boardroom, both also thinking I had overreacted, and shaking their heads: 'Oh dear, she could at least knock herself up a cheese sandwich and sign that e-petition on female circumcision. How very disappointing.' No matter, I would hold firm.

Will didn't come to bed until 11.30 p.m. I waited, pretending to sleep, and listened for the monotony of his breath, the short puffs of air that escaped from the corner of his mouth, making him sound like a miniature steam train. It wasn't loud, just irksome enough to make me think about the sound of ripping duct tape. I slid out of bed and sneaked downstairs to devour two pieces of butter-laden toast and a cup of tea. I went online and signed the e-petition on female circumcision, thanked the suffragettes for my freedom and tiptoed into the bathroom to attempt a silent wee.

Oh—my period.

8

SUSANNAH MADE A beeline for me in the playground at drop-off, her expression suggesting she had either a mind-blowing proposition or a delicious morsel of gossip to impart.

'So glad I caught you. Is everything alright? You look awful.'

'Cramps.' I rubbed my abdomen, hoping to tame the relentless pulse of my uterus. 'Have you got any paracetamol?'

Susannah opened her highly organised handbag and inspected its contents. 'I've got codeine.'

'What's that?'

'Here, take one, you'll love it. Anyway, it's a bit last-minute, but what are you doing tonight?'

'Tonight?'

'The reason I'm asking is that Teddy went back to London with Simon today to go and see some dinosaur thing at the History Museum. So Tilly and I are having a girls' night in: pizza, nail-painting...you get the picture. Why don't you and Charlotte come over? I could really do with your help with something too.'

'Oh?' It was doubtful that I possessed any skills that could help someone as self-sufficient as Susannah, unless she wanted advice on emotional outbursts or Persian carpet gardens.

'I've got this problem with a case of Argentinian malbec that Simon had the audacity to dump in my garage.' She pulled a heart-wrenching face and a voice to match. 'They're so sad and lonely and far from home. But together, Eliza, we can make a difference.' She clasped my hands in hers. 'By donating just a few hours of your time you can bring a sense of purpose to these poor little lambs, offer them the warmth and sanctuary that they deserve.'

'Wow. That does sound like a worthy cause. I'm not sure I could bring myself to look the other way.'

'I'll take that as a yes then. Bring your PJs and I'll set up the guest room.' It should be noted that Susannah's version of 'setting up the guest room' involved overpriced mineral water and truffles nestled in a sea of sumptuous white towelling. 'Do you think Will can survive the night on his own?'

'He'll be grateful for the peace and quiet. I'm trying to hide the fact that I've got my period, so good timing.'

'Hide your period? Why on earth would you do that?' Susannah's eyes lit up. 'Does he want you to have another baby?'

'What? No. I'll tell you later.'

'Sounds like a psychiatrist's dream.'

By 9 p.m. the girls were in bed. Susannah's lounge was a welcome sanctuary of deep plum furnishings and opulent Liberty cushions. The soft lighting and chilled Ibiza playlist left me feeling entombed, and more than ready to offload.

'We are officially middle-aged now, you know,' said Susannah. 'Things do change.'

'I'm forty-five, not eighty-five and I feel like I've got dementia. I can't remember anything and I'm always wandering around in a haze. It's like I need reading glasses for my brain, to sharpen everything back into focus.'

'Are you getting enough sleep?'

'Five or six hours. I'm always awake at 3 a.m., boiling hot and stressing about random stuff. I'm exhausted and angry and Will just doesn't get it.'

'Does Will have a vagina?'

'No.'

'Then he's not going to get it.'

'I'm not expecting him to understand it. I just want him to listen and be supportive.'

'I'm sorry, Eliza, but you're giving him too much credit. You're expecting Will to fumble his way through the complex maze of female emotions? He doesn't want you to be sad or worried or angry.'

'Because I might forget to do his laundry, or cook his dinner?'

'Because he loves you, and he doesn't want to see you not coping.'

'Yes, this must be a terrible inconvenience for him.'

'Men just want to find the simplest solution.' Susannah shrugged. 'That's the way they're made.'

'I'm sorry, Suze, but it's a bullshit excuse.'

'Hey,' she raised her hands in defence, 'don't shoot the messenger. Let me tell you what Simon told me when I broke up with Mr Musician.'

'Go on.'

Susannah poured more wine and adjusted herself on the sofa to reveal the life-changing statement: 'Men require three things in life and three things only: food, sex and sleep, preferably in that order. If you're looking for anything deeper, you're going to be bitterly disappointed.'

'Oh.'

'Oh indeed. But it's the best piece of advice I've ever been given.'

The balloon of hope that had nestled somewhere between my heart and diaphragm let out a sorry little squeal before being absorbed back into my bloodstream. The statement, for all its severity, made total sense. I had baffled Will for years with my inane rantings of whys and whats, and whose and ifs. He'd always reacted in the only way he knew how—to give me a little pat and blame my hormones.

Then he could return to his simpler life of eating, wanking and snoring.

'But that's so depressing.'

'Why do you think I live on my own?' Susannah said. 'Anyway, how long have you been feeling like this?'

'I don't know. Probably over the last year or so. I seem to have lost all my coping mechanisms.'

'Okay, let's look at this as an outsider, just for a minute. A happy and balanced woman has her first baby at forty. She stays at home and gets into the whole housewife gig, because she thinks it's the right thing to do. Then the baby goes to nursery so she works a few days a week, still keeping up the housewife gig. Then the baby goes to school and she sets up her own business, which involves hard physical labour. She also does admin for her husband and keeps up the housewife and mother gig. She has now reached her mid-forties and feels exhausted and resentful. Why the hell can't she just snap out of it?'

'I see what you're saying, but there are quite a few mums at school who work full time and have more kids than I do and they seem to cope just fine.'

'I'm sorry to break it to you, but they're not in their mid-forties. It's just you, me and Melanie Mulrane rocking that trend.'

'Who's Melanie Mulrane?'

'She's got Freddy in Year Three,' Susannah sighed, appalled at my ignorance of playground who's who. 'You know. On the PTA, awful hair.'

'Oh her.'

Susannah leant over to pour the last dribble of wine into my glass. 'If I was working full time with two kids in my thirties, I'd have squeezed in a pottery class and some sordid affairs.'

'Or an Open University degree in Environmental Science.'

'Emily's not immune to hysteria either, you know.'

I was certain Organic Emily was immune to hysteria—and debauchery.

'What you've got to remember is that a lot of those women are probably looking at you, thinking: *Wow, she's got her own business, works her own hours, isn't stuck behind a desk all day answering to some arsehole of a boss, or going home to some arsehole of a husband.* The grass always looks greener.'

'But you're raising two kids on your own and you manage fine. You're always so organised and together.'

'I'm organised and together now, but remember that I worked my arse off for twenty-three years to achieve this. Believe me, I'm grateful to be in the position that I'm in, but I envy you...a lot.'

Susannah jabbed the corkscrew into another bottle and waited for my reaction.

'What, me?'

'Yes you. Don't get me wrong, my London years were a lot of fun. I knew my Krug from my Cristal and met some very important *tossers*, but I haven't done half the things you've done. I've not seen Komodo dragons or hatching turtles, or climbed to the top of a volcano to watch the sunrise.'

An image of that glorious morning in Maui filled my head: high above the clouds, shades of violet fused with orange and gold, all the ease and excitement that a new day used to bring back then. What would we eat for breakfast? Where would we go later? Should we get the ferry to Lanai or a flight to Kauai? I'd met up with an old work friend who was also travelling alone, albeit in the opposite direction. We'd had three whole weeks to explore the Hawaiian Islands before she flew home to a cold and wet November. My trip was just beginning and I was giddy with freedom. 'Oh that,' I said, dragging myself back to the present day. 'You could easily do those things now with the kids. Or just wait until they've buggered off to university.'

'When I'm sixty-three? Let's hope I'm still here and fit enough. There's nothing like doing it when you're young and carefree. You bring all that worldly experience to your parenting and your relationships, even your work. You're always so open-minded and accepting.'

I felt awkward and slightly ashamed, but didn't know why. 'Ah, thanks, Suze.' I reached out for a clumsy hug, but we were interrupted by a noise from the top of the stairs.

'*Mummy*.'

'Oh god, whose was that? Yours or mine?'

'Yours hopefully,' I said.

'Yes, sweetie, what's wrong?' Susannah called up the stairs.

'I've wet the bed.'

I'd forgotten that Tilly still had the odd night-time accident and it selfishly made me feel better about having such a disorganised life.

Susannah huffed and made a face. 'Fuckity-fuck. Why tonight?'

'Because they know we're having fun. I'll come and give you a hand.'

'Absolutely not. I insist you stay here and tend to pouring duties.'

I followed my orders and snuggled up under the generous faux fur throw. *Did* the mums from school think I was lucky? I didn't think Susannah envied me, not really. She was just trying to make me feel better about myself, like a true friend. Maybe I had taken my twenties and thirties for granted, whooping it up, working to live, blissfully unaware of the word 'responsibility' until the day I gave birth to Charlotte.

Susannah burst back into the lounge.

'That was quick. Everything okay?'

'Fine. It was barely a dribble. I've changed her pyjamas and stuck a towel under her.'

'She'll be fine. They'll be up in six hours anyway,' I said, loving this other, slightly reckless side of Susannah.

'So, I take it you haven't been to the doctor then?'

'The doctor? How on earth would I explain this to my doctor? She'd think I was a danger to society.'

'Tell her everything you've told me in a nutshell. Lay it on thick about the night sweats, see if you can get some HRT.'

'HRT? Suzie, what the hell are you on about? I'm only forty-five.'

'Eliza, your periods are all over the place, and you're an angry insomniac with hot flushes and memory loss. Hello?'

'Hang on a minute. I am *not* going into the menopause. I don't have hot flushes, I just get hot at night when I've had a bad dream. My periods have only been irregular in the last few months or so.'

'How long is a few months?'

I think back to the time when I'd had to do a pregnancy test because I was two weeks' late, it was the Christmas before last. 'Well actually it's probably more like a year or so, but that's because I've been so stressed. And I'm angry because I'm tired—and stressed.'

'Fine, you're stressed. Go to the doctor for that instead.'

'No, sorry. I would not feel comfortable telling her about this. What if there's a misunderstanding and I get sectioned? I'm certainly not asking about HRT. Hilarious. That's for old people.'

'Well I've been on it for two years and it's a lifesaver, if you ask me.'

'You? On HRT? You are kidding me.'

'Ha, you see, you don't know the real me at all, do you? A few months before Tilly started at nursery I was on the verge of a nervous breakdown.'

Susannah told her story and I had to admit there were some alarming similarities, although I'd never had a hot flush on a first date nor got down on all fours and sobbed in a supermarket car park on Christmas Eve. Not yet.

Susannah's tale went way beyond what little I knew of her; her childhood in Devon, a premature baby brother when she was twelve whose poor health dominated the last of her child-hood; her resentment, then guilt; all the failed relationships, mirrored by her parents' growing disappointment and conse-quent horror regarding the turkey baster.

The conversation felt nourishing and insightful, it would deepen the dynamics of our friendship; drag me out of my self-centred world and make me think about others for a change.

Susannah's voice was rich and soothing. I curled up my legs beneath the throw and dared to rest my eyes, just for a moment.

9

'To be perfectly honest, darling, I can't quite remember.' Georgie furrowed her brow. 'Fifty? Fifty-two, maybe? I was definitely irregular by fifty because I got caught short on my surprise birthday party and had to ruin a perfectly fabulous Hermès scarf.'

'I don't remember you having a surprise fiftieth, where was I?'

'Goodness knows. Maybe you were away. It wasn't my finest hour: a surprise skydive with everyone watching. Honestly, what was your uncle thinking?'

'That's right, I was away for that.' Borneo to be exact, bathing in a hot spring with Luciano, his toned shoulders glistening in the sun. 'I know a cool bar back in Kota,' he'd said, 'we can toast your aunt's birthday.' God he was hot.

'I'm not sure I've ever seen the photos,' I said, pushing aside smutty flashbacks and trying to stay focused on the discussion at hand.

'Some things are better left in the past and that skydive was one of them.'

Luciano wasn't better off left in the past and I wondered what he looked like now. Maybe a little grey at the temples; crow's feet that made him look sexier rather than older? A jolt of lust burnt my cheeks. If I'd bothered to find out his surname, I could've looked him up on Facebook. I imagined an outrageously flirty exchange on Messenger. Stop it. What was the matter with me?

'The only upside of the day was the man I was strapped to, who looked like a young Robert Redford, but I was too concerned by the prospect of double incontinence to flirt with him. Then I got to the ground to discover that, somewhere around 3,000 feet, I'd had a damned period.'

'At least you still wanted to flirt at fifty.'

'I'm sure it hasn't escaped your notice that I still like a flirt at knocking on seventy. I don't feel a day older than twenty-five. I may be showing signs on the outside, but on the inside everything works just tickety-boo, if you know what I mean.'

How did we get back to this? I picked up the menu and chose the first thing I saw.

'I'm going for the crayfish salad.'

'Is that all you're having? It's barely enough to feed a flea. I hope you're not on some faddy diet.'

'You order salad all the time.'

'That's different,' said Georgie. 'I'm older than you.'

'You just said you didn't feel a day over twenty-five.'

'Yes, but my metabolism has slowed down.'

'What does that even mean?' I asked. 'That you lose the ability to burn fat? That you have to choose between obesity and starvation?'

'It just means that you have to be mindful. Why all the questions about ageing? Can't we talk about something else? How about that Anderson couple, do you still see them?'

'Yes, he wants me to recreate one of the gardens at Highgrove on his lawn, but I don't think I'm up to it. I've spent hours staring at images and trying to create mood boards, but I can't seem to get motivated.'

'Nonsense, he's lucky to have someone as clever as you to do that for him. I'm fancying a little glass of the Sancerre. Will you be joining me?'

'No, definitely not today. I've got a meeting at nursery in two hours,' I said, holding firm.

'What a bore. Well, I shall have myself a large glass and the meze plate. See if you can grab her attention, will you? They're dreadfully slow today.'

'Did you ever take HRT?' I asked.

'HRT? Absolutely not. Utter poison.'

'They can't prescribe it if it's poisonous.'

'Oh yes they can: devious advertising and bogus drug trials. It's what killed my mother.'

'I thought she died of cancer.'

'All I'm saying is she took this wonder drug, thinking that menopause was some kind of shameful disease that you had to treat, and two years later she was dead.'

'You think that caused her cancer?'

'I *know* it caused her cancer and she wasn't the only one. They were dropping like flies in the seventies. Then some medical expert announces they botched up the oestrogen balance. It was all over the news.'

'That's outrageous. Did anyone sue?'

'Don't be ridiculous, darling. People didn't sue in the seventies, you just had to get on with it.'

'It can't be that bad these days, surely? One of my friends is on HRT.'

'I wouldn't always trust what the doctor tells you,' Georgie said.

Should I be talking to Susannah about this?

'What makes you say that? Don't you ever go to the doctor?' I asked.

'Not unless I've broken a leg. There's no need, I'm perfectly healthy. Everything in moderation, as they say.'

'Aren't you even on blood pressure tablets? I thought everyone over sixty was on blood pressure tablets.'

'I take nothing apart from a good-quality vitamin C. I've got my Pilates and my tennis, a healthy diet and a little wine every day. Did you know that moderate drinkers have a lower risk of stroke, heart disease and diabetes?'

'Where did you read that?'

'It was an article in the *Daily Mail*,' Georgie said.

'It must be true then.'

'Oh don't start. It's a light-hearted read and I enjoy the Sudoku.' I didn't push it any further. The last time we had discussed Georgie's choice of daily newspaper, we'd ended up in a scathing debate about Brexit and didn't talk for two weeks.

'I thought I might go to the doctor, actually,' I said.

'Gosh, really?' Georgie's face dropped, making me wish I'd never brought it up. 'Is everything okay?'

'I think so. It's hard to pinpoint. I'm just a bit stressed and I'm not sleeping well.'

'I'm hardly surprised, you work like a donkey along with everything else you do. Why don't you drop a couple of days? Get yourself a cleaner and come along to Pilates with me.'

The thought of lying in a room full of ladies from the Rotary Club, tensing my pelvic floor and discussing the state of the NHS held little allure.

'It's not that easy. I just need to learn to cope better. I can't...'

Without any prior warning a pair of jumbo tears sprang from my eyes and I had to bury my face into a brochure about a forthcoming event involving someone from *Master Chef.*

'Goodness me.' Georgie was on her feet, thrusting an embroidered handkerchief into my face. 'Waitress, gin and tonic, please, straightaway. My poor darling, I had no idea you were feeling this awful, what a dreadful aunt I am.'

'I'm alright really; just over-emotional and tired. I keep waking up in the night all frantic and sweaty.'

'Ah, now I understand all the questions about HRT. Well, you're far too young for the menopause so you don't have to worry about that. Now, I'm all ears. Tell me everything.'

I had to admit that the gin and tonic hit the spot, all giant ice cubes and generous wedges of lime. Maybe I too needed to become a moderate drinker, as opposed to my current all-or-nothing approach to alcohol.

I began to offload my barrage of ailments. 'I'm always fishing around, trying to find the right word. I asked a supermarket assistant which aisle the fridge-washer detergent was in the other day. It's embarrassing. I can't tolerate certain foods anymore and I've grown a spare tyre around my waist.'

'Nonsense, there's nothing of you. Make an appointment with the doctor anyway, just to put your mind at rest. Barbara from tennis knew a lady who had night sweats and it turned out to be leukaemia.'

'That's awful. Is she okay?'

'No, died unfortunately. But anyway, I doubt it's anything like that. If you're gaining weight and not losing it, I'm sure you'll be fine. Just don't get fobbed off with some prescription you don't need, that's all.'

'I never thought that it could be anything serious.'

'It's not anything serious,' Georgie said, attempting to waft away the leukaemia bombshell with her hand. 'Forget I even mentioned it. Anyway, talking of serious things, I need you to confirm that you're coming to dinner next Thursday.'

'We are?'

'Yes, you are. It's when Tom and Tara are bringing the children and I wouldn't mind a bit of moral support, if you know what I mean.'

'Okay, we can do next Thursday. Have you spoken to them recently?'

'Only by text to sort out arrangements. They're bringing everything for Leo. I've just got to make up beds for the girls.'

'Have they seen anything of Uncle David?'

'David?' Georgie asked, as if I had mentioned some distant relative she could barely remember. 'I didn't ask. So what time shall I expect you? Around six? Come a bit earlier if you can and help me set the table.' Although I suspected that Georgie would have set and reset the table three times already, ensuring it was fashionable enough for Tara, or classy enough for Tara, before going back to fashionable enough for Tara according to *Vogue Living.*

'What time are they arriving?'

'Around 6.30 p.m. Dinner has been requested for 7 p.m. sharp so the children can be in bed by 8 p.m., else their routine is completely messed up apparently.'

Georgie went on to tell me what she had planned for the children at the weekend, a lot of which I found myself involuntarily involved in. I went along with it, trying to sound enthusiastic, but found myself distracted by the giant life chasm that had unexpectedly cracked open at my feet. It was the chasm that separated the young from the old, and I wouldn't be looking for a bridge anytime soon.

I was late for my meeting because I was sat in the car in a road beside the nursery, searching for night sweats on the Internet. A healthcare website advised me that night sweats were most probably due to one of the following:

1. Menopause. Yes okay, I can relate to a lot of symptoms, but I'm far too young.
2. Sleep apnoea. What's that?
3. Diabetes. Nah.
4. Tuberculosis. Surely I'd know if I had that?
5. Leukaemia. Yes, that's definitely it. I've got leukaemia.

I phoned the doctor and the nearest appointment I could get was in two weeks' time. I told the receptionist of my probable diagnosis and asked if I could be moved to the urgent list. She said that if my symptoms were that bad, I should go to A&E, which was absurd as by the time I'd got there all the sweat would've dried up and I would come across as some sort of hypochondriac.

Later that evening, I sat beside Charlotte's bed and stroked her hair until she fell asleep. Tomorrow I would buy all of her birthday cards up to age eighteen and write a special message in each of them; something along the lines of: *My beautiful daughter, I can't believe you are seven/eight/nine/ten etc. Even though you can't see me, know that I am always there for you, like a ship that has just sailed over the horiz—*

Will clattered into the bedroom, frowning. 'What's the matter now?'

'Ssh, Will, she's asleep,' I snapped, ushering him into the hallway. 'I think I've got leukaemia.'

'Okay. What's for dinner?'

'What? Nothing. I haven't made dinner.'

'Oh.' He retreated back downstairs, obviously having misheard me. I went into our bedroom, pulled the curtains and threw myself onto the bed to carry on with my sombre fantasy: *...like a ship that has sailed over the horizon to see another dawn. Mummy will be with you in the whistling of the wind and the rays of the sun. Always there for...* Hang on. What if Will met someone else and Charlotte liked her more than she ever liked me and they got married really quickly and Charlotte wore a flouncy dress from Monsoon? Everyone would be so pleased for them. Charlotte would ask her if she could call her 'Mummy' and she would cry and say, 'Yes, darling', and then get to play the fairy fucking godmother in games.

'Will?' I shout down the stairs.

'Yes?'

'Who will you marry when I die?'

'Scarlett Johansson.'

Scarlett Johansson would make a pretty good fairy fucking godmother.

10

'ARE THOSE NEW school photos?' I nodded at the toothy grins of Dr Chaudhry's clever-looking children. 'They're growing up fast.'

'How can I help you today, Miss Hamilton?'

'Eliza.'

'Eliza. What seems to be the problem?'

'Umm, it's all a bit silly really.'

'Go on,' Dr Chaudhry adopted a wide smile and blinked impatiently.

'Well, it's not silly at all actually. I don't know why I said that. It's probably very serious but I'm no doctor of course, that's your job.'

'Why don't you start by telling me some of your symptoms?'

'Symptoms. Okay, I would say the main one is a sort of night sweat.'

Just saying the words 'night sweat' made me feel like I'd been propelled into the body of an ageing bank clerk with greasy hair and ill-fitting clothes. I looked down at my red Zara jeans, which were snug around my waist and a tad vibrant, given the occasion. I should've worn my cotton yoga pants— far more sensible and ill-like.

'Let's have a look,' Dr Chaudhry tapped away at her computer. 'So, forty-five years old, you don't smoke and you're not on any medication. Fantastic. Lots of people your age are.'

'My age?'

'Well, *our* age actually. I'm only five years behind you,' she said, grinning with excitement, as if we qualified to join some swanky middle-aged society. 'Now, regular periods?'

'Umm, sort of, give or take the odd month.'

'Fantastic.' Dr Chaudhry was fond of using the word 'fantastic', possibly as a polite alternative to: *There's sod all wrong with you. Now please go home and stop wasting my time.* 'Any recent changes in weight?'

'Yes. I'm fat now.' I grabbed a handful of flesh which spilled over the waistband of my jeans, but Dr Chaudhry remained blasé.

'That's perfectly normal for a woman of your age. Have you been feeling more tired than usual?'

'Absolutely. I'm exhausted all the time, but that's because I can't sleep, which makes me anxious and moody. I pee a lot and I can't think straight. Do you think I've got leukaemia?'

'No, I don't think you've got leukaemia. Any other symptoms?'

'Yes. I've been crying a lot and feeling a bit...'

'Go on.'

'Agitated.'

'I see. How's your home life? Do you work?'

'Yes, I've got my own business, I have a five-year-old and I help my partner with his admin.'

'Do you have support from family?'

'Not really. My sister lives in New York and my mum spends a lot of time there looking after my niece and nephew. It's not a problem, but sometimes I just—' My voice began to crack. I blinked hard and tried to clear my throat.

'Is there any domestic abuse?'

'What? No, of course not.'

'Domestic abuse isn't confined to tower blocks, you know. It doesn't have to be physical; it can be verbal or emotional.'

Well, now you come to mention it, I often thought about throwing household items at Will. I once threw a ramekin at him because he didn't notice my new haircut, he ducked and it hit the door frame; it was surprisingly durable. I can't promise you that I won't move onto something heavier should he commit a more serious crime, like blowing all our savings on strippers and recreational drugs. Or suggesting that my tears were somehow related to my menstrual cycle.

'I have a very stable home life, thank you.'

She jabbed at her keyboard and handed me a slip of paper, spat out by the printer.

'Now, I've started you off on a very small dose, but I can easily up it if they're not doing the trick. We'll take a look at your bloods to check for anything nasty, but you look like the picture of health to me—just a little stressed with modern-day life perhaps.'

'What's this?'

'They're marketed as an antidepressant, but I'm prescribing them to help you sleep.'

'I'm not depressed.' *Am I?*

'I'm sure you're not, but sleep deprivation affects your coping mechanisms. This will ensure you get the rest you need, so you can wake up refreshed, ready to embrace another day. Take one just before going to bed.'

'Right. I'm not sure I want to start taking sleeping pills.'

'They're not sleeping pills. They're not addictive, but they will help you sleep. Just fill the prescription, you don't have to take them, but you know they're there when the going gets tough, okay? Anything else I can help you with?'

'I don't think so.'

'Great, get your blood test done ASAP, just to put your mind at rest. We'll let you know if there's cause for concern.'

I sat in the pharmacy and stared at my reflection in a Perspex cabinet filled with cold and flu medicines. Who was this middle-aged woman, awaiting her prescription for antidepressants, with wiry grey hairs and the early signs of jowls? I thought she was energetic and fearless. When did her optimism and lust for life decide to jump ship and live on someone else's beach?

11

'Tom!'

'Liza!'

We acted out the usual over-the-top bear hug and play punch. It'd been six months since I'd last seen him and my ordinarily well-groomed cousin appeared dishevelled and exhausted.

'Liza-Loo!' Tara squeaked at me in her *I'm not a ball-breaker, I don't know what all the fuss is about* tone.

'Hi, Tara.' My voice was distorted with fraudulence as we exchanged a stiff double kiss and I mimicked her sweet, fake grin.

'It's been an age. Look at you, all wild and ruddy-faced.' She pinched my cheek a little too hard. 'How amazing to be in the great outdoors every day, you lucky thing.' She placed a piece of eye-wateringly expensive luggage at the bottom of the stairs. 'Madeline, Isabella, take your belongings upstairs please, and don't make a mess.'

The girls shuffled past me and bounded up the stairs where Charlotte was waiting to jump out at them. Ear-piercing shrieks ensued. Tara frowned, as if having excited and sociable children was just another one of life's frustrations. 'Not too much noise up there, please, and remember, I said no mess, and no jumping on the beds.'

'So, you made good time. Did you come straight from the school pick-up?' I asked, before remembering that Tara was completely unfamiliar with the term 'school pick-up'.

'No, no, the girls broke up last week and they've been with the new nanny. Lovely girl: she cooks like a dream and is great with Leo.'

'He's so chunky.' I stroked his perfect, soft cheek. 'Can I have a cuddle?'

'Not tonight I'm afraid. We're so behind schedule. He should have been fed half an hour ago, but he fell asleep in the car even though I told the girls to try and keep him awake and now everything's up the shoot.' She batted her hand back and forth to suggest this was a minor setback, but her grimace said otherwise. 'Tom, get the bottle ready and then set up the cot so we can attempt to repair any irreversible damage.'

Forty minutes later, Leo was fed and asleep. We sat at the table in silence for a few moments, slurping our soup, until Will felt obligated to rescue us with small talk.

'So, what time do you set off tomorrow?'

'We need to check in at eight, so we're leaving tonight and grabbing a hotel at the airport. Sorry, Mum. I did tell you that, didn't I?'

Georgie looked at Tom as only a mother could. 'Of course, darling. I understand. Do tell us what delights await you in Krakow.'

'There's a lot to fit in,' Tara said, in an attempt to sever the steadfast mother–son adoration. 'Absolutely fascinating place; so much history. The shopping and nightlife's amazing too, of course. He-he-he.' I'd forgotten about that grating laugh.

Georgie reached over to squeeze Tom's hand. 'Well, you deserve to have some fun. Are you taking a river cruise?'

'Um, I can't remember the exact itinerary. Are we, darling?'

Tara cleared her throat. 'We arrive at 12.30 p.m. We have a light lunch at the hotel and then get a private taxi transfer to Auschwitz, where we will spend the afternoon touring the museum and paying our respects.'

'Mummy,' Charlotte piped up, 'what's a house witch?'

'It's a museum, darling.'

Tara turned to face Charlotte. 'Auschwitz is a very important part of history, Charlotte. It was the site of the systematic extermination of over a million Jews, Soviet prisoners and homosexuals by the Nazis in the Second World War.'

'Oh. Are there any dinosaurs there?'

Everyone except Tara laughed and Charlotte's face flushed red with humiliation. 'Don't laugh at me.'

'Don't get upset, sweetheart,' Will said. 'It just sounded funny.'

'Well, it's not bloody funny.'

'*Charlotte*!' I barked. 'Do not say *bloody*. Where did you learn that?'

'From you, Mummy. You always say it when you're cross.'

'Well observed, Charlotte,' Will said, applauding her.

'I don't know if she should be praised for swearing, Will.' He ignored me and poured Georgie a glass of wine. I smiled sweetly and presented him with my empty glass, pushing aside thoughts of smashing it over his head. 'Are you driving home tonight?'

'Yes, sweetheart. I can drive if you wish.'

'I do wish.'

Tara remained poised, staring at each of us in turn, waiting for us to shut our foolish little mouths. 'After the tour we shall go back to our hotel and shower. Then we will walk to the market square and eat dinner in one of the oldest restaurants in Poland, which dates back to medieval times.'

A collective 'Oooh' exuded from the table, which seemed to please her.

'On Saturday we take in the Cloth Hall and have lunch in the Jewish District.'

Georgie stood up and began stacking the soup bowls. 'Is everyone ready for their main, or do we all want to wait a while?' She turned to face Tara with a wide smile. 'I'm aware the children must be in bed by eight.'

'Don't worry too much, Mum,' Tom said. 'It doesn't matter if they're a bit late.'

'*Tom*!' was all Tara had to say on the matter.

'Yes actually, Mum, let's eat our mains now. Would you like a hand?'

'That would be lovely, darling, thank you. Sorry, Tara, do go on.' Georgie grabbed her wine glass and headed off into the kitchen with Tom.

'Later that afternoon, we take a private yacht along the Vistula to see the sunset.'

'Great,' I said. 'What's a Vistula?'

'It's a river, Eliza; the largest river in Poland.'

'Really, Liza, you didn't know that?' Will feigned shock at my ignorance.

'Sorry, my knowledge of European rivers is very poor. Then you're home on Sunday?'

'We land at two, back down here by five. Anyway, enough about our trip. When are you two planning your next romantic break?'

Next?

'We don't really go on mini breaks do we, Will? We go to Cornwall for the odd weekend, but we always take Charlotte with us.'

'Remind me to send you a link to that place in Milan we stayed in last October. It's perfect for a long weekend. You two would *love* it.'

Yes, Tara, I'm sure we would.

'*The* best manicures in the world,' she said, stealing a glance at my substandard fingernails.

Gales of laughter from Tom and Georgie echoed from the kitchen. Tara prickled. Her tension seemed to crawl across the table and seep in through my pores, pinching at tiny involuntary muscles and nerve endings.

We made our way through the lasagne and moved on to dessert.

'I spoke to my nomadic little bro yesterday,' Tom said, before spooning a colossal portion of tiramisu into his mouth.

'Well, lucky you,' Georgie said. 'I can't get through to him, I can never work out the time difference. Is he okay? When's he coming home? And don't speak with your mouth full.'

'I didn't know you'd spoken to Dan,' Tara snapped, quite furious that she was unable to go ahead and answer for her husband.

We all waited patiently for Tom to swallow his dessert and fill us in on Dan, called 'the nomadic little bro' because of his inability to settle down and who, although he stood at over six foot, was a whole seventeen minutes younger than Tom.

'They're eleven hours ahead, Mum, and it's best to phone him in the morning our time. He was on good form and he's met this great girl.'

'He's always meeting great girls. If he'd only stay in one place for five minutes he might keep hold of one.' Georgie rolled her eyes. 'He'll be fifty next year, for heaven's sake.'

'That's actually why I called him. I was thinking about having a big party. I was going to talk to you about maybe having it here.'

'That's a fantastic idea. What did Dan say?'

'He seemed up for it, so I said I'd run it past you.'

'What about that venue we looked at on King's Road?' Tara asked, who'd passed up on Georgie's home-made dessert, choosing instead to heighten her irritation with strong black coffee.

'I liked it,' Tom said. 'I'm just not sure how comfortable Dan would be in a place like that.'

'You've got to remember that it's your birthday too.'

'I would love to have it here,' Georgie said. 'The weather's always glorious at the end of July. We could get a marquee!'

Once dessert was over with, Tara barked childcare instructions at us all while obsessively checking her watch. Ten minutes later, they were out of the door and Tom was on his guilt trip, all the way to Gatwick airport.

12

THE WEEKEND HAD very few hiccups. We'd survived Build-a-Bear on a Saturday morning; we'd fed ducks in the park and paddled in the sea. Leo slept and ate at the times specified in his instruction manual. Everything went swimmingly until Sunday morning's phone call.

'Their flight's delayed,' Georgie said.

'By how long?'

'I don't know. Tom said he'd text me later when he knows more.'

'Okay. Are they all being good?'

'Angels. Are you coming over today?'

'It might be tricky. Will's parents are coming over at some point. I'm not sure what time.' Certain situations justified small fibs. I was tired. Charlotte was tired. And besides, Will's parents often popped in on a Sunday afternoon.

'I understand. I'll keep you updated.'

I logged on to Krakow airport's flight status. There was only one flight to London Gatwick that morning. Status: *On Time and Boarding.* I checked arrivals at Gatwick: *Flight expected on time.* Small fibs were one thing, gargantuan black lies were quite another.

'Don't get involved.'

'I'm not getting involved, Will. What if I text her and casually suggest she looks up the flight status herself?'

'Because she'll suspect you've already done it, *or* she'll ask you to do it for her. Either way you're back to square one, which, in case you hadn't noticed, is a *drama*.' Will shook his hands in the air in a way which I might ordinarily have found funny.

He was useless in these situations. I called Susannah.

'Absolutely do not tell her. It's none of your business.'

'But it is my business, since I've looked online and discovered the truth.'

'But you don't know the truth, do you?' Susannah said. 'Maybe that's not the correct information, or they missed their flight by accident, or something urgent came up.'

I pondered this new angle. Maybe they'd had a wild night out, overslept and hadn't made it to the airport on time. Tara would absolutely lie to save face. I could live with that. I'd enjoy the smugness it afforded me the next time I saw her. Maybe I'd even pop round when they got back, quiz her about the delay, see if she maintained eye contact. I bet she wouldn't even flinch.

I checked the flight status page again to see when the next flight got in.

There were no more flights from Krakow into Gatwick that day.

'I should let Georgie know.'

'Do not text her, you need to stay out of it.'

'But that's what I would normally do, Will, if I didn't know anything.'

'Eliza, just forget you even went on the bloody flight status page, will you?'

'Okay, I'll forget I even went on the bloody flight status page and text her anyway, because that's what I would do under ordinary circumstances.'

Hi, any news?

Nothing. Tried calling but both phones switched off
xx

OK, keep me posted x

Phew. Done.

Will took Charlotte to the park in yet another attempt to teach her to ride her bike without stabilisers. I carried on with my day as if nothing had happened and did some early preparation for Will's parents' visit.

Halfway through peeling a bag of potatoes, it occurred to me that Will's parents' visit was something that I'd fabricated to avoid going over to Georgie's. Everything felt oddly uncertain in that moment and I had to stand very still to concentrate and play back what I'd said throughout the course of the day, but it was all a thick blur. I sat down in the lounge and googled middle-aged dementia, which was quite depressing.

The web of lies seemed suddenly overwhelming so I chose to distract myself by cooking. I flicked on the oven and looked for the peeled potatoes, I was certain that I'd put them in a saucepan, but I eventually found them in a bag in the bin. I was thinking about opening a bottle of red when my phone rang.

It was Georgie.

I decided to ignore it.

My phone could be on silent.

I could be on the toilet or in another room.

Just answer it. Get it over and done with.

I reminded myself to forget that I'd even checked the bloody flight status.

'Hi, Georgie.'

'Hi, darling. Well, I've heard from Tom.'

'And?'

'The flight's been cancelled due to engine problems. Can you believe it?'

'No.'

'There're no more flights today so they're putting them up in a hotel and flying them home first thing tomorrow. I mean, what a to-do.'

'Are the children okay?'

'They seem delighted. We're just on our way to the park to feed the ducks. I'm actually quite good at this grandma business, even if I say so myself.'

'I know you are. Have a great time.'

She didn't sound at all upset. She was enjoying having the children and wasn't wasting time missing or hating Uncle David. I inhaled deeply, expanding my ribcage and filling it with positivity and light, then I breathed out tension and anxiety and responsibility and frustration and guilt because I hadn't done enough reading with Charlotte or washed the floors in a month or designed a Persian carpet garden. I took another deep breath just so I could exhale the fact that covering up other people's bullshit made me think I had dementia. I opened the red wine that also needed to breathe and allowed myself a small glass before sitting down with the Sunday paper.

I was right in the middle of a juicy article about a dominatrix in Los Angeles, whose net worth was $20 million, when the front door burst open.

'Mummy, Mummy, where are they?'

'Where are who, darling?'

'Nanny and Grandad?'

'Nanny and Grandad?'

'We saw Aunty Georgie and Maddy and Izzy in the park, and they said Nanny and Grandad were coming over for dinner.'

'Oh no, my sweet, they said they might pop in, but it wasn't certain.'

'But, Mummy, we rushed home especially.' We stared at each other; Charlotte presuming that any minute now I would erupt into laughter and produce gift-bearing grandparents from the folds of my magazine. She burst into tears and ran upstairs to her fluffy lilac sanctuary where I could hurt her no more.

I started by apologising to Will for not letting him know about Lie Number One.

I then appeased Charlotte by letting her have a chocolate biscuit and cocoa in her bedroom. I was unprepared to admit responsibility for Lie Number One to her because I was older and so decided that's how it should work.

After dinner, I made Will phone his parents and ask them tactfully if they wouldn't mind going along with Lie Number One in case Charlotte brought it up the next time they were down. I then had to get on the phone myself, apologise about making up Lie Number One in the first place and answer ten minutes of questions regarding hardy perennials.

Lie Number Two was actually Tom and Tara's lie about their flight and I refused to be part of it. I placed Lie Number Two in an imaginary bubble and sent it high up into the earth's atmosphere.

Lie Number Three, which was complete knowledge about Lie Number Two, went into the bubble as well, because if it wasn't for Lie Number Two, Lie Number Three would have ceased to exist.

I could now have a guilt-free sleep. I settled into bed and finished the article about the dominatrix. She'd written two books: *Lick My Boots* and *Lick Her Boots Too*. She'd made a killing in kinky merchandise and earned ten times the average national wage just to jab her stiletto heel into some idiot's face while he begged for mercy. Meanwhile I shovelled manure into other people's vegetable patches and could just about pay the council tax.

I shared the article on Facebook and tagged some girl-friends, asking who'd like to join me in my new business venture, on condition that I could be called 'Mistress Raven' at all times. Once posted, I flicked through my newsfeed and read an article about recycled decking, then watched a video of some panda cubs. Susannah was the first one to comment on my status with a picture of a gimp mask: *I'll only work for you if I can wear this.*

But it was the post below that caught my attention. There was something far more sinister and underhand about those familiar faces, smiling at me, champagne flutes at the ready. Two hours ago: TARA HAMILTON and TOM HAMILTON were tagged in a post with LINDSAY SHERIDAN and 1 OTHER at THE SHARD, LONDON.

I didn't know Uncle David was on Facebook. I'm not even sure if Uncle David knew he was on Facebook.

And Georgie wasn't wrong—those tits were unquestionably plastic.

13

'You need to stop going on about it now.'

'I am not going on about it, Will. If they hadn't lied about their flight, then I wouldn't have lied about your parents coming over and Charlotte wouldn't have got upset. And I wouldn't have been exhausted with guilt and needed an early night and read that article and opened up Facebook and seen *that* picture.'

'I've really got to get going. Don't let it spoil your day.'

'Spoil my day? I'm fucking livid, Will.' I felt a gentle tug on the sleeve of my top. 'Oh hello, darling. Brushed those teeth already?'

'Mummy, what does *fuck invalid* mean?'

Will glared at me, 'Jesus Christ, Eliza. Well done.'

'*Daddy!*'

'What now?'

'Don't *ever* use the Lord's name in vain. Bad Daddy.'

'I'm going to work.' For the first time in a long time Will slammed the door and no one got a kiss. And for the first time in a long time, I felt genuine pity for him.

'Why is Daddy angry today?'

I sat on the stairs and pulled Charlotte onto my lap. 'Sometimes Mummy says things that make Daddy angry.'

'Why?'

'It's just something that grown-ups do.'

'Well, it's silly. Miss Parsons said that words are not for hurting.'

'I think Miss Parsons is very wise. Let's text Daddy and tell him we love him and that we'll make tacos for dinner tonight.'

'Hooray. And I will sing him a song about dolphins.'

I would make a lousy dominatrix and so would my daughter.

We sat at the bottom of the stairs for a while and stared at the torn jumble of *National Geographics* that had been gathering dust in the hallway for over a month. I imagined someone from a hip interior magazine with a headscarf and bright red lipstick standing in the doorway, smoking a cigarette. 'I love the eclectic bookshelf and the peeling wallpaper,' she would shriek. 'But these magazines are a step too far, I'm afraid.'

I moved them into the back of my car and took Charlotte to school.

Further discussion with Susannah at the school gates confirmed that my web of deceit must go on. Tom and Tara's treachery was absolutely none of my business and guilt was a useless emotion. She said something about unlocking my shackles and turning the page, but I'd zoned out by then, preferring to berate myself inwardly over menial tasks that I hadn't completed, and the fact that my sister would be humpy because I'd forgotten to reply to her text message yesterday, but I couldn't do it now because of the time difference and I was bound to forget again later and she would be really disappointed in me. But it was alright for her—she had unlimited access to her husband's PA and only worked four fucking hours a week.

'Are you okay?' I jolted as Susannah touched my shoulder.

'What?'

'Are you okay? You look like you're about to scream or cry, or both.'

'I'm fine. I don't think I got enough sleep last night, that's all.'

'Try not to let it get to you too much, okay?'

'Thanks, I won't.'

Easy for her to say. And Will.

If they were having an affair, maybe they would discuss it this afternoon when they were in bed together.

Ridiculous.

Although if that were the case, I'd like to think that Susannah would fight my corner and tell Will that he should be more patient and understanding with me. It's the least she could do. I wondered if he'd fall asleep instantly like he did with me, or if he'd go straight in for another round.

I'd considered cancelling lunch today with an ear infection, then a migraine. I eventually dragged myself to the restaurant, along with Tom and Tara's deception, which still lingered about my aura like some foul hacking cough that I couldn't seem to shake off.

'I can't tell you how refreshing it was to see Tom without *her* yesterday.' Georgie was rapturous and I'm ashamed to say that, at that moment, I loathed my beloved cousin. 'I find it difficult to believe that an afternoon's work was more important than seeing her children after four days away but, still, none of my business. He did look tired, though.'

'I thought that on Thursday.' Not to mention the late night he'd had at the Shard the night before, necking champagne and gawping at the tits of his mother's antagonist. 'Did you get to talk about things?'

'Yes, we caught up on all sorts. There's a colleague at work who's being very difficult at the moment. Tom's literally losing sleep over it and it's always him that gets up to feed Leo in the night.'

'Did you talk about Uncle David?'

'No, I didn't ask. You know they all move in the same circles, that banking lot. I've always wondered if Tom might know *her*.'

'Who?'

'The manufactured old trollop that's screwing my husband. I don't know why he can't sleep with his dentist or maybe our accountant; she's recently divorced and is a very attractive woman. The PA seems so sleazy and clichéd—the quick and easy go-to when your wife just isn't cutting the mustard, I'm embarrassed by it all.'

'I think you should ask Tom his opinion on the situation.' I did not intend to dip the statement in vinegar and my tone did not go unnoticed.

'I don't think he's got anything to hide, if that's what you're implying,' Georgie snapped. 'I'm sure he's very upset by it all, as is Dan.'

'Of course, and when's Dan planning on coming home?'

'Heaven knows. He's still working in that rehab centre and he's got a girlfriend now. I might never see him in the flesh again and he'll just become my cyber son.'

'Why are you even talking like that? Get on a plane. Go and see him.'

'Eliza, you know how much I love my Dan. Some might even argue that he's my favourite, but I cannot deal with being cooped up in a metal tube for twenty-four hours so I can sit in a desert with a bunch of funnel web spiders and recovering alcoholics, thank you very much.'

'Byron Bay is nowhere near the desert. Mum flies back and forth all the time, and it doesn't bother her.'

'Flying to New York is very different from flying to Brisbane, Eliza.' Georgie was defensive. I'd pushed her on the affair, on going to see Dan, and now I'd had the audacity to throw my mother into the mix. Our lovely civilised luncheon nearly ruined by my idiotic quips on home truths and an offhand comparison with her cold-shouldered sister-in-law.

'That's a fair point.' I backed down.

Our food arrived, but Georgie sent back her salmon because the lemon sauce was too runny for her liking. I waited, munching on the occasional crouton to break the silence, and we eavesdropped on the table next to us: a couple in their fifties; first date. He'd taken early retirement and was a keen sailor. He talked about rig dimensions and Solent winds while she nodded politely. She caught my eye and smiled. I got the impression she wasn't looking for anything serious at the moment.

'How are you feeling now, anyway? Did you go to the doctor?'

'Yes.'

'And?'

'She tested me for leukaemia.'

Georgie gasped. 'Really?'

'It was negative. The doctor says that I'm stressed with modern-day life.'

'You see, I was right. You're overdoing it.'

'I thought you didn't trust doctors?'

'That was a generalisation. So, what are you going to do about it?'

'She gave me a prescription for antidepressants.'

'You don't need antidepressants, what a load of old nonsense.' Georgie shook her head. 'Why don't you order a gin?'

'She said they would help me sleep.'

'Gin will help you sleep. I'll say the same thing to you as I said to Tom yesterday: you're working too hard, cut down your hours before you keel over. But he won't take any notice. We all know she's the main breadwinner. He could be a stay-at-home dad and keep hold of his health. Let her be the one to drop dead of a heart attack.'

'You don't think it's genetic, do you?'

'What? Overworking?'

'No, heart disease.'

'You can't start worrying about that as well. Your uncle is only on heart pills because he's seventy and still working in the city—and sleeping with someone twenty years his junior. And your father had a lot of stress before he died. It's all down to lifestyle.'

'He always seemed happy enough to me. Maybe I should ask Dr Chaudhry for an ECG.'

'You don't need an ECG. You're just giving yourself more stress. And your father always seemed happy because he hid it from you. That's what parents do, even as adults. We're good at it. I expect you hide your stress from Charlotte all the time without even thinking about it.'

I thought of Charlotte's face, guarded and vigilant, when I was slamming things around and growling at various electrical appliances that weren't performing to the quality or speed that I expected of them. And I decided that no, I didn't think I'd inherited that particular trait.

I also thought of Dad, lying in the hospital bed in Hamburg, cracking jokes and talking about what we would be doing that Christmas. But was he secretly aware of his fate? Mum and Jess had been somewhere in the air above the Atlantic when he'd taken his last breath. They'd tried to get there sooner, Jess said, but she had a husband and a toddler to think about. It was alright for me: free as a bird and only two hours away. Mum had agreed and I wondered whether the relatively peaceful scene may've been drastically different had they arrived earlier and scrutinised the faultless staff with intense questions and embarrassing demands.

'I think he was stressed around Mum, if I'm honest.'

Georgie forced a smile and raised a quizzical brow. 'Well, that's hardly surprising.'

Her dig propelled us into uncomfortable silence once more. A wave of exhaustion washed over me and my paltry life. Unscrupulous relatives, lame medical opinions and prickly family relationships all seeming shallow and insignificant. Just one tiny human on one tiny planet in one tiny universe in one infinitesimal speck of time.

I ordered the gin.

14

I'D BEEN TRYING to convince Mr Anderson that letting a couple of students from the Arts University decorate the fountain for the Persian carpet garden would be a cost-effective, forward-thinking and overall foolproof idea.

'You don't think they'll mess it up, do you? I mean, they are only students.'

'It's very difficult to mess up mosaics, Mr Anderson.' What did I know? Maybe it was very easy to mess up mosaics and my throwaway comment was brutally insulting to the fastidious tiling artisan.

'Well, if you say so, Eliza. I'll have to trust your judgement on this.'

Good, because I could not waste another hour gazing at a blank CAD worksheet or doodling nonsense on pieces of A4. If I could get hungry young students to make a start for me, I could ride on their gnarly wave of creativity and reclaim the ambitious mindset of my college days. Maybe.

'Please do. Johnno has known one of them since primary school. He's extremely diligent and polite. You'll love him.'

'I say, Mr A, won't it be lovely to have some strapping young men about the place?' Mrs Anderson said. 'Out there, working in the sunshine. I can spoil them rotten with my baking.'

'Stop trying to make me jealous, Mrs A. You know it'll never work.' He pinched her ample waist and she giggled. 'Another thing I'm keen to incorporate is use of natural fertilisers, like they do at Highgrove. Have you considered that in your plans? I presume you're familiar with organic sustainable gardening.'

No.

'Of course, it's becoming so popular these days. Look, I could show you the ideas I've worked on so far,'—if you like looking at sketches of Scooby-Doo cocking his leg on a buddleia—'but I think it's far better to spring-board from the fountain design; work from the inside out. What do you say?'

'Sounds like a cracking idea, Eliza!' Mr Anderson gave me a thumbs-up and chuckled to himself.

'Great. I'll arrange the plumbing work for next week and the fountain delivery the week after. The students can start tiling at the beginning of May.'

Which bought me an entire month to produce the master plan; a plan which would turn a lumpy lawn into a Middle-Eastern Shangri-La, inspired by a Turkish rug in a royal drawing room—an entire month of trying to stay focused and not put a sledgehammer through my computer screen and run away to live in a jungle.

That night I drank Valerian tea and went to bed early, dousing my pillow in lavender oil, determined to get a solid eight hours. I woke at 2.58 a.m., hot and drenched, with palpitations. I threw off the duvet. My damp skin cooled quickly and I was suddenly chilled. I pulled the duvet back over me, tight into my neck, and almost dozed off. Too hot again. I got up and walked downstairs, placed a paper towel under each breast and stood naked, next to the open back door. I remembered a story on the local news about a series of night burglaries in the area and slammed the door shut, locking it quickly. I caught a glimpse of my reflection in the glass door and turned to study it further, hoping that the dappled moonlight would cast a flattering spell over my profile. It did not.

I worried that the burglars might have seen me and rushed back upstairs and into bed. I spent the next hour playing out a chilling scene where they broke into the house and murdered Will. I had to defend Charlotte because they were going to abduct her and sell her into the sex trade. The scene ended with the awakening of my inner lioness: I killed the burglars with my bare hands using a technique I'd seen on a Netflix thriller a couple of years before. Charlotte and I went on to become minor celebrities who appeared on some talk shows, before everyone decided that we should have the privacy we deserved and basically forgot all about us.

Will's funeral was featured in the local paper with the head-line: LIONESS HUSBAND'S FINAL ROAR. Except he wasn't my husband. They'd love that, the papers. What would they say? Life Partner? Boyfriend? Fuck buddy? What if they thought I'd murdered him and cashed in on the life insurance? I might have had unsavoury thoughts about Will from time to time but I'd never kill him...not intentionally anyway.

I thought about Will's death and started to cry. I thought about all of the people in the world who actually *were* being murdered and whose children *were* being sold into the sex trade, and I became inconsolable, hugging Will's back and soaking his shoulders with my tears. He stirred, mumbled something about PlayStation and then started snoring.

I was hot again and perspiration spiked at my pores.

I got up, opened a new blank worksheet on the laptop and mapped out some pathways for the Persian garden. I stared at it for twenty minutes before deleting it. I was cold. I went back to bed and continued the repetition of throwing the duvet on and off until I fell asleep at around 6 a.m.

15

Organic Emily was hosting an organic oils skincare party and I didn't want to go. I'd told Susannah that I was tired and strapped for cash, but she was having none of it. What I hadn't told her was that I felt like a dragon, ready to breathe fire on anyone who stood in my path. I thought of all those lovely products, a blue molten mess over Emily's lounge carpet, everyone's charred faces looking back at me in disappointment: *Well if there was ever a time we needed the Rose Hip Saviour Serum, this is it, Eliza, thank you very much.*

'Welcome, welcome, make yourselves comfortable,' Emily chirped. 'My home is your home.'

Great, maybe I can sling my bra over the back of the sofa and catch up on *Bake Off* while you're passing round the prosecco.

'What can I get you to drink? A glass of champagne? Freshly squeezed orange juice? Kombucha?'

Susannah answered for me. 'We'll most definitely be having champagne.'

Organic Emily was delighted by our choice and swiftly returned with two flutes of bubbles. 'Enjoy, ladies, and do help yourself to nibbles. The demonstration will start as soon as everyone arrives.'

I cast my eyes around the kitchen, hunting for something to pigeonhole, to tut at. I had expected to find a predictable oak country kitchen, but it was surprisingly modern, which annoyed me. No saucepans hanging from hooks or quirky vases of lavender. She'd even got a boiling water tap. But I did spot some rustic little pots of culinary herbs: rosemary, sage, lemon thyme, basil. I was poking my finger into the basil to make sure it wasn't drying out, when Emily tapped my arm.

'You don't think I've overwatered, do you? I was really nervous about you coming over and inspecting my foliage!' She held her hand up to her mouth in a self-deprecating pose, making it difficult for me to judge her.

'Sorry, bad habit. It looks healthy enough to me.'

'I would love to talk to you at some point about urban farming. I plan to do my thesis on it next year and wouldn't mind running a couple of things past you—only if you've got time.'

'Of course, but I don't know how much help I'd be really.'

'Just an hour of your time would be *amazing*. I saw what you did with Sally Harper's vegetable patch the other week, so clever. I'd like to introduce more companion planting into my own garden this year and I wouldn't mind picking your brains on that too.'

'No problem.'

Apprehension lurked in my chest. What the hell did I know about urban farming?

'Great, let's get our diaries together and sort out a date.' Emily inspected the lack of content in my glass. 'Ooh, that went down quickly, didn't it? Let's get you a top-up.'

Although I'd eaten an hour earlier, I made my way around the nibbles, systematically taking something from each plate and stuffing it into my mouth: olives, sushi, grapes, smoked salmon and cream cheese crackers. I even gnawed my way through some carrot sticks in a somewhat feeble attempt to meet my five a day.

I was midway through gawping at some family photographs (Organic Emily's husband was not what I expected— all suited and booted, with a slight whiff of axe murderer about him), when 'Chrissy' tapped on her glass to announce the start of the demonstration.

'Okay, ladies, take your seats, please, I'm going to start this evening with us all playing a little *game*.'

I was not in the mood for *games*.

I positioned myself between some Kettle Chips and a woman I'd never met before, who immediately introduced herself. Great: games and getting-to-know-you small talk with someone in a stripy top called Sarah.

Sarah told me that she used to babysit Emily when she was fifteen and Emily was three, and that she wrote articles for home and lifestyle magazines. Sarah also told me that the last time she'd come to a party like this, she had made an inappropriate suggestion regarding an alternative use for the silicone-coated sauce whisk and been asked to leave.

I made a mental note not to be so presumptuous about people in future and we fell into an easy, low-pitched patter about our mutual loathing of direct sales parties.

Chrissy passed around tiny bottles of essential oil. 'Now, without looking at the label, I'd like you to try and guess the plant from which the oil is derived.' Chrissy was very excited about the game, as were a handful of guests. Even Susannah seemed to be lapping it up.

Lemon.

Bergamot.

Rose.

Couldn't give a shit.

Lavender.

Sarah handed me an oil without even bothering to sniff it. 'Here, pass me those crisps before I lob this at her head.'

'And this is a very special *oil blend*. An *oil blend* is a combination of essential oils tailored to suit your needs.' Chrissy held her head high with superiority and scanned the room. 'Now, let's see if anyone can pick up on the dominant ingredients.'

Organic Emily gingerly put up her hand. 'I think I might be getting geranium?'

Chrissy pursed her lips. 'Yes, well done, Emily. Geranium is one of the ingredients. Others are sage and frankincense.' *Just in case any of you other witches are thinking of upstaging me.* 'Now does anyone here suffer from hormonal problems? PMS? Irregular periods? Maybe some of you ladies are reaching an age when you become bothered by the heat?'

'Menopause!' shrieked Sarah. 'Sweaty old menopause. Sorry, Chrissy love, I think you should just cut to the chase.'

There was a momentary pause where Chrissy was stumped for words and all the guests turned to look at Sarah. It probably only lasted for a second before someone laughed, and then we all laughed. What was it about that word that made us laugh? Chrissy blushed, like it might never happen to her. If she'd just said the word 'menopause' instead of 'bothered by the heat', we wouldn't have been in this bizarre circle of canned laughter. It made me want to stand up on a chair and shout it over and over at the top of my lungs. Menopause. Menopause. Menopause. Probably best not to.

Chrissy giggled. 'Okay, well thank you for that. What was your name again?'

'It's Sarah, Chrissy: Sa-rah.'

'Well Sarah, *menopause* it is then.' Chrissy went on to tell us how the Women's Synergy oil would level our emotions, restoring composure and grace, which I thought was an excellent selling point, until it occurred to me that, in order for composure and grace to be restored, you probably needed to have them in the first place.

I decided not to buy any.

Sarah seemed unfazed by her outburst and continued her critique in hushed tones between mouthfuls of crisps. 'I mean, fancy coming into a room full of women over the age of thirty and asking them if they have hormone problems. It's like asking a room full of sex offenders to volunteer at a Scout camp.'

The woman sat next to Sarah gave her daggers before making a trip to the bathroom. Susannah was swift to jump into her place. 'What are you two ladies gossiping about? I bet it's far more scandalous than the benefits of beeswax.'

'Hi, Suze.' I was overexcited because I thought I'd maybe found someone more hacked off than myself. 'This is Sarah.'

'I know Sarah. We got ourselves into a spot of trouble at last year's Farewell Summer barbeque.'

I'd not been invited to that.

Sarah let out a filthy laugh, 'Hey, I didn't force you to drink tequila.'

Chrissy waited for everyone to calm down before resuming the exfoliation of Melanie Mulrane's oily T-bar. Apart from the occasional dash to replenish crisp and booze supplies, the three of us didn't move from our spot on the sofa. I spent the best part of fifty quid ordering a facial oil and a hair mask I would never use.

The champagne had run out and we'd moved on to prosecco. I was scarfing down crisps to take away the aftertaste, then drinking more prosecco to wash down the crisps. Other people had started dull conversations about school staff changes or exam results, but the three of us were holding out, still managing to crack the odd joke about penises or farts. Susannah leant in and talked from the side of her mouth. 'Sarah, did you ever end up going to that support group you were talking about the last time I saw you?'

'Yes, and still am. Good memory.'

Sarah told us about the hormone support group that met every other Wednesday in her local church hall, run by a lady called Marion who'd come through the other side and now wanted to help other members of her troubled, perimenopausal community. The group was called GLOW.

'What does that stand for?' I asked.

'It's just a nod to the old hot flush. She knows damn well we don't all tiptoe around, fanning ourselves daintily and making quips about the weather. How I would love to simply *glow*.'

Susannah nudged me in the ribs. 'Seems like you two have got more than a few things in common.'

'Not really. I get night sweats, but my doctor says that I'm stressed with modern-day life.'

Sarah raised her eyebrows. 'And did you get given a prescription for antidepressants?'

For a fleeting moment I was convinced that Susannah had been talking about me behind my back and I stumbled over my words. 'Well yes, but I haven't taken any.'

'Good, don't,' Sarah said, changing her tone, making me think we were about to enter a serious discussion which I wouldn't fully understand.

'Excuse me,' Susannah sighed and got up to talk to Chrissy, clearly unimpressed with the direction of the conversation, but after hearing Georgie's conspiracy theory, I was intrigued.

'Did you know that your progesterone levels start dropping from the age of thirty?'

'No, I didn't know that.'

'Do you know what progesterone is?'

'Is it a type of hormone?'

'Progesterone is a very *important* hormone.' Sarah chopped her hands on the table with each word and I concluded that she'd put away slightly more alcohol than myself. I pressed my finger into the bowl to get the last of the crisps and tried to picture something from a long-forgotten biology class.

'I thought that it was oestrogen that we had to be worried about?' I said.

'Yes, we have to be very worried about oestrogen, especially too much of it. It's everywhere: in our food, in our water. Did you know that girls as young as seven are starting to menstruate?'

'Really?'

'Then we're all so stressed these days.'

'That's me! I'm stressed with modern-day living.'

'And stress sends all that lovely progesterone straight to our knackered old adrenals, leaving the oestrogen free to go on a wild rampage.'

'Okay.' I was out of my depth and looked around for help.

'I wasn't getting any sleep,' Sarah continued. 'The sleep I was getting was broken because I was sweating like a horse. I couldn't remember what I'd done three minutes ago, and the anger...my god, the anger. Put that together with two miserable teenagers and an ungrateful husband—it was quite the cocktail.'

Thankfully Emily walked up to me with her diary. 'I'm glad you two are getting on so well. Eliza, realistically, I'm looking at the second week in May to meet up. Does that work for you?'

Emily and I arranged our brunch date. Sarah and I swapped numbers and she told me to call her, should I need any advice.

Will was asleep when I got into bed. He flopped a heavy arm over my chest, trapping me, making me fretful and clammy. I pushed him off, wafting the duvet up and down to generate airflow.

Hormones. Huh. I was only forty-five.

But now I couldn't sleep.

No sleep, sweating, the anger...my god, the anger.

I decided that it was different for Sarah because she was older than me. I was just stressed with modern-day living. I went down to the kitchen to find the pills prescribed by Dr Chaudhry. I popped one with a tot of last year's sloe gin and sloped off to bed.

16

'MUMMY, MUMMY, WAKE up. Daddy, is Mummy still alive?'

'Possibly. Let's have a look at her.'

Will tried to lift up my eyelids. I wanted him to stop but I couldn't seem to move. I must've had a dreadful accident and be in a hospital somewhere.

'Mummy is in a bad way, Nurse Charlotte. We should treat her immediately.'

I forced open my gritty eyes to see Charlotte by the side of the bed, holding a toy stethoscope and wearing her nurse costume.

'Lie very still, Mummy. I'm saving your life.'

Will was standing over her, making an offensive sound with his car keys at what was surely four in the morning.

'What are you doing, Will? I'm so thirsty. What's the time?'

'It's 9.30 and I'm late. How did your *It's going to be really tame and drink chamomile tea all night* make-up party go?'

'It was not a make-up party. It was a skincare party. Can I please have some water?'

'No, I'm late. What's for dinner tonight?'

'What?'

'I fancy one of your home-made curries. I've really got to go.' Will kissed us both and raced down the stairs and out of the front door before I'd even had chance to ask him about my prognosis. When I realised that I was able to move my legs and make it to the bathroom unaided, I enticed Charlotte back into bed to watch some cartoons.

She woke me at midday because she was hungry and I prayed that she wouldn't report me to the child protection services. I dragged myself around the kitchen, mouth arid with sticky white globules of saliva dried into its corners. My skull felt loose and disconnected, like the contents had been sucked out with a Dyson and replaced with Hungarian goose down. I called the surgery and managed to get a telephone appointment with Dr Chaudhry.

'I don't think there's any cause for concern, Miss Hamilton. What time did you take the tablet?'

'Around ten.' Or twelve.

'And had you consumed any alcohol?'

Yeah, loads. 'I had one small glass of champagne.'

'I see. Well, I would suggest that you drink plenty of water today and rest up as much as you can. Have tonight off, then tomorrow take half the dose, no later than 9 p.m.'

Was it wrong to question Dr Chaudhry's authority on this? If I was actually suffering from depression and not merely stressed by modern-day living, would these tablets be helping me on my road to recovery or throwing me off the nearest cliff?

All I really wanted to do was curl up under my duvet with ten gallons of water and stay there for a week. I'd heard people swear by Prozac: just a short course to get you through that divorce or bereavement or miscarriage; back to normal in no time. A colleague I used to work with at the garden centre had even taken it to get through her menopause. Not that that was applicable to me. And even if it was, I would never resort to antidepressants—I'd just get on with it.

I am a terrible mother; slovenly and neglectful. Charlotte did something creative with glitter and then we walked to the shops to buy some sweets. She bounced around the garden on her space hopper for twenty minutes while I snoozed on the lounger. We went back inside to watch *Toy Story 3* and I cried at the end, when Andy went off to college and left all his toys behind. Wasn't everyone supposed to live happily ever after? Why weren't Woody and Buzz cosied up in Andy's dorm, playing *Fortnite* and smoking marijuana?

Will came home. I had not made a curry. We had fish and chips and no one seemed to care. Charlotte told Will that we bought sweets and watched movies and that it was her favourite day of the holidays so far.

I concluded that I was prone to overthinking and self-persecution.

17

It was Easter Sunday and also my birthday. The last time my birthday had fallen on Easter Sunday, I had been thirty-four, skinny and having a massage on a beach in Bali. Today, I was forty-six with a muffin top and a prescription for antidepressants. I was also cooking lunch for nine people.

Charlotte was jumping up and down on the bed at 6.30 a.m. 'Happy birthday to you, happy birthday dear Mummy, happy birthday to you. What shall we open first: chocolate or presents? Chocolate, presents, chocolate, presents, choc…?'

Will slept through everything. The bed was actually moving up and down and Charlotte was shrieking. He wasn't even pretending—he was dead to the world. And it was my birthday. He could at least have had the decency to not sleep through this level of madness on *my birthday*.

I pulled Charlotte in for a cuddle and some conspiratorial whispering. 'Why don't you jump on Daddy and tell him that he has to make tea. *Then* we'll do chocolate and presents.'

I had only taken half a tablet the night before but I still felt like I could guzzle a river. When Will finally rose to make tea, I took the opportunity to slip back into a deep, dream-filled sleep.

I opened my presents: a pair of Converse from Mum which you could only buy Stateside; the latest Martha Stewart cookbook from my sister, which promised to reset my health (Good luck with that, Martha). Charlotte gave me a novelty shower cap and a new teddy called Plum, who wanted to sleep in her room. I received a pair of embellished Monsoon flip-flops from Will, along with matching sunglasses and some bathroom scales.

'You keep banging on about how fat you're getting, so I thought they'd come in handy.' He was genuinely pleased with himself.

I was preparing a cauliflower cheese while Will peeled the potatoes. He had wildly underestimated the importance of a thorough briefing: who knows what and to what degree; and which subjects should be avoided altogether.

'Susannah knows the whole story, but I've already talked to her about what *not* to say. I spoke to your mum on Thursday, she knows about the little lie I told Georgie and is happy to go along with it, so as not to hurt anyone's feelings.'

'And about Flightgate?' Will asked.

'Your mum doesn't know anything about Flightgate; she only knows that I used her and your dad as an excuse for not going over to Georgie's on that Sunday.'

'Mum and Dad know about Flightgate. Charlotte told them on Friday.'

'Charlotte? How the hell does Charlotte know about Flightgate?'

'From you, I would imagine; it's all you've been banging on about lately.'

'I certainly didn't discuss it in front of Charlotte.'

'She must know something because she told them that Tom was naughty because he tells lies.'

'Great, just great. Anything else?'

'Dad doesn't know about Simon.'

'What about Simon? Simon's not coming.'

'I mean he doesn't *know* about Simon; Mum knows, Dad doesn't. She said it's best not to tell him because he'll only get confused.'

'I'm sorry, Will, but I'm not telling Susannah that she has

to cover up Simon's sexuality in order to appease your father's puritanical views.' I stabbed at the cauliflower, irritated by its refusal to be cut into perfectly equal-sized florets.

'Please don't get upset, I just don't want him to start asking loads of stupid questions, that's all.'

'All you're doing is enabling him, Will, do you realise that? You and your mum are waving the patriarchal flag, rolling out the red carpet for ageing heterosexual white men worldwide, so they can continue on their destructive path of power and oppression.'

Will stopped peeling the potatoes and turned to face me, my accusation of patriarchy leaving him dumbfounded.

'There's a car pulling up, can you see who it is please,' I said, distracting him so I could have the final word. It was merely an observation so I wasn't going to apologise. No one should have to apologise on their birthday.

Susannah arrived with Georgie. They scurried past me into the conservatory with a large covered plate, while I bustled the sugar-high children outside to play.

'Guess what?' Georgie said. 'Dan called me this morning. He had the day off and they were at the beach having a bar-beque, on Easter Sunday! Can you believe it?'

'Good for them.'

'And he's growing a beard. Fancy that. What about you then, darling. Heard from anybody across the pond, hmm? From your mother maybe, on your birthday?'

'I've had gifts and texts. They're going to call later.'

'Oh well, better late than never I suppose. When are Mike and Marilyn arriving? I thought we could pop open some fizz and sing you "Happy Birthday" before lunch.'

I tried my best to look joyful.

I had to go through it all again after lunch when they unveiled the cake. I let the kids blow out the candles. Marilyn hated that—all those invisible droplets of spittle landing where she couldn't see them; all those germs, picked up from class-rooms and swimming pools and play parks.

Georgie was doing the honours. 'Now, Marilyn, a nice big piece for you?'

'No thank you, Georgie dear. It looks delicious, but do you know, I'm absolutely full to the brim. Delicious chicken, Will. You must give me the recipe.'

'Actually, Mum, I didn't—'

'So modest, my little boy. You need to take credit where credit's due. Mike, you'll have some cake, won't you?'

'Okay, well here,' Georgie placed the tiniest of slithers on Marilyn's plate. 'Just have a taste; it's one of Delia Smith's finest. Absolutely delicious, if I do say so myself.'

Marilyn cleared her throat. 'Thank you, Georgie.'

'Teddy!' boomed Mike, quite out of the blue.

Teddy looked up, understandably petrified.

'Teddy, a funny name for a little boy, isn't it?' Mike had had one glass of cava and two glasses of red wine, but that was gen-erally all it took. I had been harsh on him earlier: he had a good heart but was from a bygone era; an era when a man knew where he stood, a time when one could shoot from the hip and speak to children they didn't know without being given a tag and a curfew. He broke into song: 'Aaand, today's the day the Teddy bears have their picnic.'

'*Mike,*' Marilyn faked a laugh through her gritted teeth. 'Try not to scare poor Teddy. Your voice is very loud and he's only got little ears, haven't you, sweetie?'

We all turned to look at Teddy, whose bottom lip was beginning to quiver.

Susannah lifted him onto her lap. 'He's officially an Edward, like my father, but he's always been *Teddy* to us, hasn't he, Tilly?'

'Yes and Daddy says that he looked like a teddy when he was a baby, because he had fluffy hair and sticky-out ears.'

'Oh, Tilly. Now that *is* a pretty little name for a pretty

little girl,' Mike said, turning his attention on her. 'I hope your Daddy sent you an Easter egg today, from up there in big fancy London.'

'Mike.' Marilyn jolted up from her seat. 'Help me clear the plates, please.'

'Oh, Maz, sit down. It's Easter Sunday for Christ's sake.'

'Yes, and it's Eliza's birthday. Help me clear the plates, darling.'

Tilly whispered something to Charlotte and they both collapsed in giggles. 'Grandad, Tilly says you're funny. *And* her Daddy always gets her an Easter egg from Harrods *and* her Daddy has met Ed Sheeran *and*—'

'Okay, girls,' I clapped my hands loudly, which was uncharacteristic enough to make Charlotte stop talking. 'Enough cheekiness for today. Why don't you go outside and play.' And in one fell swoop I had joined the march for patriarchy: silencing the girls and endorsing Mike's ignorance of modern parenting. I might as well have torn up my voting card and chained myself to the sink. 'I've got a cheeseboard if anyone's still hungry.'

'You sit down, birthday girl. I'll serve the cheese.' Georgie disappeared into the kitchen with Mike and Marilyn and I let out a sigh of relief.

Mike poked his head round the door, brandishing a turkey baster in his left hand. 'Where does this go, love?'

'What?'

'The turkey baster; where do you want it?'

'Err ...' I stared at the baster, and the only thing I could think about was what a logistical nightmare it must've been for Simon to ejaculate into the end of one, especially tanked up on champagne.

Will came to the rescue. 'Just stick it anywhere, Dad.'

Mike waved the turkey baster at Susannah with an exaggerated wink. 'I say, steady on.' He walked back into the kitchen, chuckling to himself.

Susannah looked at Will and me in disbelief. 'Does he know about—?'

'No.'

'No?'

'No, definitely not.'

I was happily smothering a water biscuit with St Agur and fresh fig when Mike came out with another, potentially difficult, conversation starter. 'Eliza tells me you had a nice few days with the grandchildren the other weekend, Georgie.'

'Yes, thank you, Mike, I did. It was wonderful and they were so good. Did you hear about that ghastly flight debacle? Poor Tom being stuck in Poland an extra night.'

I reminded myself to forget that I had even looked on the bloody flight status page.

'And I'm so sorry I missed you that weekend,' Georgie continued. 'The baby's in this strict routine and it's all very complicated. But still, none of my business.'

Mike frowned and looked at Will. Marilyn saved the day by diving in with a napkin. 'Look at you. A grown man with gorgonzola all over your moustache, I don't know.'

The conversation was quickly diverted to Mike's brother and his recent exploits in the Arctic Circle. Will, once again, got to explain what causes the northern lights and Will's parents, once again, got to bleat about how clever he was.

When Mike and Marilyn finally left, Georgie and I sipped coffee in the sunroom. I was slumped on the lounger, feeling like my mind and body had been pummelled into a flat, bland pebble.

'I had lunch with Valerie yesterday,' Georgie said.

'Valerie?'

'David's old PA.'

'Yes I remember her. Did you go up to London?'

'No, she was visiting an uncle in Romsey and she called me; said it would be nice to meet up.'

'And was it?'

'It was informative, let's put it that way.'

The FaceTime call that was supposed to have happened an hour earlier, and that I hoped had been forgotten, happened.

I endured 'Happy Birthday' for the fourth time in twelve hours.

Were the shoes the right colour? That Martha Stewart book will change your life. What did Will buy you this year? Is Georgie there? Jake got into Yale! So proud. Lydia's fine; working hard for her ballet exams. It's so gruelling, but she seems to cope.

She didn't look like she was coping. She looked gaunt and miserable. After the singing she pulled a desperate face and sloped off.

'Where's Lydia gone, Jess? She didn't look very happy.'

'She's fourteen. It's compulsory to be miserable when you're fourteen.'

'Is she still eating?'

'Yes, she's still eating. I'm her mother. I don't starve her just because she's miserable. Liddy?' Jess called after her. 'Come back and say hi to your aunt *properly*.'

I remembered Jess at fourteen: a snack, homework and then ballet bar until bedtime. Happy. Focused.

And then there was me:

I'm sorry, Mrs Hamilton, but she just doesn't have the coordination for ballet.

She'd fare better if she paid attention.

Sorry, Mrs Hamilton, Eliza should not be choreographing her own routine.

Maybe Eliza should consider another hobby?

Mrs Hamilton, I cannot tolerate nose-picking girls in my class.

We'd tried most of the schools in the area, with my mother systematically falling out with every teacher until she finally blamed me. She couldn't understand it: why couldn't I be more like my sister?

Within two years Jess had gone, off to a top London school that most ballerinas could only dream of. Dad took more overseas jobs to foot the bill. Mum and I ticked off the calendar continuously, living for either of them to come home, even for a weekend.

Jess had breezed through and, at nineteen, was snapped up by a company in New York where she gave her all for ten years, before marrying Mark.

I chose a more colourful route on my career path: A BTEC in Art and Design led me straight to the checkout at a local supermarket. I worked behind a bar for a few months, before finally leaving home to live in what my mother referred to as 'a squat', with seven other people. Then came the window-cleaning round. Then the travelling. Then the garden centre. Then the horticulture degree and the inevitable move back into my old bedroom at home for three years.

Horticulture? For heaven's sake, isn't that a man's job?

Dad always said I should do what made me happy.

Lydia plonked herself in front of the screen, twiddling her hair and chewing gum. 'Hey, Aunt Liza. Happy Birthday. Does it stink to have your birthday on Easter Sunday?'

'It's total bollocks.' Lydia tried to conceal a grin, but failed. We were close, despite there being an ocean between us. She was sharp and adored everything British: the fish and chips; the humour, especially the swearing; impressing her school friends with the likes of *bloody*, *bugger* and *wank*, all courtesy of her English aunt, and very much to my sister's disgust.

'Are you okay, my sweet? You look exhausted.'

Before she could answer, my mother returned, monopolising both screen and conversation.

'She's fine. Just working hard, aren't you, darling?'

I felt rage surging up through my chest. I thought about Dad's frazzled heart and breathed in deeply and slowly. It didn't work. I wanted to tell her to move out of the way. That wasn't entirely true: I wanted to tell her to fuck off out of the way. But that wasn't entirely true either: I wanted to scream it at her, with a contorted face, spit flying everywhere.

Lydia would have loved it.

'Thanks, Mum. Can I see Liddy again, just for a minute?'

She complied, but with little point. Either she or Jessica consumed every question until Lydia was finally drowned out and she slipped away. I would go out to see her again this year, even if Charlotte and I went on our own, if just to see Liddy.

I took my sleeve and wiped away the layer of moisture that had gathered on my upper lip and at the nape of my neck—too much wine; too much cheese.

Mum reminded me that it was only three more weeks until she came home and that she was looking forward to seeing us all, which basically meant: Can you please go to the flat, run the vacuum around, fill the fridge with supplies and collect me from the airport? But not from the pick-up point. I'd like you to park the car and be waiting to greet me in the arrivals lobby, preferably with flowers and a *Welcome Home* banner.

18

CHARLOTTE WAS BACK at school. The sleeping-in and general dossing of the Easter holidays had come to an end. I had sketched out and consequently torn up over twenty designs for the Persian carpet garden, opened and deleted around twelve CAD worksheets, and spent around five hours working out how many hours I'd wasted on not coming up with any ideas for the garden. Add that to the hours wasted on social media; it totalled around fifty-eight hours. I continued to take half of the little red pill at 9 p.m., slipping into a coma at 10 p.m. I was aware of disturbances throughout the night—the odd car, my sweating, Will's snoring—but they weren't sending me into the spiral of fury I'd experienced in previous months.

I was no longer angry because I was monotonic, and no longer stressed by the Andersons' garden because, somehow, I was no longer bothered whether or not I pulled off the most exciting and challenging project of my landscaping career so far. Maybe I was still upsetting people, maybe not. I didn't care.

I couldn't be bothered to cook because I couldn't be bothered to eat. Charlotte and Will were making do with a default fare of sausage and mash, chilli and lasagne.

'You don't think it's those tablets you're taking, do you?' Will tried his best to make out the idea had just popped into his head.

'What? You think the antidepressants are making me depressed?'

'You weren't depressed before you started taking them, were you?'

'No, but I *was* stressed with modern-day living, and now I'm not, I suppose.'

'I see. So instead of being *stressed* with modern-day living, you now just can't be *arsed* with modern-day living, or maybe you're *indifferent* to modern-day living? I can see what an improvement that must be for you. Maybe you should up the dose, then you could just *sleep* through modern-day living.'

This level of sarcasm would ordinarily have resulted in an explosion of suppressed anger regarding Will's lack of cooperation with mundane household chores. But I noted that the shrew had gone into hibernation, and the new, emotionless me couldn't be bothered to argue.

'Good idea. I'll up the dose and see what happens.' Back at you, Will.

But he was already wandering into the kitchen, opening up cupboards and whingeing about the lack of chocolate biscuits.

'Are you even listening to me, Will?'

'I'm listening. Yeah, that sounds great. I'll go to the pub if you're having an early night. Some of the old college crowd are getting together.'

'You should've told me. We could have got a babysitter.'

'I wasn't going to go, to be honest. Partners aren't invited and I didn't want you to get funny about it.'

'Why would I get funny about it? I'm not funny about it. Go and have a good time. I don't mind.'

Will stood in the doorway of the kitchen and bit into an apple, trying to gauge me, trying to catch me out, but I held firm. I could huff and puff to my heart's content once he'd gone. I'd pour myself a glass of merlot and call Susannah for a rant.

'So who's going?'

'Just Ben and Chloe. And now me. Lexie might pop in for one or two.'

'How lovely. Who's Lexie?'

'Don't you remember Lexie? She ditched photography to study acting, so maybe she'd left by the time we got together. I'd better go if I want to catch the 7.30 train. Be careful with those pills.' Will kissed me on the head and ran out of the door.

I plonked myself onto the sofa. The thought of opening the wine and ranting to Susannah seemed like rather a lot of effort now. I turned the television on and flicked mindlessly through the channels. How dare Will say that I was indifferent to modern-day living. I might have been tired but my finger was still firmly on the pulse. And I'd never been funny about him going to the pub. I prided myself in being liberal with our independence. Heaven forbid I should be lumped into the camp of the needy insecure woman at home. And who the hell is Lexie?

I conjured up an image: mousy hair, sunken eyes, undernourished. I opened up Facebook and scrolled through Will's friends. I found her easily, but she hadn't posted anything for over a year. I nosed through her previous posts anyway; may as well, nothing better to do.

Lexie likes lots of indie bands that I had never heard of.

For her thirty-fifth birthday, Lexie went to cool bars in Budapest and shot vodka with some artists.

Lexie spent New Year in Stockholm with her parents. Her father is Iranian and her mother is Swedish, giving her dark glossy hair, green eyes and fucking spectacular cheekbones.

Lexie had read a book called *Oryx and Crake* which she found to be 'spellbinding' and 'effervescent'.

I imagined myself at the pub, sandwiched between her and Will as they embarked on a boring debate about post-communism and the free market, while I tried, unsuccessfully, to lighten the tone by making stupid jokes that no one found funny except me.

I felt grateful that partners hadn't been invited and that I wasn't wasting my valuable time. I took a full dose of the prescription and went to bed at 8.30 p.m. I would have a ten-hour sleep and, in the words of Dr Chaudhry, would wake 'feeling refreshed and ready to embrace the day'. The list of side effects on the information leaflet caught my eye, but it was unlikely that anything would bother me—I don't do side effects.

I scanned the numerous symptoms that one might experience after taking the medication, which included mood swings, excessive sweating, lack of libido and weight gain. I should also watch out for an irregular heartbeat and suicidal tendencies.

I considered self-induced vomiting to rid my body of this poison which I had been blithely ingesting for the past three weeks, but the lethargy so kindly given to me by the medication prevailed and I allowed my body to succumb, falling into a dense, dreamless sleep.

I woke, sluggish and leaden at 7.30 a.m., to find Will and Charlotte in the bed. Will informed me that, when he'd arrived home at almost midnight, Charlotte had climbed into our bed because she'd had a nightmare. She'd called out but couldn't wake me.

Dr Chaudhry eventually returned my call at the end of the day.

'Those particular side effects you're listing are rare, Miss Hamilton. Now, I'm glad you've given your body time to adapt to the medication and that you're taking the correct dose.'

'But I could hardly string a sentence together this morning. I've got a business to run and a child to raise. Why the hell would an antidepressant drug make someone want to commit suicide anyway? How is that even legal?'

'That's only in very extreme cases, concerning people who are already clinically depressed, which doesn't apply to you. The pharmaceutical companies have to make people aware of the risks.'

'What about all those other side effects, most of which were the reason I came to you in the first place.'

'Again, those only affect a handful of people. Are you sleeping better now?'

'Only because I'm doped up to the eyeballs. I'm still having night sweats.'

'Okay,' I could hear Dr Chaudhry tapping away at her keyboard over the phone. It echoed, loud then quiet, then loud again, like she was typing the blueprint for the second half of my life directly into my psyche and I was powerless to stop her. 'I'm going to send you for another blood test to check out your FSH levels. Just make sure you have it done on day three of your cycle.'

'What are my FSH levels?'

'Follicular Stimulating Hormone. If they're high it could suggest that you're close to physiological ovarian failure.'

'What?'

'Menopause, Eliza.'

19

GEORGIE WAS RUNNING late because Barbara from tennis had stubbed her toe and had to be driven to A&E. It was 8 a.m. in New York so I took advantage of the spare time to check in with Lydia:

> *How's it going over there? Miss you xx*
>
> *Just got to school, which totally sucks btw*
>
> *Not long til summer break, look on bright side? How's Mum/Nanny?*
>
> *Nanny leaving next week. Can't wait, Mom chills out when Nan goes home x*
>
> *I bet ;) What're your plans for the summer?*
>
> *Watching ballet, doing ballet, teaching bloody ballet. Yay, Christmas in July x*
>
> *Give it up then? x*
>
> *You're hilarious. Gotta go, class starting xx*

'Darling, I'm so sorry, what a carry-on down at A&E. You've never seen anything like it.'

'Was it broken?' I asked.

'No, just badly bruised. The doctor told her to rest up for a few days.' Georgie settled in her seat and I couldn't figure out why she looked so different.

'Have you had your hair done?'

'Eliza, my hair's a complete disaster. I barely had time to put a brush through it.'

'It looks good. Is that a new top?'

'It is. I had my colours done last week. Do you know, all this time I've been wearing warms when I should have been wearing cools. No wonder my husband left me.' She waved to the waiter, 'Jacob, a small glass of Pouilly-Fumé, please.'

She'd finally said it out loud. She'd finally said, 'My husband left me.' Not in the desperate, gorged-on-wine manner that I'd always expected; more with a *hey-ho, life goes on* approach.

'So you went shopping?'

'We certainly did. Barbara and I went to Selfridges and got one of those personal shoppers, which I would highly recommend by the way.'

'You went to London?'

'Yes, after we had our colours done on Friday. I said to Barbara, we can't possibly go on this cruise wearing the wrong colours and she agreed, so we hopped on the next train. Honestly, what a hoot.'

'Cruise? What cruise?'

'Ten nights around the Med. Didn't I tell you?' Georgie looked at me as if I was in a time warp. 'Barbara was originally going on her own and I thought, what the hell; you only live once.'

She looked genuinely excited.

'When do you leave?' I asked.

'In two weeks. This personal shopper really made me think about my wardrobe. I didn't have any of the right bag–shoe combinations and I think she was secretly appalled.'

I didn't know what had brought on this new and exciting burst of optimism, but I could do with a slice myself. I was itching to dig deeper. I thought back to the last time I had seen Georgie, just over a week ago, on Easter Sunday.

'You didn't ever finish off the story of the *informative* lunch you had with Valerie the other week.'

'Yes, well, get comfortable. Now, as you know, I've always liked Valerie. She was so kind and helpful whenever I called David at the office. But she was suddenly relocated when his mistress arrived on the scene and she now works on the floor below.'

Georgie sat back in her chair and laced her fingers together. Any talk of this previously and she'd have brushed it aside and ordered a double gin.

'And?'

'The mistress moved to the compliance department from the City just over a year ago.'

'Is that when you think it started?'

'It started the minute she set foot in David's office and he came home like some love-sick puppy. It was pathetic. Anyway, you're missing the point.'

'And that is?'

'The *City*, Eliza; she worked in the City.'

Still too cryptic for my scrambled brain, which was a fog of menu choices and various buildings in the financial district. I'd been awake half the night thinking about all sorts of scenarios surrounding my forthcoming hormone test. They all seemed ridiculous now, but at 3.48 a.m. Will had impregnated Lexie on their stupid night out where partners hadn't been invited, and they were moving to Stockholm. 'I'm sorry, Georgie, I'm not quite getting it.'

'Tara's *Little Linny* is David's mistress.'

Of course. Lindsay Sheridan, aka 'Little Linny'. That explained a few things. We'd never met Little Linny, but there had been a time when she'd been infamous.

When Tara had returned to work after Izzy was born, *Little Linny* was an assistant to the traders. She was responsible for giving Tara back, what they liked to call, her 'freedom'. There were endless parties and dinners out. The nannies didn't last more than a month and a family counsellor was hired. Eventually it was recommended that Tara spend three weeks in a 'health spa'.

'Does Tara know?' The words were caked in nervous energy.

'Oh come on, Liza. Everyone bloody well knows. They must have been having a right royal laugh at me up there, sat at home waiting patiently for him to get over his silly little affair. Well, no more.'

She downed the rest of her wine and Jacob was there in a flash to refill her glass. She had a fire in her eyes that I wasn't sure I'd seen before. I found it unnerving but thrilling at the same time. She obviously didn't know about Flightgate. And I reminded myself that nor did I. The flight had been cancelled and they'd stayed in Krakow for an extra night.

'Remember when I found those photos of her on David's phone, did I ever show you?'

'No.'

'Hmm, well you didn't miss much. Let's just say, you can't buy class. Anyway, I told Tom and he acted all disinterested. He obviously knew then, so why didn't he just tell me? I'm his *mother*, for heaven's sake.'

'To be fair, he must have been in an awkward position.' Why was I defending him?

'I can't think he'd be that impressed, considering all the trouble that woman has caused. And I can't believe your uncle; one glimpse of those ghastly great melons and he'd found his soulmate, very disappointing. I just don't understand why no one told me.'

'Have you spoken to anyone else about it?' I ask.

'I can't bring myself to speak to Tom about it yet. I'm too angry. And as for *Tara*—'

'What about Dan?'

'I really don't want to involve him; he's done nothing wrong. The only person I've spoken to is Barbara from tennis. The woman's a one-stop shop when it comes to gossip: once Barbara knows, the whole damn tennis club will know.'

'So why on earth did you tell her?'

'Because it's done, and it's *liberating*, Eliza. When I decided to give up smoking twenty years ago, I told everyone I met, which meant I had to follow it through. And this is the same.'

'What did Barbara say?'

'She was rather indifferent, which was a bit of an anticlimax. She told me that when her Robert was alive, he had three affairs. *Three!*'

'That's awful. Why did she stick it out?'

'For ease. She said she was grateful to the mistresses for saving her a job, and we all know what sort of job she's talking about. She threw herself into friends and hobbies. I mean, look at her now—she's having a whale of a time.'

'And what are your plans, apart from a cruise and a new wardrobe?'

'My plan, my dear, is to be utterly selfish. I shall do whatever, with whomever I choose. And I am starting with my online profile.'

'Are you finally joining Facebook?'

'No. Barbara's signed me up for mysinglefriend.com and I'm joining Tinder. What do you think?'

'Wow. Amazing.'

Dating apps, shopping trips, cruises, zest for life. I thought about laundry and what to cook Will and Charlotte for dinner, and there was a possibility I was slightly jealous.

20

'SORRY FOR THE wait today, Miss Hamilton. I hope I haven't delayed you too much.'

'No, I'm meeting my mum for coffee in a minute. She's just got back from New York and I expect—'

'Well, let's not keep you any longer. Now, I've had your blood test results through and it seems we have a solution to our little mystery.'

'Is it my heart? My father died of heart failure.'

'We didn't test your heart. We tested to see what your hormones were up to and it appears that your FSH levels are rather high.'

'Does that mean my ovaries have failed?' I thought of them hanging there, all crestfallen and dejected. I put my hand on my abdomen to protect them from Dr Chaudhry's harsh words.

She inhaled sharply. 'They're not taking their driving test, Miss Hamilton. What this means is that your ovaries aren't always getting the message to release an egg, which is to be expected in a woman of, let's see...' She scanned her computer screen and I had a fleeting thought about strangling her with her stethoscope.

'I've just turned forty-six.'

'So I can see. You're slightly young to be in full menopause, but I would say that you're well on your way.' For a moment, it looked as if she might congratulate me. 'We call it the *peri-meno*pause.'

'Oh.' This couldn't be right. 'Are you sure?'

'Yes. Your test results clearly show that you haven't ovulated this month. Now that doesn't mean to say that you won't next month, so don't use it as a form of contraception.'

'So I could still get pregnant, if I wanted to?'

Dr Chaudhry switched to her concerned yet authoritative tone. 'Eliza, do you seriously want to have another baby at forty-six?'

'That's not what I meant. I was just checking. It's all very final, isn't it?'

'Not really, no. My last patient has two months left to live—that's all very final. Menopause is a perfectly natural process that we will all go through. We wouldn't want to be messing about with periods in our seventies, now would we?' She smiled at me like I might smile at Charlotte after she'd scraped her knee and I'd applied a Mickey Mouse plaster.

'The good news is that we can treat your symptoms.'

'I don't want to take more antidepressants.'

'I'm suggesting that we start you off on a low dose of Hormone Replacement Therapy.'

'HRT?'

'Correct.'

'My aunt says that it can cause cancer.'

'I'm highly unlikely to prescribe you something that causes cancer. These modern-day drugs are marvellous—no more brain fog or anxiety. Your night sweats will be non-existent and you'll be feeling brighter in no time.'

'I think I need to digest it all.' I got up to leave, heart pumping, head burning, top lip glistening. Was I to have a full-on humdinger of a hot flush right there in Dr Chaudhry's office, just as I was trying to side-step a prescription for HRT?

'That's absolutely fine, but before you leave...' She tapped away on her keyboard. 'Take this.' She handed me a prescription. 'And this.' She handed me a leaflet with the word 'menopause' in a swirly font with a flower in place of the 'O'.

There was a photograph of an attractive woman on the front: early fifties, shock of silver hair, laughter lines. She was, ironically, gardening. *'It's okay,'* she said to me through the lens, *'my ovaries have withered away too but here I am, living my full and happy life. My vagina might be saggy and parched, but by Jove, look at my clematis.'*

'Will everything just dry up now?'

'Eliza, please, take the prescription and you won't have any problems, I can assure you.'

'Sorry, Mum, I got held up at the doctor's.' I bent down to give her an awkward hug. 'You look well.'

'Thanks. We were over at the house in Brookhaven all of last week. The weather was amazing. What did the doctor say?'

'That I am perimenopausal.'

'Oh well, never mind, you'll just have to get on with it; at least you've got Charlotte. Your sister's periods are like clockwork and she's forty-nine next month. Still, she's lived a much healthier life than you, so I expect she'll sail through menopause, just like I did.'

'I'm sure.'

'What did Will say? Is he upset?'

I hadn't considered Will. What *would* he say? He would fold me in his arms and tell me he loved me of course, and that it didn't matter. Presuming that he hadn't actually impregnated Lexie on their stupid little night out where partners weren't invited, and I'd nearly overdosed on prescription drugs. I pictured Lexie with a neat little pot belly poking out of the top of some exquisite harem pants that you could only buy in Tehran. She was giggling and handing Will some Scandinavian fish extravaganza that she'd knocked up in her rustic and whimsical-looking kitchen. She would use weird filters and smear the photographs shamelessly all over Instagram: #swedishcuisine #instafish #hungrydaddy #imsofuckingfertile.

Fine. Let him set up a new life with Lexie and her effervescent literature.

The thought stabbed me in the chest and I had a stern word with myself: knee-jerk reactions and social media stalking were not beneficial to one's wellbeing and I needed to stop. I would practise some meditation when I got home and cook Will something other than sausages for dinner.

'I haven't told Will yet.'

'Hmm, I expect he wanted you to have a son at some point, didn't he? All men would like to have a son. I know your father loved you dearly, but he secretly wished you'd been a boy.'

'Oh.'

'Well, try not to look so glum about it, dear. It's got to happen at some point.'

'I did think I should get an ECG, in case I've inherited Dad's heart condition.'

'You won't inherit your father's heart condition. It was that heavy German diet: too much meat and potatoes and beer, plus all of those contracts he kept taking on. I'm all for instilling a good work ethic, but your grandfather pushed those boys to the limit. Look at your uncle: still working at seventy. You'd think he'd have more sense after seeing what happened to his own brother.'

'You know the affair's out in the open now, don't you? Georgie's happy to talk about it.' I had a sudden urge to blurt everything out to Mum, to tell her about the Facebook photo and the fact that Tom had lied about the flight home from Poland. But she couldn't be trusted, it would get back to Georgie in some warped way or another and I'd somehow end up with the blame. 'She's even going on a cruise.'

'That's nice for her.'

Mother's haughty response marooned us in silence for a moment and we observed a man outside who was removing a toddler from a seat attached to the back of a sleek-looking mountain bike. The toddler refused to take his helmet off even though the man had said that he would get too hot. The man tried to take matters into his own hands by physically removing the helmet. The toddler won.

'So, are you jetlagged?'

'Not at all. I had a fabulous surprise waiting for me at check-in. Mark had put me in first class, to say thank you for all my help!'

'Wow.'

'He has *got* to be the world's best son-in-law. It was amazing. I slept all the way home and I couldn't believe it how polite and discreet my fellow passengers were.'

'Why? Did you think you'd be sharing the cabin with the Kardashians? Seven hours of Kayne West screaming out demands for diamond-encrusted caviar?'

'Don't be sarcastic. What is it with this country and sarcasm? Americans aren't like that; they're just nice to everyone.'

'Even when they're shooting people?' That was enough.

Mum paused.

'I take it you're not planning to visit anytime soon, then? Jessica's been asking, and Lydia.'

'I want to go this year, maybe at Christmas,' I said, exhaling slowly. I tried to practice a calming exercise taught by my prenatal yoga teacher: *channel a healing light through the top of the head and let it melt down through the chakras.* But I couldn't decide on a colour. I think it's supposed to be white or yellow but mine was a weird murky brown and was giving me a slight headache. My chakras would have to remain in darkness for now.

'Fabulous. I'll be there then. All the family together on Christmas Day.'

'Well, I don't know if I mean Christmas Day. I mean around Christmas. You know how Will likes to be at home.'

'Yes, well, it's not all about Will, is it? We'll go ice-skating in Central Park. How exciting for Charlotte to be with her cousins at Christmas.'

'I texted Lydia last week. She sounded okay, a bit bored with school though.'

'She does her best. She's never going to be as academic as her brother, but then who is? The boy's a genius. She's a natural ballerina, of course. She just needs to put in that extra effort to make it to the top.'

'Are you sure that's what she really wants to do?'

'She'd be crazy not to. Jess has all the contacts. Lydia will get there, she just needs to mature and push herself a little.' She looked at me, clearly irritated, and downed the rest of her coffee. 'Did you say you had to be somewhere this morning?'

'I need to be at work by midday.'

'Well, I won't keep you.' She gathered up her bag and a newspaper. 'I must get home and get on with some jobs. When's a good time to pop in and see Charlotte?'

'The weekend?'

'Great. I'll call you tomorrow night to arrange.' She blew me a kiss and headed for the door.

An iron-pumping barista, who had a Celtic tattoo which swirled around his ear and disappeared down the back of his t-shirt, called out to her: 'Excuse me, madam?'

'Yes'

'I'm sorry, but the newspapers are for our customers to enjoy.'

'Well, aren't I a customer?'

'They're for our customers to enjoy *here*.'

'Outrageous! This would never happen in New York.'

She slammed the paper on a table and flounced out of the cafe, leaving me to nurse my embarrassment with a lukewarm cappuccino and a shambolic reproductive system for company.

21

I STARED AT the front of Elm Tree care home, but I could not figure out what was different. I noticed Linda marching out from the side door, her gloved hands rubbing away at a brass jug.

'Morning, Linda.'

'Everything alright, Eliza?'

'Yes, fine. Have you had it painted?'

'Have I had what painted?'

'The woodwork. It looks brighter.'

'What makes you think I'd have time to paint the place? I've got too many care plans and not enough staff.'

I zoned out from her frustrations and started to plan my day. I liked to work from the front backwards: weeding, pruning, watering, mowing, and then on to the hanging baskets. The baskets, that's what it was—or wasn't.

'Linda, what's happened to the hanging baskets?'

'Ah, yes, the baskets. Sorry about that. You know our lovely little Dorothy? She told me they needed dead-heading and I thought the fresh air would do her good. I should've kept an eye on her but I had so much to do. You know how it is.'

We both regarded the baskets which, only last week, had been brimming with colour and vitality, now they were barren and fruitless like a pitiful assembly of menopausal ovaries.

'Is it just these ovaries?'

'I beg your pardon?'

'Sorry. Is it just these baskets, or did she have a go at any of the others?'

'I think she may've had a little go at the ones at the sides and back as well. But you'll work your magic, won't you?'

'It's not quite that simple, Linda, I've got a trowel not a wand.' I tried a laugh to offset my caustic tone. I wanted to refill all the baskets with an abundance of young, budding petunias, which would bloom all through the summer until the first frost of autumn. Maybe that's why Dorothy had picked all the primulas in the first place; a senseless grudge against their brazen fertility.

'May I suggest that if they are such a precious commodity, you hang them higher,' Linda said. 'Then the next time my residents want to help out, they'll be unable to reach them.'

'What if they decide to stand on a chair? We wouldn't want that now would we? Health and safety.'

'Are you sure you're alright today, Eliza? You seem a little touchy.'

'I am absolutely fine today, thank you, Linda. And how are you?'

'I, *Eliza*, am very busy. I need you to check up on those conifers again, please. They were a total mess when I went down there yesterday; weeds everywhere.'

'Of course, Linda. Will Mr Withers be joining me today?'

'No. Mr Withers has been admitted to hospital with pneumonia. I'm not sure if he's even coming back.'

Before I could utter another word, she strutted up the path, rubbing away furiously at the jug and shouting orders at Brian to hose down the decking. I blinked back some tears while making my way down to the conifers. I thought about burying Linda under the rockery. What would Brian say? Would he be secretly delighted? Would Brian and I have an affair?

Just when I'd finally got my tardy arse into gear and put the *National Geographics* in the back of the car, lovely Mr Withers had ended up in hospital. I would find out the number of

Mr Withers' ward and take him a few copies, making sure I'd got the one about the giant redwoods. I'd make a cake and take him some bananas—he'd love that. I imagined myself sitting by his bed and reading the article to him and a glow filled my heart.

The glow also filled my chest, my neck and then my ears and the rest of my head until sweat had soaked the top half of my t-shirt. I tried to mute the recollection of Dr Chaudhry shrilling the word 'perimenopause' in my face. I had read an alarming article yesterday about global warming and if what it said was true, it was no wonder I was in such a mess.

Global warming and stress from modern-day living—what a terrible combination.

22

'So far, I'm chatting to Trevor and Andrew. Let me show you.' Georgie opened up her phone. 'Now, you may think Andrew's not much to look at, but he's an absolute hoot. We've been messaging each other about five times a day. I think he really gets my sense of humour, or *GSOH* as they say on the website.'

The waiter delivered our food. I was ravenous and got stuck in to a burger and chips. I wasn't comfort-eating; I just fancied a few carbs—the refined, filthy kind.

'First of all, let me show you Trevor, he's the looker.' She passed me her phone and I saw a man of about my age wearing a white linen jacket and a debatable haircut.

'Handsome or what? Can you believe he's sixty-seven?'

I zoomed in. 'Georgie, this is about twenty years old, he's taken a photo of a photo.'

'I asked him when it was taken and he said it was two years ago, on his boat in Corsica. He owns a second home there.'

'Hmm. What about Andrew?'

Georgie peered down her glasses and swiped to a photo of a respectable-looking man of her own age. 'This is Andrew.'

'He looks nice *and* you have a laugh with him.'

'Yes, but I'm not sure about anything else. He retired five years ago, but does a few hours a week as a Sainsbury's delivery man.'

'Good for him. At least he's keeping active.'

'Yes, but a delivery man? Shouldn't he be playing golf or something?'

'Maybe it's not his bag,' I said.

'Maybe it's not his *carrier* bag.' She laughed and clicked her fingers in the air and I was reminded of when I was a child and we used to dance around her living room and on her coffee table. It was always so much more fun than being at home.

'No, I don't think I could go on a date with a delivery man.'

'What about a platonic coffee? He must have other strings to his bow.'

'He does take swing dancing lessons, which I thought sounded rather fun. I messaged him and said: *I hope you're not going to invite me to go swinging with you, are you?* He messaged back saying, *No, but don't be alarmed if I ask you for a Carolina shag*. Barbara and I were in hysterics over it all.'

'He sounds like great fun. I don't know what's stopping you.'

'But what if he's a weirdo? Now Trevor on the other hand...' She swiped back to the first man and we scanned the photo once more.

'Looks like a *Miami Vice* villain.'

'Eliza, stop it. He seems to be a little more refined, with a place here and in Corsica. He runs an import–export business with his son and he's hoping to retire next year.'

'He sounds like a two-dimensional liar. Message him now and get him to take a selfie and send it to you. Go on. See how quickly he replies.'

'Why are you so suspicious? Trevor says he keeps to a strict diet and exercise routine. That's probably why he looks so good.'

'So, he's a boring as well. Anyone else?'

'Goodness, no. Two's plenty to be getting on with. I've had a few other requests, but they were either bald or had a funny look about them. We board the ship tomorrow so I won't want to be bothered with any of them then.'

'I hope you've got your bag–shoe combinations sorted.'

Her phone pinged, and I was pulled into her frenzy of excitement.

'Ooh, it's Trevor.'

'What did he say?'

'He says: *I hope you enjoy your cruise. Shame you don't stop in Corsica. Maybe we can have dinner on your return? Keep in touch.*'

'Ooh.'

'Well I have to reply, don't I? It's only polite, and there's a question mark. He's asking me out, Eliza. I haven't been asked out on a date in fifty years.'

Although I suspected this man to be a rake of the highest order, her face brimmed with joy and it would have been ruthless to quash it at this stage of the game.

'What are you going to say?'

'I'm going to say yes!'

'Good. Say yes and that I want him to send a selfie.'

'Okay, here we go: *Dinner sounds good. Having lunch with my niece. She says hi and send us a selfie.* That sounds okay, doesn't it?'

'Sounds perfect.'

'Well, I know we're being good,' Georgie said, 'but this calls for a toast. How about a small glass of bubbly?'

Ping.

'Oh, that was quick. He says: *Great, I can't wait to meet you. Can't take selfie at present as dropped phone while lobster-diving and having to use an ancient pay-as-you-go. Enjoy.*'

'Lobster-diving?'

'Yes, apparently that's quite tricky.'

I watched her drift off into thought and onto the deck of Trevor's boat. Her: white one-piece, wide-brimmed hat, cool gin cocktail. Him: tanned, muscular, seventies wetsuit, hand-feeding her lobster to the sound of the accordion.

She raised her glass. 'Cheers, darling. To the next chapter.'

'The next chapter.' I chinked her glass and took a swig of Veuve, hoping it would block out the negativity that whispered in my ear, feeding the cynicism that is slowly becoming part of my everyday repertoire.

23

EMILY HAD CHOSEN a new place in town called 'Free Range Franny's' for our brunch date.

I ordered a Happy Hen Omelette, which was delicious although I wasn't sold on the name. I'm sure the hen concerned was quite happy when she was pecking away on juicy little grubs in her toxin-free pasture, but how did she feel when she returned to find that all of her eggs had been whisked up into an omelette? Probably more of a horrified hen or a heartbroken hen. What if she was a perimenopausal hen and those were her last eggs?

Franny was telling us about her new 'Time of the Month Tea'– a fusion of ginger, chamomile and cinnamon—which should probably have been called 'Bitchy Brew' or 'Irritable Infusion'. Franny and Emily had a brief, hushed conversation regarding their hectic little ovaries, bustling with juicy eggs, all waiting their turn to be propelled into no doubt spotless fallopian tubes.

I pictured my own eggs loitering around in dusty corners, belching, swearing, swigging cheap lager from a can before slumping into an oestrogen-starved coma.

'I'm going to bring you some over, on the house,' Franny said, interrupting my morose fantasy. She gave us a reassuring smile before wiggling her tiny saronged bottom back into the kitchen.

'She's so amazing,' Emily gushed. 'Everything you see on the menu is locally sourced. She even makes her own gluten-free vegan pastry.'

Thankfully much of the advice Emily required from me today was about design which I considered—Persian carpet gardens aside—my forte. She showed me some of her ideas on Pinterest and I sketched a rough design, which she made a big fuss about and showed to a customer on another table, who then asked for my business card. I was mortified by the whole scene and wished I'd never drawn the damn thing in the first place.

Emily told me more about her thesis, and assured me that she was a member of the Permaculture Association, as she was sure I was. I listened carefully and nodded, making the correct noises at the appropriate time, and somehow managed to pull it off.

I was meeting Mr Anderson later who would most certainly have more questions on sustainability, so I could take Emily's knowledge and present it as my own; impress him with information that I myself had been too lazy to look up.

Mr Anderson strode toward the car as I arrived, holding a spade and wearing a high-visibility jacket.

'Eliza, I'm so glad you're here. I need you to come and take a look at this garish erection.' There was no irony in his tone. Mr Anderson was a perfect gentleman and simply used old fashioned language. No need to laugh and make things awkward.

The students had erected an orange tie-dye tent around the fountain. One side of the tent was emblazoned with the words GLASTO ROCKS, while the other hosted a giant pair of tits.

'I did speak to whathisname about it.'

'Ben?'

'That's the one. I've had a quiet word. You know I don't like to complain, it's just that we've got people coming for dinner this weekend and—'

'Absolutely. It's really offensive. I'm so sorry.'

My head was a muddle of screaming abuse at Ben and anxiety about what the hell the fountain looked like. Did I remember to bring my so-far crappy drawings with me? I was certain that I'd got a green tent in the loft without tits on.

'You know us, we're quite open-minded about the youngsters. It's just that it's not quite fitting in with the landscape and the visitors are a little straight-laced.'

'Of course. I'll make sure it's replaced by the end of the day. Have there been any other problems? Have they been polite and tidied up?'

'Oh yes, they've been great fun. Mrs A's been plying them with cakes and flirting outrageously, especially on those warm days when they worked without tops on.'

'I see. And how's the fountain coming on?'

'Ah, well. Let's enter the garish erection and have a look, shall we?'

Mr Anderson winked and slowly unzipped the door of the tent. I changed my mind on the perfect gentleman bit—filthy old bastard.

'Now close your eyes, please.' I was comforted by the degree of excitement in his voice and tried to push aside fears of controversial images of religious icons with giant mosaic testicles.

'May I present to you, the almost finished centrepiece...of my very own...Persian carpet garden!'

I opened my eyes and took in the sight before me. The centre of the fountain was the deepest midnight blue, spiralling out into teal and sapphire and turquoise. The bowl of the fountain was packed with tiny tiles, forming a jewelled whirlpool which, at first, gave the impression that the tiles had all been chucked in and swirled around with a wooden spoon. On closer inspection, the painstaking work and patient steady hand that had been required to create such a masterpiece became obvious. Crimson and mahogany flashed through barely noticed, until they spilled over the edge to dominate the base. The effect was nothing short of stunning and I was temporarily speechless.

They would still get a bollocking about the tit tent.

'What do you think?'

'It's absolutely beautiful. I had no idea—'

Mr Anderson grasped my shoulder. 'That it would be so spectacular?'

'Yes. I don't know what to say.'

'Well, I say that it's a beautiful day and there's some of last year's sloe gin chilling in the fridge. So, let's throw down a rug, toast the fountain and have a good look at these fabulous designs of yours.'

Before I could protest, a car pulled up, vibrating with an old B-side Nirvana track.

'Speaking of the golden boys, here they are now.' Mr Anderson gave a high wave and headed back toward the house.

I stomped over to the car. 'Aren't you rather young to be listening to Nirvana?' I asked, secretly hoping they'd be impressed by my nineties Seattle grunge scene knowledge.

'Nirvana are sick,' Ben declared.

They both looked inherently happy.

'Are you two stoned?' I asked.

'What? No, we're not stoned. Are *you*?'

'Don't you think it's high time you showed a little respect? And what is that tent all about?'

'Hey, that's my tent,' Bill said. 'It's seen some killer action.'

'I really do not wish to know about any action your tent has been involved in, Bill. I just want you to take it down.'

'Hey, his name's not Bill, okay. It's Tim. Why do you always keep calling him Bill?'

'Well, it's... I'm sorry. They sound similar.'

'They do not sound similar. What's turned you up?' Ben was moving from foot to foot, my lecture quite obviously *messing with his chi* or whatever it was that one messed with these days.

I can't tell them that I'm incapable of remembering mono-syllabic names, they wouldn't understand and it would leave me feeling weak and exposed. I go in for the attack instead. 'And what's this about working without your tops on? Is that really necessary?'

'Mrs A seemed to think so,' Ben said and they both sniggered.

'Please tell me you don't call her Mrs A?'

The barn door swung open and there she was, sporting a denim jumpsuit and a straw hat.

'Boys, you're here. Hurrah!'

'Alright Mrs A, what's cooking?'

'Some rather scrumptious buns, if you must know. I'll let them cool and then I'll make you a nice lunch. Anything else I can get you? Coffee? A cold beer?'

Lunch? A cold beer?

'We're all good thank you, Mrs A. Thanks for taking care of us so well.' Bill or Tim, or whatever his name was, put his hands together in mock prayer and shot her a killer smile.

Okay, it all made sense now: fresh-faced, poverty-pleading students being nauseatingly courteous to older lady, with a sprinkle of lothario charm thrown in for good measure. Mrs Anderson skipped back into the house wearing a slightly dazed expression.

'Can you please remember to conduct yourself in a professional manner at all times?'

They ignored me and Ben pulled a cow-print tent bag from the back seat.

'What is *that?*'

'What? It's my sister's, and it fits in with the countryside.'

I spotted the rug and the sloe gin and didn't have the energy to argue.

'I've got some important matters to discuss with Mr Anderson,' I said.

'Eliza?'

'Yes?'

'What do you think of the fountain?'

'The fountain's very nice, well done. Now excuse me, please.'

I marched over to the rug with my work folder, trying to come off as righteous as one could sat on a rug with a tumbler of gin at one in the afternoon, holding what is essentially a business meeting.

I laid out the plans and waited for Mr Anderson. We'd gone past the preliminaries but still weren't at the master plan stage; I blamed the students of course, nothing to do with me.

Text from Susannah:

> *You, me and Sarah going to the White Lamb tonight for half-price burgers xx*
>
> *That does sound good, but need to check with Will x*
>
> *Have already checked with Will. He says yes! See you at 7? xx*

When did she check with Will? When she had sex with him in our bed while I was discussing compost heaps with Organic Emily over a cup of Period Tea?

Stop it.

> *Great, see you then x*

24

THE WHITE LAMB was a ten-minute bike ride away. I hadn't used Bessie since the incident involving the forgotten car keys, which had turned out not to be forgotten at all; just one more oversight in a compilation of oversights which had cemented themselves into my daily routine. I found myself holding some kind of illogical grudge against her, becoming infuriated by unfamiliar squeaking or the fact that I had to change gear.

When I arrived at the pub, I slammed her against the railings and I reminded myself of a stressed-out, chain-smoking young mother, yanking a toddler's arm. I needed to give myself a brief lecture to regain some composure before mixing with other humans:

Bessie was simply a metal and rubber structure which I had humanised by naming. She did not feel emotion.

Sarah was not trying to lure me into menopause in order to make herself feel better; I was hurtling towards it on my own. It's a perfectly natural process which we all experience eventually, anyway. And I was only perimenopausal, which is different.

Susannah is a dear friend who is not sleeping with Will. These stupid insecurities had begun to rampage through my conscience like rabid beasts, with little regard for the dearest people in my life. Apart from Lexie; I wouldn't put her into the dearest people category, but that's because I'd never met her and because her Instagram posts made me want to boil her alive.

It had become clear that my almost-nightly 3 a.m. social-media stalking habit needed to stop; the triggering of such violent emotions would surely be damaging to my adrenals, not to mention my possible genetic heart condition.

Inside the pub was packed. Youngsters hogged the bar, ordering complicated cocktails and pushing out the older locals, who remembered the place when it had been privately owned and served a simpler fare with traditional ales. I found Sarah and Susannah wedged into a corner table. They both jumped up, genuinely delighted to see me and it was only then I realised how much I needed a change of scenery—a change from work, cooking, the school run, and the never-ending drudgery of sorting shit out.

We had a light-hearted moan about men and messy kids. Sarah made us howl with stories about her recent visit to a retreat, where the vegan menu had her suppressing a fart for the best part of ninety minutes while a hot Italian masseur worked on her tight hamstrings. By the time our food arrived, the conversation had inevitably moved onto the state of everyone's hormones.

'I don't take the support group that seriously,' Sarah said. 'But it would be great to have more fun people; some of them really need to lighten up.'

'I no longer have any issues to talk about,' Susannah replied through a mouthful of chips, 'thanks to the wonders of modern medicine.'

Sarah held up her hand. 'Don't get me started on HRT. I don't want a political debate to ruin the evening.'

Susannah shrugged. 'Hormone replacement has come a long way. That cream you use is still a form of HRT, and you swear by it.'

'What about you, Eliza?' says Sarah, swiftly steering us away from what has obviously become a bone of contention. 'You don't have to do anything, you could just listen or maybe talk about how you've been feeling that week. It's surprisingly cathartic.'

'I don't really think it's me, if I'm honest. I don't mind having a rant to you two, or friends I've known for years, but not a roomful of...well—'

'I know exactly what you're thinking,' Sarah said, 'because I thought it too: a load of sniffling women trying to pull off animal print who can't cope with unloading the dishwasher.'

I nodded.

'There's probably one of those, but the rest are a mixed bag. One of them is a plastic surgeon, then there's this crazy psych nurse; she gets really animated and always stands up to speak. Last week she got so enraged about school catchment areas that she flung a Bible across the room and it really upset Marion.'

'Sounds like a riot, although I'm only perimenopausal at the moment so I'm not really sure if I'd be suitable.'

'Oh come on, Eliza, get a grip, would you?' Sarah laughed but I took it personally and felt my face burn, hopefully with humiliation and not anything hormone-related—that would be dreadful timing.

I quickly downed the rest of my beer. 'Okay, maybe I'll come for one session, but I can't promise I'll speak.'

'Hooray!' Sarah lunged forward to give me a hug. 'I'll get another round in.'

'So how was Will when you told him?' Susannah's question caught me out and had an air of interrogation about it.

'He was great thanks, supportive.' My answer felt dismissive and I broke eye contact. Not that there was anything to hide. Will had been great, as he always was in these circumstances. He reminded me of the line he'd used when we went out to celebrate our first year together, when he promised that he'd still love me when my tits were where my arse used to be and I had laughed so hard that I snorted wine out through my nose. When I'd regained my composure, I thought he was going to propose but he ordered a salted caramel cheesecake instead. I was okay with it...ish. I knew Will was far from traditional and that's what I loved about him. But last week when I'd told him about the blood test results, something made me doubt him and part of me wanted to spew out all of my irrational thoughts right there and then. I opened my mouth to speak but Susannah beat me to it.

'You could always freeze your eggs.'

'What?'

'In case you want another baby.'

'Another baby?' Will and I had never used a conventional form of contraception: me thinking that pregnancy was something that happened to other people; and Will not being fussed either way. Charlotte had taken us both by surprise and we had been beyond delighted, but we hadn't entertained the idea of having any more and had successfully relied on the rhythm method for the last five years.

'I've got eggs stored in a clinic in London. Not that I'll ever use them, but it's nice to know they're there.'

'Why have you stored your eggs, Susannah?'

'I don't know. It seemed like a good idea after Teddy was born, just in case I wanted any more.'

'I don't think I want any more and I certainly don't want to freeze my eggs.'

'Suit yourself.' Susannah shrugged off my disdain as if I was the weird one. 'It was only a suggestion.'

Once Sarah had come back, Susannah filled us in on the latest with Simon, whose commitment-phobic boyfriend, Gerald, was finally moving in. Gerald was going to rent out his house for six months and had suggested that they use that as a trial period, to see if it worked out. Simon had told him to man up or fuck off.

We arranged a repeat meeting in three weeks before Sarah and Susannah hopped in a cab. I rounded the corner and got my keys out, ready to unlock Bessie, only to find her gone.

I looked around for her, as if someone might have politely moved her or she had wheeled herself off to a more comfortable area of the railings. I walked the perimeter of the pub, looked over some walls and asked some girls smoking roll-ups in the pub garden, who shrugged their shoulders apologetically. My beloved bicycle had been stolen and I would never see her again.

I slumped to the ground and let the memories of the last eleven years flood my mind. Getting home from travelling and being broke but super-fit thanks to a hike up Kilimanjaro. I'd bought Bessie for twenty quid from an old school friend who was moving to Ireland. She'd only used her three times.

I thought of the carefree days of the garden centre and how I'd vowed never to buy a car. I remembered how firm my buttocks were, not the flaccid, underdone pancakes which hang from my hips today. I remembered my boss and his girlfriend who ran the cafeteria; the laughs we'd had in the neighbouring beer garden on warm summer evenings. Why hadn't I stayed in touch with them?

I used to take Bessie on the train to get to and from the station when I went to college; even the guard knew her name. She had been the conversation starter between Will and me on a standing-room-only journey home, one snowy Friday afternoon. Will told me I needed to be careful cycling in the snow. I said, thank you, I would.

After some awkward small talk, he asked if I would like to go sledging the following day, but the snow had melted so he suggested we went to the cinema instead to see a horror flick where they made the girl cut open her own stomach. It was so disturbing that I didn't sleep for about a week afterwards. Will kept apologising, calling every night to see if I wanted him to keep me company, and it became our party piece first date story.

The following weekend Will put candles and wild flowers on the table and remembered that I didn't eat mushrooms. He introduced me to pinot noir and made the most delicious linguine I'd ever tasted. We had chocolate ice cream for dessert and I never wanted to go home.

'Are you alright, love? I'm locking up now. Need a taxi?' I looked up to see the pub landlord and felt appalled that I probably looked like one of those women in a *Drunken Britain* documentary, minus the grazed knee and gladiator-style stilettos.

'Sorry, I'm okay. My bike was stolen. I left it right there.' I motioned to the railings.

'Did you lock it?'

What a stupid question.

'Of course I locked it.'

I'm sure I did.

'So do you want a taxi then or what?'

I stood up and dusted off my bottom. 'No thank you. I'll walk.'

Did I lock it? Honestly.

'You did lock it, didn't you?'

'For Christ's sake, Will, of course I locked it.' Will was trying, unsuccessfully, to comfort me.

'Look, don't worry, it was old anyway. Why don't we go out tomorrow and get you a new one? My treat.'

'I don't want a new bike, Will. I want Bessie back. And even if I did want a new one, I'm perfectly capable of buying it myself.'

'Fine. Did you report it?'

'Not yet. I was really horrible to her when I got to the pub. I shoved her handle bars into the railings and now she's gone for ever.' I knew this would do nothing except fuel Will's concerns about my mental health, but I had to get it out, had to confess my shameful behaviour.

'I'd try not to worry too much. Aluminium isn't prone to hypersensitivity. You should report it—they won't do anything, but it's good to make them aware just in case it turns up.'

I called the police to report it but they seemed to have more important things to get on with. I talked too fast and probably came off as slightly hysterical and they didn't really take me seriously. Will said that he should have called them instead, which I found offensive, and we somehow ended up having a heated discussion about how the ancient Greeks labelled most female ailments as hysteria, with me saying that things had not moved on much and Will missing the point completely by insisting that I was being overdramatic. I ended up calling him a wanker and we went to bed not really speaking.

25

'Mr Withers? Hello, it's me, Eliza.'

His eyes were shut and his mouth open, there was a tube coming out of his nose and another from his wrist. I held his hand. I had never held his hand before and was acutely aware that I was crossing some kind of social boundary. His skin was waxy, and he had a yeasty aroma about him. The whole scenario took me back to Dad and the last precious hours we'd spent together in the Hamburg hospital: me keeping it light, trying to hide my shock at his purple, swollen face; Dad assuring me that he would be discharged soon, once the doctors had sorted this whole silly palaver out.

The man in the next bed craned his neck to get a better look. 'You can talk to him, he can hear you alright,' he rasped, before falling back into his mound of pillows. At least Dad had had his own room, which was like a hotel suite with fresh orange juice and cable TV. This place felt like one step up from the morgue. I drew the curtain around the bed.

'Sorry I haven't been in sooner, Mr Withers, but you know how it is: weeds to pull, dirt to be hidden. I would say primulas to be watered, but you'll be glad to hear there're not many of those left now, thanks to Dorothy.'

Mr Withers' eyes remained shut, and his chest continued to rise and fall in the same steady motion.

'Linda told me to work my magic and I wanted to tell her to get lost. Actually that's a lie, Mr Withers: I wanted to tell her to fuck off and stick her contract up her gigantic wobbly arse, but I know that's very unladylike and I hope you're not disappointed in me. It wasn't the same when I went last week, knowing you weren't there. It felt a bit pointless, like it was just a *job* and I may as well have been working in a call centre, or driving an underground train.'

The curtain twitched and a young girl with a badge saying 'Cathy Milligan: Healthcare Assistant' poked her head in and checked a chart at the end of the bed. She spoke with a soft Irish accent. 'Are you okay there? Would you like me to fetch you a cuppa tea?'

'Don't be silly. You've got enough to do,' I said.

She smiled, warm and gentle, then disappeared. I took the *National Geographic*s out of my bag. I'd brought three, in the ludicrously optimistic notion that Mr Withers might have been able to sit up in bed with his glasses on and flick through them.

'I've finally brought you the magazines, only three for now, the rest are waiting for you back at Elm Tree. Better late than never, I suppose. I found the one about the giant redwoods, so, if you're sitting comfortably, I will begin. They are the earth's living giants, some taller than the Statue of Liberty, some with seedlings which were believed to have been around when Jesus was alive. Now, I've been up to the crown of the Statue of Liberty and, let me tell you, it's bloody high.'

I'd never talked to Mr Withers about travel. I'd spent several hours with him every week for the past three years and we'd covered topics from potatoes to politics, but apart from wartime stories, I knew very little about the places he'd visited and I suddenly found myself wanting to know everything.

'Have you ever been to New York, Mr Withers? I could quite imagine you on the *QE2*, all dapper, swirling Margot around in the ballroom. Anyway, recent research by scientists—'

Cathy Milligan slid in through the curtain and, without words or eye contact, placed a cup of tea and a box of tissues on the table next to me. She paused to squeeze my shoulder and then left.

'Where was I? Okay, a 350-foot-tall redwood might absorb as much as 1,500 pounds of water through its leaves via coastal fog...'

I spent two hours sat by the bed, watching Mr Withers' chest rise and fall. I read him the article peppered with other snippets from my life to keep it interesting: the Persian carpet garden; Will and Susannah's imaginary affair; Will and Lexie's imaginary baby; the stolen bike; ovarian failure.

Then there was nothing left to say. I'd purged every one of my sins onto poor Mr Withers, who was minding his own business with his charts and tubes. I gathered up my belongings and left the magazines on the bedside table in the hope that when he woke, he'd know I'd been. I leant in to kiss him on the cheek and reached up to pull back the curtain.

'Li...Li...'

I turned to see one crusty eye open and a papery hand reach out.

'Mr Withers, you're awake. I've been here for ages.'

I held his hand as he attempted a nod and a smile, but his grip was weak and his eyelids heavy. Cathy Milligan appeared and yanked back the curtain, exposing our makeshift confessional to the rest of the starkly lit ward. 'Give him another week and I'm sure he'll be right as rain, don't you worry.'

'Thank you, Cathy,' I said, before kissing her on the forehead, which, at the time, seemed like a perfectly reasonable thing to do. It was only when I got into the car that I was struck by how inappropriate a gesture it had been and I then worried about it for the rest of the evening.

I woke at 3.06 a.m., my mind flooded with images of the Andersons' fountain and the blue and red planting theme I'd been so sure of yesterday, now clashing, looking predictable and lazy. I moved back toward violets before going off on a tangent with oranges and yellows, then back to blue and red. I threw off the duvet. Will threw it back over me in his sleep and attempted a half-hearted grope. I slid out of bed and stood in the cool air, thinking about where Bessie might be, hoping she'd been sold to someone who was kind and needed her more than I did. Ridiculous, obsessing over a piece of metal. I returned to bed and imagined myself old, in a hospital bed, with my life slipping away, no one there but a nurse who had never known a world without social media or cars that drove themselves.

Will farted on my leg.

I turned on my phone.

A text from Georgie, three hours ago:

> *Back on ship after night with 'Pierre' at casino in*
> *Monte Carlo, OMG!!! XX*

I thought about texting her back, but worried that she won't have turned her phone off and I would wake her, then worried that she was in *Pierre's* cabin doing things that she'd regale me with on her return as I choked back a regretfully ordered cassoulet.

I flicked through Instagram and fretted that my baking skills were poor and that I never wore lipstick. I drifted off again at around 5 a.m.

26

Sarah was calling, probably confirming tonight. Or hopefully cancelling.

It's been such a busy day today; I'd be exhausted by seven. There was so much to sort out, what with reading to Charlotte and cooking dinner. And did I feel a cold coming on?

'Hi, Sarah.'

'Hi, just checking you're still on for GLOW tonight. I can pick you up if you like?'

'Don't be silly, it's out of your way. I'm sure I can find it.' *Oops, got lost, no map, left phone at home, I'm such an idiot, maybe next time, eh?*

'Nonsense, I'm dropping someone else home later who lives near you.'

Great. That was the car trouble lie out of the window, which only left me with sudden illness or an immediate family crisis.

I pictured myself sitting mute in a circle of crazed women. 'Let us welcome our newest member,' Marion would say. I would stand up, look at my toes and murmur something like: 'My name is Eliza and I'm perimenopausal.' There would be an assembly of flimsy laughter before everyone went back to throwing Bibles and moaning about dishwashers. Then I would come home and have a large glass of merlot with Will and never have to go through the whole charade ever again.

'My daughter thinks I'm a witch and I can't blame her. I mean,

I'm awful to everyone I meet.' I was making a strange gulping sound like the call of a mating seal. 'Things just pour out of my mouth. My social filter has vanished, along with my ability to reproduce. I expect Will wanted a son—all men want a son. One of his friends gave us some baby rugby boots when I was pregnant with Charlotte, and now I'll have to put them on eBay.'

'Eliza, there are plenty of women in their mid-forties having children. There's really nothing stopping you,' the surgeon said, delving into her Mulberry and handing me a box of tissues which had clearly been stolen from the hospital.

'I don't want another child.' I stopped to blow my nose and a sea of perplexed faces stared back at me. 'I can't even remember to lock my bike up, let alone look after a baby. I'm sure my sister could cope with another baby, but not me. I'm just so tired.'

I could have lain on the musty wooden floor of the church hall, sobbed myself to sleep and stayed there until the next meeting. Marion gently praised my ability to share. But I wasn't finished.

'I can't sleep unless I'm doped up on pills. What's that about? I still sweat, but I'm just too stoned to care, let alone design some ridiculous Persian garden. I haven't got a clue what I'm doing.'

Sarah reached over and draped an arm around my shoulder. 'Shall I talk now?' she whispered into my ear. I nodded, taking in the concerned expression of the woman opposite.

'Before I start, I should mention—shameless plug—that Eliza is a garden design *expert*, should anyone need their lawn sprucing up or a spot of topiary,' Sarah said, hoping to lighten the atmosphere. A couple of the women laughed and some nodded, but I don't think anyone really wanted me anywhere near their homes or families.

As I sat there, listening to Sarah wax lyrical about a new cream she had stumbled upon, the shame of everything that'd come out of my mouth started to hit home. An hour before I'd had no idea who these people were and now they knew me more intimately than Dr Chaudhry, who, over the last ten years, had inserted either a gloved finger or medical instrument into every single orifice I possessed.

'Excuse me, Sarah?' Older lady, lumberjack shirt, convent school education. 'Where on earth does one put it?'

'What?'

'The cream. Where does one, you know, apply it?' Lumberjack lady raised her eyebrows in that habitual way that we all still do when embarking on a discussion regarding our reproductive organs; as if the equipment which was vital for maintaining life on earth should really be locked away in a dusty old cupboard and never spoken of again.

There was a moment's silence. We were all thinking the same thing but no one had said it. Why not? We were a room full of women discussing our bodies and our feelings, but our uptight Britishness made me want to stamp my feet and scream the word 'vagina' in everyone's faces.

Someone coughed.

'Oh right. You're supposed to alternate, I think: one day on your legs, the next on your arse, that sort of thing. As long as it absorbs into your bloodstream.'

There was a general response of: Ooh, okay, interesting, hmm, yeah. No one said 'vagina'.

Marion moved on, asking others about mood swings and food intolerances. The woman opposite me spoke softly. 'My husband just doesn't get it. He sleeps for eight solid hours while I toss and turn and worry about my bad back and the kids' exams and work stress. And when he gets up, he asks me where all his clean shirts are and I just want to... Grrr.' She gritted her teeth and clenched her fist. We knew what she wanted to say but Marion did not encourage profanity or violent fantasies in the meetings and I was beginning to wonder whether we'd all be better off down the pub or in a kick-boxing class.

Simone, the psych nurse, clattered in twenty minutes before the end, complaining about teenagers and traffic jams. When asked how she'd been feeling she'd replied, 'Paranoid. Really bloody paranoid.'

'Tell us more,' Marion said, tolerating the mild expletive.

'My husband always removes his wedding ring when he showers, but recently he keeps forgetting to put it back on, and now I'm convinced he's having an affair. What's wrong with me?' Simone shrugged, mocking herself, and some of the other women joined in the banter. The surgeon said she often felt paranoid at work, especially around her male colleagues, and some others agreed. Colleagues, friends, partners—nothing was quite as stable as it used to be.

'But *is* he having an affair?' Everyone turned to look at me before I realised that I'd actually said what I was supposed to only think.

'Hi, I'm Simone.' She stretched out a hand and embarrassment devoured me.

'It's... I'm Eliza. I'm so sorry, I...'

'Don't worry about it. We're all in the same boat, aren't we?'

Some more than others, I'd wanted to say.

There was a brief group discussion on anxiety, which Marion said she would like to touch on more next time. She asked everyone to bring an item of clothing to the next meeting for a homeless women's charity she's collecting for. We said our goodbyes and I said that I'd be back in two weeks, knowing full well that I'd never set foot in the place again.

Sarah dropped me home. There was no other woman to drop home who lived near me and I decided that Sarah had made the story up just to get me there. She lent me a book about perimenopause and bioidentical hormone cream, which I promise to read.

I lay in bed, too hot to sleep. At least I wasn't out on the street, cold and hungry. At least Will was gentle and kind.

An attitude of gratitude, that's how it'd be from here on in.

27

AN HOUR INTO a new CAD worksheet and I'd made good progress on borders and shrubs. I allowed myself a quick break to make another coffee and check my emails. Facebook reminded me that an old school friend had her birthday today, so I spent the best part of twenty-five minutes flicking through images, trying to find the perfect 'Happy Birthday from Simon Le Bon' photo.

Should I push the boundaries and make the pathways leading to the fountain diagonal? No. It's not traditional and Mr Anderson would think that I'd missed the whole point. Was Simon Le Bon still married to Yasmin? I had a quick look, just to set my mind at rest, and according to *Red* magazine, Yasmin has been through the menopause too (turns out she didn't rate it much), but she was in her fifties, so that was to be expected. She hadn't just turned forty-six. She looked bloody amazing and I tried to imagine what it must be like to be born with stupidly long legs, glossy hair and superhuman bone structure, to marry a famous pop star and have professional photographers snap you in designer gowns. Very stressful though—all those nubile young girls wanting to sleep with your husband. But on the upside, if you looked like Yasmin, you'd also have lots of hot young men wanting to sleep with you, which would be fantastic.

I put a wash on, ate some cheese and sighed at the empty fridge.

I thought of the homeless women and hated myself for ever

feeling discontented. I placed a large refuse sack next to my wardrobe to fill later. I would be ruthless.

I returned to the task at hand.

Berberis, buddleia, globe thistle and pelargoniums. It was a start even if I had absolutely no idea where to put them. Had I got on with it eight weeks ago, I could have adopted the usual approach of leaving the plan to simmer for a few days before going back to it and finding all the gaping holes and obvious flaws.

But as it stood, I needed it by tomorrow morning and although Mr Anderson was terribly understanding about my paper jam last week, additional excuses regarding ink cartridge levels or software viruses could be pushing my luck.

'I'm having the green salad,' Georgie said. 'I've got my date tonight and I'm still undecided on what to wear, I've got it down to three possibilities.'

'Are we talking men or outfits?'

'Don't joke. I'm seeing Trevor tonight. He's been texting every day, even on the ship.'

'And what about the swinging delivery driver?'

'I've had a couple of messages from Andrew through the website, but he doesn't have my number. Now let me tell you about Pierre.'

'Is this Mr Black Jack?'

'It certainly is.' Georgie oozed frivolity.

The most calorific thing I could find on the menu was seafood linguine, so I ordered that and made myself comfortable.

'Pierre is French.'

'Really?'

'Pierre is also fluent in Italian and Spanish.'

'The French are generally good at Romance languages.'

'And Cantonese.'

'Fair enough.'

'Pierre is only fifty-eight.'

'Closer to my age then.'

'Pierre is rather good at kissing.'

'You didn't?'

Georgie flicked her serviette across her knees and held her head high in glory. It was the most joyous I'd seen her in years and I was incredulous. 'You snogged a bloke on a cruise ship?'

'Eliza, don't make me out to be some slapper on an Ibizan party boat. We'd been drinking vintage champagne in Monte Carlo. It was all so glamourous.'

'What was Barbara doing? The captain?'

I'd never met Barbara, but the image of a lady in tennis whites and the captain's hat splayed across the bridge controls came to mind.

'No, Barbara was down at the karaoke bar by then. She does a cracking Tina Turner, you'd never guess by looking at her.'

Georgie sipped her mineral water and peeked at me over the rim, encouraging more questions.

'So did you, you know...? How did you leave it?'

'I didn't sleep with him if that's what you're asking, not that he didn't try, mind you. He was quite the pest. It was a bit of fun, that's all; an ego boost.'

'So where does he live then, this *Pierre*?'

'Antibes. He's recently divorced. His wife had an affair with a diamond-hunter, poor thing. She wrecked his life, so he went on the cruise to try and piece things together again.'

'What's a diamond-hunter?'

'I didn't ask too many questions; he was clearly devastated by the whole situation. It made me realise that I'm further on the road to recovery than I thought. David can have his plastic mistress and his Docklands shag pad for all I care. And I shall have my fabulous house by the sea.'

'So, do you think you'll see Pierre again?'

'He has some business to take care of in London next week,

so I said I might be available for dinner. I'm playing it very cool. Heaven forbid one should come across as desperate.'

'Well, you're not desperate, so I wouldn't worry. Have you spoken to Tom?'

'No, but I sent David a text, to tell him I was going on the cruise.'

'And?'

'He wished me a good time. Little does he know. Tom's being very cagey at the moment. I expect Tara's got some sort of gagging order on him. But Dan and I have been chatting on Instagram.'

'You're on Instagram?'

'Yes, I joined on Sunday. It's so much fun.'

'Why haven't you followed me yet?'

'I'm only just getting to grips with it. Hashtag patience please.'

Georgie had inspired me to put an end to my habitual procrastination and general melancholy. I was only forty-six and, if I sorted myself out, I could live another forty-six years in rapturous harmony, without constantly stressing about ovaries and affairs and the wrong species of begonia.

I informed Will of what to expect: the healthy eating and fitness regime; the orderly state of the house; and the fun activities I would be planning for us at weekends. But Will was far more interested in the adventures on board the love boat.

'I bet she shagged him.'

'Stop it, Will. She's my aunt, for Christ's sake.'

'She did get married young. You wait—she's about to unleash herself on the unsuspecting pensioners of Hampshire. I'm going to start a Facebook campaign called *Lock up your Grandad*.'

'She's just having a bit of fun, that's all. Now, as I was saying, my six-month goal is to—'

'Good for her. Where's she going on her date tonight? Shall I don my Groucho Marx disguise and follow them?'

It occurred to me that Will no longer takes anything I say seriously. Gone were the days when he would peer at me, all twinkly-eyed over a glass of pinot while we planned our idyllic future. Susannah's words of wisdom popped into my head: all Will cares about is food, sex and sleep.

'I'm going upstairs to read.' I slammed a bowl of pasta down in front of him and took my hormone book into the spare room where I planned to spend the night. If Will needed to take his carb-bloated stomach off to bed and masturbate himself to sleep, then fine. I wouldn't have anything to do with it.

I read for over two hours. I learnt that, in the time before my period, I wasn't crazy but had heightened sensitivity and even psychic abilities; that at forty-six, I lacked progesterone, my air freshener was killing me and drug companies ruled the world. There were several complex diagrams to illustrate hormonal pathways, with some baffling terminology and I admit to skimming over those bits. The general consensus was that I needed to take better care of myself and learn to say 'no'.

I was shocked to discover that my younger years of free living (cigarettes, vodka, the occasional dabble in recreational party favours) had not helped my hormones one iota. But if I made changes now, I could live the rest of my life in perfect harmony; my failed ovaries and our plastic, polluted planet at one. I would need to throw away the contents of my cleaning cupboard and use lemon and vinegar from here on in. I would eat an organic diet, stop using pesticides, cut out coffee and alcohol and order an expensive pot of cream from somewhere in middle America.

On reflection, it was probably wise to reduce the coffee and alcohol slowly, in case I had a healing crisis. I wouldn't want that. And Linda would never allow me to use anything less than an Agent Orange degree of poisoning on her pesky dandelions.

I snuggled down into the lumpy single bed, pulled the duvet up under my chin and tried to recall why I was sleeping here in the first place. I couldn't really remember, but thought it was something to do with Will's attitude and some overboiled tagliatelle. I looked to the suffragettes for guidance but sensed that they too had become annoyed by my recent apathy and general lack of chaining-myself-to-railings mindset.

I picked up my phone and looked at Lexie's Instagram account. She was on tour with a puppet company and had 2,487 likes of her standing in front of a wall of graffiti. She was wearing ripped dungarees and holding a puppet which had one giant pink eye and fluorescent-green hair; the perfect accessory to help win the affections of your secret lover's five-year-old daughter: #puppet #puppets #puppeteer #puppeteerintraining #crazygreenhair #puppetshow #lovemyjob #bristol #banksy #streetart #lovethiscity #worknotwork

Will had not liked her post.

The room was cold and the duvet thin. I lay shivering for a while, longing to have Will's arms around me. I felt ridiculous. I tiptoed across the hall and climbed into our bed. Trying not to wake him, I snuggled into the position of little spoon and began to thaw.

28

MR ANDERSON RUBBED his chin with grave concern. 'I'm not sure about the red at all. I thought we were going to go with the more traditional lilacs and purples of Highgrove.'

'I see your point, but we're not copying Highgrove, are we? We're merely taking inspiration. This fountain has little resemblance to the fountain at Highgrove, yet it's stunning in its own right and deserves to be framed in swathes of robust blooms.' I'd watched a couple of episodes of *Gardener's World* before leaving the house and my turn of phrase was on fire.

'I just wonder whether it will have quite the same presence.'

'The garden will be exuberant in its own presence; a mere respectful nod to the original idea.'

Mr Anderson frowned, no doubt imagining His Royal Highness popping by for an impromptu cup of tea and nearly choking on his oaten biscuit when he noticed the distinct lack of violet hues surrounding the fountain. 'Will there be some green? I don't see much on here at the moment. And what about centranthus?'

'There's nothing stopping us throwing some in. Maybe cut out the buddleia or the pelargoniums. They'll be plenty of green, of course.' I grabbed the worksheet. Did I honestly forget to add green? Yes, I did.

'The pelargoniums can go. I'm not too fussed about them. Maybe the centranthus can be lilac or pink.'

'Maybe. Or blue and red.'

'I'm sorry, Eliza, but I'm just not sure. Let's run it past Mrs A; get a different perspective on the whole thing.'

He marched up to the house to retrieve his wife. A futile move; she always sided with me. I would dig my heels in regardless; blue and red would add a much-needed boldness to the whole theme. I kept getting drawn toward red as a colour more and more recently; in clothes or home furnishings, even the fridge was full of beetroot and radishes after last week's shop. Possibly a subconscious connection to my waning menstrual cycle. Would I cling to it like a jilted lover? A tragic image flashed through my mind of a woman splayed on the floor with her skirt hitched up and mascara running down her face, cradling her wrinkled uterus.

My phone pinged: A text from Linda, probably distressed about a few crumbs of unsightly earth around the conifers. I opened the message with a huff and wished I had a different job.

> *Eliza, just thought you should know that Mr*
> *Withers took a bad turn and passed away at 4 this*
> *morning, Linda.*

I imagined him lying there, all alone in that corner bed, while the night staff were having their umpteenth caffeine fix of the shift. I hoped Cathy Milligan had been on duty. She wouldn't have let him die on his own. She'd have been right there by his side, squeezing his waxy hand and telling him it was time to see Margot.

'Eliza, dear, whatever's the matter? Has Mr A upset you with all this nonsense?' Mrs Anderson pulled me into a cinnamon-scented embrace and I sobbed into the tea towel draped over her shoulder. 'My advice is to listen, then ignore. You're the professional around here.'

'I'm sorry, it's not that. I've just had some sad news.'

'My poor girl. Come inside and let's get you a brandy. That'll sort you out.'

She guided me into the house where Mr Anderson was shuffling around in the larder. '*Harold,* stop behaving like a bumbling idiot and do something useful for a change. Can't you see she's upset.'

'Yes, well blues and reds it is then, Eliza dear. I'm sorry I was being such an arse.' Mr Anderson, mortified at the thought of being responsible for my distress, rushed to the sink to fill up the kettle and I considered using the situation to my full advantage.

Mrs Anderson produced a small tot of brandy which I duly knocked back. Once I'd finished my tea and the long-winded story about Margot, I regained some composure and entertained them with tales of Linda's rubber-glove obsession.

Mrs Anderson set down her cup and squeezed my hand. 'Eighty-nine's not a bad age to pop off, you know.'

'I know. He was just so, well...sprightly, I suppose.' Just like you, I wanted to say.

'That's why we try to live a full life and laugh every day, don't we, Mr A?'

'Too true. Never know when the Grim Reaper's going to wander up the driveway.' Mr Anderson got up and patted me on the shoulder. 'About the colour scheme, I think we'll go along with your original idea, Eliza. I'd hate to put His Royal Highness' nose out of joint by making a carbon copy of his garden.'

He retreated into the porch to pull on his wellies. Mrs A waited until the barn door slammed shut behind him. 'Of course, we were always going to go with your idea. I don't know who he thinks he is sometimes.'

'I just think it'll complement the fountain nicely.'

'And you know best. I hope you don't mind me asking, Eliza, but how old was your father when he passed away?'

'Dad? He was fifty-eight.'

'So young. Did he enjoy life?'

The question caught me unawares, not just because I'd never discussed anything deeper than the most basic family dynamics with the Andersons, but because I honestly didn't know. My parents' relationship seemed like a blur of pressure and contracts and bickering about making ends meet. The memory made me want to sell the house, buy a camper van and escape this crazy rat race. We could travel the globe and Will could sell his photographs to unsuspecting tourists. Charlotte would grow dreadlocks and be really good at surfing and spearfishing. I'd throw my phone away and never feel intimidated by anyone's fake life ever again.

'I'm afraid I don't really know the answer to that.'

Mrs A laughed. 'Of course he did—he had you. And you must make sure you get hold of life and enjoy it too, just like Winifred's got hold of that bone.'

We looked over at Winifred snuffling away at the bone, blissed out, eyes shut, letting out putrid dog farts without the slightest concern.

It was an odd metaphor, but I could see where she was coming from.

29

WE WERE BACK at Susannah's having tea and brownies after a day out at a country show. It had been the hottest day of the year so far and the air was filled with chattering birds and all the possibilities of a long hot summer. We sat on the deck, enjoying views of the surrounding poppy fields as I regaled Susannah with Georgie's online dating exploits.

'Good for her. I can barely be bothered to look at a man these days.'

'I do worry about her meeting the wrong type of person, but she seems to be enjoying herself.'

'How about you, Liza? How are you doing?'

'After my complete breakdown in front of a roomful of strangers? Couldn't be better.'

'Isn't that the whole idea of a support group?'

'I suppose so, but I can't believe I talked about having another baby, and then my *sister* having another baby. I sounded like a lunatic.'

'Mummy, Mummy, Mummeeee.' Charlotte charged straight for me, wearing a frizzy blue wig, her eyes filled with excitement.

'What on earth's the matter, darling?'

'Tilly has just asked me for a sleepover. Say yes, Mummy, please, please, please.'

'Hang on a minute, Charlotte. You can't just invite yourself to someone's house for the night. You have to speak to us.'

Susannah began to clear away the plates. 'It's fine with me.'

'Well, I'm not sure. Let me phone Daddy. He might be waiting for us at home.'

'Oh please, Mummy, please.'

The hot day and lack of hydration had caught up with me and I didn't want to make decisions. Susannah reappeared with a bottle of gin and two glasses crammed with ice and freshly cut limes, which she slammed on the table in front of me. 'Go on, Mummy,' she whispered, 'phone Daddy and see if you can have a sleepover.'

I thought about Will, coming home from his wedding, exhausted and moaning about precocious bridesmaids. All he'd really want to do is have a beer, eat some pizza and get an early night. I compared this prospect with Susannah's fluffy guest towels and fully stocked refrigerator.

'I'll send him a message.'

'Good idea. Charlotte, come here, please,' Susannah pulled her onto her lap. 'Ask Tilly to get you a pair of her pyjamas and a new toothbrush from the guest room. Then you can eat dinner and watch a *Tinkerbell* movie in the snug.'

'Yes!' Charlotte leapt off and did three star jumps before bounding up the stairs.

I texted Will:

> *Hi darling, good day? xxx*
>
> *Excruciating. You? Why did you call me 'darling'? What have you done/broken?*
>
> *Nothing, just being loving xxx*
>
> *You're sat on Susannah's deck drinking gin, aren't you?*
>
> *No actually. Sat on Susannah's deck drinking a cup of tea xxx*

Knock yourself out. Won't be home til gone 9. Is there pizza?

Top drawer of freezer xxx

Thnx. Stay there if you like, am knackered. Just want to eat and sleep X

And have sex. Or a wank. Let's not forget that part. Quite frankly I might as well stay here and drink gin. Will wouldn't want us at home, interfering with his weird masturbatory rituals.

Maybe he was thinking about shagging one of the bridesmaids in our bed. He wouldn't, would he? What if he did it in Charlotte's room; that would be abhorrent. Knowing Will, he'd go for the floor in the lounge. Yes, that would be better. I could use some carpet cleaner and give it a good vacuum, throw the windows open for a few hours.

Susannah reappeared with a chopping board full of stuffed peppadews and other delicious offerings. 'All sorted?'

'Sleepover it is.' I took a long sip from the highball glass and allowed myself to speculate on the bridesmaid's dress; a dusky pink fishtail number, tricky to take off. She'd be wearing a full-body-control slip underneath, which would be incomprehensible to Will and they'd become entangled in a maze of Polyamide straps and diamanté hairclips. Surely by this point he'd come to his senses and send her home?

What if she was some smouldering Scarlet Johannsson type in a killer set of Agent Provocateur and he fucks her brains out on the breakfast bar?

She'd find herself with jam-sodden toast crumbs up her arse crack, that's what. I took another long slow slurp of gin, allowing the soothing botanicals to seep into my aching muscles. The thought of the toast crumbs and the fact that Lexie was on tour made me happy and relaxed.

'So do you think you'll go back?'

'Where?'

'The support group.'

'Not a chance. I've got an interesting question for you, Suze. Did you always trust your boyfriends?'

'What boyfriends?'

'You've had a few relationships. Were they monogamous?'

'As far as I know, apart from that time I was seeing Reliable Robert and I accidently shagged a waiter from Pizza Express, but that doesn't really count.'

'Why not?'

'Because it was only three weeks into the relationship and Robert was reliable and dull. And the waiter was definitely *not* dull.'

'What was his name?'

'Jesus, Eliza, I can't remember. Todd or Brad, maybe? Something American.' A filthy smirk lit up her face, exposing a secretive side of her. She probably was having sex with Will. I pushed the ludicrous thought far from my mind, longing to be back to my old, undelusional self.

'Why do you ask anyway? Do you think Will's having an affair? Or hang on, are *you* having an affair?'

'I might be. Would you care if I was?' I was trying to come off as witty and playful, but the gin had gone to my head and I just sounded catty.

Susannah eyed me with genuine concern. 'Yes, I would actually.'

I downed the rest of my drink and delved into the ice bucket for a generous top-up, with the vague notion that I was charging into the abyss, the shrew at the wheel, waiting to inject her venom into anyone who crossed her.

The clock in the guest room read 04.37. My head was stuck to the pillow by a crust of dried saliva. I couldn't recall going to bed. I sat up and it took a minute for my head to catch up with the rest of my body.

I reached for the glass of water on the bedside table and guzzled the lot. I went to pull my knees up to my chest but discovered that my right knee had a thick bandage around it, which was enough to spark the recollection.

I'd been riding Tilly's scooter and had fallen off on the gravel path. Susannah had come to the rescue, bathed and dressed it. I could remember that—no big deal. We had moved onto white wine at some point. There was no more water. I needed more water. Susannah normally left out a large bottle on nights such as these. I got to my feet and waited for my brain to stop swimming. Some acid crept into the back of my throat. I recall being slumped over the toilet, Susannah rubbing my back. She had been oddly silent, but I had been really quite drunk on gin and wine.

When I see her later, she'll tell me that it was good it all came up; that I probably had a touch of heatstroke and that we didn't eat a proper dinner—nothing that some smoked salmon and scrambled eggs couldn't fix.

I made my way toward the stairs, grasping hold of door frames and other available surfaces. I knocked over a framed photograph on the sideboard of Susannah's parents holding her as a baby. They looked up at me from the floor in disgust. I left them there, fearful that bending over could result in more vomiting. The rug. Had I puked on the beautiful ivory rug? My knee made me wince as I attempted the stairs and I ignored the still-drunk version of myself that suggested I should slide down the banister.

I was in the lounge on my hands and knees, feeling the rug for damp patches, when I noticed Susannah in the doorway, looking gorgeous in a silky white camisole and matching shorts.

'Oh. Hi. You look nice.'

'What are you doing now?' I sensed irritation in her voice. 'Let's get you back to bed shall we? It was a heavy night, you should get more sleep.'

'Okay, I just wanted some water.'

'I'll bring you some. Go on, up you go.' She addressed me like a child using delay tactics at bedtime. I sloped back upstairs, reminding myself to pick up the photo of her parents, but Susannah had beaten me to it.

I was back in bed when she brought in the water. 'I'm so sorry, Suze. Was I a hideous mess?'

She pulled the cover up over my shoulders. 'I've seen you better. I'm sure you'll be fine after some sleep.'

I lay awake, enduring another two hours of self-flagellation. Just as I started to nod off, Charlotte ran in and sat on top of me. 'Mummy, Aunty Suzie said you had a bad tummy, is it better now?' She nuzzled into my neck and I marvelled at her pure, unpoisoned body, oozing with health and vitality.

'Almost darling, yes.'

'Good because she's making pancakes!'

She got up and ran out, slamming the door hard behind her. I squeezed my temples and prayed that she would grow up to be a teetotalling square.

The next time I looked at the clock, it read 09.58 and I was feeling more upbeat. I stood in a steaming shower for longer than necessary, hazy flashbacks filling my mind: I showed Susannah Lexie's Instagram and, at first, we laughed. But then she began to question my motive and, at some point, it went sour. Susannah told me that I was overreacting and I told her she'd hurt my feelings. I couldn't recall much after that; after I'd said the words: *actually, Susannah, I find that very offensive.* I only remember crying. I dried off and climbed into my clothes, which hung with the shame of the night before. I made my way to the kitchen, to the sounds of clattering pans and lively children demanding more pancakes, and noted that Susannah appeared cheery and not at all hungover. I slipped in silently between Charlotte and Tilly at the table.

'You look better. Ready for some breakfast?' Susannah

offered a terse smile and a flicker of eye contact and I felt like we were a feuding couple, trying to behave normally in front of the kids.

The doorbell rang and Charlotte leapt to her feet. 'Daddy! Daddy's here!'

Why would he be here?

'Go and let him in girls.' The children ran to the door and Susannah turned to me. 'I hope you didn't mind that I called Will, but I thought he could drive you home, in case you weren't feeling up to it.'

'I think I can drive home, Suze.'

'Eliza, I told him about last night, not everything, but—'

Will makes his entrance into the kitchen looking fresh and virile, flanked by adoring children wanting to play on his skateboard.

'Why have you got your skateboard, Will? Did you forget that you're a grown man?' I hated the sounds that were coming out of my mouth.

He glared at me in what I think was contempt. 'To get here from the train station. I can remember my age, unlike some people around here. How's your head?'

'It's not her head, Daddy, it's her tummy,' Charlotte said. 'Mummy ate a funny prawn and it made her sick, didn't it, Mummy?'

'Yes, darling, it did,' I said, looking at Susannah, trying to thank her with my eyes.

'Naughty prawn,' Will said, with a coarse edge that he seemed to think Charlotte wouldn't pick up on. He and Susannah exchanged a quick glance, then they both turned to look at me and I felt like a trauma patient in a low-budget medical drama.

I despised everyone.

I demanded that we take a long walk in the forest on the way home to blow away the cobwebs. I wasn't so revoltingly hungover that I longed, more than anything else in the world, to lie on the sofa all afternoon, with the curtains shut and the television on, neglecting my motherly duties.

The forest was packed with tourists, scouts and general do-gooders enjoying a smashing day out. There were sumptuous picnics, yapping dogs and rosy-faced children wielding cricket bats and squealing with delight at the top of their adorable little lungs.

We walked for ten minutes before deciding that it was too hot. Then we stood in line at the ice cream shop for another twenty minutes. Will had not brought enough cash to buy me a bottle of water and they didn't take cards. Charlotte had a toddler-on-meth scale of meltdown because they'd run out of chocolate flakes. We went home.

Once home, I texted Susannah because I couldn't face a phone conversation; couldn't face feeling even worse than I already did:

> *Hi Suze, epic memory failure. Was I a nightmare??*
> *Sorry if I snapped...all a bit mental at the moment.*
> *Hope you had a good rest of the day xx*
>
> *Hey no problem, catch up soon x*

Only one kiss. Susannah never put one kiss, especially when I'd sent two.

Once Charlotte was in bed, Will and I had a takeout curry which I wolfed down due to the return of a ravenous appetite. I had started to contemplate a small glass of red when Will said something unusual: 'So, shall we talk?'

'If you like. What would you like to talk about?' I asked.

'You. Us.'

'What about me and us?' I felt a lecture coming on.

'Okay, let's be more specific shall we. Number one: your drinking. And number two ...' Will pushed his half-finished plate to the side in an uncharacteristic show of sombreness. 'The fact that, according to you, I'm having an affair with Lexie.'

30

'You look rather peaky today, darling. Everything okay?' Georgie was eyeing me with suspicion and I needed to act sharp to throw her off the scent.

'It's been a busy week. So, I gather from your text that Trevor wasn't quite up to the mark?'

'Why don't you have a little glass of wine, hmm? That'll perk you up.'

'I'm fine with water and stop changing the subject. Now, Trevor?'

'Yes, Trevor. Well, I hate to admit it, but I think you may've been right. He didn't look quite as youthful as he did in that picture. He supposedly couldn't get a table at Limewood, so we ended up meeting at some pub in Southampton.'

'Nice?'

'No, not really. The food was awful and he had sweat marks under his arms. He drove a rusty convertible with a personalised number plate and spent half the night talking about his PPI claim.'

Jacob placed the ice bucket next to Georgie and poured a taste of the Pouilly-Fumé into her glass. 'For heaven's sake, Jacob, just pour me a proper glass.' Aware of her tone, she softened and touched his arm. 'Be a poppet and pour a glass for my niece, will you? Thank you.'

'I really won't drink anything. I'm detoxing.'

'Now we've talked about this before, Eliza: detoxing is not good for you. The human body doesn't work like that. You

can't binge drink and then expect to take a week off to neu-
tralise the damage. Consistency and moderation are key. Take
my grandmother for example: she drank every day from 8 a.m.
until 2 p.m. and lived to one hundred and five.'

'That's six hours of drinking. I couldn't drink for six hours
every day. I'd be annihilated.'

'Well she didn't guzzle it back like you do; she took lady-
like sips—just enough to keep her pepped up and busy with
the housework without getting too downbeat.'

'I do not guzzle it back.' Jacob poured a perfect measure of
crisp, lemon-gold nectar into my glass. Nothing but water had
passed my saintly lips in the last three days and I planned to
keep it that way for at least two weeks. I tried to ignore the
wafts of honeysuckle, which were making their way up through
my nostrils and hitting the roof of my mouth, causing me to
salivate and question my relationship with alcohol.

'Well. Cheers.' Georgie raised her glass, 'Here's to, as you so
rightly called him, the two-dimensional liar.'

I took a sip of my water and she downed her wine. She'd got
some gall to say that I guzzle. I passed her my glass. 'Have this.
I've got to go to Elm Tree this afternoon.'

Georgie made a face, 'How dull for you. Is Susannah picking up Charlotte?'

'Will's collecting her today. Susannah and I are a bit weird
at the moment.'

I didn't mean to blurt it out, I just did, guzzling wine on my
way and dreaming up excuses as to why I'd now be turning up
to Elm Tree in a taxi. It felt so good to get it off my chest:
Georgie would offer me a balanced view and not be overly
judgemental. Susannah was giving me a wide berth and I was
glad; I was fuming with her. I may've been unreasonable the
other night, but it hadn't justified calling Will and telling him
everything I'd said. What kind of a friend did that? Will and
I had hardly spoken a word since Sunday. I'd explained that it

was just wine-fuelled drivel, that I felt off balance and unattractive. I admitted to being paranoid and that I hated myself for it. That I didn't really think he was sleeping with Lexie or any of the bridesmaids.

'Why the bloody hell did you say it then?' Will had, quite rightly, asked. And the truth is that I simply don't remember. I'd tried hard, scratching around my memory, certain I'd wake in the middle of the night with a clear, or even vague, recollection of my silly, intoxicated slur. In the clear light of day, the prospect of Will even having the time to indulge in an affair was stupid.

'Can you believe she called Will and told him what I'd said?'

'Maybe Susannah thought that talking to Will would help get it out in the open and, for the record, I agree with her. You're definitely overreacting. Try not to worry about it too much. It'll all sort itself out.'

Had I become so deranged that my best friend had to stage some form of intervention? I had heard Georgie's default line of: *Try not to worry, it'll sort itself out in the end*, many times over the years and I was comforted by the fact that she was usually right. I would apologise again to Will and Susannah, admit to overreacting and try, again, to explain that I don't remember an awful lot about it and that I wasn't myself, probably because I'm perimenopausal.

'And Will thinks I'm drinking too much. I don't think my habits have changed, but I can't seem to handle it like I used to. I can't seem to handle anything like I used to.'

'Well, now *he's* overreacting.' She poured the last of the bottle equally between our glasses and signalled to Jacob for another. I suggested she just order a glass but she ignored me. 'If you want my opinion, you're not drinking enough. If you had a little drop every day like I do, you'd have more tolerance and could cope with the odd overindulgence here and there.'

'Will was furious that it happened when Charlotte was there, and I agree with him, it was really irresponsible.'

'You've got to remember that children are very resilient and that Susannah handled it perfectly,' Georgie said.

'Of course she did.'

'It's okay at Charlotte's age when they're none the wiser. I don't think Tom and Dan ever forgave me for getting tipsy at their eighteenth birthday party.'

'I vaguely remember that. Didn't you embarrass one of their friends?'

'I danced on the patio table, which ended up being more of a striptease, but I think your mother had taken you home by then.'

'That's a shame.'

'The boys were mortified at the time, but, as I said to them the next day, I couldn't have been that bad because all their friends were cheering me on and Matthew Coombes-Taylor quite clearly had an erection. Funnily enough, I ran into his mother in Waitrose the other day; she's still frosty toward me, after all these years.'

'Pouilly-Fumé, madam?'

'Hervé, how lovely to see you.'

'And you, madam. How are you? And how is Mr Hamilton?'

'Mr Hamilton is having himself a *wonderful* time, Hervé, in London mainly. And I'm having a rather fabulous time myself, if you must know.' She raised her shoulders and gave me an excited wink as she waited for Hervé to probe further. He didn't.

'Excellent, madam. I am most pleased for you.' He smiled and headed back toward the kitchen, but Georgie remained blasé.

'What on earth made you think there was something going on with this Lexie girl anyway?'

'I didn't really think there was anything going on. I suppose

I've just been feeling a bit flabby and frumpy. Lexie's all fun and skinny and theatrical.'

'So you're saying that Will's going to leave you and Charlotte for someone with no tits and a puppet on her hand?'

I laughed out loud and the couple at the next table stared at me, obviously revolted by my ability to find humour on a Tuesday lunchtime. I laughed even louder, just to annoy them.

'Eliza, is that you?' A voice I recognised, but couldn't quite place, was calling from a table opposite.

'Linda! Hi. I didn't see you there. How are you?'

Linda was sat with a dour-looking couple in their sixties I'd seen before, visiting the care home. She came over. 'I'm fine. Weren't you planning on popping in this afternoon?' She talked in a whisper, as if she was embarrassed to be associated with me.

'I still am. Linda, this is my Aunty Georgina.' Georgie stood to shake Linda's hand, but was ignored so she sat back down and refilled both our glasses.

'I would've hardly recognised you like that,' Linda said, gesturing to my attire, seemingly appalled that I'd brushed my hair and changed out of my muddy work clothes to visit a restaurant.

'Actually, Linda, if I may be so bold as to interrupt?' Georgie had a fiendish twinkle in her eye.

'Yes?'

'I brought Eliza here today to tell her some sad news about her uncle.' Georgie stopped, inhaled deeply and looked down into her lap. 'You see, he's had a ...a diagnosis ...'

'I'm sorry to have bothered you,' Linda said, rather abruptly. 'Don't worry about coming to see the conifers later, Eliza. You're obviously busy. I've got another gardener coming over in the morning to give me a quote. I'll see if he can come up with a better solution.' She flounced off back to her table.

Georgie recovered quickly and raised her glass once again.

'Well that's that little problem taken care of, isn't it, darling? Bottoms up.'

'Shush, Georgie. She might hear you.'

'So what? I didn't say what he'd been diagnosed with, did I? He could have been diagnosed as a dickhead as far as anyone's concerned.'

I tried to conceal my laughter. 'What do you think she meant when she said about that other gardener coming?' I whispered.

'Well how would I know? Maybe you've got some competition. Isn't that the woman you're always moaning about anyway?'

'She's a pain in the arse, but I can't afford to lose eight thousand pounds a year. Should I go and ask her?'

'Absolutely not,' Georgie said. 'You've had too much wine and she'll only manipulate you if she thinks you're desperate.'

We picked at our food and polished off the second bottle. I tried to guzzle more water than wine and then finished with a double espresso, thinking of how disappointed I would make Will later.

'It's ironic, isn't it, darling?' Georgie said. 'I've spent the last year pretending that my husband's *not* been having an affair, and you've been pretending yours *has*. Or maybe you want him to have an affair.'

Georgie had a theory: That a lot of unhappily married women want their husbands to have affairs; they'd get a green light to leave them, they'd get to have all the freedom with half the cash and zero guilt. I got that. But I didn't want to leave Will. Maybe I was looking for a green light to fly off the handle. An excuse to emotionally detonate without apology or justification.

'Changing the subject, I've got an exciting update on Pierre.'

'Go on.'

'He's coming to stay for a while.'

'That's exciting, how long for?'

'He's undecided at present, but we had lunch at the Eastern Continental in Knightsbridge last week, as you know.'

'And how was that?'

'We had so much fun together and the food was excellent. Mind you, the bar's teeming with overpriced prostitutes, even at lunchtime.'

'How did you know they were overpriced?'

'No amount of cashmere and designer handbags can offset the fact that you've had five dicks in your mouth since breakfast.' Georgie had become rather animated now and I realised that her drinking-every-day-to-increase-tolerance theory was tripe. The three tables in my direct line of vision stopped to stare, including Linda's.

Some of the customers smirked and exchanged whispers, others stopped their conversations; trying to tune in to what promised to be a riot of a story.

Linda got to her feet, stony-faced, and walked over to the table.

'Eliza.'

'Hi, Linda.'

'It may not have escaped your notice that I am meeting with some prospective clients, who are looking to move *both* sets of parents to Elm Tree. I really don't wish to be embarrassed by your drunken frivolity.'

I pictured her scrubbing away in Mr Withers' room, throwing away his personal items with disgust and strangers putting their clothes in his wardrobe, sleeping in his bed.

'Gosh, I'm sorry, Linda.' I put on a Texan drawl. I thought it was funny. Linda did not.

Georgie was right behind me in full swing. 'If you hadn't decided to rudely interrupt our lunch, you could've pretended you didn't know us.'

Linda looked her over. 'In hindsight, that would've been preferable.' She turned to walk away.

'No wonder her husband plays golf all the time,' Georgie said, loud enough for Linda to hear. It was then I remembered the golfer joke—the perfect antidote to diffuse any fractious atmosphere.

'Hey, Linda, what do you do with your arsehole before having sex?' I thought I'd been subtle, but other diners were staring in expectation so I felt compelled to finish.

She turned, aghast. 'I beg your pardon?'

'I said, what do you do with your arsehole before having sex?'

Linda stared at me with her mouth open.

'You drop him off at the golf club! Get it?'

Georgie let rip raucous laughter, along with a few other diners. Linda sat back down and signalled for the bill, completely unamused by my peace offering.

31

'WHAT WERE YOU expecting? A bunch of flowers? An invitation to dinner?'

It was 6.45 a.m. and I was slumped across the breakfast bar, holding the letter confirming Elm Tree care home's wish to terminate its contract with Bay Leaf Garden Design, presumably delivered in the midst of the night by Brian, who would've skulked up the garden path by order of the rubber-gloved finger.

'Why did I even call it Bay Leaf Garden Design? Did I just pluck the name out of thin air?'

'I don't know, Eliza. Maybe you were drunk at the time.'

Will was offering no sympathy for the fact that I'd been lying awake, hot and anxious, since 3.30 a.m. No sympathy for the lost contract.

'Come on, Will. You're making a bit of a meal out of this. Can I have more toast please?'

Will glared at me and slammed a slice of bread into the toaster.

'Thank you. Was Charlotte okay last night?'

'She was great; thoroughly delighted by her mother serenading her with a heartfelt rendition of 'Hakuna Matata' before bedtime.'

Oh yes.

'And I'm not making a meal out of the fact that you've been drunk and obnoxious twice in four days, it's like having an overgrown teenager in the house. Does it not frighten you that you can't remember anything?'

'I can remember perfectly well what I said.'

'I'm referring to Saturday night.'

'I said sorry. How many more times do you want me to say it? Sorry, sorry, sorry, sorry.'

'I don't want you to apologise, Eliza. I want you to sort yourself out. Sobriety's very on trend at the moment. It's all over Instagram.'

'Is Lexie doing it?' I mumbled.

'What?'

'Nothing.'

'And what about this menopause situation?'

'Perimenopause.'

'Whatever it's called. Can't you take those new tablets the doctor gave you?'

'The HRT?'

'Yes.'

'I don't want to take HRT.'

'I don't want you turning into an old lush.'

'You think I'm a menopausal old lush?'

'I didn't mean it like that.'

'Thanks a lot, Will.' I marched upstairs and threw myself back into bed, fully intending to have an operatic sob before calling the Andersons and feigning a migraine. But tears refused to fall and exhaustion took over.

The relentless ringing of the landline woke me at 10.05 a.m. It clicked to answerphone, to Mr Anderson apologising because he'd thought I was coming over this morning, but he must have got the date wrong. He'd been doing that a lot lately, he said. It must be his age.

There was a text message from Sarah:

Remember GLOW meeting tonight, 7 p.m.

I'll call her to cancel. There was another from Will:

*Remember that Charlotte finishes early today for
half term. Can you confirm that you're able to pull
yourself out of bed in time to collect her?*

'I won't take no for an answer. Just come like that.'

'I can't come like this, Sarah. I'm in my pyjamas.'

'Style it out with a scarf or something. Come on, I'll take
you for a beer after.'

'Oof, no thank you. I'm on a detox.'

Sarah had kindly driven all the way here to pick me up,
so I sloped off to the bedroom to get changed, trying to feel
grateful that she'd made the effort. I heard her chatting to Will
downstairs, their voices low and covert. People often refer to
menopause as the second adolescence and now I could see
why: tantrums, a breakdown in communication, concerns over
substance abuse, everyone talking about you behind your back.
I slumped onto the bed to put my socks on. Everything was so
much effort. I ached. I didn't feel like a teenager even if I was
behaving like one.

In the car, I tell Sarah about Saturday night at Susannah's.

'Do you really think Will's having an affair?'

'No.'

'Then why'd you say it?'

'*I don't know.* Susannah hates me.'

'She doesn't hate you, don't be daft. You just had a ding-
dong. Give it a week and you'll be fine.'

'Has she said anything to you?'

'No. Eliza, this has absolutely nothing to do with Will, or
Lexie, or Susannah. It has everything to do with you and your
unchecked hormones.'

That was harsh.

'Maybe,' I said, looking out of the window.

'Definitely. You're exhausted and you keep telling me that

you're fat and angry all the time. Hmm, what else? Not sleeping, can't remember anything, can't take your drink anymore. The not-sleeping part alone is enough to send most people psychotic.'

'I don't think I'm psychotic.' Not yet.

'Off balance then.'

'Yes, off balance. I like that.'

'Have you read any of that book I gave you?'

'Some. I know my hormones are all over the place. I told Emily that I wanted to shag every dad in the playground at drop-off on Friday. I thought it was funny, but she seemed pretty repulsed.'

'Hilarious. It could have been worse.'

'Really?'

'You could have told her you wanted to shag every mum in the playground, including her. That would've made her spill her fair-trade latte over her ethical footwear.'

We cackled like witches around a cauldron and I was secretly pleased at Sarah's dig.

A nutritionist called Helen ran the first part of the meeting. Helen was a bright-eyed, glossy-haired, flawlessly skinned beanpole. She was here to advise us how to improve our eating habits throughout our 'change of life'. She used taglines such as Protein Power, Fantastic Fibre and Wondrous Water.

We should be eating quinoa, spinach and more broccoli. We should be drinking at least two litres of water a day and less than ten units of alcohol a week. I wanted to put my hand up and tell Helen that I didn't particularly want a change of life, that I had been quite happy a few months ago, going about my business, eating crap, ovulating, quaffing wine and making an idiot out of myself. I wasn't ready to grow up just yet.

Helen handed out vouchers entitling us to a twenty-five per cent discount on our initial consultation. She reminded us that we all held the power to regain our balance and health, that we would emerge fitter and stronger; the poster girls of mid-life vitality.

The minute she left, Simone exploded into a summary of the past two weeks: the lack of sleep; her husband's erectile problems and details of the full-scale public row she'd had with her son's PE teacher. Sarah talked about her dealings with a chauvinistic editor, and someone else I'd not seen before recounted an embarrassing flushing episode at a family wedding.

I'd initially planned to omit recent events and offer some snippets about poor sleep and weight gain, but I ended up a pathetic heap in Sarah's arms, discussing the lost contract and insecurities surrounding my sex life.

'You're in good company,' Simone said. 'Not only does my husband forget his wedding ring, but now he can't even get it up. I am on full mistress alert.'

We all laughed. We knew we sounded preposterous, but tonight, within these four walls, preposterousness would suffer no scrutiny.

'Do you get dry?'

I looked up from blowing my nose to see Lumberjack Lady staring at me in genuine concern. 'I'm sorry?'

'Do you have a problem with dryness? You know, downstairs?' She nodded toward my lap. 'Because I did and it affected my sex life terribly.'

'Er no, not that I've really noticed.' Did I? Maybe I should ask Will; the present time not being ideal.

'Charles and I were using lube for a while, but I have sensitive skin so I got hold of some cold-pressed coconut oil and bought Charles a super little handbook on foreplay, which has been a real eye-opener I can tell you.'

A few people laughed nervously because our tendency toward social stereotyping told us that she should be selling chutneys at a church fete, not discussing marital fiddlings at a local support group.

'You can borrow it if you like. Charles seems to have got the hang of everything now.'

'Great,' was all I could say, trying to picture Will's expression on me handing him a dog-eared copy of a foreplay manual. What would he do, roll his eyes? Laugh in my face? Ignore me and carry on watching *Deadly Sixty*?

On the way home, Sarah insisted on pulling in to the pub. I requested a juice but got a pint of cider. 'There we are, grown-up juice.'

'Will thinks I'm an alcoholic.'

'Are you drinking vodka for breakfast?'

'Of course not.'

'Then you're not an alcoholic, you're menopausal.'

Ouch.

'Just don't go mad. Chances are, you're oestrogen-dominant too, so your liver's got enough work to do. Just rein it in a bit, realise that you're not twenty-five anymore. Now, I'm interested in this Persian carpet garden. I reckon I can get an article out of it.'

'I thought you only wrote for interior mags?'

'I do, but it's becoming harder to get published. The market's saturated with people like me, so I need to branch out.'

'Yes, but it's only me. I'm a crappy little local business with part-time help from a bartender, who I'm probably going to have to make redundant.' I'd been thinking about that all day. Johnno was saving up to spend the winter backpacking around the Pacific Islands. Thanks to my overindulgence and tactless humour, he'd probably have to stay at home and work extra hours at the pub all winter to make up for my recklessness. I desperately wanted to fix it, but my mind was blank and I pined for the woman who would've picked herself up and found a solution; the woman who would've used the opportunity to her advantage and found something more profitable and less stressful.

Sarah was adamant and wanted me to speak to the Andersons tomorrow. She wanted to follow my progress, discussing everything from inspiration and the creative process to practicality and overcoming obstacles. I wanted to throw all my gardening equipment on a bonfire and live in a van in Costa Rica.

32

WILL HAD TAKEN it upon himself to book me an appointment with Helen, the holier-than-thou nutritionist who had come to lecture us at the GLOW meeting.

'It's all booked and paid for. My treat,' he informed me over breakfast one Sunday, with all the excitement of a smooth-talking Casanova whisking a lover off to Paris. I couldn't say anything or throw anything. I had to accept that I'd pushed my luck far enough. If I wanted to keep my friends and my business, if I didn't actually want Will to run off with some fruitful bohemian waif, a transformation of sorts needed to take place. And this was as good a time as any to start.

The appointment was not for another two weeks and she'd already sent me reams of paperwork and a comprehensive questionnaire regarding my fruit and vegetable intake, exercise routine and alcohol consumption. There was an intrusive section on my bowel movements, which I'd tried to answer as honestly and graphically as possible. Upon its completion, I'd come to the conclusion that I needed to eat less and shit more. I failed to see how this warranted a seventy-five pound fee from some sanctimonious health freak who looked like she only ate carbs on her birthday.

After almost three weeks of tactically avoiding each other on the school run, Susannah and I got together with the children over half term and endured the horrors of soft play on a rainy afternoon. A few texts had been passed back and forth, but it was the first time we'd met up in person since our little tiff and a cloud of unrest hovered over us. I asked for more details about our conversation on that fateful night and she laughed it off, saying that it wasn't important and we should just forget about it. The children were tetchy, our coffees were tasteless and the usually delicious brownies were stale. There'd been no more invites to stay in the guest room, to knock back Argentinian wine and put the world to rights.

Sarah had delighted in the Persian garden project and had visited twice already, allowing the Andersons to lavish her with their hospitality and enthusiasm for life. Thanks to the lost contract at Elm Tree, the garden was back on schedule and looking better than I could have imagined, with the fountain now complete and the paving slabs down; separating the plot into four neat quadrants. The edges were cut and we'd started preparing the soil for planting. Sarah had already written an initial draft, using only the master plan, but it had given me the kick up the arse that I'd so desperately needed to take it further. Sentences such as, *The fusion of colour and cleverly discreet borders which flow seamlessly throughout the garden create the perfect refuge from a frantic world,* made me feel like I was about to do something right for a change.

The effort to drink more water and less wine had been made easier by the lack of social interaction with both Susannah and Georgie, who had kept a low profile since the much-anticipated arrival of Pierre. And, apart from the day when I'd foolishly volunteered to chaperone for a child's birthday party at an indoor waterpark on a Saturday afternoon, my hormone imbalances had been few and far between.

I'd had two lunches with Mum since her arrival back home: one with Charlotte at Pizza Express in half term and the other last week, at Free Range Franny's.

'Well I must say, I'm impressed with your choice of restaurant this time. It's just like the place in Tribeca, but of course the staff are much friendlier there.'

'They work on a tipping system, Mum. Of course they're friendly.'

'Well I know that. This lot could learn a thing or two, that's all I'm saying. Anyway, how're things? Do you still see Georgie on a Tuesday?'

'Not recently. She's got this French toy boy staying at the house. I'm not sure when he's going back.'

'I see. Is he married?'

'Married? I should hope not. He's been here for ten days already so I don't know how he'd explain that to his wife. Georgie wouldn't date anyone who's married, not after everything she's been through.'

Mother pursed her lips and raised an eyebrow, dining on some undisclosed past knowledge of which I would never lower myself to enquire. Today, armed with a particularly aggressive bout of PMT, I was struggling to negotiate my way over her ever-challenging hurdles. Franny did not serve gin at her cafe, so I opted for the Time of the Month Tea instead.

'What about you, Mum? I'm surprised Jess hasn't tried to set you up on some dates over there.'

'I can't be doing with any of that nonsense. I'm too busy going back and forth to start a relationship. I'm happier on my own. Janice was set up with this man her daughter worked with and he tried to molest her in the taxi on the way home.'

Mum went on to list every worst-case scenario dating story she'd ever heard and I wished I'd just asked about the kids or the weather. And maybe she was simply happier on her own— nothing wrong with that. Her relationship with my father wasn't close, not like Will and I. Not like Will and I used to be.

'Mum, if I book to go away with Will for a couple of nights will you look after Charlotte?'

'Where are you going?'

'I don't know yet. Maybe a little inn somewhere in the forest.'

'Of course I'll look after Charlotte. But can you to afford to go away, now you've lost that care home contract?'

Oh.

I'd cooked up a dreamy world of log fires and cosy dinners, of make-up sex without the threat of a six year old walking in and demanding pancakes or a puppy. We would take long walks and I would be able to explain myself to Will in a calm and lucid manner. Will would smack himself on the forehead and apologise for not understanding me sooner. Then he would tell me that Lexie was a twat and unfollow her on Instagram. But anyway, none of that mattered now as I'd forgotten that, due to my own stupidity, I was flat broke and would probably never stay in a cosy country inn for the rest of my life.

'And how are your hormones? Any more problems with your menopause?'

'It's *peri*menopause actually, Mum. I've been a bit up and down, to say the least, and I've had a couple of ...' I stopped, not wanting to expose myself to scrutiny.

'A couple of what?'

'Nothing. I'm having the tofu salad. What about you?'

33

IT WAS 6.15 a.m. and the sun was already shining. I had the urge to spring out of bed and start my day.

I flicked on YouTube and followed a ten-minute yoga tutorial before nipping out to buy fresh fruit for breakfast. By the time Will staggered downstairs, banana smoothies were in the blender and Sister Sledge boomed out of the radio.

'Christ, Eliza, been on the sherry?'

'No, Will, I have not been on the sherry.' I handed him a smoothie and inwardly congratulated my calmer self for not telling him to fuck off. I'd worked hard at keeping a lid on the outbursts and, like many habits, it had become easier with each day. 'I'm merely reaping the rewards of a good night's sleep, of which you are the beneficiary. Try this.'

'Mmm, that's really good.' He wrapped an arm around my already slimmer waist and kissed me on the lips. I surprised myself by feeling warm and strangely unrestricted—a tiny glimpse of the old me.

I pushed him away nonetheless. I didn't want him getting ideas of me mutating into a submissive Disney princess type who'd burst into song the moment a sparrow appeared on the window sill. 'I've got a productive day planned: I'm dropping in on the Andersons to show them the first draft of Sarah's article and I'm meeting Georgie for lunch—'

'Does she know you can't drink wine?'

'Yes, she knows. After lunch I'm going to meet a couple

from the Andersons' bridge club, they've got half an acre which needs a complete renovation.'

'My, we are on top form, aren't we?'

'Thank you, Will.'

Will was extremely pleased with himself for having booked and paid for my appointment with the nutritionist, for stepping up and taking the reins. I'd initially found it excruciating to admit defeat, to push aside irrational fears that I was merely the co-star in Will's private taming of his own shrew.

The morning of my initial consultation with Helen had not started well. I'd woken up three times in the night, drenched in perspiration, and at 6.20 a.m., Charlotte had plonked herself between us and proceeded to pull out her wobbly front tooth. There was a lot of blood and my much-loved Egyptian cotton bedding was no longer brilliant white.

I'd sat at the breakfast bar in silence, cradling the cafetière and savouring my last-ever piece of butter-laden toast. When the time came, like Anne Boleyn to the chopping block, I bade farewell to my family and walked bravely out of the door.

I had feared the glossy hair and the flawless skin and the vast knowledge of all things saintly, presuming I'd be judged by my bloated stomach and love of cheesecake; that I would be lectured, shamed and banished to a life of raw kale.

But that's not what happened.

I mentally ticked off every symptom that Helen listed when explaining the effect that sugar had on hormones. I learnt how the health of my gut influenced my weight, moods and overall immunity. We talked about tiredness, night sweats, childbirth and brain fog. I was educated and inspired, praised for my love of avocados and given empathy for my love of wine.

'I've got an amazing cheesecake recipe which I'll email over to you. It's made of avocado and lime and it's the most delicious thing you'll ever eat,' Helen promised me.

I hadn't been given a strict, no-bending-of-the-rules programme: 'Trust me, those never work. We're going to gently introduce a new way of eating: that bag of sweets you keep in the car is now a bag of walnuts; that second coffee is a ginger tea. If you want a big roast dinner on a Sunday, go ahead. Just make sure you have sweet potatoes instead of white, and stick to the one glass of wine.'

Helen did not specify what size that glass of wine should be, which I appreciated.

By the time I returned home two hours later, I had my tailor-made menu, bags of exciting, colourful ingredients and a fresh new purpose in life.

Even the Tooth Fairy arrived on time that night, leaving shiny, glitter-coated coins under Charlotte's pillow. A stark contrast to the last time Charlotte lost a tooth, when she'd been far too involved in a Netflix box set and a bottle of pinot noir to remember her duties and I was forced to make excuses for her, blaming Brexit labour shortages for her slapdash negligence.

All was quiet at the Andersons. The spaniels were out on the lawn, content with bones. They ignored me, apart from Winifred, who offered three wags of her tail. I knocked and pushed open the barn door into the kitchen.

'Hellooo? Mr Anderson?'

I could hear classical music being played at high volume in an upstairs bedroom. I didn't want to alarm them, so I called up the stairs, 'Hello, it's me, Eliza.'

There was a brief pause in the music, and that was when I heard the first scream.

It was undoubtedly Mrs A, sounding very distressed. My heart began to pound. Should I call the police, an ambulance? Both their cars were here, had intruders murdered Mr Anderson? The beginnings of a trumpet crescendo muffled her cries and all I could make out was, 'God, Harold, no.'

I took off my flip-flops and raced up the stairs. The commotion was coming from a room at the end of the hallway where the door was shut. I tried to catch my breath. Full flight-or-fight mode had kicked in: shaking hands, tight throat. I'd armed myself with a flip-flop, which, albeit an absurd choice of weapon, I gripped tighter. I channelled the soft words of my online yoga teacher: big breath in through the nose, out through the mouth. I walked slowly and silently up the hall and heard Mrs A crying, 'Oh Harold, please.'

There were no other voices and I remembered Dr Chaudhry's words: *Domestic abuse isn't confined to tower blocks you know.* The fear quickly turned to anger. Mr Anderson: the middle-class wife-beater.

I reached for the door handle and had pulled it down just a notch when I was struck by something abnormal, yet vaguely familiar, about Mrs Anderson's cries: they were rhythmic.

I stood rigid, ears ringing, head pulsing.

'Harold, stop. I can hear something.'

'It's just the dog. Piss off, Daphne.'

'It's not the dog. Someone's here.'

I was a cartoon character frozen to the spot in an unexpected blizzard, my hand still holding the door handle with pinpoint precision.

'No one's here. Now let's turn you over, you naughty girl.'

Mrs Anderson giggled. 'Oh, Harold, you are wicked. What would the headmistress say?'

Beads of perspiration formed around my temples. They dripped down my face and into the corners of my mouth, they ran from the back of my knees, down my calves and between my toes, as my sweaty palm slowly lost its grip on the door handle.

Daphne appeared at the top of the stairs, her claws skating toward me on the wooden floorboards and her stump of a tail wagging furiously. I was momentarily suspended as she licked the sweat from my feet, slurping up my horror with little care for the antics of her owners, just a few feet away.

As Beethoven's 9TH entered a cymbal-crashing climax, I

gently released the door handle and high-tailed it back down the hallway, the soles of my feet slipping on the stairs. They were elderly, why the hell did they have high-glossed stairs? Why the hell were they playing kinky sex games?

I ran across the grass and into the safety of my car, let go of the handbrake and glided silently down the driveway and onto the street. I caught a glimpse of myself in the rear-view mirror: frizzy damp hair and a face as crimson as the wilting rhododendron spilling over the front wall. I succumbed to the fact that I'd left my other flip-flop at the bottom of the stairs, started the engine and roared off down the street.

I would discuss this with Georgie over lunch, being careful not to discriminate about old people having sex.

'There's absolutely nothing wrong with old people having sex, Eliza.'

'I'm not bothered by that at all. But how do I explain my flip-flop? What if they looked out the window and saw my car?'

'Well you could always just tell them the truth.'

'What? Like, *Hey, if you're wondering why a flip-flop is at the bottom of your stairs, it's because I swung by the house unannounced earlier and thought you were being murdered. There was a brief domestic violence theory before I realised that you were simply having filthy role-play sex in the privacy of your own home.*'

'Something like that, yes. I would probably leave out the bit about Harold being a wife-beater though. You don't want to lose another contract now, do you? Glass of wine?'

'No. And no.'

'How long's this silly diet going on for anyway? I hope you're not going to get all obsessed like these celebrities.'

'It's only for three weeks, then I can get back to cheese and wine.' I said, knowing that I felt much better without either, but desperately missing them nonetheless.

'I'll drink to that.' Georgie chinked her wine glass against my tumbler of mineral water and I was relieved that I had a good excuse not to join her.

'So, how's it all going with Pierre?' I asked.

'Very well, thank you. He's taken my car to meet a business colleague in Wimbledon today.'

'What exactly is his business?'

'Something to do with aerospace and satellites. He did explain and I pretended to understand but, anyway, who cares? He does a lot of work on his computer.'

'And when does he leave?'

'Well, funny you should ask. He said that he might stay a while longer, we're having such a wonderful time.'

I knew what she meant by 'wonderful time', but she spared me the details, thankfully. I'd had enough voyeurism for one day and was beginning to feel quite inadequate.

I bumped into Susannah on the school run and, for the first time in a long time, she looked genuinely pleased to see me. She was buzzing with excitement as she had a date tonight with an equestrian vet called Lars.

'I've known him for three years and something's just clicked between us. The kids are with my parents, so I think I might shag him.'

34

'WHY DON'T WE drink some champagne?' I suggested to
Will as he poured away the remains of the revolting soup I'd
made for dinner.

'But it's a Tuesday. What about your diet?'

'What about my diet? I'm forty-six years old. If I want
champagne, I'll have champagne.'

Will and I have not had sex since the night before I lost the
plot at Susannah's. Everyone I knew was having sex: new sex,
old sex, kinky sex, first date sex. I had decided that I too would
like to have sex, and champagne would help me navigate the
road to sex, which I'd found, in recent months, to be quite dis-
orientating.

Will reached up to the top of the wine rack and pulled
out a bottle of Mumm which the Andersons had given me for
Christmas. 'I'll chuck it in the freezer for twenty minutes,' he
said, attempting to conceal a smirk as the champagne–sex connection slowly crept into his mind.

I remembered that I was wearing my period pants. Not
because I had my period, but because I had not given much
thought to laundry in the last week, due to the mountainous
task of food-planning and endless visits to the supermarket to
pick up goji berries or quinoa. Will wouldn't give a toss about
my underwear, but I did. They were faded and baggy with a
stray bit of elastic hanging from the trim, making me feel all
careless and mumsy.

I made an excuse to check on Charlotte and crept into

our bedroom to inspect the contents of my underwear drawer, which was a sorry sight indeed—a mishmash of ill-fitting bras or tasteless matching sets that Will had purchased on birthdays past. I made a vow to treat myself to a re-stock, once I'd got rid of the spare tyre that had lassoed itself around my waist. I decided to stay in the ones I was wearing and cut off the stray elastic with some nail clippers. I found some old lipstick in the bathroom cabinet and decided to try a tip I'd seen in a magazine, where you pressed the colour into the cupid's bow using your finger, creating the illusion of natural bee-stung lips. I looked like Barbara Cartland. I scrubbed it off and used Chapstick instead. I gathered up a pile of laundry and trudged downstairs in my slippers, feeling about as saucy as Kim Jong-Un.

We sat in the garden so I ditched the slippers and went barefoot. We chatted easily and sipped at the champagne. I tried not to guzzle. We listened to the blackbird and I felt the tension of the last few months edging away. 'I'm going to bed,' I announced in my best seductress voice, which I may have pulled off had I not stubbed my toe on the table leg.

After some awkward foreplay, we found a lackadaisical rhythm but, by this point, I'd rather gone off the idea. The thought of the Andersons doing it doggy style was proving to be somewhat of a stumbling block, but Will seemed to be having a wonderful time, no doubt fantasising about Scarlett Johansson in some swanky LA hotel room.

I didn't know if I was entirely happy about that. What about me? Who was I fantasising about? I hadn't had a crush since a rather longstanding one on Hugh Fearnley-Whittingstall some years back, and I was horrified that I had nothing else to hand. I scanned through a portfolio of suitors, finally settling on Hugh Jackman.

Will and Scarlett could have their sterile hotel room. Hugh and I were cosied up in a beach cabana in Costa Rica. That's better; back on board. I briefly imagined myself as Scarlett, but she had showed up as the peasant girl, scrubbing dishes in *Girl with a Pearl Earring*. Did she get an Oscar for that movie? I had gone to the cinema to see it when I was in Sydney with a girl from the hostel and now I couldn't remember her name. Lauren or Laura maybe?

Anyway, back to Hugh Jackman. His beachfront cabana was surrounded by lush bamboo and now I was beginning to think that I should speak to the Andersons about introducing bamboo along their right-hand fence. It would solve the privacy issue and add some well-needed interest.

We switched position so I was on top.

I hoped Susannah's date was going well and she'd remembered not to eat yellow peppers, as they gave her dreadful wind.

I needed to add peppers to my shopping list, and flaxseed.

Will was making a succession of short squeaks, which indicated that he was rounding the corner to the finish line. Why couldn't he grunt like a real man? That's what Hugh Jackman would have done. But Hugh was nowhere to be seen and instead my mind was a horrific casserole of Audrey Anderson's bottom and Colin Firth in period costume.

I faked it while Will had the time of his life.

He spooned me and I lay perfectly still, thinking about hardy species of bamboo and the fact that I might never go to Costa Rica.

35

I'd not been to the Andersons' since last week's incident involving the flip-flop. I had to swing by the nursery to pick up more buddleia, but then it was time to face the music. Johnno had been there since eight that morning and I'd not had a text yet saying that anything was weird, or that Mrs A had asked him if I'd heard her yelping to Beethoven while she and her husband frolicked around in the bedroom.

'Ah, here she is!' Mr Anderson strode across the lawn towards me. 'Looks like you've got a car full there, Eliza. Let me grab a wheelbarrow.'

I wanted to get this over and done with as quickly as possible. Georgie was right: I should just be honest.

'Coo-eee!' Mrs A popped her head out of the window. We waved to each other. She didn't seem off in any way. Maybe they were secretly pleased I'd heard them having sex. 'I'll put some coffee on.'

I busied myself with the new plants until it was coffee and cake time. Thankfully it was bright so I could avoid any awkward eye contact by keeping my sunglasses on.

I was showing Mr Anderson Sarah's first draft of the article, remaining professional and trying not to think of him with an erection, when Mrs A hovered above me, holding an envelope and wearing a somewhat sullen look on her face. 'I think we need to tell her, Mr A.'

Heat pumped up through my neck, engulfing my head and

face. She sat down on the rug and passed me the envelope. 'Please open it and then I will explain.'

I wiped my face with the bottom of my t-shirt. I began to well up but I swallowed hard, bracing myself for another contract termination. I tried to appear cool as I opened the envelope and pulled out a fifty-pound gift voucher from Monsoon.

'Eliza, please accept our utmost apology,' Mrs A said. 'I came down the other day to find Daphne in her basket with one of your flip-flops torn to shreds. I'm so embarrassed.'

'Gosh, really?'

'I'm so sorry. I have no idea how she got hold of it.'

'I must've left them by the car when I put my boots on. It's my fault, there's really no need for this.'

'Eliza, there's every need for this: they were your birthday present from Will. We've yet to find the other one. We've hunted high and low. Mr A thinks Queen Mary's buried it, so it could be anywhere—not that it's much use to you on its own, I'm sure.'

Daphne ran over to me and started to sniff my toes, waiting for more hormone-rich secretions to feast on.

'Daphne, no! Naughty dog, go and lie down,' hollered Mr Anderson. Daphne scampered off with her head hung low, looking back at us with huge forlorn eyes.

I absolutely loved that dog.

Later, when they went inside with the empty cups and plates, I walked over to Daphne and rubbed her tummy. She licked my hands and wagged her tail. My secret was safe with her.

36

SUSANNAH AND I met at The Lamb. We bypassed the 2-for-1 burger offer, opting for salads and mineral water. I couldn't deny that the atmosphere was somewhat drab; both of us behaving like we were on a sober blind date. We laughed awkwardly about what we were going to order and were unduly apologetic about interrupting one another. I think we both wished that Sarah was there to crack some inappropriate jokes and take the strain off.

I was keen to move the conversation on to her date with Lars, hoping some juicy details might lighten the mood a little, but Susannah wanted to quiz me about my diet.

'I'm not gonna lie: days two and three were a hideous caffeine and sugar comedown, and I was bloody miserable and exhausted. But there's been no night sweats and, I have to say, there's been a big improvement in mental outlook, you'll be glad to hear.'

'Thank fuck for that.' Susannah laughed. We both laughed and in a matter of seconds I felt back on track with her for the first time in over a month.

'Sorry—again. I really don't know what happened.'

'I don't know what happened either. We didn't actually drink that much, but it really hit you. Anyway, stop apologizing, I'm over it now. Besides, I was secretly flattered by the fact that you felt threatened by me.'

'Threatened by you? What do you mean?'

'You know, with Will.' Susannah eyed me with amusement.

'No I don't know.' Panic rose within me. Surely I didn't go there? I remembered getting defensive because she'd challenged me, but nothing much else. I imagined myself verbalising all those stupid little thoughts, 'Susannah, what did I say? Please tell me.' Tears threatened, making me feel like I could fall back down to the foot of the mountain at any moment.

'For god's sake, don't get upset. It's fine. I've forgotten all about it.'

'Please, Susannah, I have to know.'

I hadn't stopped at Lexie. Or the bridesmaids. I was pigheaded, stubborn as a mule. And because Susannah suggested that my behaviour toward Will was unreasonable, then she would have to be thrown into the pit along with everyone else.

I felt sick to my stomach. 'Please tell me I didn't accuse you of anything.'

'Of course you didn't. It was more of a suggestion, if I remember rightly. More of a: *Well, if you think he's so bloody perfect, why don't you go and join the queue?*'

'Oh, Susannah, I'm so sorry.' I gasped and held my hands over my mouth, like I could somehow unsay the words.

'Then I thought I'd be clever and ask if I could get a Fast Pass and you burst into tears. Don't you remember that?'

I put my head in my hands and we laughed again, this time stupidly, like we used to, like we did when we thought we might never stop. Sorrow stirred within me when I considered all the idiotic words I could've spoken; words that would have damaged our friendship at a much deeper, much more personal level. 'A bloody Fast Pass? Susannah, that's genius, why didn't I laugh at that?'

'You were not in the mood for black comedy that night, I can assure you. And I'm sorry I called Will the next day. I thought I was being helpful, but looking back it was the wrong thing to do.'

'I'm glad you didn't tell him the whole story. That could've been awkward.'

'Yeah, I thought the edited version would be better.' Susannah's smile faded and she looked away. 'After you left, I just felt so flat for days afterwards.'

I reached over and squeezed her hand. 'I'm so sorry. I don't know what came over me that night. I think I felt overwhelmed with work and the perimenopause thing, and then Mr Withers dying, which just reminded me of Dad.'

'We all have our wobbles, Eliza, don't let it get to you. Now, can we please move on to something more scandalous?'

My body slumped with relief from the tension I'd been lugging around for the last six weeks as I spilled the beans on the Andersons' bedroom exploits. I hoped this might prompt her to reveal her shenanigans with the vet—it did.

'It's funny. I've known Lars for so long and I can honestly say I've never thought about him romantically, but halfway through dinner I looked at him and just knew we were going to have sex.'

'To be fair, I think you'd already decided that before you left the house.'

'Yes, but I didn't know if he'd feel the same way about me.'

I wondered how Susannah rated herself aesthetically on a scale of 1–10. These new insecurities had naturally made me question if I was jealous of her and I could confidently say that I wasn't. But I was, without a doubt, a little in awe and there's a big difference; a difference because I loved her and she was a decent, kind, no-bullshit friend.

'So did you invite him back?'

'Kind of. There was a lot of intense eye contact and when the waiter took the plates away, he asked for the bill immediately, saying we had to get back for the babysitter.'

'That old chestnut.'

'Yep. Then we did it in the doorway of that Methodist church near Tesco Express.'

'*Susannah!*'

I was genuinely outraged. What had got into everyone?

'I'm seeing him again tomorrow. It's all a bit of fun really. I've reduced my HRT dose so I hope it doesn't all start going weird downstairs.'

'Why? What do you mean weird?'

'I don't know. What if I dry up?'

'You won't dry up.' I said, not admitting that I'd asked the same question myself not so long ago. 'You're still getting periods, right?'

'About every three months or so, although I'd be happier without them. I'm just so tired all the time.'

'You should see my nutritionist. This diet's been boring as hell but I feel amazing. It's like the whole of my insides are calm and balanced, although my cycle's still all over the place: last month it was twenty-one days; this month it's thirty-five; and if I don't come on soon I think my tits will explode.'

I'd missed this, talking at ease about all manner of gory bodily functions; Susannah being one of those few friends that still laughed out loud about farts. We had a bitch about some uptight school mums, made some loose camping plans for the summer holidays and discussed Simon's relationship with Gerald.

Simon was bringing Gerald down at the weekend. Gerald was a born city boy, favouring arthouse cinema and Korean food over rural life. He had, however, formed a delightful bond with the children. Tilly, especially, seemed fascinated by his every word and was often heard quoting random cultural references far beyond the realms of her vocabulary, complete with Gerald's comical gesticulations. It worked out well for Susannah, having them stay for the weekend and take care of the children, leaving her more time to have long rides in the country or hot sex in doorways.

When I arrived home, Will was engrossed in a martial arts film and barely acknowledged me.

'I had a lovely night, thanks for asking.'

'Great,' he said without looking up. 'It's nearly at the end.' Which was irrelevant, given that he'd seen it twenty times already. The lead role, who was playing a female assassin, being another one of his crushes. I stood in the doorway and allowed myself to be briefly sucked in:

The assassin was explaining to some older guy how her pregnancy had affected her ability to jump a motorcycle onto a speeding train: 'Once that strip turned blue, I could never do any of those things, because I was gonna be a mother. Can you understand that?'

The man said that he could understand but she killed him anyway, which I was pleased about.

Having a job as an international assassin might sound very cool and glamorous but, in reality, it would be a logistical nightmare during pregnancy and I felt grateful for my humble choice of career.

'I'm making tea.' I floated into the kitchen, feeling as if the weight of the world had been lifted from my shoulders. I flicked the kettle on and took the milk out of the fridge, noticing with bittersweet empathy that it too had gone past its sell-by date. I took the lid off and gave it a sniff before vomiting into the sink.

37

THE STRIP TURNED blue.

At forty-six, the strip turned blue.

'Well firstly, congratulations, Miss Hamilton.'

Dr Chaudhry's pronunciation of the word 'Miss' was playing havoc with my emotions; *Missssss*, all viperish and taunting. *Look at you: forty-six, still not married and now pregnant. Dear, dear, dear. You should've been more like me: a qualified GP at twenty-nine, and married with two kids by the time I was thirty-five. Look how neatly life has panned out for me and my cardiothoracic surgeon of a husband. You wouldn't find me wanting to smash crockery over his head now, would you?*

'I can't have a baby at forty-six. I'll have my bus pass before it reaches puberty. Surely it's dangerous at my age?'

'Complications can arise with any birth; I would try to take a more positive approach. Look upon it as a gift. It wasn't so long ago that you were upset about being perimenopausal.'

'Yes, sorry, I'm just a bit shocked, that's all.'

'I'm sure. But we also talked about not using that diagnosis as a form of contraception, do you remember?'

I clenched my jaw and pushed savage thoughts aside. Dr Chaudhry was just doing her job.

'Yes, I remember.'

'I suggest you go home and have an open and honest chat with your husband—sorry, *partner*. I'm sure you'll come up with some solutions to raising another child. People always do. Let me give you this leaflet.'

'I'm forty-six. I don't need a leaflet.'

'Fair enough. You can fill in a self-referral form for the maternity hospital on the NHS website and they'll take it from there. There's really no need to see me again unless you have a problem.'

I picked up Charlotte from school in a daze and a pair of dark sunglasses to veil my growing madness. Organic Emily waved frantically and pointed to something in the front of her bicycle basket, which looked like it needed an excitable reaction. I pretended not to see her and drove off before Charlotte even had the chance to fasten her seatbelt.

Later, as Will put Charlotte to bed, I slumped on the sofa in utter exhaustion. I remembered feeling the same way the last time I had been pregnant six years ago, when I could have curled up on the floor of Victoria Station at rush hour and slept for twenty years.

I'm not sure I should be having a baby. The risk of miscarriage at my age was high and, besides, I couldn't cope with the night feeds. I should be hiking the Great Wall of China in my bifocals when I'm sixty, not worrying about acne medication and mood swings. What about dysfunctional breast pads? What about giving birth?

Amongst the chaos of my thoughts, there was a small spark of joy deep within me that I allowed myself to explore and, by the time Will came downstairs, I was all soft blankets and birthing plans.

'At least Charlotte's going to have a sibling. She'll have nieces and nephews and someone to help her choose our nursing home when we're doubly incontinent.'

Will sat beside me and slipped an arm around my shoulder. This was the first time that he'd not looked ashen with horror since I'd broken the news four days ago. 'I'm glad you're feeling better.'

'I wouldn't go that far, Will, I'm pregnant. I won't feel better for another nineteen years.'

'Liza, you need to get off the emotional roller coaster. It'll be fine. We can deal with this.'

'That's easy for you to say. I need wine.'

'I don't think wine is a good idea.' Will looked at me with an expression of deep concern, making me want to reach up and smooth out the lines of his furrowed brow—with an iron.

I snapped out of it and offered him a hopeful smile. 'At least if it's a boy he can wear those rugby boots that are in the loft.'

What if it *was* a boy? How would I know what to do? He'd be obsessed with football and I'd have to spend my Saturday mornings standing beside a cold, muddy field, shouting things that I didn't understand. And wasn't there some special procedure for washing their foreskin?

'I'll make us some tea. Then I think you need some sleep, young lady.'

'What if it's twins?'

'You're not going to have twins.'

'No, *we're* not going to have twins, Will, unless you think this whole charade does not involve you in any shape or form? Maybe I should get an abortion.'

Will huffed and broke eye contact. I'd pushed it too far. 'That was a stupid thing to say Will, sorry. I'm scared.'

I lay my head on his lap. Will half-heartedly stroked my hair because he didn't know what else to do. We went to bed at 9.30 p.m. and Will fell asleep within minutes.

I did not fall asleep.

I went on Google.com.

As an older mother I could expect to have a higher risk of birth defects, cardiac complications, diabetes, pre-eclampsia and twins—or even triplets. On the upside, I was more emotionally and financially stable—apart from the fact that I was quite clearly neither.

I lay there ricocheting between good and evil: would I be a wise and balanced earth mother or a psychotic, screeching old hag? I thought of the reaction at the school gates: the

Lycra mums would snigger; the over-forties would be secretly impressed with the fact that I was still having sex. 'Oops, an accident, but we're both delighted!' I would blatantly lie through my serene smile.

My mother would feign joy and then promptly call Jessica to rant about how irresponsible I was. Jess would be genuinely elated. Susannah would laugh her head off. Will's parents would be bemused and say something like 'Oh. Well, that's good news, isn't it?' and I had no idea how Georgie would react.

Will farted in his sleep and I rushed to the bathroom to throw up.

38

WE WERE HAVING Sunday lunch at Georgie's. Tom, Tara and the children were there. And so, for some inexplicable reason, was my mother.

'Mum, this is a surprise.'

'Isn't it just? I was dropping off some old photos I found of the twins when they were babies and Georgie kindly invited me to stay for lunch.'

Twins ran in the family. Why had I not googled the stats on that the other night?

Georgie appeared from the kitchen and presented Mum with an elaborate Bloody Mary. 'I thought it'd make a fabulous little impromptu family reunion!' Georgie clasped her hands together in a faint attempt at glee.

I could see Tom and Tara out on the decking, Tara was wearing oversized sunglasses and they were laughing at something the girls were doing at the back of the garden. For once, neither looked painfully harassed which was quite admirable, considering their deceit.

Mother riffled through a pile of photographs on the table. 'Eliza, have you seen this one of Georgie when the boys were tiny? Oh dear, she does look tired.' She thrust a faded photograph into my hand of a very young, very bloated-looking Georgie with a baby in each arm, sneering at the camera beneath a heavy auburn fringe. Imagine having twins at nineteen. Imagine having them at forty-six.

Georgie leant in to take a look. 'Ah yes, I remember that,

I was getting about an hour's sleep a night back then. I think your dad took that photo, Eliza.'

'Really, Georgie? Then I'm surprised you weren't looking a little happier,' sniped Mum, plonking herself at the top of their hypothetical scoreboard.

'Goodness me,' Georgie said, stirring her drink with a slither of celery. 'It's the dig that never wears thin!'

They both threw their heads back in mandatory laughter before Georgie took her jubilance and the dregs of her Bloody Mary back into the kitchen to check on the potatoes. My father had always quite fancied the idea of twins. Reading between the lines, there had been other things my father fancied too, but I wouldn't be addressing that right now.

We all came to the table to eat. Mother pulled out every unflattering photograph of Georgie that she could find and showed them to the entire family. Even the children weren't spared. I imagined her at home, sifting through old albums with pursed lips, ripping up all the pretty photographs and making herself a neat little pile of pre-digital humiliation.

I'd pulled the 'I'm driving' card and was sipping at a modest glass of rather lovely organic rosé that was currently Tara's favourite: 'Now, I can promise you there are no added sulphites and it's far richer in nutrients and anti-oxidants than non-organic wines.' (An ideal pregnancy wine, if you ask me). She scanned my face. 'Eliza, I must say you're looking extremely well.'

'Thank you, Tara, I—'

'Have you put on weight?'

No need for that.

'I really couldn't tell you. I don't weigh myself obsessively. You must tell me about Poland. How awful that they cancelled your flight home.'

'I know.' She put down her knife and fork and stared at me wide-eyed, appalled by the apparent memory of the whole ghastly affair. Oh, she was good. 'All I can say is we were so thankful that the children were in safe hands.' She looked over at Georgie, squeezing up her face in affection. Even though this was the first time she'd seen Tara since she'd discovered the identity of Little Linny, Georgie seemed genuinely touched.

But I wasn't. I suffered from a strong urge to lean across the table and hack Tara an extremely short fringe, using only my left hand and a steak knife. It must have been a hormone surge, testosterone maybe?

'Mum tells me your big design project's almost complete, Liza,' Tom stuttered, hoping to steer the conversation away from their whopper of a lie.

'Yes, finally. It was really behind schedule due to one thing and another.' Me not getting my arse into gear. 'We're doing the photoshoot in the next couple of weeks and then Sarah can finish her article and hopefully sell it to a magazine.'

'Ah, so my little cousin will be famous: the acclaimed landscape gardener who's not afraid to give the royals a run for their money.' He meant well.

'The Andersons are throwing an official opening party over the bank holiday weekend and they're trying to get the local press involved. Come along, if you like.' I said this confident in the knowledge that Tara wouldn't be seen dead at something so provincial, where I might be considered to be more important than her.

Pierre was nowhere to be seen. Everybody knew about Pierre, but no one had asked as to his wellbeing or, indeed, his whereabouts. I decided that it was safer to keep my mouth firmly shut and observe everyone else instead.

My mother was on her soapbox, boring Will with how intellectual her other grandchildren were, Georgie was opening more wine and little Leo had the furrowed brow and stern stare of a child whose only concern was to fill the contents of his nappy in the most catastrophic fashion. Tara spotted this and felt compelled to start clearing away the plates.

'So,' Tom pressed on. 'How do you manage in the summer

holidays? It must be great to have your mum around to help out with Charlotte.'

'It doesn't make that much difference really, Tom. Mum's only been able to have her for two afternoons so far.' I felt Will's hand on my leg giving two pats and a squeeze, which was code for: *Shut the fuck up.*

'Eliza, honestly, you make me out to be a monster. There's always so much to sort out when I've been away. You must know, Tom, you're always on a plane. How is *your* job going, still stressful?'

'Daddy, Daddy, look at Leo.' All three girls had a look of delighted horror as we turned to face Leo, who was rocking back and forth in his high chair, shit oozing out of every possible opening of his designer baby grow.

Tom jumped to his feet, whisked Leo out of his chair and carried him, at arm's length, upstairs. Will and I stared at the high chair and then at each other. We communicated silently:

You know baby shit makes me retch, Will said.

I'm pregnant and it will make me retch too, you selfish wanker, I replied.

I smiled as sweetly as I could and took the chair outside to hose it down. My mother told the girls to go and wash their hands while Will poured himself another glass of wine.

Through the kitchen window, I could hear Tara confiding in Georgie about how distressing it'd been selecting a senior school for Maddie. Apparently, she'd been to hell and back. Thankfully, the *Tatler Schools Guide* had come up trumps again and they'd managed to narrow it down to three, the favourite being an all-girls equestrian in Berkshire where she would weekly board.

I grabbed the hose and called to her through the window, 'Tara, could you pass me some detergent and an old cloth, please? Leo has had a little accident.'

Tara poked her nose out of the window and raised her hand

to her mouth in shock. I could easily have turned the hose on to jet mode and blasted it in her face.

Because it was fresh shit and soft shit, it came off with relative ease. I scrubbed away at it regardless, my t-shirt pulled up over my nose, hoping the exertion would ease my psychosis.

Tara ambled over after about five minutes to see if she could take over. Gosh, was it all done? I shouldn't have. How grateful she was. By the way, dessert's ready, she hoped I'd be able to stomach it.

The children ran outside, opting for ice lollies and Swingball over homemade cheesecake with irritated grown-ups.

'Mmm, delicious, Georgie. Is it a Hemsley and Hemsley recipe?' Tara dabbed at her mouth with a napkin and straightened up in her chair, confident in her prediction.

'Who? No, this one's a tried and tested Nigella.'

Tara's demeanour faltered as she did a brief mental calculation of the saturated fat content and the effect it would have on her thighs. Nothing that a 10k run and a two-day fast wouldn't fix, I'm sure. Or a week-long cocaine binge. No, that was unfair. I was certain Tara wasn't involved with that crowd anymore.

'Have the two of you been out anywhere nice for dinner recently?' I asked; a perfectly acceptable, innocent question.

'Not really,' Tom said. 'I'd rather be at home at the moment. This deal in Tokyo's really taking its toll.'

'Oh, Tom, you make us sound like terrible old bores. We went to a fabulous Sri Lankan tapas bar last Friday.' Tara smiled and waited for us to express our intrigue, when my mother dived in with what could mildly be described as a bombshell.

'Now, Tom, Jess showed me a lovely picture of you and your dad on Facebook. I think you were all in the Shard. How is your dad? I must say, he did look well.'

'What? No that wasn't, err, I don't think—' Tom had quite

obviously expected his wife to conduct herself with some decorum on social media.

'And who was that other girl you were all with? She can't have been much older than Eliza—dark hair, big boobs?'

Tom coughed as beads of sweat sprang up all over his forehead. Tara sat perfectly still, fingers laced together, in demure silence. Even Will looked nervous.

Georgie made a dramatic show of holding the cream jug high above her plate, pouring a generous amount over her cheesecake. 'That would have been David's mistress, Lindsay Sheridan, or *Little Linny* to those who know her well.' She looked directly at Tara, any affection from earlier now wiped clean from the slate. Tara remained composed, offering only a thin smile in return.

I'd never been so grateful to see two sobbing children burst through the patio doors, wailing in a sea of unfathomable accusations. Will and I simultaneously leapt to our feet in a bid to be first on the scene.

'Izzy, Charlotte, what on earth happened?'

Charlotte, red-faced and furious, pointed her finger right at Izzy's nose. 'I hate her.'

I grabbed her face in my hands. 'Charlotte, what a dreadful thing to say.' I realised that all of today's frustrations could easily be taken out on my innocent six-year-old child, right there and then.

'And you're a liar-liar-pants-on-fire,' shouted Izzy before hammering upstairs to sob in the bathroom.

I couldn't get any sense out of Charlotte, who was at the stage of devastation where she was struggling to even breathe. Tara stared on nonchalantly, while Tom remained speechless. I called out to Maddie, who was engrossed in a lip-syncing app on her phone, and she wandered in without looking up.

'What happened, Maddie?'

She let out a big sigh, irked to be dragged away from her

cyber stardom. 'Charlotte said that our mum and dad had told a big, fat lie because they weren't really stuck in Poland.'

The four of us who knew the truth burst into canned laughter. Tara turned to look at Charlotte. 'Oh, sweetie, what a funny thing to say.'

'Then,' Maddie looked me up and down and it was the first time that I'd ever seen her truly resemble her mother, 'Charlotte told us you had a secret baby in your tummy, so Izzy called you liars too and said they were even.'

39

'I'M SIX WEEKS' pregnant.'

'What?'

'I can't come to the wine-tasting next week because I'm six weeks' pregnant.'

'What?'

'Can't you take Sarah? Or what about Lars? I bet he's good with wines.'

'Eliza, can you shut the fuck up about the wine-tasting for one minute. Oh my god, congratulations!' Susannah threw her arms around me but we both knew this was staged: me having to explain how weird I felt; her feeling morally obliged to tell me that everything was going to be okay.

'Enough of that.' I said. 'Can we sit down?'

'Of course. Are you alright? Shall I get you some water?'

'I'm fine. Please don't make a fuss.'

Tilly had dived face first into the ball pit and was shouting for Charlotte to follow her into the soft play tunnel which lured them into an underworld of anarchy and disease. Charlotte was unsure, hanging back and trying to stay in earshot.

'Go on, darling, Tilly's waiting. Have fun.' She lowered herself in and waded somewhat listlessly over to her friend, her face still heavy with emotion from the day before.

We'd left Georgie's on a good-enough note. I'd caught Tara stealing a glance at my stomach, but everyone else had opted to laugh it off: *Honestly, how do they come up with all this stuff? I expect they've all had a bit too much sun and sugar.*

But Charlotte had cried the whole way home before falling asleep just as we'd turned into the driveway at 5 p.m. Twelve hours later, she ran in and plonked herself in the middle of our bed, wide awake and ready to take on the world.

'Is there anything you want to talk about?' we'd asked her in unison.

'Are you having a baby, Mummy?'

'Why do you think that, darling?' asked Will, trying to sound surprised.

She turned to address him like the idiot she quite obviously believes him to be. 'Because I heard you talking about it the other night.'

Will looked at me for help.

'Sometimes Mummy and Daddy talk about things, but they might not always happen,' I said. 'A bit like when Daddy says he's going to clear out the garage.'

'Or like when Mummy says she's going on a detox,' countered Will.

'Or when you say that we'll go to Disney World but we never go because Daddy would rather stick pins in his eyes,' Charlotte said.

Will laughed, tickling her and trying to deny all knowledge. The mood lightened, but I was left questioning what other conversations Charlotte had been privy to, when we'd assumed that she was fast asleep in her bed.

Susannah returned with two mochas; the diet having been put on hold in this time of crisis. 'So, how are you feeling?'

'Indifferent.'

'Oh.'

I confessed my paradoxical state of mind; that I couldn't seem to get excited or upset, which she warmly accepted.

'Well you *are* forty-six. People do it, I know, but I would freak out if it happened to me.'

'That's comforting.'

'Not feeling like her then?' Susannah nodded to the shiny thirty-something sat at the table next to us, who was sipping on a carrot juice and lovingly rubbing her perfectly round belly.

'The antithesis. Let's change the subject. How's Lars? Tell me something exciting.'

'Lars is good.'

'Just good?'

'No, he's great. We have amazing sex. He's still got a photo of him and his wife in the bedroom. Is that weird?'

'Yes, that's weird. Is it a wedding photo?'

'Hell no, not that bad. It's a photo of them skiing a few years ago. They're holding hands.'

'Ew, that's not right. Have you said anything?'

'Of course not. How can I?'

It was a sensitive issue. Two years ago, Lar's wife had left him in a blaze of glory and moved back to Germany, then died in a horse-riding accident five weeks later.

'How the hell am I supposed to have an orgasm with *her* judging me from the grave?'

We discussed tactics for raising the photograph topic with Lars. Should she do it over dinner? In the bath? Over the phone? Susannah had read somewhere that you shouldn't bring up relationship problems just before or just after sex— and certainly not during. We dined out on the latter for a while, cackling as we acted out various inappropriate scenes to the occasional disapproving glare. But when we stopped laughing, reality was right there to spank me in the face.

'Do you think I should keep it?'

'Keep what?'

'The baby.'

'*What?*'

I tried to read her face. Concern? Pity? Annoyance at my attention-seeking behaviour?

'What if I'm not even pregnant, if I just made it up?'

Susannah wiped her hands up and down her face and it dawned on me that I'd seen Will use the same display of exasperation, more times than I cared to remember.

'Have you made it up?'

'I'm pretty sure I haven't. I've thrown up and I've done a test. It's just that I don't feel pregnant or joyful. We had lunch at Georgie's yesterday and I felt completely unhinged. If anything, I'd say I'm even crazier than I was before.'

Susannah smirked. 'Is that possible?'

'Evidently. Can you get *pre*natal depression?'

'Definitely. You should look into it. I think I had it with Teddy.'

'Really, what happened?'

'Another time. Look, it's probably just the shock of it all, it is okay to feel pissed off you know, so try to be nice to yourself.' Susannah looked distant and exhausted, and my neediness was probably not helping.

'Sorry, I'm being an idiot. Again.'

Susannah touched my hand under the table, which was unlike her; tactile behaviour being strictly reserved to coincide with wine consumption. 'Try to stop judging yourself, Eliza. You're a good person. The battle you're fighting is with yourself.'

'Well yes, I think I know that.'

'Do you?' Susannah said. 'Because it's draining. Not just for you, but for everyone else around you. I feel if I offer you a solution, you'll offer me ten problems in return.' We locked eyes and Susannah appeared oddly defeated, like she'd probably had enough of my bullshit.

'*Mummeee!*' Tilly was trying desperately to extract herself from the ball pit while simultaneously pulling her trousers down. 'I need a wee-wee, now.'

Old habits told me I should be huffy and defensive: who did she think she was, talking to me in that way? I was pregnant—at forty-six. Surely in my condition I was exempt from the naked truth?

But thoughts cast back to that Saturday night and acted as a stark reminder that sticky negative emotions did not serve me well. By the time Susannah returned from the bathroom, there'd been a shift in gratitude and I thanked her for her honesty.

40

'Do you think Izzy was alright in the end?'

'Izzy was fine,' Georgie said. 'What about you then?'

It would have been perfectly acceptable to have denied the whole thing, considering that most people didn't go public until they'd had the twelve-week scan.

'What about me?' I said, avoiding eye contact.

'Well it's certainly a turn-up for the books. I've never seen your mother so lost for words. How are you feeling?'

I shrugged. 'I just feel terrible about Sunday. I don't know what got into Charlotte.'

'Hmm, well it's surprising how insightful children can be sometimes. Tara seemed very pleased for you both anyway.'

'Didn't she just. She sent a huge bunch of flowers yesterday, which I promptly donated to the hospice.'

'That's rather extreme. Are you not in the slightest bit excited?'

'I can't explain it. I know Charlotte was a surprise, but when I was pregnant with her, I felt lucky, like someone had given me an amazing gift that I wasn't sure I deserved. This is different.'

'You'll be alright. When's your scan?'

'I don't know, another month maybe. I can't focus on it right now. I've got the Andersons' garden opening in a couple of weeks, and Charlotte's in holiday club for the next three days and is hating every minute of it.'

'You could have asked me to have her. Is your mother not helping out?'

'No, too busy interfering with everyone else's business, I expect. What was she doing with those photos?'

'Just trying to comfort herself, darling. It's water off a duck's back to me now. Talking of photos, what's this photo of them at the Shard? Have you got it on your Facebook?'

'I don't really look at Facebook these days,' I lied.

'Yes, but do you think you could find it?'

'I doubt it. It would be so far back on my newsfeed.'

'What about if you went onto Tara's page? Couldn't you find it on there?' Georgie persisted.

'Maybe. Actually no. Why do you want to see it anyway? You know what she looks like.'

'I'm just curious to know when they had their cosy little dinner, that's all.'

I was so shocked about being outed for my pregnancy that I'd brushed aside the fact that Charlotte, in return, had outed Tom and Tara about Flightgate and now Georgie was starting to piece things together. I felt a dull pain in my lower back and used this as an excuse to visit the bathroom.

I sat on the toilet, staring at the braille on top of the sanitary bin and wondered what it said. *Place sanitary wear on tray and close lid,* probably. I considered what it must be like to deal with a period as a blind woman and remembered the attitude of gratitude. I rubbed my stomach, but felt void of emotion.

I should get back to Georgie. I didn't need to feel guilty about other people's actions. I would be assertive and tell her that Facebook only stored posts for two weeks and then I'd ask her about Pierre as a diversion. I wiped myself and caught sight of something red on the tissue. I threw it in the toilet, left the cubicle and washed my hands. Well, that was that then; a false alarm. We could brush it under the rug and get on with our lives.

When I returned to the table, Georgie was engrossed in her

phone. Except that it wasn't her phone, but my phone and it was open on Tara's Facebook profile.

She looks up. 'Bingo.'

'What?'

'I found the photo.'

'What?'

'Except that they're not in the Shard, they're in the Dorchester, so your mother got it wrong. Linny looks like she's had an overzealous makeover in a cheap department store. Here, look.'

I grabbed the phone. There they all were again, but a different photo on a different date. I imagined the aftermath of Sunday, Tom furiously insisting that Tara delete all evidence. She'd let one slip through the net though. I didn't imagine their thousand-thread count cotton sheets had been of much comfort that night.

'Georgie?'

'Yes, darling?'

'I think I need to go to the doctor.'

41

Darcy, the sonographer, scanned my notes. She made reassuring gestures, nodding her head and smiling gently.

'So, you're forty-six?'

'Yes.'

'And your last period was eight weeks ago?'

'Yes.'

'Have you noticed any bleeding before yesterday?'

'A bit here and there,' I lied. It was a streak, that's all. Dr Chaudhry had fobbed me off over the phone, telling me that it was 'perfectly normal' and that I should 'try to relax'. But there were other reasons making me push for the scan. My boobs had gone from buoyant balloons to pitiful sacs, I'd stopped feeling sick, and I just didn't *feel* pregnant. I needed to know and, when I'd called the early pregnancy clinic, there was a possibility that I might have exaggerated my symptoms.

I couldn't see the screen but Will could. I saw the face of the sonographer and her assistant who both looked neutral yet pensive; an expression they must have had to perfect as part of the job.

'Hmm, alright. Well, this isn't giving us the best view,' Darcy said, 'so I think we'll go ahead and do an internal, if that's okay with you?'

'Of course.' I removed my pants and placed some austere paper towelling over my lap. Darcy put a condom over an instrument that, childbirth aside, would surely never fit inside my vagina.

'Okay, Eliza, try to relax.'

Relax? While she inserted that in me? I was aghast to find that it slid in with relative ease.

Darcy delved around my cervix, pointing out my ovaries and the fact that I had a full bowel. She pushed several round buttons beneath the keyboard, before showing an image to the assistant. They both fell quiet. The atmosphere in the room was static. I sat up and craned my neck round to look at the screen.

'Is anything coming through?' I asked, as if attending a séance.

Darcy touched my arm with her Latex-gloved hand. 'I'm afraid your pregnancy hasn't developed.'

'What does that mean?' I contorted my face to mimic hers.

She turned the screen toward me and showed me a series of lines which I presumed I was meant to interpret. She pointed at two different areas of the screen. 'You can see here and here that the embryo hasn't formed correctly. There's no heartbeat. I'm so sorry.'

The three of us sat and looked at each other for what seemed like an eternity while the assistant tapped something into a keyboard. Numbness was the only thing I felt.

'Are you going to take it out now?' I asked, breaking the silence.

'There's a couple of options we can look at, Eliza, but we can discuss this when—'

'No, I mean the scanner. Can you take it out now, please?'

'Yes, of course, I'm so sorry.' Darcy flushed red upon realising her faux pas and my instinct was to reassure her by laughing it off.

'That's okay. Easy mistake.'

Will looked at me in bewilderment as she removed the scanner. For some reason I'd wanted to laugh again at the sound it made on the way out, but thought better of it.

'I'll give you a few moments alone,' Darcy said.

Will threw his arms around me and squeezed me tighter than he had in years. I knew I should cry but I couldn't seem to let go. I imagined Will's sprightly sperm, standing like a soldier, vigilant and ready for the task at hand. Then my listless egg, half-asleep and a bit hungover, probably hadn't showered or brushed her teeth for a week. They had been a fun and quirky couple for a while, but it was never going to work long term.

Will held my shoulders and looked deep into my eyes. 'This might not be the best time to ask Liza, but did you really want to have another baby?' I knew the answer but I wasn't sure I could bring myself to say it. 'Because if you do, we can try again.'

I took a deep breath. 'I don't think I can handle it.'

Will pulled me close while all the emotions of the last year swirled around my head: all of the terrible things I'd thought and said; the failures, the anxieties and the anger. The fear—fear of losing my grip, of growing older.

Darcy returned to the room. She offered her condolences once again and advised us of our options. 'Take your time to think it over. You don't need to make a decision today. Best of luck.' She smiled warmly before leaving the room and I wondered whether she saw a couple engulfed in grief or absolved from the weighty responsibility of bringing new life into this messed-up world.

42

'And then he had the audacity to tell me that I'd be good for him. What about me? What about what's good for me?' Susannah had knocked back her first mojito in a matter of minutes and was checking her watch, signalling the bartender for another before the end of Happy Hour.

'He *is* a man and English *is* his second language,' I said. 'I think I'd struggle if I had to express my inner emotions in German, especially if I had a penis.'

'I'm not putting my heart on a plate for him to feast on while he's grieving over his wife. She left him for someone else, for fuck's sake.' Susannah handed me my second cocktail as I hurried to finish the first. 'Don't rush. Actually no, do rush. Let's get drunk.'

'I'm out of practice.'

Apart from that night when we'd drunk champagne and Will had accidently impregnated me, I'd not touched a drop since my lunch with Georgie when I'd lost the Elm Tree contract, so I was trying to approach the evening with an air of caution.

'Damn, these are good,' Susannah said. 'So enough about me, what's going on with you?' She nodded toward my navel. 'Anything happening?'

'Nothing yet. I feel fine though, really healthy. I don't think I want to have an ERPC. You have to be under a general anaesthetic while they hoover out your uterus.'

'No, I wouldn't go there. I had an abortion at seventeen and it felt like someone had taken a shovel to me. What are your other options?'

'Some pills which I didn't like the sound of. I'm gonna sit it out, let nature take its course.'

'Have you spoken to Emily?'

'No. She's coming to the opening party on Sunday, but she doesn't know anything about this.'

'Yes she does. I told her,' Susannah said.

'Oh. Thanks.'

'It's only because she had the same thing a couple of years ago and Emily being Emily didn't want to take pills so she took a load of herbs and did some visualisation on the side of a mountain somewhere wearing a string of mystic beads.'

'Really?'

'I may've embellished that a bit, but I know she took some herbs.'

'What kind of herbs? What did she say about me? Was she shocked?'

'Not really. She's not like that. You should talk to her about it.'

I tried to imagine having a conversation with Emily about my pitiful uterine activities and worried that she would find me flippant or irresponsible. What if she took me to one of those red tent meetings where someone in a long robe with hairy armpits blessed my womb and told me to connect with my inner goddess?

'Do you think drinking mojitos is a good idea?' I said, suddenly concerned for the baby that never was.

'That depends. Do you plan on trying again?'

'I don't think so. Part of me feels devastated, but another part feels like I've turned a corner.' I was trying to be upbeat, to not offer ten problems to every solution, and it was easier than I had expected. 'I'll speak to Emily.'

'Do. By the way, I told Sarah too, just so you didn't have to.'

'Oh, great. I don't really want anyone to make a fuss. It's not like we were desperately trying to have a baby.'

'No one's going to make a fuss. People just want to know if you're alright, that's all. Before I forget, Sarah has left GLOW and started a WhatsApp group called Old Girls. She wants us to all meet once a month in the pub; it'll still be a support group, only with swearing and a bar. Self-help with jazz hands is how she described it. She wanted to add you, but thought you might not be feeling up to it just yet.'

I sent Sarah a text:

I'm up for it... Add me to Old Girls please xx

We talked about the Andersons' opening party and Susannah got me quite enthused about the day, asking me what I was going to wear and say to the press and other fairly important factors that hadn't even crossed my mind. We made our way through another mojito and cracked bad-taste gags about the photo of the ex-wife, with Susannah claiming that she'd been involved in some ghostly *ménage à trois* and would sell her story to the *Enquirer*. I stayed positive, which became easier as the night went on and had absolutely nothing to do with rum consumption.

I was in bed by ten, making Will laugh with tales of harassed barmen and metaphysical voyeurism. I made him promise that when I died and he was having sex with Scarlett Johansson, that he would turn me face-down on the mantelpiece and not make too much noise.

'Eliza.'

'Yes?'

'I feel like I'm getting you back.'

Will spooned me and fell asleep. I lay awake, pondering his poignant words.

43

When Johnno and I arrived at 7.30 a.m., Mr and Mrs A were already outside setting up tables and chairs. They kept us topped up with coffee and pastries as we carried out last-minute pruning. We'd both worked hard in the last couple of days, mowing the lawns and pulling out weeds, and the garden was looking the best it could be. But I'd had a fitful night, worrying about the general public's reaction and whether I'd chosen the right species of rose. There was the almost obligatory dream where I'd arrived only to discover that there was no fountain, that I'd meant to call the students to book it in, but had forgotten, and in its place was a muddy hole and a dead shrew.

Although we'd completed the project over a month ago, I hadn't felt anywhere near satisfied until Will had taken the final photographs last week and managed to borrow a camera drone. When I finally saw the result—Will would not show me until he'd printed them as they would, hopefully, appear in a magazine alongside Sarah's article—it was hard to believe that it was our garden; the one I'd huffed and stressed about and told myself I couldn't do.

The students arrived at 10 a.m. to give the fountain a final polish. Mr Anderson had made an arrangement with them earlier in the week to man the bar and they looked rather smart in their black aprons and crisp white t-shirts. Tensions between us had lifted since the tent fracas and we'd built a good working relationship, with the students learning how to work in a professional environment and me having bigger fish to fry.

When Johnno and I were happy, we took a final walk around and tried to view it with fresh eyes.

Painted Lady butterflies busied themselves amongst the clusters of tiny red centranthus flowers, which lined the borders and spilled softly onto the paving. The diagonal lines of berberis that I'd been so unsure about while planning, had settled in to provide a loose symmetry within the quadrants; we'd kept them cropped to allow for the silvery foliage of the dwarf buddleia, whose now-tapering blooms of ivory, indigo and magenta mingled with the oregano and chives. But it was the globe thistle, the tallest of the main starring plants, with its tiny spikes exploding into sky-blue spheres, that now took centre stage. We walked in silence, taking in the aromatic scents and the hum of bees. White cosmos, Johnno's idea, had been scattered throughout and added delicate movement, giving an almost sensual tranquillity to the whole area.

Johnno let out a huge sigh of satisfaction. 'We did alright, didn't we? For a bartender and former window cleaner.'

'Thanks, Johnno, there's no way I'd have survived this without you.' We had a quick hug and went back to work, clearing away tools and polishing the large glazed terracotta pots filled with Felicia rose and lavender which marked the four corners of the garden.

Guests drifted in at around midday; a mixture of friends, relatives and curious neighbours taking full advantage of the free food and booze, while the Andersons' beloved Beethoven tinkered away in the background.

Mr Anderson ushered over a frantic-looking lady in a fleur-de-lis-patterned maxi dress. 'Eliza, I'd like you to meet Gail from the *Daily Standard*.' Mr Anderson was very excited by the introduction, hopping from foot to foot and interrupting with amusing anecdotes of the past few months, including the flip-flop debacle.

But we don't want the flip-flop debacle to be included in the article, do we, Mr Anderson? Not my version anyway.

Gail asked a lot of irrelevant questions regarding my thought process and inspirations for the garden. 'Are you influenced by modern architecture?'

'Er, no, not really.'

'Okay, good. What about colours? Do you close your eyes to picture the layout of colour? And what about churches? They're always inspiring, don't you think?'

I'd never been interviewed before and instead of embracing it, I found it invasive and rather embarrassing. I was glad to see Organic Emily wave and wind her way towards me through a sea of children and dogs. Emily gave me a warm embrace and one of her *Are you okay?* glances before introducing herself to Gail.

'Emily is designing her own garden at the moment,' I said, 'and is also studying environmental science.' They embarked on a conversation regarding the Open University and I took the opportunity to escape and get myself a refill.

Until now I'd stuck to lemonade, in an effort to remain appropriate for various exchanges with journalists and posh people. I was hot and tired, and should probably drink some water, but I found myself wandering over to the bar, where there was a handwritten notice: *Espresso martinis now being served*. Mrs A was sat in a deckchair squealing with delight as Ben poured a cocktail into her champagne glass.

'Eliza, look at what this clever boy has just made me. It's a fabulous pick-me-up apparently—coffee and vodka,' giggled Mrs A. 'I learn something new every day. You should have one, you must be exhausted.'

'I'm on it.' Ben pointed at me and for a moment I found him quite charming in his cool Ray-Bans, perspiration making his t-shirt cling to his chest.

'I may just take you up on that,' I said.

As he set to work, flexing his biceps and making overzealous gestures with the cocktail shaker, we made polite chit-chat about the so far positive response and how pleased we were with the finished result.

He handed me my drink. 'Enjoy. Oh, Eliza, before I forget...'

'Yes?'

'One.' He took back my glass and with the same strong, steady hand that had created the fountain, placed three perfectly aligned coffee beans on top of my martini.

'Oh, thank you.'

'And two.' He flipped off the top of an Amstel on the edge of the counter, removed his sunglasses and leant toward me. 'Cheers. It was an absolute pleasure to work with you.' He shot me a filthy smile, raised an eyebrow and chinked my glass.

'Yes, you too,' I said before turning away. The cheeky sod. Who the hell did he think he was? He was nineteen, for heaven's sake. No one's that confident at nineteen.

'Darling, look at you, you're positively beetroot. Do you need some factor 50?'

'Hi, Georgie. No, I'm fine really.'

'Eliza, I'd like you to meet Pierre.' Hovering behind Georgie was a man wearing a straw boater who I'd noticed earlier and taken an immediate dislike to.

'Ah, the beautiful Eliza. *Enchanté*. I hear so much about you.' Pierre lifted my hand to kiss it, far too tenderly for my liking.

'Nice to meet you too, Pierre.'

'*Le jardin, c'est stupéfiant*. Amazing, just like your aunt.' He smiled at Georgie and she offered a coy giggle in return. '*Excusez-moi*, I get us some champagne.'

'See you in a minute, darling.' Georgie waved and he tipped his hat at us before heading off in the direction of Ben, who seemed to have attracted quite an audience. Georgie turned to me. 'Good god, he's getting on my nerves.'

'Pierre?'

'It was all very well for the first few weeks: cooking me dinner, reading me poetry. Now we're three months down the line and all he does is borrow my car and use my Wi-Fi. I'm seriously thinking of turning him out.'

'So do it.'

'It's not like he's actually done anything wrong, he just doesn't do anything *at all*, except freeload. But anyway, how are you? Have you had...you know?' She leant in closer and whispered, 'The abortion?'

'Georgie, I'm not having an abortion, it's an ERPC, and no, I'm hoping it will happen naturally.'

'Are you sure that's wise? Don't you think it would be better to just go and get it sorted?'

'Excuse me, I'm sorry to interrupt,' Emily put a delicate arm around my shoulder. 'Could I have a quiet word with Eliza, just for a moment?'

Georgie gave Emily the once-over. 'Anything you've got to say to her, you can say to me. I practically raised her.'

'Sorry, Emily, let me introduce you. This is Georgie, my aunt. Emily's children are at school with Charlotte.'

'Does she know?' Georgie piped up louder than necessary. She leant into Emily, disregarding any personal space etiquette. 'Do you know?'

Emily, cool as a cucumber, touched Georgie's arm and nodded gently. 'Yes, I know. It's so lovely to meet you, Georgie. Eliza's told me lots about you.'

And she'd won her over.

'So what's your opinion, Emily? She can't just walk around with some—heaven knows what to call it—inside of her forever, can she?'

'I think the correct term is *products of conception*,' said Emily, meaning well.

'Products?' said Georgie. 'Products are what I put on my skin.'

'I *am* here, you know,' I said. 'Can we keep it down a bit, please?'

Products of conception. They'd kept using that term at the hospital after the scan and it made me want to sob. Will and I had made those products. They might as well have called it the 'aftermath of a shag' or a 'consequence of coitus'.

Emily produced a paper bag from her jute holdall, that was bursting at the seams with tinctures and herbs. 'I've brought you a little care package to help things along. There's a sheet of paper explaining everything. I would start it as soon as you can. I could give you some acupressure this afternoon if you'd like? The evening primrose oil really needs to be done when you go to bed.'

'Shall I take some now?' I asked, realising that I wanted to pry myself from this bizarre limbo sooner rather than later.

'Wait until you get home,' whispered Emily. 'The primrose oil needs to be applied to your cervix.'

Georgie threw her head back and laughed. 'How the hell's she supposed to do that?'

'Well, you could use a medicine syringe, or—'

'Will could put some on the end of his pecker,' shrieked Georgie. Emily looked at me with concern, failing to see the funny side.

'Ignore us,' I said. 'Tasteless humour is a Hamilton trait. We're truly terrible people.'

A member of Emily's angelic brood called for her and she excused herself gratefully. I too was grateful to move away from the elephant in the room. The espresso martini was starting to take effect and I wanted to relax and, as Georgie would say, *just have some fun.*

I endured another line of questioning from Gail, but I sent her in Johnno's direction to gather the finer technical details. He had been a rock while I had been a mess; doing all the hard labour and politely pointing out the many flaws in my plan. I preferred him to have the glory over me. I meandered around, grazing on canapés and chatting to various people until I eventually found Susannah and Georgie, huddled over a bottle of wine and looking very cloak and dagger.

'Excuse me, ladies. Mind if I join you?'

Susannah looked over the top of her sunglasses and spoke in a low, monotone voice. 'It's classified.'

'Oh, sorry,' I stuttered and felt a sting of sensitivity as I turned to walk away.

'Eliza, you idiot, get back here.' Susannah yanked me by the arm and thrust a glass into my hand. 'Are you alright?'

'Yes,' I said. 'What's going on?'

'Drink that please,' she ordered sternly, gesturing to the glass. 'Now, we're working undercover on Operation Dump Pierre. Are you in?'

'Most definitely.'

We spied on Pierre, who was making clumsy attempts to charm women who could see straight through him, until a young girl in a jumpsuit steadied herself on his arm and whipped off his hat, placing it at a jaunty angle on her own head. He poured her more champagne and clearly forgot that he was there with Georgie.

'Good Lord, he's almost old enough to be her grandfather. Has he no shame?' Georgie said, not particularly upset by the scene unfolding before her.

'This is an ideal development in Operation Dump Pierre,' Susannah declared. 'You can just throw him out now. No explanation needed.'

We laughed and conspired for the next half an hour, then I hit a wall. I'd had enough cocktails, enough gossiping, enough compliments and enough of humans. I needed to find Will and go home that minute.

Susannah came to the rescue as always. 'Just get in the car. I'll get Will and bring Charlotte home later.'

'I can't just leave.'

'Yes you can. It'll be all mysterious and celebrity garden designer-ish. I'll make your excuses. Now get in the car.'

I did. And Susannah made my excuses.

Will drove me home and I collapsed into bed, overcome by a range of emotions. I missed Dad, and I realised how much I'd wanted Jess to be there today, to see what I'd achieved. She would have been proud of me.

It would've been nice for Mum to have been there today too, but she'd gone to the Notting Hill Carnival instead. 'Oh, that's a shame,' she'd said when I told her about the opening, 'Janice and I have already booked the hotel.'

Will tried his best, with camomile tea and random sprinklings of lavender oil, making helpful suggestions such as, 'Just don't worry about it' or 'Try not to cry.'

Charlotte arrived home elated and exhausted at 8 p.m. I could hear Will speaking to Susannah quietly in the hallway as Charlotte jumped into bed with me.

'Mummy is ill, oh poor Mummy.' She lowered her bottom lip while holding my face in her hands, as if to study the extent of my ailment. 'Was it a funny prawn again?'

The door slammed and Will came back upstairs with more tea. He climbed into bed with us and everything felt a little more complete, until Charlotte sat bolt upright, wearing her deadly serious expression, one I expect she will use to tell us that she's a drug addict or is leaving home at fifteen.

'Mummy and Daddy, something happened at the party and there was an argument.'

My thoughts immediately jumped to Georgie and Pierre and I panicked that there had been a scene. 'Go on, darling. Was it some of the children?' I asked, optimistically picturing a fiasco involving the last packet of salt and vinegar Hula Hoops.

'No, Mummy, it was the grown-ups, and one of them was Aunty Georgie's *boy*friend. But he's not a boy, is he, Mummy? Boys don't have grey hair.'

'Try to stay focused, Charlotte. Who was he arguing with?' I asked, stroking her arm, trying to smooth over my angst.

She looked me square in the face and spoke slowly, 'Aunty Georgie's *boy*friend had an argument with the man who was making the drinks.'

'You mean Ben? The student?'

'I don't know his name, but he called Aunty Georgie's *boy*friend...' Charlotte looked wide-eyed and whispered, 'a twat.'

I gasped, trying not to snigger, while Will shamelessly laughed out loud.

'And then Aunty Georgie's *boy*friend said something to him in French, but the man who made the drinks understood French and someone had to go and talk to them. Jasmine in Year Five said that everything was about to go pear-shaped.'

Great, now Emily's children were involved.

'Now, darling, were you okay? You weren't caught up in anything?'

'No, Mummy. I went to find Aunty Suzie, she was with Aunty Georgie, and she said it was time to go home.'

'And what about Mr and Mrs Anderson? Were they upset too?'

'Mrs Anderson was having a little sleep in the deckchair and Mr Anderson says it will all come out in the wash.'

Both Pierre and the students had been at the party because of me and, even though I hadn't been there at that point, the weight of responsibility fell firmly on my shoulders. I'd need to call someone to find out the finer details. Georgie would quite possibly be arguing with Pierre, so I'd try Susannah or Sarah. Maybe a courtesy call to Mr Anderson wouldn't go amiss either. I'd apologise for my early exit and innocently enquire how the rest of the day had gone. Yes, that was a perfectly normal and acceptable thing to do.

44

'WHAT YOU'VE GOT to understand, Eliza, is that slapping someone's arse is perfectly acceptable behaviour for older French men like Pierre, they wouldn't know about the MeToo movement if it smacked them in the face.'

'Georgie, you can't say that. Why are you protecting him? I thought you'd had enough of him anyway.'

'I'm not protecting him; I'm just making the observation that it was a two-way street and she was doing her fair share of flirting.'

'But she was only about eighteen and he was plying her with champagne, where exactly do you draw the line?'

'I hardly think she felt violated if that's what you're insinuating.'

I attempted to grasp the sentence, to come back with an answer that would make her see sense, but my mashed-up perimenopausal brain told me not to bother. *It's not important for you to identify with this* it said. *Just let her get on with it and see if you can manage to choose something from the menu. And don't be adventurous, just stick to what you know.*

'I'm having the spinach risotto.' I announced, hoping to steer the conversation away from her chauvinistic toy boy.

'Good choice. I think I'll join you. Did I tell you I saw a barrister last week? Someone from the tennis club gave me his card. Lovely young man; angelic face but ferocious in the court room apparently.'

'Do you think it'll come to that?' I asked. 'I'm sure Uncle

David will be fair.' It was hard for me to imagine my uncle dragging Georgie through the courts, he had always been so kind to me growing up. I was the youngest of the cousins and spent a lot of time staying with them when Mum was busy with Jessica's dance school and Dad was away.

'He's already sent some over-excitable young suit round to value the house. I told him I'm not moving. I'll chain myself to the silver birch and they'll have to get a team of firefighters in to remove me. Imagine that?'

'But you've been married for so long and he's had an *affair*. Surely it's fairly cut and dried?'

'Who knows what he'll pull out of the bag, but let's just say I've got a few things up my sleeve. Now, what's going on with you? Have you had your abortion yet?'

'I'm not having an abortion.' One of the Lycra mums from school was sitting at a table opposite. She stared and I spotted her suppressing a sly grin. 'Can you stop calling it that, please?'

'Just go to the hospital and get this *thing* out so you can move on.'

'There's nothing to move on from and it's not a *thing*. It's a little clump of cells that Will and I made by accident. End of story.'

'I disagree,' Georgie said firmly. 'You've never had a miscarriage and I have, so I know what I'm talking about. You're managing to hold it all in now, but you're going to be an emotional wreck.'

'I will not be an emotional wreck. I'll throw myself into healthy eating and exercise. I've downloaded that Couch to 5k app.'

'You're putting your head in the sand.'

'I've just been so busy with the opening party and the new term. Charlotte's already decided she doesn't like her teacher.'

'Stop changing the subject,' Georgie said.

'I'm not changing the subject. I'm just done with talking about it now.' I really was. I kept getting texts from people in the know, checking if I was okay or if anything had happened yet. They were loving, thoughtful messages but I really just wanted to turn off my phone until it was all over and done with.

Georgie started talking about some of the guests she knew at the garden party: who was married to who, who'd had an affair or a bankrupt business and whereabouts their children had been educated.

I was half-listening, half-wondering if she was right about me being an emotional wreck. That little clump of cells had bound Will and I together somehow, forced us to connect when we could've so easily detached. I muffled the thought and sent it back down to the depths, thinking instead about the Persian carpet garden.

'Do you think the garden looked alright in the end? There were times throughout the day when all I saw was a jumble of foliage that we'd thrown around a fountain.'

'Eliza, what are you talking about? The garden was magnificent.'

'Was it though? Be honest. I know I spent months on it, but anyone with half a brain and a spade could have done the same. The newspaper reporter asked me some really bizarre questions, probably trying to make it sound more interesting than it actually was.'

'Eliza, you've created something truly wonderful, how many more people need to compliment you before you can accept this?'

'I don't need compliments, I'm just saying that I probably could have made it better, that's all.'

'But everyone was taking photographs, you're going to be in the local paper and hopefully in a national magazine. And look at all the feedback you've had from Instagram since Sunday.'

'I just feel a bit flat now though. It's all over with; everyone's seen it and I didn't get to make it quite as perfect as I'd have liked, if I'm honest.'

'*Perfect?* I didn't know you were looking for perfection, Eliza. For heaven's sake, don't turn into your mother.'

'What?' Lycra mum stared once more.

An awkward silence descended on the table.

'That was harsh.'

'I'm sorry, I didn't mean it to come out like that,' Georgie said. 'I'm a little oversensitive right now, and I'm worried about you: how you react, the things you say—you're not yourself at the moment.'

'I've had a lot going on, to be fair.'

'I know you have, but I think you need to find some sort of happy medium. One minute you're up and the next you're down, you ricochet between apathy and perfection. It's not good for you. And then there's those accusations against poor Will.'

'Why are you bringing all this up now? I've said sorry to Will, and Susannah, and everyone's fine. And I'm alright as long as I don't overdue the coffee or the sugar. Or the wine.' I said, raising my saintly glass of mineral water.

She sighed. 'Look, there's something I keep meaning to talk to you about, but it just never feels like the right time.'

'Is everything okay? You're not ill, are you?'

'Gosh no, fit as a fiddle. It's just nonsense from the past, so let's do it another time.'

'No, let's do it today.'

Georgie put down her fork and took another mouthful of wine. 'I don't want you to blow it out of proportion.'

'Of course I won't blow it out of proportion. Tell me.'

'You would only have been about eleven. The boys had not long left for boarding school so I was suffering from an empty nest. Children shouldn't be allowed to leave home at thirteen and I often wonder whether I would've had a stronger relationship with them now had they stayed at home, but your uncle was insistent.'

I tried to relax and let the story unfold naturally, rather than jump to any wild conclusions.

'Do you think that's when things started to go wrong?' I asked.

'That's when things started going wrong with your parents.'

'*My* parents?'

'Your father had started working away and your mother was not coping at all well. Jess was going through those arduous auditions for that ballet school. And then you were just left to get on with it.'

'But what's this got to do with me being up and down and accusing Will of adultery? Which I know is nonsense, by the way.'

'You and I developed a close bond in that time, Eliza. People used to think you were my daughter when we were out and about, and I admit that I didn't always correct them.'

I remembered that happening on a few occasions too and we would giggle; it was our secret little joke. 'I still don't understand.'

'Your mother didn't like it very much and she started saying things—unpleasant things.'

'What kind of unpleasant things?'

'Accusations...about your father and me.'

45

'WELL, I MUST say this smacks of familiarity,' Will laughed falsely. 'Familiarity being the optimum word in this instance.'

I'd wondered how to present this new piece of information to him, without having to endure this most obvious form of sarcasm, and I'd come to the conclusion that I'd simply have to pull up my big girl pants and take it on the chin.

'Have you finished, Will?'

'No. So Georgie's concerned that you're turning into your mother? Wow, that's got to sting. But I can see where she's coming from.' Will was in his element. He'd bang on about it all night if I let him. 'I suppose you could have accused me of sleeping with your *sister*. That'd be tricky though, given the geography.'

An image of Will and Jess naked on the lounge floor at the house in Brookhaven flashed through my mind and made me shudder.

'Will,' I slammed the cupboard door shut, 'can you please be serious for one minute and just listen.' I'd rounded off lunch with a coffee. I'd asked for decaf, but it was becoming obvious now that this had been overlooked, as I wanted to rip Will's head clean off his shoulders using only my teeth.

'Okay sorry, I'll stop,' Will held up his hands. 'Look, I know Georgie's a handful, but I don't think she shagged your dad.'

'Please stop saying that.'

'Alright, I don't think Georgie and your father ever made love.'

'That's even worse. Can't we just refer to it as an affair or something?'

'What? You're saying they had a full-blown affair now?'

'I'm going for a run.'

'When did you start running?'

'I'm starting now.' I charged upstairs, pulled some mouldy trainers from the back of the wardrobe, grabbed my wallet and headed out the door. 'I'll be back in an hour.'

'Okay, Paula Radcliffe.' Will appeared unfazed by my latest act of rebellion.

I hadn't run for twelve years, so I'd envisaged it being more of a light jog around the block, ending up in the pub garden with a cold beer if I'd done well. I started gently, finding my stride, loving the monotonous sound of my shoes hitting the asphalt. I rounded the corner and surveyed the hill in front of me. It was only about two hundred metres; surely I could sprint up that in one burst? I made it a third of the way before I slowed, coughing and gasping, into a lumbering walk.

I passed the retail park and noticed a sign in the sports shop saying '20% OFF BIKES'. I bought one, defiance pumping through my veins and smashing into my overdraft with ease.

I flew down to the promenade and began to organise my thoughts: I expect Mum was stressed and not thinking straight at the time. She was known for her jealous streak and it was no secret that Dad and Georgie had got on like a house on fire. But Georgie had some morals. And, if I remember rightly, so did my father. His marriage may've been on the rocks, but he wouldn't have slept with his brother's wife. No, Mum was being crazy. She resented Dad and Georgie's easy relationship, and wanted someone to blame for the breakdown of her marriage. And that person was Georgie.

And here I was, thirty years later, clambering along the same rocky path; a thread of DNA that was as predetermined as my turned-up nose and frizz-prone hair. Would Charlotte now go on to accuse other slightly more attractive women of sleeping with her husband? Would I feel for ever wretched for having passed on this disgraceful chromosome?

I pondered this for some time—the cycle of behaviour from parent to child; that our mothers were merely older versions of us, with the same fears and insecurities; just other human beings making the same stupid mistakes along the way. But we were not newly socialised baby boomers. We were not too nervous to admit when we'd messed up or too proud to apologise. We were Generation X and it was up to us to break the mould.

It was dark now. I could see the yachts bobbing up and down in the marina and I wondered how easy it would be to commandeer one, to sail away and only return when everything made sense again. I decided it was probably rather difficult, given the legality issue and the fact that I had zero sailing experience. I turned around and headed for home.

The gears on the new bike were impressive and I glided effortlessly up the incline towards the house. I thought about poor old Bessie and wondered where she was now with her rusty chain and squeaky pedals. By the time I turned into the driveway I felt purged. The exertion had calmed me and I was ready for bed. I might even apologise to Will for storming out of the house. Yes, that's what I'd do. I'd start breaking the mould.

I rang the doorbell and waited for Will's surprise reaction to my new purchase.

'Eliza, where the hell have you been? I've been worried sick. Why didn't you take your phone?'

I ignored his interrogation and presented the bike in what I perceived to be a comical game show type fashion, 'Ta-da!'

'Jesus Christ, what's happened to you?'

'Chill out, Will. I only bought a bike.'

'Why are you covered in blood?'

46

THEY'D SAID IT would be like a heavy period. They'd said I'd feel emotional and maybe nauseous. No one said it would feel like labour.

I'd taken a shower and sat on the toilet for two hours. There were contractions, first every ten minutes and then every three. The Mumsnet forum informed me this was normal and had given me the clearest advice of anyone so far. The stranger behind the screen was a far cry from the professional, diplomatic hospital staff and not afraid to discuss all of her misfortunes in graphic detail for the world to comment on. No question was too taboo—we were in this gruesome mess together; an anonymous coven supporting each other in a virtual world of blood, guts and cyber hugs.

Will had been good up until midnight with sympathy, paracetamol and cups of sweet tea, but then I heard him snore. I could see him through the crack of the bathroom door, mouth open, his head lolling over the end of the bed. 'Will, wake up. Will?' I whispered, my tone scathing, not wanting to wake Charlotte by hollering, 'you fucking arsehole' at full volume.

I threw a toilet roll at him and missed. It hit the dressing table and knocked over a jar of expensive, unused face cream that Georgie had given me for Christmas. I watched helplessly as it clattered to the floor and the toilet roll unravelled itself in a long stream, finishing up in a dusty corner somewhere under the bed. It was the last toilet roll left in the house.

My eyes began to fill—a huge relief. I had not cried up to this point and was beginning to think that I'd morphed into an emotionally crippled potato.

I used the sleeve of my bath robe to wipe my face. I couldn't even get up and retrieve the toilet roll without leaving carnage across the bathroom floor. We'd recently had it retiled in an off-white textured design and it was a bugger to clean at the best of times. Will and I had fallen out over it: I'd wanted a simple Victorian check, but Will eventually got his own way, using cheap scare tactics about how perilous my tiles would be, how Charlotte would surely slip and crack her head wide open. But now I had a fair argument: *the Victorian check would've been a damn sight easier to clean after I'd trailed the products of our conception all over it because you'd fallen asleep and I'd had to try and wake you with a toilet roll, Will.*

Dark, mad thoughts whirled around like miniature cyclones, until there was just a void; a skull full of nothingness. For a short time, I remained motionless, almost bored, as tears slid down my face and into the grisly depths of the toilet. A feeling of disorientation washed over me. I called out to Will, but could only manage a gasp as I gripped the side of the bath, sweat pouring from my body. I cried out in pain, the waves of contractions now a constant low throb. I bent my head forward, toward my knees, ready to throw up or pass out. Will was suddenly upon me, enveloping me in his arms. 'Liza, I'm so sorry.'

I panted with exhaustion. Everything slowed down. The worst was over.

'I hate you,' I sobbed into the crease of his neck.

'I know,' he said. 'It's okay.' We stayed there for what seemed like an eternity, crying, hugging and rocking together, the shape of the toilet seat permanently embedded onto my arse cheeks.

47

A Right Royal Knees-up
by Gail Hooper

The August bank holiday saw the much-awaited opening of Harold and Audrey Andersons' Persian Carpet garden. Inspired by a Chelsea Flower Show silver medal winner in the royal gardens at Highgrove House, this stunning display of botany is a phosphorescent jewel in the crown of this well-heeled estate in the heart of the Hampshire countryside.

With an array of wild foliage, from humble herbs to the delicate rose, the creation is the brainchild of internationally renowned garden designer Eliza Hamilton. Eliza, a surprisingly down-to-earth and rosy-faced forty-six-year-old, says that she often imagines what buildings would look like if they were left to decay and flora took over, and how the hues of stained-glass windows feature heavily in her work.

There was a photo of Johnno and me standing by the fountain with the Andersons and the students. My mouth was wide open, making me look like a cheap inflatable sex doll, and I had something resembling a slug stuck to my collarbone.

'What a pile of shit. How can she get away with writing this?'

Will was spoiling himself in over-the-top laughter. 'Sorry, Liza. I'm still getting over you being rosy-faced and internationally renowned.'

'Only because I told her about the rockery I'd built in the garden at Brookhaven seven years ago. Here we go. Listen to this: *Harold Anderson, who had visited the gardens at High-grove last year, said he wanted to create an eye-catching, yet simple addition to his already mature plot.*

'Simple? How dare he call the last five months *simple.*'

'Maybe he didn't, maybe Gail Hooper just made it up along with everything else,' Will said.

The doorbell hailed the arrival of Susannah and Will jumped to his feet. 'Okay, I'll leave you to it. Sure there's nothing else you need?'

'I'm sure.'

'Just call me.' Will tilted my chin to meet his gaze. 'Eliza?'

'Yes?'

'You've been amazing.' He planted a kiss on my forehead and headed for the door.

'So have you.' I called out after him.

And he had. He'd made all the right noises at all the right times: he'd fetched, carried and served. But I needed him to go back to work now. If he cleared his throat or asked me if I was okay one more time, I might say or do something quite unforgivable. Even his thoughtfulness was beginning to grate on me and I found myself pining for the Will who left his socks on the bathroom floor and moaned about the lack of food in the fridge.

Susannah barged into the lounge carrying a large cardboard box and I sat upright in a burst of anticipation. She dumped it on the coffee table and sat on the sofa next to me. She squeezed me tightly and emotion surged through me.

'I'm not going to ask if you're okay, because you'll probably tell me to go fuck myself.'

'I might be hormonal, Suze, but I'm not an ogre.'

'Alright then.' She stood up and took a deep breath. 'Are you okay?' Susannah's face was intense, searching for something in mine which I tried to swallow back down. There was an uncomfortable pause.

'Go fuck yourself. What's in the box?'

'That's my girl.' She clapped her hands, back in her element of nurturer and provider of all-things gorgeous.

'First and foremost, we're going to sample a large slice of my home-made chocolate cake with a cup of tea. Then we'll plough into the Haribos I brought for Charlotte. She'll never know.'

Within ten minutes I was howling with laughter. Everything she produced from the box came with its own backstory, including a lasagne which was slightly burnt due to Lars rudely interrupting her while she had been bent over the Aga. Tilly had made me a stress ball from a balloon filled with dried lentils and Teddy had drawn me a picture of what looked like an ejaculating snowman.

'You really didn't have to do all of this, Suze.' I was rubbing some bath crystals between my fingers which had come in a gift pack with body oil and a selection of lip balms.

'Of course I have to do all of it. That's what friends do.'

'It's not what *I* do. I'd be crap at this.'

'But you're good at so much more. Do you remember Paulton's Park? I was so bloody ill.'

'I won't forget that in a hurry.' I'd only known Susannah for two months. I'd arrived at her house and she'd opened the door, her face white as snow, heat radiating from her layers of clothing and hats. 'Better wrap up, Eliza, it's freezing today.' She was beyond delirious and I had to frogmarch her back to bed. I then spent four long hours being dragged around Peppa Pig World in the rain, and Teddy had puked in the back of the car on the way home because I hadn't been aware of his dairy intolerance.

'What's going on with you anyway? How's Lars?'

'Lars is alright. It's a bit of fun but I'm not getting too involved. The kids just think he's a very friendly vet.'

'Photo still up?'

'Yep. I was going to mention it last night but I ended up cancelling our date because I had a bit of a funny turn.'

'A funny turn? Aren't they for old people?'

'I just had this cracking headache that came out of nowhere and I was all disorientated. It was so strange.'

'Why didn't you call me?'

'Eliza, you've just had a miscarriage—I wouldn't call you.' Susannah waved her hand around, wishing the whole conversation would vanish into thin air. 'Simon was there with the kids anyway. I took some aspirin and went to bed. I feel fine today.'

We had a glass of sherry and ate more cake.

'The first Old Girls meeting is next Thursday. Think you'll be up for it?'

'Of course,' I said. 'Why wouldn't I be?'

'I just thought you might be a bit tired or, you know, upset.'

With that exchange, I knew we had opened the door and I could no longer shut it without an explanation. It was hard to get going, but once I'd gathered some momentum it was hard to stop.

'I'm exhausted, mentally and physically, and I feel empty, like the ability to bear fruit has been snatched away from me by an early frost.'

Susannah listened without judgement while the words poured out of me: sorrow about losing the little clump of cells that Will and I made, but also the quiet relief at not having the responsibility that those cells carried with them. And the guilt associated with both of those emotions.

'Embrace it. Acknowledge how you feel and stop beating yourself up because society dictates you should feel something else.' Susannah read a lot of psychology articles on the Internet.

'Is it callous of me to want to go back to work?'

'No, I would say that's constructive. You're not a surgeon or a pilot, it's not the end of the world if you lose the plot and massacre a rosemary bush.'

'I'm not good at sitting, I need to get outside and move around. There's this kind of optimism amongst all the chaos, which makes me think that something good is about to happen. But how do I acknowledge that?'

'Because maybe something good *is* about to happen. For goodness' sake, Eliza, start living your life. You never know what's around the corner.' Susannah was using her bossy voice now; the voice no one wanted to argue with. 'You've got the weekend to rest up, do a few hours on Monday and see how you feel. Have you still got Johnno?'

'Yes, he's already offered to pick up the extra hours, he's been a godsend.'

'Perfect, there you go. It's all great timing. Ease back in slowly and if you get stuck, you can always ask me.' Susannah grinned with excitement but her eyes told me that she didn't really mean it.

When she left, I lay on the sofa and pulled a blanket over me. Susannah had opened the chaotic filing cabinet of my mind and put everything back neatly and in alphabetical order. Johnno was going away in November and was desperate to work as much as possible before then. I'd use this opportunity to ease off for a few weeks, do a little manual labour in the morning and maybe some design work in the afternoon before picking Charlotte up from school, rather than shoe-horning it in around dinner and before bed. Somewhere along the way I'd slipped out of my daily yoga habit too, I'd work this back in before breakfast maybe.

I flicked on the TV and watched an old episode of *The Simpsons* before falling asleep for the rest of the afternoon.

48

'Now tell me honestly, are you okay?'

I took a deep breath. 'Yes, Georgie, I really am okay.' I thought I was; maybe a little fragile here and there. I'd worked a few hours at the Andersons' the day before and then slept like the dead. This morning, I'd jumped out of bed and cracked on with a yoga class and a few chores, and it felt like life was beginning to take shape again.

'Well that's good to hear. Of course, when I had my miscarriage no one would discuss such things. One had to keep a stiff upper lip and there were certainly no online forums. Nowadays everyone's beside themselves, demanding IVF and hating other pregnant women because the Internet says it's acceptable to do so. You've handled it very graciously.'

'Thanks. Now can we change the subject? Is there anything you need to get today?'

'Do they sell Christmas decorations?'

'In September? Thinking about it, yes, they probably do.'

This was Georgie's first trip to IKEA. I had cancelled today's lunch because I couldn't face further discussion on Mum's accusation right now; it didn't really fit in with my new, stable lifestyle and I'd also had time to reflect on our Tuesday lunches, which had become a regular occurrence for over six months now. She might have been able to approach the whole thing with an air of European sophistication, but for me it spelled a sugar and carb disaster ending in night sweats and lost contracts. Georgie had been more disappointed than I'd bargained for, so I invited her along on my quest to find a storage system for Charlotte's catastrophe of a bedroom. I would use my recovery time to restore order to my home: unused items would be given to charity; clothes would be hung or neatly folded; toys would be tidied away in boxes; and, by the time Christmas was upon us, I would be calm and organised, with my life perfectly back on track.

'There's an odd smell in here, Eliza. Is that some kind of organic air freshener?'

I'd got up early to vacuum out the car for the trip. I'd left the doors open for two hours and sprinkled lavender oil on the seats, but it still stank of rotting plant matter.

'It's lavender. Any news on Pierre?'

'Pierre is out.'

'Out where?'

'Out the door. Ditched. Back in the Channel Tunnel.'

'Well done. Now tell me everything.'

Georgie launched into a tirade involving Pierre's lack of evidence of pretty much everything; the ex-wife, the Antibes penthouse, the job. I listened to her scandalous tale—a stark contrast from her melancholic state of denial a few months earlier. Pierre might have been a smarmy, philandering bull-shitter, but he'd certainly given Georgie her mojo back.

'And the only thing he can say in Cantonese is: *Sorry, I don't speak Cantonese.*'

'You must've been upset, to think you'd been lied to like that?'

'Not really. An optimist sees the opportunity in every difficulty, my dear.'

'Dalai Lama?'

'Winston Churchill, for heaven's sake. Before I forget, I won't be around next Tuesday. Barbara and I have booked to see an exhibition at the V&A and we're staying in Sloane Square overnight. We're hoping to meet Valerie, you know, the old PA, for dinner.'

I sighed silently with relief. I was off the hook for next Tuesday and if I made an excuse for the following one, we could break the habit. We pulled into the car park.

'It's huge.' Georgie closed the car door and looked up in awe.

'Four floors. Still not as big as Selfridges.'

'Is there a personal shopping service?'

'No.'

We wandered around aimlessly, touching the fabric of chairs we didn't need, running our hands along dining tables and admiring decadent-looking throws which tempted us into thoughts of the impending winter, of cosying up in front of a fire with cocoa and a loved one, pretending that we were Swedish and cool and totally at one with ourselves. I thought of Lexie. *There you go, Lexie, I'm not a dried-up old hag just yet. I could still hit the odd ball, even if I couldn't quite manage to knock it out of the park.* Thoughts of the miscarriage made grief and anxiety jump up out of nowhere. I pushed them aside, thinking instead about whether monochromatic cushions would work in the lounge. It was hot and the screams of a nearby toddler were making my skull vibrate.

'Do you think I should get a new kitchen?'

'Georgie, why would you want a new kitchen? Your kitchen is amazing.'

'But look at this one. I can get the whole lot for less than three thousand pounds. It'll be good to have a change, a new start. Where's the sales assistant?'

'There isn't one. Why don't you pick up a brochure and have a think about it?'

We browsed the children's department and Georgie loaded the cart with rugs and giraffe lamps, foldable storage and glove puppets. What was it with the Swedes and puppets?

'I need to freshen up the children's room and I'm thinking about turning the office into a bedroom for Leo. What do you think about these curtains?' I went back outside to get another cart and cool down. I thought about getting into the car, driving home and going to bed for the rest of the afternoon, but decided that it was not conducive to getting one's life perfectly back on track.

Back inside I was sucked into the mass consumer vortex, picking out jungle-print bed canopies and duvet covers and other toys that weren't puppets. Charlotte needed an update to her room. I'd not been the best mother of late and this would help make up for it. Surely some vibrant scatter cushions and an oversized toy snake would negate the fact that I'd been a lunatic for the past six months?

The carpark was rammed and the air was clogged with fumes from nearby traffic. I lowered the back seats and slid the panels for Charlotte's new wardrobe through the middle of the car, where they nestled between the front seats with an inch to spare. We bolstered them with an assortment of soft furnishings; shot glasses and candles; a wok with quirky red handles; and canvas prints of Manhattan. All these pointless items bought to bring a sense of comfort and security to our lives. I drifted back to my idea about living a simpler life in a van or camping out under a canopy of trees with only the buzz of crickets and the calling of birds to assault my ears.

The blast of a car horn brought me back to reality. 'Are you moving, love, or what?' I turned to see a greasy-looking man with a roll-up stuck to his lip leaning out of a car window. He looked me over with indifference. 'I ain't got all day.'

I got into the car, started the engine and attempted to put it in reverse.

'How on earth are you supposed to drive home like this?' Georgie pushed the wardrobe panels back and forth.

'I'm sorry, Georgie, but you're going to have to rest them on the edge of your seat for a minute, just while I change gear.'

'Are you sure this is safe? Why don't you get them delivered?'

No matter how hard I rammed the gear stick against the panels, there wasn't enough room to engage it in reverse. Georgie was becoming impatient. 'This is terribly uncomfortable, Eliza.' The man honked his horn again, this time in long, continuous blasts at two-second intervals. Each blast reverberated through me, beating out the last of my patience. I got out of the car and stormed over to his window.

'Why don't you stop honking your stupid fucking horn and let me move my stupid fucking car so you can have your stupid fucking parking space, you rat-faced little prick?' My voice echoed around the car park and I saw a mother scoop up her young children in a panic and run into the store. She was about thirty-one.

As I walked back toward the car, he blasted the horn again, craning his neck out of the window. 'You need a big fat cock up your arse, you frigid bitch.'

Tears stung my eyes. When I climbed back into the car Georgie had moved the panels over to her seat and I reversed out.

We drove home in silence.

49

'Welcome, everybody, to the Old Girls' inaugural meeting. Cheers.'

We clinked our glasses. Sarah gave off an air of authority as she stood up with her notepad and pen. 'Is there anything anyone would like to discuss?'

We all talked at the same time about a variety of woes, the most common theme being tiredness and ungovernable rage.

'Last night I wanted to kill my husband,' Simone declared. 'That's really bad, isn't it?'

'No.' I was, naturally, first on the scene to defend her, but the others looked unsure. 'No, it's not bad to want to kill your husband. Well, it is bad if you *really* wanted to kill him and you hired a hitman or just did it yourself.' I laughed but no one else did. 'I think what you're feeling here is frustration. Outside influences such as lack of sleep, sugar intake and environmental toxins can play havoc with hormones and emotions.' I was repeating my consultation with the nutritionist word for word, but loving how sophisticated it made me sound, and the clever way it had defused the hot potato of husband-slaying.

'This is fantastic, Eliza, thank you,' Sarah said. 'And this is what I want to steer toward on these meetings. It's great that we can all come here and let off some steam, but I want these meetings to be productive. Yes, we might be angry or tired, but instead of just moaning, let's find out why and do something about it. And I'd also like to add, that all suggestions should be welcome with open arms, from modern medicine to natural remedies to gong therapy.'

'Hallelujah!' Susannah waved her hands in the air and there was a collective sigh of relief that their differing opinions had been put to rest. 'And what the hell is gong therapy?'

Sarah shrugged. 'No idea, just heard about it on a podcast and liked the sound of it.'

The meeting was all very business-like for a while, everyone putting their two cents in regarding the different items we shouldn't be using, from deodorant to nail polish. We talked about alternatives we'd tried and products that we'd found effective. It was sensible and productive and I could tell that Sarah was pleased.

Simone talked about a heaviness which many of us could relate to. 'I can't really explain it, but driving to school, remembering people's names, everything's such an effort. One of my patients wanted to talk about his traumatic childhood the other day and it took everything in my power not to tell him to shut the hell up. It's dreadful.'

'You need to look after yourself in order to care for others,' offered Emily, who, at thirty-five and with her optimism still intact, didn't quite fit the criteria for our meetings. 'Have you ever tried breathwork? It leaves you so energised.'

Simone showed no interest and sloped off to the bar to order a Guinness.

I recounted the IKEA car park scenario. Will had laughed too when I told him, but it had shaken me: the fact that I had let an arrogant, weedy little man get under my skin so much that I'd had to yell abuse at the top of my voice in the middle of the day in a public car park. I asked Susannah to retell her story about the time she got down on all fours and sobbed in a car park on Christmas Eve. Susannah laughed. Everyone laughed and congratulated us for actually following our true emotions. And I felt a little less crazy.

'That's something we'd all like to do,' Sarah said, 'but none of us do it because we've been taught to be nice girls, who aren't supposed to show anger or despair. We're going to implode if we're not careful.'

'That's what I keep saying,' Susannah said. 'There's nothing wrong with being angry every now and again, it's healthy. And if someone's pissed us off, why shouldn't we tell them?'

And that remained the topic of conversation until it was time to put another date in the diary and say our goodbyes. All in all, the first meeting was successful and hopefully beneficial for all of us. I cycled home to a Motown playlist and a feeling of optimism.

'I thought the whole idea of these meetings was about regaining your health. Why don't you call yourselves the Sauvignon Blanc Six?' Will laughed at the brilliance of his own wit.

'Because there were only five of us, we didn't drink wine, and, as a matter of fact, we did discuss health issues. Sarah thinks that I'm oestrogen-dominant. Did you know that weed killer has been found to produce gender changes in frogs?'

'Yes, I knew that. Then what? Did you spend the rest of the evening bitching about men?'

'Will, I'm serious. Male frogs have been turning into female frogs and I use weed killer all the time at work.'

'So you'll turn into a frog? No big deal, I'll still love you. What else? Any scandal?'

It was pointless trying to have a sensible conversation with Will when he was in this sort of mood and I knew better than to persevere. 'No scandal.'

'Oh. You feeling okay?'

'Yes, Will, I feel okay. Why shouldn't I?'

'Just checking. I'm glad you had a good time.'

I made tea and took myself off to bed to read what was left of last Sunday's paper. Tonight had been good fun and I felt happier for the most part. Sarah had suggested earlier that I talk about the miscarriage, saying it would be good to air it out; that maybe it would encourage others to open up about their feelings surrounding the loss of fertility. But I had decided against it and I was glad now—that was mine and Will's skeleton and I wasn't ready to regurgitate it for the sake of group discussion. I was ready to heal and move on.

50

'I CAN'T BELIEVE we flushed our baby down the toilet, what were we thinking?'

'Eliza, this is crazy. We did not flush our baby down the toilet.' Will reached forward to sweep the hair out of my face. 'I don't understand, you were so happy last night, what's changed?'

I was sitting on the bed, rocking back and forth, hugging my knees. I wasn't crying for a change and this confused Will, but there was an impish little corner of my brain that found it enjoyable: Mr Capable, not knowing what to do or say. I wondered if I had narcissistic tendencies.

'Do you think I'm a narcissist?'

'No, narcissists lack empathy; they certainly don't feel guilty all the time. Do you want me to call the doctor?'

'What on earth's she going to do? Fish it out of the drain with a net?'

I knew that I was being unreasonable and Will knew that I knew that, but I needed him to indulge me nonetheless.

'I'm not answering that. I'm going to make you some tea and then you need to tell me what happened.'

'I promised the Andersons that I'd have their lawn finished by this afternoon. Their grandson is flying in from Italy tonight.'

Will stopped dead at the top of the stairs, rubbed his hands over his face and shouted, 'Fuck the Andersons' fucking lawn.'

Will never shouts. Or swears.

I remained in an almost catatonic state while he slammed every possible cupboard door and piece of cutlery in the kitchen. The truth was, I'd no idea what had happened. One minute I had been standing outside the school gates chatting happily to Organic Emily about the upcoming Harvest Festival (She thought if we must give beans and soup, then we should try to buy brands that were packaged in BPA-free cartons, as not only did they carry less health risks, but were kinder to the environment and lighter for the children to carry up to the church. She got hers from Ocado.), and the next, my head was pulsing, vibrating.

'Okay, so what happened between talking to Emily and calling me?'

'I can't remember.' And that's what frightened me; I actually couldn't remember anything. All I knew was that I'd felt scared and had difficulty breathing. And driving. 'It felt like another person drove home. What if I jumped a red light or ran someone over without realising?'

'I'm phoning the doctor.'

'Please don't, Will.'

He ignored me. I was aware that I was talking drivel, but it was cathartic drivel. I didn't want to sit in the surgery's waiting room with all those other people. I'll never get an appointment today anyway, they're far too busy. What if Dr Chaudhry's on call and she comes to hiss at me on my own sofa?

'Hi, I'm Dr Hughes. Dr Chaudhry's in the surgery today and I'm on call so you'll have to put up with me, I'm afraid.'

'Nice to meet you, Dr Hughes.' It was very nice indeed to meet Dr Hughes: thirty-two maybe, lashings of dark glossy hair, soft stubble. I imagined that when he wasn't committing middle-aged women to psychiatric units, Dr Hughes played bass guitar in a local rock band.

I was sitting crossed-legged on the sofa and was trying a jovial approach to hide my embarrassment at the whole situation. I'd made a catastrophic decision to wear grease-stained joggers and not brush my teeth or hair. Not that my appearance mattered; he was a professional and I'm pretty sure it's not possible to be cured of a mental ailment the minute a hot doctor walks into the room.

'I'm just going to check you over. You can start by telling me what you remember. Take all the time you need, Eliza.' He smiled warmly. I thought about snogging him and our future life together: everyone would be shocked and naturally side with Will. I'd have to confess to Dr Hughes that Charlotte had not had her MMR booster because of something I'd read on the Internet and he would be very disappointed in me. No, that would never work.

He took my blood pressure and shone a torch into my eyes while I tried to retrace my steps from leaving the school. I regaled him with other tales of work stress and sleepless nights.

'Alright. Now, Eliza.' He rested his hand gently on my arm. 'Your husband told me about—'

'We're not married, just, you know, living together.'

'Alright, well your partner, Will, told me that you've recently miscarried. About two weeks ago, is that correct?'

'Correct, but the pregnancy was unplanned.'

'Which doesn't mean that it's any less traumatic physically or emotionally for you both, and I'm sorry for your loss.'

'Thank you, I've made a good recovery.'

'And you've gone back to work?'

'Yes, but I'm only doing six-hour days. I feel quite normal most of the time. I don't think I need to be locked up or anything.'

Dr Hughes broke into charming, gentle laughter. 'That's a shame. I had the straitjacket all ready for you.'

Quite clearly a hint at bondage. Outrageous.

'Eliza, I think you may've experienced a minor panic attack earlier. It's nothing to worry about and, as long as you heed the advice I'm about to give you, I'm sure you'll be back to your old self in a few days.'

Panic attack? I thought they were just for neurotic people?

'Okay, I'm listening.'

Dr Hughes adopted a serious, yet devastatingly sexy expression. 'You need rest and a lot of it. I would suspect that what happened earlier and how you're feeling now is a direct result of you pushing yourself too hard. A miscarriage is a major event to go through and you'll experience fluctuations in your hormone levels: one minute you'll be feeling fine and the next you'll not. Does that sound familiar?'

Oh yes. 'Um, sort of.'

'This is hard enough to deal with on its own, but when you're charging around doing school runs and mowing lawns, it's bound to come along and bite you in the bum at some point.'

I imagined Dr Hughes biting my bum while I protested feebly.

'Drink lots of water, eat a balanced diet, try to get some fresh air and gentle exercise. Avoid stress at all costs. Have you got someone who can pick up the slack for you at work?'

'Oh yes, that's not a problem.' I waved my hand nonchalantly, hoping to give off the air that I had a large and willing team of employees at my disposal.

'Excellent. Try to recognise how much you take on, Eliza. So many women are guilty of overdoing it these days. You need to make sure you look after yourself, as well as everyone else.'

If Will had said this I'd have called him a sexist twat.

'I'll try. Thank you, Dr Hughes,' I attempted an innocent smile which probably just made me look a bit simple and I made a mental note to double-check in the mirror later.

'I'm at the surgery on Tuesdays, Wednesdays and Fridays, so if you have any more problems, don't hesitate to call. Now you take care of yourself.' He stood up. He was about six foot one at a guess, muscular forearms. 'I'll see myself out.'

'He was pretty cool for a doctor, eh?'

'Yeah, he was alright.'

'How're you feeling?'

'I'm fine, Will, much better now.'

'So, panic attack then, eh?'

'It seems that way.'

'And you're working too hard.'

'Will, were you listening?'

'I was sending an email in the next room. I couldn't help but overhear the odd snippet. I've always thought you work too hard.'

'Well it's quite convenient to ease off for a while. Johnno's happy to work as much as he can before he goes away.'

'And we'll manage. Oh, by the way, I spoke to Susannah and she's going to help Johnno out at the Andersons' this afternoon,' Will said.

'Susannah? Really?'

'Yes, she seems really keen. That's alright, isn't it?'

'It's fine. I just know that she's been feeling a bit off-colour recently and I don't want to put on her.'

'Look, if she didn't want to do it, she wouldn't have offered. Please think about what the doctor told you and stop stressing about everything.'

Taking four of those little red pills that Dr Chaudhry prescribed and sleeping for the rest of the week would probably be the only way to *stop stressing about everything*. I'll take half of one later, they can't be that bad.

'Were you even going to tell him about the miscarriage?'

'You'd already told him, so I didn't need to.'

'Because I was worried you wouldn't. You need to face up to what's happened. It's been a big strain on us all.'

I slumped into Will's arms and, at last, the tears fell steadily. Will and the hot doctor were right, of course; it had been tough on him and Charlotte as well. I'd just been too self-indulgent to see it.

51

I CALLED JESS on FaceTime. She was at the house in Brookhaven packing up for the winter. Her iPad was propped up on the dressing table and I was watching her fold the bedding.

'I don't understand why you're stressing about something that happened thirty years ago. You should be resting.'

'I'm not stressing about it.' This was a big, fat juicy lie. I hadn't planned on discussing it with Jess but I'd had too much time on my own of late; too much time to overthink. 'I just want more information. Surely Mum wouldn't have said something like that if there was nothing in it?'

'There *was* nothing in it, Liza. I remember discussing it with Dad a couple of years after it all happened. You know he would never do anything like that. Mum was just a bit erratic when she was younger. She's much better these days. If you want a positive side of menopause; it definitely chilled Mum out.'

'But why didn't Dad discuss it with *me*?'

'Because you were like twelve or something, and you didn't know anything about it. We all thought it was best left that way. It was just you and Mum most of the time back then.'

'So you went off to school, Dad went off to Germany and I was left at home with a paranoid role model? That would explain a few things.'

'Oh come on, Eliza, it wasn't that bad. You used to stay with Georgie when Mum came to London, which was probably another reason not to upset the apple cart over something so petty.'

'It was alright for you.' As soon as the words were out of my mouth I wanted to gobble them back up again. Jess was fully aware of how her leaving home at fourteen affected me, and now, almost forty years later, it was a cheap shot and I needed to drop it. 'Sorry. Look, whatever you do, don't mention it to Mum.'

'Mention it to Mum? Are you crazy?' Jess said. 'Georgie should never have brought it up in the first place, not while you're going through all this. That woman's a damn drain on you.'

'Well, it was sort of relevant to something else we were talking about.'

'What then? What was it relevant to?'

Maybe I should tell her, lay it on the line. Who's to say Jess wasn't doing the same thing three thousand miles away? Her Facebook life looked like a whirlwind of charity balls and inspirational quotes, but what if her reality involved standing on the dining table, glass of wine in hand, charging Mark with adultery?

'Nothing. How's Jake getting on at Yale?'

'Jake's fine.' She zipped up a vacuum bag and sat down on the bed to give me her full attention. 'I'm worried about you, Liza-loo. I really wanted you to come over this Christmas.'

'Yeah, well, I can't.' I had taken a little red pill last night and was not in the right frame of mind to deal with my outwardly together, albeit slightly neurotic sister.

'Listen, I've spoken to Mark. He's more than happy to help out. He's got some Airmiles that need using up.'

'No, Jessie, I just can't. Please thank Mark, but neither Will nor I would feel comfortable with that. And, besides, he's got a lot of work on around Christmas.'

'Then why don't you and Charlotte come out?'

'And leave Will on his own?'

'Sorry, no, I'm not suggesting that. I'd just like to see you, to chat and laugh and catch up.'

'Then come to England.'

'It's difficult, Liza, with Mark's hours and Lydia's classes.'

'How's all that going?' I asked, unable to disguise my disdain.

'Well if she wants to audition for Juilliard next year, she'll need to buck up her ideas. She'll nail the ballet, but her Modern is frankly appalling.'

'Maybe she hates it.'

'Eliza, don't be ridiculous. Just because you hated dance doesn't mean that everyone hates dance. I don't think you appreciate how talented Lydia is.'

'I didn't say she wasn't talented, I'm merely asking you to explore the idea that she might like to participate in other hobbies. What does she really love doing?'

'She really loves dancing, Eliza.' Jess was starting to lose patience and, as I was trying to avoid stress, I changed the subject.

'How's the temperature there at the moment? It looks sunny.'

But it was too late: she pulled *the face* and we were probably better off saying goodbye. But we didn't: we battled on through, trying to pretend that I hadn't upset her.

'It's pleasant; high sixties.' Jess slapped on a fake bright smile and went back to stuffing pillows into bags. 'Tell me about all the good clean living you're going to do to get back on your feet. I hope you're using that cookbook I sent you.'

'Of course. I love the juices.' As luck would have it, through the utter boredom of resting at home, I'd picked up the book for the first time two days ago and, conveniently, it was resting on the arm of the sofa. I held it up to the camera. 'Look, see.' I flicked it open to a random salmon recipe. 'This one looks amazing.'

Her face lit up. 'Oh, I've done that one. Now, you must

make sure you get the freshest asparagus you can find.' And, just like that, Jess was restored to her former place of glory. And maybe that's just how it would always be with my sister.

I told her that I was seeing Helen, my nutritionist, the following week and Jess asked me about her qualifications, of which I had no idea. She strongly advised me to find out. She also thinks that:

Will and I should have some counselling regarding my miscarriage and the fact that I was perimenopausal with only one child;

I should limit time spent with Georgie and put my own family's needs first;

I should get Charlotte tested for dyslexia;

I should seriously consider rebranding my business;

I should give up coffee.

My lethargic state enabled me to nod my head in agreement to her every word, so we ended the call on a happy note. Jess was satisfied in her role as my transatlantic life coach and would carry on ignoring what was happening to her own daughter on home turf.

Susannah was doing the school pick-up and popping in for a cup of tea in just over an hour. I flicked through the recipe book and was amazed to see that I had all the ingredients for a roasted vegetable quinoa dish and so set to it in the kitchen.

I took great comfort in carefully chopping up the vegetables into small, perfectly even pieces, mulling over Jessica's words; on how our mother had been erratic when we were growing up. What did she really mean by *erratic*? Is that what Georgie meant when she said I was always so up and down? Was this what was referred to as deep-rooted behaviour patterns?

I was so engrossed in scrubbing the grime off of the roasting pan, that the doorbell made me jump out of my skin. The children charged in and dived onto the sofa, all appearing slightly deranged. 'They had Haribo on the way home,' explained Susannah without apology.

She waited for them to disappear upstairs. 'Did I tell you how much fun I had on Friday?'

'What, mowing the Andersons' lawn?'

'Johnno and I got on *really* well.' Susannah winked.

'Susannah!' I had a shocking image of them doing the unmentionable atop Mr Anderson's sit-on mower, partially disrobed and covered in grass clippings. 'He's twenty-two years old.'

'So? I had a great-aunt who married someone twenty-five years her junior. Not that I'm suggesting that Johnno and I will marry...not yet.'

'Please tell me you didn't.' I feigned disgust.

'Shag him on top of the mower? Of course not. He'd never be the same again.' Susannah looked better today, with a healthy complexion and a spring in her step.

'I've made us dinner.'

'Eliza, you're supposed to be resting. If there was ever a time for ready meals, this is it.'

'I was bored and it's the least I can do when you're mowing my lawns and running around after my child.'

'And lusting over your staff.'

'Stop objectifying Johnno, the last thing I need is a tribunal on my hands.'

But she didn't. She spent the rest of the evening cracking brazen jokes and making me glad I had such inappropriate friends.

52

'Each night, I'd like you to ask yourself this question: Do I really need to take these pills?'

'I only ever take half. I've read about the side effects but they can't be that bad if my doctor prescribed them.'

'The doctors are practically trained by the pharmaceutical companies.' Helen slammed the palm of her hand onto the desk, causing me to jolt in my chair. 'You need to stop thinking that kind-hearted scientists in white lab coats are sitting around tables with concerned faces trying to cure cancer.'

'Oh, okay.' That's exactly what I thought happened.

'I know it's harsh, but Big Pharma shareholders don't give a shit about your health.' She stopped herself and sat upright in her chair. 'I apologise. That was very unprofessional.'

'Not at all. I'm a big fan of swearing.'

Helen had just returned from a course in Luxemburg outlining food–drug interactions. 'You take a drug because you think it helps you sleep or keeps you alive, and that same drug will prevent your body from absorbing nutrients needed by cells to keep the body healthy. We're on a senseless hamster wheel.'

'I hear what you're saying, but Will's always telling me to stop stressing about everything. I suppose it's just an easy option.'

'All I'm saying, Eliza, is that you're not ill and I don't think you need medication. You know the clean diet works for you;

you've done it before. Just talk to Will. Tell him when you're feeling crazy and stop trying to dull it all down with pills.'

'I do talk to him. I just thought he might need a break from me ranting on all the time.'

'What about friends? Do you meet friends for coffee? On second thoughts, I'm banning that. You'll be meeting for herbal tea.'

Banning coffee? Again?

I told Helen about our Old Girls group.

'That's such a great idea.'

'Thanks, yes, it's really beneficial.' No need to mention that it's held in the pub, not interesting.

'Try and do a quick catch-up with someone at least once a week, even if it's just for an hour. You're working on your own a lot and it's easy to overthink.'

'Is that why I had a panic attack? From overthinking?'

'We'll get on to that in a moment. For now, you're going to cut out all the usual suspects, just for a couple of weeks, and then reintroduce them slowly, with a view to everything in moderation, except sugar of course. Oh—and coffee, but we'll get to that.'

'What are usual suspects?'

'Dairy, gluten, sugar, alcohol, caffeine, any additives and processed foods.'

'What about sourdough bread?'

'No sourdough, not yet. Let's get you back on track and kickstart that gut health. We'll get a supplement programme together to support that. I want to see rainbow salads, home-made soups, everything organic and clean, clean, clean.'

'When can I start having coffee again?' I was trying not to sound desperate.

'Ah, yes, the coffee.' She put down her pen and turned her chair to deliver the prognosis. 'How many cups are you having a day now?'

'Two or three.'

'I see.' She didn't fall for it. 'Well let's cut that down to one a day for the next few days and then none when you start your programme next week. You can start weaning yourself off of the other culprits over the next few days too, just to prepare yourself.'

'Yes, good idea.' I tried to sound excited.

'Your symptoms strongly suggest that your adrenals are depleted. You're running a business, raising a child and you've just had a miscarriage. A panic attack is a red light to slow down and take better care of yourself. It's tempting to knock back a few coffees to wake you up in the morning and have a glass of wine at night to wind down, but both cause stress on the adrenals.'

'So no more wine then?'

'One glass won't hurt, but I'd like you to go without for at least two or three weeks. It'll help everything balance out. The human body is amazing, Eliza. If it couldn't fix itself, none of us would be here, but you have to help it.'

'And coffee, when am I allowed to have that again?'

'When you finish the cleanse. But I'd really like you to stick to one a day.'

'For the rest of my life?'

She smiled warmly. 'There are worse things, Eliza.'

'Of course, yes. Sorry.'

'There are some health benefits, but too much coffee has been linked with heart problems and anxiety, it can cause insomnia, irritability and aggression. Do you see where I'm going with this?'

'Yes, I understand,' I said, holding up my hands.

'On your health plan, I'm going to recommend a chicory substitute. It's delicious and I bet you won't taste the difference.'

I bet I would. 'Will it make me feel like I can take on the world?'

'Probably not, no. I'm also going to recommend a homeopath. She's amazing, specialises in hormones. Her diary is full of women like us.'

'Like us?'

Helen lowered her glasses. 'You know—skimming fifty.'

I left Helen's office with an overall feeling of excitement. There was apprehension regarding the coffee exodus, but I'd done it before and I remembered how good it felt. The caffeine, the excess wine and the soft, doughy bread from my local bakery had simply become a way of life, a little routine which could be easily broken.

I got into my car, reached into the glove box and pulled out my stash of Haribo. I ate one and threw the rest into a nearby bin, making a silent vow to loosen my grip on some worn-out old habits.

53

'Good evening, Georgina.'

'Good evening, Harry. I must say, you're looking on fine form this evening.'

'I'm feeling on fine form, thank you.' A charismatic grin lit up Harry's face before he took a long glug from a water bottle. We both remained silent, transfixed by the pulsing of his Adam's apple, the excess liquid escaping from the corners of his mouth and running down his chin to nestle into the folds of his t-shirt. Harry wiped his face and returned to the court, positioning himself for a powerful serve.

'He's got an odd gait, don't you think?'

'It's hard to tell from here. Maybe he's sprained a muscle or got something in his shoe.'

'Hmm, maybe.' Georgie studied him carefully as he tossed the ball into the air and coiled his body before slamming it across the net toward his poised opponent.

Fault.

'Why is that a fault?' I asked.

'No clue, darling. I wasn't paying attention to the technicalities. Fancy a glass of wine?'

'No, I'm on another cleanse. And I'm driving.'

'A small one?'

'I'll have a water, thanks.'

'I'll see what I can do.' Georgie slipped out of her seat and headed toward the bar. It was unusual for us to meet of an evening, but she had been volunteering at the tennis club for the men's Round Robin and had asked me to join her for some spectating. I'll admit that I hadn't banked on it being quite so much fun.

'They were out of water so I got you a wine spritzer. It's practically the same thing. So, how are you feeling, you know, in yourself?'

I hadn't told her about the panic attack so I presumed she was referring to the IKEA car park incident, which we still hadn't discussed.

'I haven't had any more public outbursts, if that's what you're referring to.'

'That's not what I meant. Are you back at work?'

'Part time, yes.'

'Well, I have to say you're looking good on it.'

Other people had told me I looked better too. One of the Lycra mums said I looked *fresher* and then asked for the number of my Botox doctor. I was sleeping for seven hours straight most nights and there'd been a sharpness to my thinking. My mind was quieter and stuff was getting done.

'Thank you.'

'Although I still think you should retire and spend more time with me, you could join the tennis club. They've got a gym here too. Think how fit and healthy you'd be.'

Financial implications aside, I didn't think retirement would suit me. I'd seen too many feisty, switched-on women become despondent when they gave up work; searching for fulfilment in gyms or Buddhism or affairs. I briefly entertained the idea of becoming a lady of leisure, driving to the tennis club in a white convertible with Shellacked nails and a leopard-print scarf. The air around us was thick with testosterone and I imagined having a casual fling with a young tennis coach. I studied Harry, who was wiping the sweat from his brow with the bottom of his t-shirt, revealing shiny ripped abs.

A pleasant thought, but I'd become a predictable monstrosity of a person and all my friends would hate me.

'How's that spritzer going down? You could always leave your car here if you fancied having a few drinks; we could share a taxi home.'

'Georgie, no. I've got to take Charlotte to school in the morning and then I'm going to see the Andersons.'

'Oh well,' Georgie sighed, disheartened by my lack of frivolity. 'And how are the Andersons?'

'They're great, I saw them yesterday. They're really pleased with the Persian garden.'

'I should think so too with all that hard work you put in. What an asset for them. I bet they'll be hosting parties every weekend next summer. Or orgies.'

Harry and his opponent shook hands and left the court to gather around a large name sheet. Georgie craned her neck to see them. 'I wonder who's up next?'

'Are there more games?'

'Of course. Each player has to compete against each other. We'll move down to the other end if it's no one interesting.'

'Are you coming to us for Christmas this year?' I asked. 'Will's parents are away but Susannah and her clan will be with us on Christmas Day.'

'Tom's supposed to be coming down for Christmas, but he's being very elusive about everything this year. I hope Tara's not hatching some plan to spend it with David and Linny. I don't think I'd handle that very well. New York's definitely off, then?'

'Definitely. I'd love to see them all, but we've made the decision and I think Will's relieved, to be honest. He's got a lot of work on right now.'

'And how did it go down with everyone else?'

'So-so. Jess is disappointed, but she understands. Mum's being...well, you know, Mum.'

Georgie said nothing, preferring to focus on the court action than return to the subject that had been haunting me for the last two months.

'Oh.' Georgie motioned toward the new players in front of us. 'The one in the green shirt is Victor Davidson. Barbara dated him briefly after her husband died; a small penis and a bad loser.'

'This could be entertaining. Shall we stay here?'

'Hmm, maybe,' Georgie scanned the other courts to see if there was anything better on offer. 'I'm getting a top-up from the bar. Anything for you?'

I was only allowed water or herbal tea on my cleanse but there was only one day left. I'd already ruined it with the spritzer and now I was in a rebellious mood. 'A Coke please, not diet.' I'd regret it later: lying in bed, wired, listening to Will's snoring, conjuring up ridiculous situations about not being able to pay the mortgage or someone dying. Or obsessing over family-related issues which continued to simmer away underneath my skin, telling me that there's more to the story than meets the eye.

Georgie navigated her way up to the mezzanine level. When she sat down, I noticed that her eyes were glazed and she wore the benign smile that always brought out her malleable side, which I decided to exploit.

'So how did David and Dad handle it then, when Mum was saying all those daft things?'

'What daft things?'

'Come on, Georgie, you know what.'

'Oh, that. Look, I don't know why I brought it up. I was just concerned that you were becoming so unnecessarily suspicious of everyone. It serves no purpose now, thirty years on.'

'Well, I think it does and I think it would help me to talk about it.'

Georgie sighed. 'Your dad and Uncle David handled it like typical men: they stuck their heads in the sand and left me to deal with it all. Anyway, let's not get into it now.'

'But how was she with you after Dad died?'

'Still bitter. Truth be told, I think she felt foolish after the accusation, as it shone the light on her...' Georgie paused, as if to catch herself.

'On her what?'

'Nothing.' She averted her eyes and looked for something to distract her. 'That ball was out. I'm surprised Victor didn't pick up on that.'

'Georgie. She accused you of sleeping with her husband, she was bitter and miserable for years, and now you think I'm following in her footsteps. You can't say it's *nothing*.'

Georgie raised her glass and tossed a mighty slug of wine to the back of her throat, like a cowboy knocking back whisky in an old Western; a lipstick-wearing cowboy with a Gucci neckerchief.

'Look, it wasn't that bad, okay. And you're certainly not following in her footsteps. Unless you're sleeping with your neighbour.'

'Pardon?'

54

'You're exhausted. You need to stop working,' Simone said. 'Believe me, I know a worn-out woman when I see one.'

'It was a one-off,' I said, 'and my job isn't exactly high-pressured.'

'I don't think work is the issue here. It's the non-stop emotional roller coaster of the last few months,' Susannah said.

I silently sipped my merlot, my panic attack being the hot topic of conversation at this month's Old Girls meeting. But a few weeks had passed and time had smoothed out a lot of the sharp edges. My mind was awash with new information from Georgie and I found it difficult to concentrate on anything else.

'My mum had an affair for eighteen years.'

'What?'

'Sorry, I know it's a bit off-topic, but my mum had an affair with our neighbour when I was twelve and it lasted for eighteen years. I've only just found out about it.' I welled up unexpectedly and Sarah hugged me. Susannah fetched me a brandy from the bar and everyone gushed their sympathy.

'Sorry, I don't know why I said that. Let's talk about something else.'

'No, tell us. Please.'

'Are you okay?'

I felt like a needy social media post with a pulse and a cognac; the post where someone you hardly knew had woken up with a head cold or a tax bill and updated their status with:

Can life get any worse? I acted it out too; everyone asked for details to which I protested, saying it wasn't important and I didn't want to talk about it, knowing full well that I did want to talk about it—a lot.

Georgie had exposed the epic saga, or rather I'd extracted it from her while she was steeped in wine, but she'd regretted telling me afterwards and become sketchy on the details: Ed, the neighbour, worked abroad too, so maybe it had been more off than on over that time, and eighteen years was a bit of a guess.

Will was matter-of-fact; 'People have affairs all the time,' he'd said, barely looking up from the TV. I'd managed to bite my tongue but a hot lava hissed and spat underneath my skin. It was only when Susannah suggested that it was actually a rather noteworthy scandal, and that maybe the group needed something other than insomnia or bloating to dissect, that I erupted.

People offered varying advice and questions: Was I angry? Did your dad know? Will I confront her? Give it time to sink in. She must've been lonely with your dad working away all the time. What about Ed's wife?

Mum and Jean used to attend pottery classes together. The four of them went on holiday to the Algarve when I was sixteen, for heaven's sake, and left me with Georgie for a week.

'Have you been feeling okay otherwise?' Sarah asked. 'When do you see the homeopath?'

'Not until the first week of November, but I've just finished a two-week cleanse and was feeling pretty good until I found out about this.'

I'd felt a range of emotions over the past few months: anxiety, guilt, grief, remorse, but, IKEA car park incident aside, not anger. But yesterday I'd woken at 7a.m. to the red shroud wrapping me so tightly that I could barely breathe. I faked an emergency sprinkler fault and raced over to the Andersons' to embark on a dawn massacre of their laurel hedge. It was long overdue and they were always up early anyway. Once finished, I had coffee, freshly baked cinnamon buns, and a heart-warming conversation about barn owls with Mrs A in the kitchen, while Will rushed around the house, trying to eat breakfast and make sandwiches and find school shoes.

'Did you have to live without wine?' Simone asked.

'Yep. And bread, and cheese.'

'Then what exactly *did* you eat?'

'I could have quinoa, salmon, beetroot, artichoke...' I was trying to remember the tasty meals from my cleanse plan, but my interpretation to the group sounded like I was reading from the menu of an upmarket concentration camp.

Everyone looked horrified apart from Emily. 'That sounds amazing, you must forward the recipes on to me.'

Emily went on to tell us about a dynamic breathwork class which claimed to shift emotion and nurture creativity. Susannah and Sarah were sceptical, and I felt a surge of empathy for Emily. She was so wise yet so innocent, learning from us older women, and probably vowing never to become like any of us.

Sarah told everyone she'd not had a period for ten months. 'It's such a relief. Hopefully they'll stop all together.' And she meant it.

'I've not had one for five months,' I said. 'Not a proper one.'

'That's great though, isn't it?' Sarah said. 'Imagine the freedom.'

I sat back, slightly breathless. No, I wasn't ready for that sort of freedom right now. I would speak to the homeopath about it and she would give me a lovely bottle of tiny pills and everything would return to normal.

I took my time cycling home, feeling somehow alien to the rest of the group. Did I honestly think, in my brush with fertility, that I'd escaped the inevitable? Had I secretly hoped to prove a point; that my perimenopausal diagnosis was all a silly misunderstanding and Dr Chaudhry had got my results mixed up with another, older patient? Had Mum shagged Ed in the bed she shared with my father? Gross. Ed smelt of wet dog and had a ginger beard which always had chutney in it. The sedative effect of the merlot and the cognac had been neutralised by my sheer fury at the hypocrisy of it all. I decided to take a detour, whacking up the gears and peddling as fast as I could. It felt good, grunting out the frustration of the last two days. As I reached the top of the hill, I decided that Emily's breathwork class was probably not as fluffy as it sounded, that near hyperventilation actually was a stress buster. I stopped and let the endorphins flood my system, replacing the anger with a nugget of righteousness, and a sense that change was on the horizon.

55

THERE WAS A comprehensive display of books on the table in the homeopath's waiting room, along with a large bowl of apples and, as I was early, I ate one. The cleanse had finished ten days earlier, but I'd surprised myself by carrying on with most of it. Recent revelations would have ordinarily sent me head first into a sea of gin and French pastries, but I'd managed to rein it in to a degree—apart from coffee consumption, which was creeping up by the day.

The door to the consulting room swung open to reveal a woman in her late fifties: formidable eyebrows, grey roots that looked almost intentional, and full lips that had no doubt mesmerised decades of admirers. She was followed by another lady: tall, slim, sharp business suit, equally sharp nose. I waited patiently while they shared a joke about the woes of running in heels. I hoped that Jane was the eyebrows. She was.

The businesswoman left. Jane walked over to greet me with a friendly handshake. 'Please come in and sit down.'

'What brings you here today?' she asked. I told her that Helen had sent me and mumbled something about my hormones. She asked questions: food likes and dislikes; was I happy indoors or outside? Bowel movements—consistency and regularity? Was I bothered by the heat or the cold? How was my sleep?

We talked about periods, or lack of them, about family health history. We moved onto emotions. What made me happy or excited? Angry or sad? What was I scared of? What did I worry about? I told her about the miscarriage and the panic attack, and tried not to dull anything down.

'We have to build up a picture,' Jane said, 'and I must understand your spirit: what makes you shrink and what makes you shine. Only then can we bring about a harmony of body and mind.'

I didn't hold back on giving her my life story.

'I'm glad to see that you take your diet seriously and that you're out in the fresh air, keeping fit with your job. Can I ask if you wear protective clothing like gloves and boots at work?' she said.

No, I wear stilettos and a ballgown. 'Yes, I generally wear gloves and boots.'

'And this recent project, this carpet garden, did you wear boots and gloves then?'

I wasn't sure where she was going with this and it felt a little like a cross-examination in a courtroom.

'No, that was different; it was summer and we weren't using any fertilisers.'

'Mmmm.' Jane nodded her head and smiled. She seemed pleased with my answer and fell silent to write some notes in her book. 'And you felt stressed during this time or happy?'

'A mixture; I was stressed doing the planning, but happy doing the planting.'

'Oh yes,' Jane enthused. 'You love feeling the earth between your fingers and are not content with sitting in front of a screen—that makes a lot of sense. This is excellent, Eliza, really good.'

'Why is that good?'

'Because you're open and honest, which makes you easy to read, and allows me to form a very clear picture. Let's go back to your emotional wellbeing and talk more about your guilt issues regarding your family.'

'I don't think I've ever been called open and honest before.'

'But life is changing; you are changing. And maybe changing allows you to be more open and honest.'

And with that prompt, I told Jane my innermost phobias; the realisations of the past few months that I'd struggled to even tell Will—that Charlotte was growing up too quickly; that I've meandered my life away, going from job to job, travelling whenever the opportunity arose; that I was too old to have another child; that I didn't phone my sister enough and an unspoken distance had grown between us.

I told Jane that everyone was disappointed in me and I'd never actually said that out loud before.

'Who is disappointed in you?'

'Just everyone.'

'Be specific.'

'Family. And some friends.'

'Let's identify them.'

I made a futile stab at dancing around this for some time, telling weak tales of a time when I may've said something wrong or let someone down, but she wasn't going to let it go.

'Let's talk about how your parents fit in to all of this, shall we?' Jane asked, with an encouraging and almost excitable smile, like it might be a fun thing to do.

And, as odds would have it, it kind of was.

I was around five or six years old, sitting outside a ballet classroom, with Mum speaking in hushed words to the teacher, a feeling of dread in my stomach. At twelve, Mum cried when Jess was away at school and Dad was working abroad. *'There's nothing you can do,'* she'd sobbed, when I'd tried to comfort her. At age thirteen, caught with cigarettes that we'd stolen from my friend's sister. I was a disgrace—Jess would never have smoked. In the Hamburg hospital, clearing out Dad's room when Mum and Jess arrived. *'You should've buzzed for the doctor sooner. They might've been able to do something.'*

On and on I whirred, about perceptions of this and reactions to that.

Jane put down her pen and turned her chair to face me, 'Let's imagine for a moment that your mother had been wise enough to accept that you were your own person; even appreciated that you were your own person.' She spoke slowly and with great authoritative tone. 'Do you think that you may feel differently about yourself?'

I looked at her for quite some time, unable to speak. It did all seem quite obvious, but no one had ever said it directly.

'People generally try to be the best that they're able to be, Eliza, but if that person's best is judging a fish on its ability to climb a tree, then that person is going to feel disappointed in the world around them, which is a sad place to be indeed. We should observe and move on, careful not to fall foul of the same trait.'

'Yes,' was all I could manage in response.

'Sit quietly for a moment while I make some notes,' Jane said.

And I did, incapable of much else. This was not at all what I'd expected. I'd presumed we'd have a quick chat about hormone balance and I'd be on my way with a bottle of tiny placebo pills. I had not been expecting full-blown therapy. I thought of the times that Charlotte had irked me by not doing something I'd expected of her: did she feel how I'd felt? Were we all destined to carry on this cycle of disappointment and attack?

'First and foremost, it would be preferable if you could adhere to your current healthy eating regime. This will keep your immune system in check and you'll get the most out of the remedy I'm going to give you. Are you back at work full time?'

'Almost.'

'Where possible, only do things you enjoy. Try to delegate the rest. I know the weather's cooling down, but as long as you're not using pesticides, try to work without gloves. You were destined to be among nature, Eliza; you need the electrical charge from the earth, it's what makes you tick. You'll feel better for that alone.'

I didn't understand anything about electrical charges but I could ask Will later; he'd know. I didn't ask any more questions. I was overwhelmed and had already been there half an hour over my time.

'The remedy I'm going to give you today is not too strong. It won't open up the floodgates, nor will it immediately fix your night sweats or cure your mood swings. But it will help you with acceptance; acceptance for who you are and the choices you have made—which were the right choices for you. You should start feeling a little more balanced, and this will support you to overcome some of the other problems. Let's see how that goes and if you feel you need to, come back and see me.'

'Thank you, I feel better already.'

'Remember not to discount other therapies if you need them. I can work with your doctor or a hormone specialist if you feel you need more help, take it one step at a time.'

She opened the door and I was relieved to see no one else in her waiting area.

'I'm sorry,' I said. 'Have I gone into your lunch hour?'

Jane shook her head and smiled. I reached out to hug her, this person I'd known for only ninety minutes, and cried. But these were different tears, these were tears of transformation, of clarity.

56

I MIGHT HAVE cooked the turkey just right this year. Usually, it was either tough as leather or I had to return it to the oven for another hour while we watched all the other vegetables turn to stale mush before our eyes. This was different from previous years, probably helped by not jumping out of bed on Christmas Eve in an overly excited festive frenzy, downing four coffees and two mince pies for breakfast then sending out a spur-of-the-moment WhatsApp inviting everyone over for an open house. The rest of the day would then be lost in a fog of cleaning and panicked trips to the supermarket because everyone replied: *We'd love to!* when we were sort of thinking half of them might have other commitments. And ten packets of puff-pastry canapés and thirty sloe-gin cocktails later, we're seeing out the last of the, usually child-free, guests at midnight when we still had to wrap presents, throw half-chewed carrots onto the lawn and tramp floury footprints around the fireplace before getting up at 5 a.m.

This Christmas Eve we had taken care of ourselves: a long, rainy walk through the forest in the morning, followed by a spontaneous lunch at Georgie's. She'd had a very special delivery and we absolutely had to pop in to see it. The special delivery was Dan, who'd arrived home for the foreseeable future. We'd heard him talk of his amazing girlfriend Nicola, from Newcastle, before. But we'd all assumed that she'd been from Newcastle, Australia, not Newcastle upon Tyne. 'Nice to meet you, pet,' she said, embracing me. 'Sorry about my big fat belly,' she pulled back to reveal a perfectly neat bump, which was probably about the size that mine would've been by now, had my pregnancy been successful.

She was due in March, and my cousin, always searching, always a bit out of place, had never looked happier. Georgie was delirious and I felt, along with my elation at this new family unit, an overwhelming sense of respite—and a quiet appreciation that things had turned out the way they had.

We were back home by mid-afternoon for hot chocolate and *Miracle on 34th Street* in front of the wood burner; just the three of us. We chatted on FaceTime to the New Yorkers. Both Lydia and Jake were there to whip Charlotte into a frenzy, telling her that, according to the Track Santa app, the big man would be hovering over our house at 8 p.m., so she'd better be asleep by then.

My mother was there, talking over them in her usual fashion, but it didn't bother me so much now: I found it a funny quirk, rather than an infuriating obsession. We'd met for lunch a couple of times, since my discoveries about her past and the insightful visit to the homeopath, but I'd not made any incriminating remarks or asked for any explanations. It was calming to simply view her in a different light, to feel a vague sorrow for her, as she sat there, judging fish on their ability to climb trees, knowing how deeply let down she must be by her own abilities, her own actions. She was quieter too, picking up on my newfound ease.

'Gerald, for Christ's sake, don't feed them any more chocolate coins.' I opened the door to Simon balancing bags of gifts and bottles of wine. He looked harassed and exhausted, just as I would've looked this time last year.

'Hey, Merry Christmas! Was this your first time waking up with the kids on Christmas morning?' I didn't even try to disguise my amusement.

'Yes, and it didn't help that *she*,' he nodded at Susannah

who was struggling to clamber out of Gerald's Chelsea Tractor, 'kept me up half the night drinking mulled wine and making this stupid bloody dessert, which you lot had better appreciate.'

'Oh we'll appreciate it, don't you worry.'

'And what is it with the 4 a.m. alarm call? They literally jumped on me, while Gerald slept through it all.'

Simon and Gerald usually spent Christmas Eve at a civilised dinner party or with one of their parents. I imagine they'd lie in the following morning, rising at around 11 a.m. for Eggs Benedict and a chilled glass of champagne. Simon would have a leisurely drive down on Boxing Day morning and arrive, armed with fresh presents and giant chocolate reindeers, to a hero's welcome.

They piled into the house. Gerald brought high-end fizz and home-made hors d'oeuvres. The children were loaded with chocolate and more gifts. Susannah walked behind them with a large covered plate—the on-trend dessert that she'd been talking about for the whole of December; the one that was gracing the household of everyone who's anyone this Christmas.

Susannah walked gingerly toward the table, snapping at the children. 'For goodness sake, Teddy, get out of my way.' It was unlike her. It must've been a very late night.

I quickly cleared a space on the table. 'Put it here, Suze. Are you alright?'

'Yes, fine. I just need to check that the—'

'That the what?'

Her mouth opened, but nothing came out and she frowned at me before she hit the floor, like I might have the answer to what was happening. She took the dessert with her and that's all I could think about for the first few seconds: about how much work she'd put into it and how excited she'd been. Now it was just a wreck of green meringue and chocolate mousse, seeping into the creases of the chairs, down the legs of the table and into Susannah's hair, which she'd taken the unusual step of putting up in a chignon.

It was Gerald who took control, who realised, ahead of all of us, that Susannah wasn't just pulling a festive prank; that she wasn't going to leap up and shout, '*Ha-ha, I had you all there for a minute*' and crack open the Moët.

It unfolded slowly: Gerald and Will putting her into the recovery position; Simon emerging from the bathroom, his face creased with confusion. I threw myself into clearing up mode, with kitchen towels and wet dishcloths. I even took a tiramisu out of the freezer, assuring everyone that it only took two hours to defrost.

But that was before we realised that Susannah couldn't actually speak, that the only sounds coming from her mouth were primal grunts, that one side of her face had collapsed and she didn't seem to recognise her own children.

But Gerald, the born city boy with his cutting humour and edgy fashion, whose sophisticated mind I tortured with my trivial chit-chat, came to life. It was Gerald who checked her breathing, her heartbeat. And it was Gerald who made the swift decision to take her straight to A&E, saying those words: 'She's had a stroke.'

57

GERALD KNEW A lot about strokes; his brother had been left paralysed by one three years previously. He knew they weren't just for the elderly or people who didn't take care of themselves. They could affect anyone at any time, even your best friend on Christmas Day before you'd had the chance to be wowed by her dessert or compliment her hairdo.

Will and I carried on the best we could. Teddy cried when they carried her to the car and Tilly became the grown-up, repeating my assurances that Mummy would be back in time for dinner. But Mummy was not back in time for dinner. We had hourly updates: waiting for this doctor and those test results. Waiting for the scan, for the prognosis. We played games and opened some presents, we tried to eat dinner. Tilly and Charlotte appeared oblivious to the catastrophe that consumed us, playing make-believe games with shiny new dolls that were getting married or working in cafes. But now was not the time to liberate them or insist that the dolls become company directors or gender fluid scientists. Today I silently observed their sectarian performance from the sofa, where I spent most of the day cuddled up with Teddy. He'd stopped crying, but was clingy, following me around the house and waiting for me every time I came out of the bathroom. Simon and Gerald came to collect the children at 9 p.m. They'd been told to go home: she'd been given a drug that could drastically help her recovery, but the recovery could be long and she would need to rest.

I was up early the following day but was not allowed to visit until noon. Will and Charlotte went to Georgie's as planned and I was disgusted with myself for feeling relieved that I didn't have to sit through another meal with Tara, who would be shamelessly taking all the credit for moving Dan and Nicola back from Australia: *'Of course I told them they should move back home. Of course my assistant arranged all the travel. Of course it was my idea that they had intercourse and made a baby.'*

I was not in the mood for Tara today.

After they left, I had an hour to kill. I tidied up the house and sorted out the recycling, I flicked through Instagram and looked at people I hardly knew standing by artfully decorated Christmas trees, holding flutes of bubbles or babies or pets. I put a toiletry bag together for Susannah with a hairbrush, a bamboo flannel and the face cream from Georgie that I'd never used. I packed fruit and chocolates and the Christmas present that she didn't get to open. I left early because I couldn't bear to be at home a minute longer. I needed to make sure I got a parking spot anyway and it would give me time to nip into the hospital shop and pick up a new toothbrush and a *Hello!* magazine for her to flick through.

I thought of Mr Withers, of how I'd marched in expecting to find him awake and sitting up in bed. What if Susannah was unconscious? What if she didn't actually recover? The beep from the car behind jolted me. I was stationary at a green light. I pulled away and stalled the car. The windscreen was foggy and the wipers battled against the driving rain as I turned the engine over. Cars swarmed around me, frantic shoppers trying to make it to the retail park before they sold out of iPads or discounted lounge furniture.

Pulsing head, clammy hands; flashing images of the miscarriage; of Will's frown; Susannah collapsing on the floor, meringue in her hair. I flicked on the hazard lights and pulled over. I'd not had another panic attack since the one three months earlier and the breathwork exercises recommended by

Emily always seemed to make everything slightly less over-whelming. With shaky hands, I glugged some water and opened the Spotify app on my phone.

Close your eyes and take time to get into a comfortable position. I pushed the seat back and reclined slightly. *Gently breathe in through your nose and deep into your belly. Exhale slowly and with ease through your mouth. Be sure to keep your breath in your comfort zone. You're doing real good.* Let's be honest, he didn't really know how I was doing because he was in a recording studio in Texas or somewhere probably about four years ago, but that shouldn't matter because the intention was good. *Let's do a four-second breath: in, two, three, four...and out two, three, four. Keep a continuous flow. Now move your shoulders up, two, three, four...then down, two, three, four, in time with your breath. That's it—nice and easy. Now let's lift the right shoulder up, two, three, four, then down...*

Hang on, I think that's actually my left shoulder but I'm sure it doesn't matter. I'd never been particularly good with my left and right. Jess always thought that there was a mild dyslexia gene that ran through the family and that's why I needed to get Charlotte tested. Now my shoulder movements were completely out of sync with my breath and Tobias, my breathwork facilitator, told me to visualise a colour before he moved onto neck rotations and I hadn't even started on the other shoulder.

It was midday already and I still wasn't at the hospital, so I hit pause and started the car, feeling a little more composed, even if I did have poor clutch control and left–right confusion disorder.

I walked behind two nurses on the way to the stroke ward. One wore a Santa hat and was telling the other about yesterday's shift: it was busy but the atmosphere was festive, relatives came in with cake and party poppers. She was frazzled from doing too many twelve-hour shifts, but that was okay because she had three days off over New Year and was spending them with her family.

I climbed the stairs, humbled and thankful, and prepared myself for Susannah: big smile, positive outlook. I'd read on the Internet that her face may still be drooped, might always be drooped, and that she might not recognise me. I looked at the fruit and the stupid magazine full of shallow celebrities and thought about throwing it all in the nearest bin.

58

'ABOUT FUCKING TIME. Please tell me you brought shampoo.' Susannah was sitting up in bed, the same bright glint in her eye, the same familiar smirk. It was all there. She was pale and her face was a bit lopsided, but she was still Susannah, and she was alive.

I couldn't say or do anything apart from throw my arms around her and nestle my tear-soaked face into her crispy, sugar-congealed hair. She didn't resist and we stayed there, Susannah clinging to me with her one good arm.

We eventually pulled away, neither of us hiding our emotions for a change. 'You look so much better than I expected,' I said. 'I haven't brought shampoo but I can go to the shop downstairs.'

'No shut up and sit down. How are the kids? Have you seen them today?'

'No, but they're fine, Simon and Gerald picked them up last night.'

'Okay.'

'Can you remember what happened?'

'I can remember segments of the morning and I know we went to your house, but I can't remember being there, if that makes sense.'

'That's really normal. I've been reading all about it and there're lots of exercises you can do and I know you'll make a good recovery from this. Thank goodness Gerald knew what to do. If it had been left to me, I'd have just given you a cup of tea and told you to peel some carrots.'

'Eliza?'

'Yes.'

'Who's Gerald?'

We spent the next half an hour going over everything: Simon was not her husband nor mine. She recognised the name Gerald, but couldn't visualise him. I showed her a photo: still nothing. She knew her parents were driving back from Scotland early to look after the children, but where was Scotland? She remembered carrying something on her lap in the car, but that could've been a child or a goat. She couldn't remember anything about a dessert, apart from the fact that half of it was stuck to her hair.

'I can't even help you out there. You banged on about this surprise dessert for two weeks and the first I got to see of it was the apocalypse left on the floor.'

'I'm sorry I made such a mess.'

'I'll let you off. I've got to confess, I tasted a bit that was stuck to the chair leg. It was delicious and there was definitely a mint theme going on: pale green meringue and minty chocolate. Ring any bells?'

'Nope.'

I got out the hairbrush and began the task of pulling apart the chignon, the strands of hair were matted together like candy floss. I worked methodically, feeling privileged in this role of carer, to wholly concentrate on another person's wellbeing without worrying about insignificant bullshit. I thought of Will and Charlotte, eating cold meats and listening to the in-depth itinerary of Tom and Tara's next ski holiday. I was sure they were having fun, but I'd rather be here with an M&S meal deal, brushing out candy floss and doing something worthwhile.

Doctors, speech therapists and nurses came and went. Susannah tried some food. She struggled to swallow, but the nurse told her it was important to keep trying. I helped her, mashing everything up to a pale grey pulp. She took her time, closing her eyes, pretending it was yesterday's turkey dinner. I brushed out most of the meringue. Simon would come tomorrow with her favourite shampoo from home, and a silk nightgown. They'd taken the kids to the pantomime today, to keep them occupied. Maybe they'd bring them tomorrow, depending on how she was. We looked at photos: she remembered everything about the children. She cried, wanting to hold them and smell them.

I stayed there all afternoon. She slept for a while and I read the magazine. When she woke, I was able to tell her all about the holiday plans of a celebrity chef and which outfit the Duchess of Cambridge was predicted to wear on New Year's Eve. We studied the glossy pages full of people from *Love Island* and *Bake Off*. We pulled apart their pretentious outfits and ridiculous eyebrows. Susannah laughed a lot, dipping in and out of lucidity.

59

'CONGRATULATIONS DARLING, WHAT wonderful news. Let's get a glass of something fabulous,' Georgie said, signalling for the waiter.

'I'd rather celebrate once Susannah's back on her feet.'

'Really?' Georgie made a pouty face. 'And what do you think Susannah would say to that?'

'I haven't told her.'

'Why the hell not?'

Susannah had made a grand declaration before Christmas that if and when the Persian carpet garden article was accepted by a magazine, she would take Sarah and I for a slap-up lunch at a new boutique hotel in the forest. We'd go early and use the spa facilities. We imagined ourselves dressed in fluffy robes, sitting around a pool sipping champagne, celebrating our success. But that wasn't about to happen anytime soon and I didn't want to rub her lengthy recovery in her face.

'I don't think she's up to it yet.'

'Of course she's up to it. It's Susannah we're talking about here, she's as tough as old boots and probably gagging to get out the house. Go and show her a good time.'

But Susannah was on a strict rehabilitation regime; a regime that didn't include champagne and pedicures and fluffy robes—physio five times a week, arm braces, ankle braces, exercises several times a day, every day. She was exhausted and reliant on Simon, her parents and Will and me to do all of the things that needed to be done when trying to manage a home and a family. But day by day, week by week, she was making improvements; tiny ones, but they were definitely happening.

'Besides, it's not all about you. We've got a few more things to celebrate other than my niece being featured in *Garden Life* magazine.'

'Ahh, of course we have, how is she?'

'Biased grandma alert...she's the most perfect thing I've ever seen.' Georgie delivered a blow-by-blow account of the birth of baby Maya. She'd arrived two weeks early and Nicola's parents were away in Dubai so she'd asked Georgie along for additional support, easily securing her place in the favourite daughter-in-law stakes. 'Nicola is such a natural, and Maya always stops crying when I walk into the room, it's like she can feel my presence.'

Georgie asked more questions about the article and it occurred to me that she was more excited about it than I was, and that's probably not quite right so I tried to convey the information with more gusto, but then I felt cheesy and fake.

'I can't wait to tell Barbara. It'll be all around the club in no time. Maybe you could sign some copies and I'll hand them out to some of the tennis ladies.'

'*I'm* not being featured; the *garden* is being featured.'

'What the heck, here's to your garden, the new baby, my impending divorce and Susannah getting back on her feet.'

I raised my glass. 'Wait, did you just say divorce?'

'I've just received the decree nisi. I should have the absolute in a few weeks.'

'Is congratulating you appropriate?' I asked. Everything in me was saying not.

'It is absolutely appropriate,' Georgie said, her head held high.

Because of Susannah and work commitments, I hadn't seen Georgie since Christmas Eve, which had been somewhat chaotic with the unexpected arrival of Dan and Nicola, and the subject of divorce had been far from the radar.

'Are you selling the house?'

'No.'

'How did you manage that? What did the boys say?'

'The boys have been very supportive. It's been a long time coming, Eliza. Your uncle will be keeping the flat in Docklands and I shall remain in the house.'

'And he was okay with that?' I asked, finding it hard to believe.

'He was very amenable and we shall remain on good terms. We've got a new grandchild, for heaven's sake. Now, let me tell you all about Christmas. I know yours was a rather sombre affair, but let's top up our glasses and spread some cheer.'

Georgie recounted the whole event in vivid detail. How well she'd got on with Nicola, and how Tom and Tara had arrived later on Christmas Eve with an elaborate Fortnum & Mason hamper.

'You've never seen so much food. I think Nicola was a little overwhelmed.'

'And how was it with Tara?'

Georgie had not seen Tara since the summer, when my mother had infamously outed her and Tom for dining with the enemy. Tom had grovelled apologies: Linny and Tara had arranged that dinner, of course; neither he or his father knew anything about it until they were at the restaurant; he was sorry but he was in an awkward position. The lie about being stuck in Poland had conveniently slipped his mind.

'It was fine with Tara; I think I've turned a corner.'

'Really?'

'Yes. Barbara from tennis thinks that it's important for one's health and wellbeing not to get caught up in other people's deceit, even if it does involve you in one way or another. It's their problem and not mine. I've chosen to love and embrace both of my daughters-in-law, wherever their faults may lie.'

'That's quite impressive. How long are Nicola and Dan staying?'

'They're not going anywhere for the next six months, which is fine by me. I'm out so much these days anyway. Did I tell you that Barbara and I are taking dance lessons?'

'What kind of dancing?'

'We've signed up for salsa and a Clubbercise class. Last time we went to London we bought all the gear, I am a vision of neon. I need to get fit now there's a new baby on the scene.'

Georgie was buzzing with anticipation and possibility; the flirting and the avid drinking had been replaced with a fascinating energy, the kind of energy that I wanted to bottle up and freeze for myself in twenty years' time—or maybe even now.

60

I TOOK GEORGIE'S advice and on a bright morning, almost two months on from Susannah's stroke, Sarah and I took her to the new boutique hotel in the forest for the slap-up lunch and the spa day. We were given strict instructions on the journey:

'If I get one offer of help or one whiff of pity today, I will beat you to a pulp with my cane.' She was eternally grateful for everyone's support and her mum moving in with her eight weeks ago, but, regardless of what her body wanted to do, Susannah needed to regain her sanity. 'I just want to be normal again.'

And from the minute we got out of the car, Sarah and I did not hold back:

'For goodness' sake, Suze, can you hurry up?' We tutted as we held doors open for her, goading the disapproving stares of other guests. We poked fun at her slut-red manicure and Joan Collins-style swimsuit. We laughed when she got into the pool, a float supporting her weak side, and realised she could only swim in a small circle.

'This has been the best day of my life.' Susannah declared as we sat down for lunch.

'What about when you gave birth?' Stupid question; no idea why I asked it.

'What, twenty hours of screaming agony which ended with me hoofing out a lump of afterbirth to a team of eagerly awaiting med students?' The waiter handed us our menus, clearly disgusted by our topic of conversation. Other tables within earshot discussed villas in Majorca or their children's university options.

'Can I get you anything to drink, ladies?'

'The Krug.'

'*Susannah!*'

She slammed her menu on the table. 'I said that I would take you out to celebrate the magazine article and that's what I am doing. We're having the damn Krug.'

The waiter nodded and rushed off, now less disgusted and more nervously excited by Susannah's extravagant demands.

'Not to mention the fact that I spent my fiftieth birthday inside a brain scanning machine.'

'I didn't know you turned fifty,' Sarah said.

'It was my birthday on the 2nd of January.' Susannah had been assessed for discharge from hospital on that day. We'd brought balloons and flowers and cards, but she was not in the mood; she was still in shock and carrying an uncharacteristic anger about what had happened to her.

'To be fair, I don't even think I knew much about it either, apart from that stupid helium balloon that Dad brought in. What was he thinking? I can remember lying in that plastic bed looking up at it: it was silver with a big orange 50 and there was this crazed woman with a party whistle jumping out of the zero, and all I could think was, *I've just had a fucking stroke, why would I want to look at that?*'

Sarah howled, far too loudly for the woman with the villa in Majorca, who stared at us, dabbing delicately at her mouth with her pompous designer napkin, as if this act of decorum would somehow morph us into submissive housewives.

Should I say something about the balloon? I didn't want to make Susannah feel bad, but there was the No-Pity Rule to consider.

'I texted Simon the next day and told him to bring scissors

so I could hack that stupid middle-aged piece of shit to a cruel death, which negated a lot of pent-up anger—'

'Susannah, *I* gave you that balloon.'

'No you didn't, it was Dad.'

'*It was me.* I went to the florist to pick up your flowers and it was just there and I don't know—it just seemed appropriate at the time. Sorry you hated it so much.'

'I didn't hate it.'

'You hated it.'

'Alright, I hated it.'

'Thanks a lot.'

'Sensitive bitch.'

'Ungrateful cow.'

'Damn I've missed this. Thank you for picking me up and taking me out and not treating me like an idiot.'

Sarah told her that she was a pain in the arse, and that we loathed skipping work to have lunches and pedicures.

'So, Lars came to see me yesterday.'

'Really?'

'Oh, do tell.'

Lars had called Susannah several times since Christmas, wanting to visit, but each time she'd put him off, not wanting to see him with her still-dribbling mouth and limp foot. I'd tried to talk her round, thinking it could be a positive step in moving the relationship forward, that maybe he wasn't just a booty call who was still in love with his late wife.

'In my head I'd kind of written him off when this happened, plus I was shamelessly vain and didn't want him to be grossed out by me. But he was always sending sweet texts and nice flowers, so I invited him over for lunch.'

'That's so exciting, Suze. I can't believe you didn't mention it before,' Sarah said.

'Well it was a bit weird. I think it was a mistake.'

'Really?' I asked. 'Is it to do with the photo?'

'No, that's old news. The photo went down just before

Christmas. I just came out with it and I think he felt genuinely embarrassed; like it had never even crossed his mind that a photo in his bedroom of him holding hands with his late wife might be off-putting to his current lover.'

Sarah held up her hands, 'Let me tell you, I've been married for twenty-two years, and I can guarantee you that it never even crossed his mind.'

'So what happened?'

'It was great to see him. Don't get me wrong, he looked hot. He'd come straight from the stables; he was all stubbly and the right side of grubby, if you know what I mean?'

We both did.

'He walked straight in, held me in his arms and told me how much he'd missed me.'

'That's so lovely Suze.' I found myself almost moved to tears by the actions of a man I'd never met.

'Anyway, then we started kissing and it got really intense, right up until the point where I put my hand down his pants, then he got all weird on me. What's that about? He made me feel like some kind of pervert.'

We jumped to his defence:

'You haven't seen him for over two months. Maybe he wanted to ease into it slowly.'

'Maybe he thought that you were still in pain?'

'Yeah, right,' sighed Susannah. 'Maybe he was on his period.'

Sarah and I cackled.

'Did you say anything?' I asked.

'Yes I said something. I was like: "Just because I can't walk properly yet, doesn't mean I'm not human, Lars, or is my disability freaking you out?"'

'What did he say to that?' Sarah asked.

'He just mumbled an excuse about needing a shower and being uncomfortable because my mum was in the next room.'

'*What?*' Sarah and I shouted in unison. 'Your mum was in the next room?'

'So what? I told her to leave us alone and she's as deaf as a post anyway. We could've gone at it hammer and tongs on the lounge floor for an hour and she'd have been none the wiser.'

Sarah was speechless and I was forced to take the reins. 'Susannah, you can't expect Lars to want to get it on, in the middle of the day, when your mum's in the house. That's outrageous. No wonder he was freaked out.'

'Yeah well, I think he's using it as an excuse. Other mammals just do it when they feel like it. They're not worried about who's around.'

'He's not using it as an excuse and we're not other mammals, otherwise everybody would be at it, right here in this dining room.'

'Well now you've brought it up, if I absolutely had to...' Susannah scanned the room. 'I'd go for 3 o'clock, white shirt, dark hair—preferably over the bar.'

Sarah and I looked around to choose our own hypothetical lunchtime suiter but pickings were slim, with Susannah easily claiming the best of a bad bunch.

We concluded that Susannah was simply having a chronic attack of old fashioned sexual frustration and we convinced her to text Lars, to maybe organise an evening out when the kids were with Simon and her mum wasn't in the next room doing a Sudoku.

'Do you know, I don't think I'd ever appreciated normal until now.'

I don't think we'd been appreciating Susannah's normal either; that she wasn't a delicate flower that needed to be quiet and cradled in soft blankets just because she had a limp and sometimes choked on her food. She was Susannah: she loved the food she choked on, and the Krug, and the inappropriate conversations in the dining rooms of pretentious hotels.

We toasted Susannah's belated fiftieth milestone; we

toasted success and friendships; we toasted being alive. Majorcan Villa looked us over, making her shallow assumptions before demanding the bill. We carried on eating carbs and talking passionately and laughing until it hurt.

61

THE FIRST SIGNS of spring were now visible in our back garden. A carpet of daffodils lay underneath the deep pink florets of the cherry blossom and deep burgundy tulips were waiting to burst into life. On brighter evenings Will and I sat out on the patio and watched the sun disappear behind the towering Scots pine of our neighbour. We huddled in blankets, drank tea and enjoyed the song of our resident blackbird.

Will had had to take a back seat in our relationship since Christmas, with me having to prioritise the business due to the new season and the magazine article bringing in a flurry of enquiries and new bookings. But he'd stepped up to the mark and had taken over the lion's share of the cooking, and didn't stress quite so much if there wasn't an endless supply of food in the fridge. It did us both good, this shift of domestic duties, with each of us feeling a little more appreciated by the other.

We laid bare a few of our vulnerabilities on those spring evenings. I'd attempted to dissect my stupid and irrational paranoia over him and Lexie; a nugget of thought I'd allowed to run amok because of my disbelief that I could be enough to make another person happy. Will admitted that he hadn't liked me very much around that time either; that he'd walked around on egg shells, worried that I'd never return to my old self. And I was able to explain how overwhelmed I'd felt without throwing it in his face as an accusation.

We hadn't taken Tara's advice and booked a weekend away in Milan with shopping and manicures. My underwear drawer remained a shambles and my fingernails still an eyesore. But we did sneak off to a cosy country inn when Charlotte stayed with Mum for the weekend. It was affirming and nourishing, with no one to focus on but ourselves—and no Hollywood actors gatecrashing our intimacy.

I had asked Mum about the affair. There were no accusations, but it was important to me that she knew that I knew, and that Jess knew. She didn't get defensive or ask where I got my information. Instead it seemed she was almost resigned to the fact that, one day, she would have to come clean. She stared into space to say her piece: 'Ed was a kind man and he helped me through a difficult time, but he was also committed to his wife.' I asked a lot of questions and she answered them fairly and, I hoped, honestly.

Mum told me that the affair had been 'off' when Dad died. I remember Ed and Jean coming to the funeral, because, despite the fact that he'd been periodically fucking his wife for the best part of two decades, Ed had wanted to pay his respects. I also remember Jean, her face ravaged, looking far more devastated than she should have been and I'd even considered, in my ignorance, that maybe she and my father had been more than friends.

Shortly afterwards, they sold their house and relocated to Portugal to help Jean's failing health; her hands so crippled with arthritis she could barely hold her own knife and fork.

My mother had entertained a few gentleman friends here and there in the years that followed, but none of them had stayed around for long. It was easier to throw herself into grandmother mode, spending as much time in New York as possible and helping out Jess when the children were young.

The conversations with Mum, and the shock of Susannah's stroke, had sparked a slow and steady change of perception. People could go through years of their life, miserable and married to the wrong person. Or they could go through years of their life looking for the right person but be too judgemental or idealistic to find them. What if we were lucky enough to spend years of our lives with someone we *were* in love with and who *did* make us happy? And I questioned why I'd always thought that so many other people got it right and I'd got it wrong.

Just because Mum spent years of her life striving for the unattainable and Susannah thought that all men wanted to do was eat, sleep and wank, it didn't mean that I had to follow suit. And I laid it on the line with Will too, telling him how happy he'd made me, promising to communicate better and not to be derailed by my own, often impetuous assumptions again.

62

Jess TRIED TO pay the cab driver in dollars. 'What's the matter with me?'

'Maybe you're jetlagged.'

'Maybe I'm losing my mind.'

'Then you're in superb company.' We laughed.

I'd laughed a lot since the arrival of my sister this morning, and the icing on the cake was that she'd come alone, after a carefully contrived plan that we'd cooked up over a late-night FaceTime chat just a week before. My mother was firmly in place on the other side of the Atlantic: *If Jess will just hop on a plane without warning then I have no choice but to stay put. Someone has to feed Mark and take Lydia to her classes. This is a crucial time.*

'So, was Mum okay with holding the fort, or are you in the doghouse?' I tried to ignore the voice that hoped she was.

'I think she was a bit shocked at first that I would do something so spontaneous. Let's face it, it's very unlike me.'

'I am expecting a spreadsheet with a breakdown of expenditure and time-tracking for the entire week.'

'Very funny, Sis. I admit it was liberating to double-click the complete booking tab and not think about anyone but myself for a change. And Mum's in her element now she's got her head around it. She's matriarch of the house, planning every inch of the week, from subway routes to menus.'

'Well, I'm so glad you're here, and you brought the sunshine.' I motioned to the final glints of daylight that flickered through the window of our favourite bistro.

'Enough small talk. Let's get to the nitty-gritty. You first.'

The evening had started with such a buzz, when Jess had done my make-up and told me which shoes to wear. I wanted to carry on the party, not be psychoanalysed. I chose to talk about the Persian carpet garden; it was relevant to the past year and the upcoming magazine article was a positive spin that would meet her full approval.

'I didn't know it was official. That's amazing. Why didn't you tell me?'

'I don't think I've felt that enthusiastic about it until now.'

'What the hell's the matter with you? Your work's in a national magazine! When's it out?' Her eyes popped with excitement.

'The end of the month. Sarah's sent me an advance copy. I'll show it to you later.'

'I can't believe you haven't already. Are you pleased with it?'

'Yes, I suppose I am.' Sarah had written a slick piece and Will's photographs had given the garden a fresh and bold perspective. 'But it kind of feels like it was someone else's work.'

'Classic imposter syndrome. Right, that's it, we're having a special cocktail,' Jess ushered the bartender over and gave him strict instructions, listing off ingredients on her fingers while maintaining intense eye contact. I felt embarrassed by her imposing these Americanisms on him without notice. 'Whatever you do, go easy on the lemon,' Jess said, 'or it'll ruin the whole thing.'

'Yes, ma'am.' He saluted Jess and winked at me. Jess had lived away from home for thirty years now and had waved goodbye to her sense of irony long ago.

As we sipped our French 75s, we both began to loosen up. Jess wanted to pry into the realms of my mental health, but I was resolute in my wish to not scrutinise the emotional scars of my miscarriage. We discussed menopause, but symptoms of scant periods and unfounded neurosis seemed frivolous now, in the wake of strokes, affairs and divorce. I was just glad to have Jess home, if only for a week, smoothing out the turbulence of the last few months.

'I don't think I'm far off the menopause myself,' Jess said. 'I came over all crazy in the subway the other day. This intense heat came out of nowhere and I stood up to check if the heaters had come on and everyone stared at me. The sweat was pouring off me and I had palpitations so badly that I had to jump off a stop early.'

Jess made me laugh with her expressions and wild hand gestures. This was when she was at her best; semi-drunk and free from our mother. 'Didn't you know what was happening?'

'No idea. When I eventually caught up with my friend for lunch she was like: *Jeez, you're forty-nine, you had a hot flash.*'

'But your periods are normal?' I asked.

'I don't think I've had one for about six months.'

'Really? But Mum said you were like clockwork.'

'What the hell would Mum know? I don't talk to her about it.'

This was the first glimpse of irritation I'd seen from Jess regarding Mum. I knew she had her moments, but Jess had always remained fiercely loyal, some might say beholden, as Mum did so much for her. I told her about the eighteen-year affair when I'd first found out; I couldn't *not* tell her. Everyone else—Georgie, Will, my second-cousin in Wales who I only spoke to twice a year—just seemed to brush it off, like it didn't matter because it had been so long ago and I should just move on. Jess was much the same. I suspected that, deep down, she had known that something was amiss at the time but, like everyone else, had chosen to turn a blind eye. But I wondered, now some time had passed, whether she might look at things from a different angle. And I wondered if tonight, I might just find out.

Jess ordered wine.

We got onto the subject of toys we had as children. 'Have you still got that manky old donkey?' Jess asked. 'You used to suck on its ears and it stank.'

'Daisy? Yes, she's in a suitcase in the loft. What about Lulu, do you still have her?'

'Lulu, no!' Jess made a sad face. 'Don't you remember? I lost her in the Odette Saga.'

'Oh my god, so you did.'

The Odette Saga. Jess had been nine when her dance school had put on a production of *Swan Lake* at the local theatre. Jess had auditioned for the part of Odette, but the part of Odette had been given to another little girl and Mother was far from pleased. Jess and I had been outside the office, listening to her arguing with the ballet teacher: '*You wouldn't know talent if it smacked you in the face.*' To make matters worse, Odette and her mother were also sat outside the office, hearing every word.

Lulu, Jess's faithful pink hippopotamus, had been wedged between us on the threadbare sofa, which had adorned the school's communal area for decades. When our mother emerged under full sail from the office, she glowered at Odette, before grabbing us both by the hand and dragging us into the car, vowing never to return. Poor Lulu had been left behind and, as much as Jess cried for days to come, our mother refused to go and collect her. '*We will never set foot in that place again. Toys can be replaced. Dignity cannot.*'

'She was a bloody nightmare.' Jess laughed whole-heartedly, but I struggled to find the humour. 'Oh come on, Liza, you've got to see the funny side.'

'But was it really that funny, Jess? She humiliated you, she humiliated me—not once, but dozens of times. You had to lose your favourite toy because she couldn't keep her shit together and you were nine. It's a big deal.'

'She calmed down once I'd got into White Lodge, I think she felt like her work was done, someone else could do the nagging.' As soon as she'd said it, Jess's smile slipped from her face. 'That's what you think I do, isn't it, with Lydia?'

I hesitated for a fraction too long. 'We're not talking about Lydia here, Jess; we're talking about you and me. Mum was really low when you moved to London. I took it for granted at the time, but, looking back, I think she was quite depressed— for years.'

'How do you think that made me feel?' Jess said.

'If you're anything like me, you'd feel guilty.'

'Yes, of course I felt guilty. I always felt guilty.' Jess reached for the wine. 'But I also felt free, Eliza. It was this wonderful freedom that I'd never had before and I worked as hard as I could just so I could stay there and stay free.'

A tear jumped from her left eye straight into her wine glass. I stood up and wrapped my arms around her. 'I'm sorry, let's go home. I'll call a cab.'

'What? No, I don't want to go home.' She sat up and blew her nose with her napkin, pulling herself together. 'I'm on holiday and I want more wine.'

We rarely had this opportunity to speak so openly and uninterrupted. Even when I'd visited Jess in New York, Charlotte had been with me or friends would be over. Or we weren't at the right time in our lives to open up to the idea that maybe there had been some glitches in our upbringing; a few snags that we should probably iron out before we inflicted the same fate onto our own children, if we hadn't already done so.

I'd never brought up my guilt with Jess, presuming she'd cast it off and accuse me of being too self-absorbed. It hadn't occurred to me that she'd suffered the same fate. But why wouldn't she? At least Mum had eventually washed her hands of me, but the pressure was still on Jess. She'd felt guilty about not getting grades or passing auditions; guilty about Dad working so hard; for not making it to the hospital on time; for not being able to say thank you or goodbye.

She offloaded for a good twenty minutes before putting her

head in her hands. 'Christ, Eliza, you're right. You're bloody well right.'

'Right about what?' I'd swerved the wine, but was still having difficulty keeping up.

'I'm doing the same to Lydia. Mark's working all the time; I'm living the goddamn *Mum and Dad Show*.'

'I don't think you're that bad. Are you shagging your neighbour yet?'

Jess managed a wry smile. 'Have you *seen* my neighbour?'

63

It was early April, the air felt fresh and exciting and I had successfully broken the habit. It all happened quite naturally, with the arrival of Dan and then the new baby. My Tuesdays had become a lot more productive, and when Georgie and I did meet, like today, I looked forward to it.

A new restaurant had opened by the marina and it was nice enough to sit outside. Georgie wanted to celebrate, but grandmotherly duties were called for later so we toasted with sparkling water. 'Here's to divorce!' The decree absolute had arrived on Friday and Georgie seemed nothing but elated.

'Cheers,' I said, rather half-heartedly. 'Have you spoken to Uncle David?'

Although my uncle's behaviour had been far from honourable, he was my dad's brother and I wanted to know that he was okay; that he wasn't smacking himself on the forehead for the most monumental fuck-up of his life. I wanted him to be happy with the outcome too and I decided, as Georgie had managed to keep the house, that he probably was.

'I spoke to him on Friday lunchtime and he's fine. He asked me to send you his love.'

'Well that's nice. I feel like I should text him. Would you mind?'

'Of course I don't mind. He's your uncle after all, although he did ask me not to tell you the full story.'

'Does he think that I don't know about Linny?'

'Oh, Eliza, the full story goes way beyond her. How the hell

309

do you think I got to keep the house?' Georgie took a sip from her glass and peered at me over the rim. 'And if he thinks I'm going to protect his reputation, he's got another thing coming. Make yourself comfortable.'

I studied Georgie with wonder as the story unfolded. I'd made the assumption that her recent jaunts to London and lunches with Valerie were just a blur of senior railcards and shopping. Now I was beginning to think that I might be ageist, possibly even sexist.

'Valerie was certain that she was reassigned to the floor downstairs to make room for Linny, and she wasn't very happy about it. She knew something underhand was going on, but she couldn't prove it, until now.'

It appeared that Uncle David had not been particularly compliant in the compliance department of the bank, and had received a few shady perks for his trouble.

'Once I'd gathered all the evidence I needed, I sent it over to him in an email. Then Barbara and I trotted off to Harrods to treat ourselves to a new Balenciaga.' Georgie held up something pink and ugly, which was probably the financial equivalent of my annual grocery bill. 'By the time we were pulling out of Waterloo Station, your uncle was on the phone, making me the offer of a lifetime before I could even say the words *Financial Conduct Authority*. Hence the quickie divorce. Are you okay? You look white as a sheet?'

'It's a lot to take in.' I wiped my top lip with a napkin and it occurred to me that I hadn't needed to do that in quite some time.

'I know, but I had to tell somebody. Don't mention it to the boys. David's being an absolute pussycat as you can imagine, so no need to rock the boat any further at this stage.'

'I wonder if you'll ever meet Linny?' I said.

'I'll meet her in July, at Tom and Dan's fiftieth. That's three months to get myself in tip-top condition. I've found this wonderful personal trainer at the club and I'm having two sessions a week. I should have the body of Madonna by the summer.'

'Aren't you nervous about seeing the two of them together?' I asked.

'No, not now I know all of their filthy secrets. Talk about having the upper hand. I'm actually rather excited and I'll have so many people to support me. Barbara from tennis is coming—naturally, she can't wait. I've invited your mother but she's busy, then there's Andrew—'

'Who's Andrew?'

'You remember Andrew. I met him on that dating website back in May last year, but I ended up having dinner with that awful Trevor man instead and then I got involved with Pierre. What a fool I was. Andrew is lovely.'

'I remember, the delivery driver. So did you go back online?'

'No, but I kept seeing this dashing chap when I was waiting to go into my salsa class on Wednesday evenings. He went to the swing class before me. Then, about three weeks ago, he stayed on for the salsa and he said he recognised me and it all went from there.'

'So, are you two, well, you know...an item?'

'Not quite. I've kept it platonic so far, but now I'm officially free to do what I damn well like, so...' Georgie trailed off with a warm twinkle in her eye.

'So you like him. Tell me everything,' I said, welcoming a distraction from my uncle's criminal activities.

'Andrew is a retired GP. He lives in Beaulieu and is a keen windsurfer.'

'Oh, sounds adventurous.'

'He's writing a book called *What Britain Eats*, about the nationwide rise of obesity, hence the delivery driver job. He still does one day a week, even though the book is pretty much finished. Very admirable.'

'Very.' I reined in the sarcasm bubbling away underneath my skin.

'He's also volunteered in several hospices since his retirement. He keeps ever so fit and has run three London Marathons.' Georgie seemed excited, but in a harmonious, unflustered way and my scepticism stayed in check.

'That's very impressive,' I said. 'When can I meet him?'

'He's invited us all over for lunch on Easter Sunday but I haven't given him an answer yet. What do you think?'

So far, nothing had been discussed about Easter Sunday. It was only a week away and I was rather hoping that somebody else would pick up the slack this year. 'Yes okay, sounds great.'

'Really?'

'Absolutely. I'll run it by Will, but I'm sure he'll be up for it.'

'I phoned Will last week, not about Easter, but the following weekend. Isn't someone about to turn forty-seven?' Georgie did a little dance in her seat.

'Maybe.' I managed a weak smile. I hadn't quite got my celebratory head on about anything much this year and I was not about to put turning forty-seven at the top of the list.

'Will and I have gone ahead and organised it,' Georgie informed me. 'I'm having Charlotte on the Saturday so you two can have a night out. Then, on Monday, I'm taking you to this fabulous spa that Barbara and I discovered in Knightsbridge. You could do with a decent manicure.'

I pictured myself sitting opposite a fashionable person who would inspect my cuticles and ask complicated questions about my beauty routine. Maybe my arms and legs would be wrapped in seaweed, which the fashionable person had recommended for my collagen-starved skin. The fashionable person would also recommend expensive products, which I would buy because I wouldn't want to offend the fashionable person. I would use them once before they started gathering dust on the dressing table, and would eventually give them to Susannah.

'Hmm, sounds great.' I tried to deliver the response with gratitude but it sounded fake and sarcastic.

'Eliza,' Georgie lowered her tone, looking every bit the formidable aunt. I shifted around in my chair and fiddled with my fish fork, feeling every bit the ungrateful eight-year-old.

'You've got a beautiful daughter and a loving husband who would never cheat on you.'

'*Partner.*'

'Let me finish,' Georgie cleared her throat and glared at me. One of those glares where I knew I must sit still and not interrupt.

'You live happy lives, you get to go to the beach, ride your bike, eat nice food,' Georgie gestured to our surroundings and I suddenly felt like a preposterous human being. 'Your work has been featured in a magazine; people *like* you. I hate to break it to you, but menopause happens, wrinkles happen and a few people get ill along the way. You really don't have an excuse, so start living your life, properly. Remember: nothing lasts for ever, so live it up, drink it down and laugh it off.'

'William Shakespeare?' I offered brightly, confident that I could smooth out the edge of her lecture with my literary know-how.

Georgie held my stare, pokerfaced and perfectly unimpressed. 'Marilyn Monroe.'

Susannah had given me a speech on *living my life properly* a few months back and I'd pretty much ignored her, presuming it was a generalised quote from a social media post and not directly aimed at me.

The waiter arranged the fish platter on the table between us. Three king prawns and a grilled sardine stared back at me, seemingly unimpressed with their fate. I sighed, pushing away the shroud of pessimism that had become a daily routine, and resolved to heed the wise words of my closest allies.

TOM AND DAN'S FIFTIETH
BIRTHDAY PARTY

SILVER BUNTING AND balloons, mismatched tables draped in lilac organza with illuminated willow twig centrepieces, jars strung from trees held softly scented tea lights and wild flowers. There was the obligatory photoboard of the boys throughout their childhood, from naked toddlers to spotty teenagers, christenings to graduations, in fancy dress and rugby kits.

Stalls mimicked a French market: charcuterie, fromagerie, boulangerie, patisserie. A decadent vegan stand adjoined another, where children could make their own pizzas. A trail of fairy lights led to a tent where children found games and activities to keep them entertained and away from exhausted, drunk adults.

Tara had taken the idea from an article in *Absolutely Chelsea and Fulham* magazine. Did I know it, she wondered? No? Oh.

But I had to take my hat off to her: the whole place looked incredible and, while I'd done my fair share of garden preparation in the week, she'd worked tirelessly the day before to give it the wow factor.

On our arrival I'd found Georgie upstairs in her bedroom, at her dressing table in an electric-blue jumpsuit, carefully applying her lipstick.

'Are you feeling okay about today?' I asked.

'Of course, why wouldn't I be?'

The opening of the bathroom door startled me, but not as much as it did Andrew, who emerged half naked with a face full of shaving foam. 'Oops, morning, Eliza,' he laughed, thoroughly unperturbed. 'I'll make myself decent.' He grabbed a robe and I couldn't help but notice that, for a man of his age, he was in very good shape.

'All ready for the party?' he asked.

'Um yes, I think so.'

Andrew walked over to Georgie and puckered his lips, his foamy chin perilously close to her perfectly made-up face. I expected her to push him away but she giggled, puckering her lips too. 'Be. Very. Careful,' she warned and they kissed gently.

'You look beautiful,' Andrew said.

I made my excuses and disappeared downstairs.

I spent the first half an hour swarmed by children. We had Tilly and Teddy for the weekend so Susannah and Lars could go to the Cotswolds, and every time I tried to start a conversation or eat some food I was interrupted by a child who was hungry or thirsty or had grazed their knee. I walked up and down the garden with baby Maya for a while, trying to wind her after her lunchtime feed so Nicola could recharge. It seemed alien that ten months ago I had been sobbing on my toilet, unsure whether to feel saved or cursed. As Maya started to grizzle and I handed her back to Nicola, I took a sip of my cool mojito and felt at peace with the outcome.

'Hello, hi. So good to see you. It's been years. You do look well. How's city life?' A hubbub of questions rang out from the hallway and I peered inside to see what all the fuss was about. People were shuffling around and speaking in high-pitched tones, like an A-list movie star had just entered the building. I craned my neck and squinted to see Uncle David, looking thinner now and a little tired. Georgie had disappeared and I was concerned that she'd had some last-minute nerves and was hiding somewhere with a gin and tonic.

Regardless of his actions I wanted to rush up and throw my arms around this man who had become the closest thing to my father, but I didn't have the inclination to compete with everyone else. Then I heard Georgie's voice, sultry and deep, 'David, you're here.' Everyone turned to face the top of the staircase where she was making a blatantly contrived entrance, like a scene from a 1980s American soap opera.

I didn't breathe until she'd safely reached the bottom step.

'How lovely to see you.' She reached out her arms to envelop him in a warm embrace and everyone heaved a sigh of relief. She looked down and changed her tone as if addressing a small child. 'And you must be Linny. I've heard so much about you.'

Some of the more cowardly guests dispersed and I moved closer to see Georgie, in six-inch Louboutins, towering over the woman from the Facebook photo. Linny didn't seem like the bullish, pilfering bribe-monger I'd imagined her to be; more of a shrinking violet whose hair was too long and whose dress was too tight. Right there, in that moment, Georgie was in her element; whisking Linny away and giving her no choice but to suffer the humiliation of being introduced to old friends and family, while Uncle David had already found himself locked into a heated conversation with Matthew Coombes-Taylor about Russian investments.

Linny was eventually rescued by Tara. 'It's been sooo long,' she lied. I watched as they embraced. Tara whispered something into her ear and they both laughed. She handed her a glass of champagne and Linny had to fish around in her handbag for a tissue to wipe her face, which was beet red with rivulets of sweat streaming down her cheeks. It hadn't occurred to me that Linny would be suffering with hormonal problems and I was hit by a rush of concern for her. Should I get my care kit out of the car? I had wet wipes, a pot of Sarah's cream and Jane had given me some homeopathic remedies to reduce anxiety.

But why should I help this woman of highly questionable morals? This woman who had wrecked the marriage of my greatly loved relatives? I mulled this dilemma over for a moment and thought about calling Susannah; she would know what to do. Then it dawned on me that I knew what to do and that, if I was really honest, I'd always known what to do.

Tara disappeared to get some ice and I made my move. 'Hi, Linny. I'm David's niece, Eliza.' I kissed her cheek and touched her lightly on the shoulder. I could feel that the top of her dress was soaked through. 'Isn't this heat appalling?'

Linny was clearly uncomfortable and I tried to put myself in her slippery shoes: she was experiencing a full-scale hot flush in the garden of the woman whose husband she'd stolen; the woman who knew the intimate details of her dirty laundry. She was putty in her hands; putty in her niece's hands. And she was probably worried that she'd started to smell, but was certainly not in a position to start sniffing her own armpits.

'Yes, I'm struggling a bit to be honest,' Linny said, quiet as a mouse, fanning herself with one of the many issues of *Garden Life* which Georgie had left casually dotted around.

'Let's go over here,' I ushered her toward some shade. She followed with trepidation as Tara glowered at me from the kitchen.

It was awkward, starting a conversation with a complete stranger about my menopausal woes and the fact that she was quite obviously suffering the same fate. Would she be outraged by my intrusion into the state of her ovaries? Would she burst into tears? Glass me in the face with her champagne flute?

By the time Tara returned, we were managing a laugh about memory loss. 'I see you two are getting on well,' she said, acidity dripping from her tongue.

'Who are you?' Linny said, looking her up and down, and I couldn't help but laugh out loud at her quick wit. I left them to it. That was enough for now. It felt good to step outside the box and dish out compassion in the most unlikely of scenarios.

I observed them from afar. Both, it seemed, felt obliged to

keep up the game with Botox, expensive colour jobs and all the other services and accessories sold to us to make us feel worthy. And I felt grateful that I didn't have to be part of it.

'Liza, you'd better come and see this.' Will took my hand, leading me toward the patio, where Georgie was standing on the large wooden table, with one leg wrapped around the umbrella pole.

'Hit it, Barbara!' shrieked Georgie.

Will and I looked toward the French doors, where a no-nonsense lady with a sharp white bob and bejewelled Fendi shades fiddled around on her phone. The first bars of a Tina Turner anthem echoed across the garden and some people gathered round.

'What's she up to?' asked Will. 'Is she making a speech?'

'I don't think she's making a speech, Will.'

Georgie beckoned Andrew to join her on the table. Some of the men were wolf-whistling and Barbara was hooting, wiggling her hips to the beat.

We took in the bizarre scene before us—euphoric, pole-dancing pensioners; Matthew Coombes-Taylor flicking his phone onto video mode; and my uncle, stealing glances at his ex-wife, the resignation in his face telling the world that he did, indeed, make the most monumental fuck-up of his life.

'I'm not sure I want to watch this,' I said to Will.

'Me neither. Let's get something to eat.'

Will squeezed my hand and I took a moment to study our fingers, entwined together, the veins now visible on the back of our hands beneath thinner, sundried skin and the many scars that had bled and now healed. These were resilient hands; hands that could stand the test of turbulent times, of grubby fingernails and loss, of flawed families and ovarian failure. These were future-proof hands.

ACKNOWLEDGEMENTS

To all the people who bought and read this book: I appreciate your time and investment, thank you. Thank you to all the women who bared their souls and shared their stories, face to face and anonymously. Eliza would be a shell of a character without you.

Thanks to Andy for your unwavering encouragement, love and support, and to Kitty for your hugs, patience and spontaneous pots of tea.

Thank you to Dorothy and Gilly for feedback on those painful early drafts. Thanks to Ali, Bec, Cariad, Lucy, Tray and Gail for your time, optimism and kind words. Thank you Dawn @soberfish for our chat, which helped me steer Eliza in the right direction.

To all the girls in the WhatsApp group: I am so grateful for your candid response to all of those random questions. I blame the tone of this book on all of the years we've spent sat around kitchen tables, spouting out childish and often tasteless humour over good food and wine. I feel lucky to call you my friends.

Thank you Gale Winskill for your critique and a huge thanks to Nicola Lovick for your reassurance and sharp editorial eye.

Thanks to Shalini Boland for your advice and encouragement early on, when I was a ball of self-doubt. And to Tim John, for setting an assignment to write about a topic we felt was often overlooked in fiction; thank you, I got there eventually.

Thank you to everyone else who gave their support, directly or indirectly, on this crazy ride.